THE SPIRITUALIST

ALSO BY THE AUTHOR

An Inconvenient Wife

Susannah Morrow

THE SPIRITUALIST

A NOVEL

MEGAN CHANCE

THREE RIVERS PRESS • NEW YORK

Copyright © 2008 by Megan Chance

Published in the United States by Three Rivers Press, an imprint of the Crown Publishing Group, a division of Random House, Inc., New York.
www.crownpublishing.com

THREE RIVERS PRESS and the Tugboat design are registered trademarks of Random House, Inc.

Library of Congress Cataloging-in-Publication Data
Chance, Megan.
    The spiritualist : a novel / Megan Chance.—1st ed.
    1. Rich people—Fiction. 2. Murder—Fiction. 3. Spiritualists—Fiction.
4. United States—History—1815–1861—Fiction. 5. New York (N.Y.)—
Fiction. I. Title.
    PS3553.H2663S65 2008
    813'.54—dc22   2007040826

ISBN 978-0-307-40611-8

Printed in the United States of America

Design by Lauren Dong

10 9 8 7 6 5 4 3 2 1

First Edition

To my sister Tonia,

a survivor, with much love

Acknowledgments

A great many thanks to Kim Witherspoon, who saw the potential of this story and went above and beyond the call of duty in helping me see it too; Julie Schilder and Eleanor Jackson, and everyone else at Inkwell Management for their hard work and enthusiasm; and Allison McCabe at Crown, who shaped the manuscript further and with whom it has been a pleasure to work. I'd also like to thank Kristin Hannah, for all the reasons she knows, and Liz Osborne, Jena MacPherson, Melinda McRae, Elizabeth DeMatteo, and Sharon Thomas for their support and friendship. And, of course, Kany, Maggie, and Cleo, who put up with a great deal and still offer their unflagging support and love—to you I owe everything.

Truth is rarely pure, and never simple.

—Oscar Wilde, *The Importance of Being Earnest*

Tell all the Truth but tell it slant—

. . . .

The Truth must dazzle gradually

Or every man be blind—

—Emily Dickinson, "Tell all the Truth but tell it slant"

THE SPIRITUALIST

1

OPEN TO THE POSSIBILITIES

The fog crept in at four o'clock. By seven it had blanketed the city so completely that the efforts of the lamplighters went for naught—the streetlamps were completely obscured, and no carriage lamp was bright enough to pierce the gloom. Beyond the misted windows of the brougham, it was as if the world had fallen away. I could almost believe my husband and I were the only ones left alive on this night, and that the muffled echo of our driver's shouts belonged to something otherworldly, as if the nightmares that plagued me had seeped past my watchfulness to follow me into my waking hours.

But I said none of this to Peter. I was so happy that he'd asked me to come with him that I would have braved any element. I even—foolishly—harbored hope that tonight might be the start of some new understanding between us.

I glanced across at him. His blond hair was bright even in the darkness, and he sat so still he could have been made of stone. I knew he was nervous—as was I—and I looked out the window and said as idly as I could, "Look how heavy the fog is. I wonder that Cullen can even see the road."

"We'll be late," he said brusquely.

"As will everyone else, surely?"

He sighed.

I tried to lighten his mood. "It's a perfect night for it, wouldn't you say? It already looks as if the world is full of ghosts."

His wince was sharp enough that I felt it. "They aren't ghosts, Evie, as I've told you before."

Another misstep. It seemed lately I made nothing but missteps. Quietly I said, "I was joking, Peter."

"Perhaps I shouldn't have brought you after all. If you can't be open to the possibilities—"

"I can be open—"

"You promised not to be the investigator's daughter tonight."

"And I won't be." I leaned forward, putting my gloved hand on his arm. With a twinge of dismay, I felt him stiffen beneath my touch. "I won't disappoint you. I want to see what you see. I do."

He moved his arm so my hand slid away, and reluctantly I sat back against the plushly cushioned leather seat. He looked out the window. His voice was soft as he said, "You know, Evie, he's a miracle worker."

There was something in his words that made me shiver. I moved my feet closer to the brazier and told myself it was due to the damp and penetrating cold, and not the disturbing reverence in my husband's voice. It was a tone I'd been hearing more and more often since his mother had died six months before, and though I'd told him the truth—that I wanted to see what he saw, if only because it would make everything so much easier—I could not hide my alarm that he'd fallen into this fashion of spirit rappers and table tiltings; he was a lawyer, after all, and I'd thought him too rational to believe in such things. Still, I knew too how irrational grief could make one, how all-consuming it could be. I should not be surprised now that he'd found comfort in the idea of his mother's enduring, communicating spirit. God knew he had not looked to me for solace, though I'd hoped desperately that he would.

"We're here," Peter said.

How he knew it, I didn't know—there was nothing outside to show we'd arrived. But then the brougham jerked to a stop, and the fashionably crenelated Gothic brownstone that was Dorothy Bennett's house appeared in the mist before us like some materializing spirit. I had not been to the Bennett mansion in some time, as Dorothy had withdrawn from society almost entirely in the last two years in deference to her invalidism. Now, the sight of it unnerved me. Every window was lit, reflecting against the fog, so the house seemed to stand alone on the block, pulsing with a weirdly macabre life. It looked as if it belonged to one of Mr. Poe's strange and eerie tales.

The carriage door opened, and the frosty damp air rushed inside to displace the heat from the brazier. It smelled oily and reedy, of coal smoke and the river, and though I told myself it was an exaggeration, in that moment it seemed as if the foundation of my marriage depended upon this night, and the mist seemed conjured especially to lend atmosphere, to whittle away at my rationality. I knew how much Peter wanted me to believe in this medium of his, and I was desperate enough to ease our vague, unspoken estrangement that I meant to try. But my upbringing worked against me—I was uncertain I had the skill to pretend, even for Peter.

He stepped out and turned to offer me a hand, and just as he did so, another carriage pulled up, coming so suddenly out of the fog that I started. Peter turned with a frown that grew deeper as a man pushed open its door and stepped out. But for the paleness of his face above his closely groomed beard, he would have blended into the night—dark coat and top hat, dark beard, eyes I knew already to be so dark brown as to be nearly black. Benjamin Rampling, my husband's law partner.

"What are you doing here?" Peter asked sharply.

"Why shouldn't I come? Haven't I been to all the other circles?" Ben's tone was equally sharp.

I'd never heard them speak so to each other. Ben was not only Peter's law partner; he was also my husband's closest friend. He'd been to dinner at our house on many occasions over the last year, and I'd never heard a harsh word between them. It was obvious that they'd argued, though Peter had said nothing of it.

"You said you had too much work."

"That was before I learned you intended to bring your pretty wife." Ben gave me a smile, a flash of white teeth in the shadow of his beard. "I own I was surprised to hear it. A spirit circle doesn't seem quite the fashion for you, Evelyn."

I tried to ease the tension with flippancy. "You think not? But you know how I enjoy spectacle—and Peter assures me I'll never see another like Mr. Jourdain."

"Ah yes. Jourdain, Jourdain, Jourdain. How ever did we live without him?" Ben stepped closer to my husband and put his hand on Peter's arm, saying in a lowered voice, "I must speak with you."

Peter shook his head and pulled impatiently away. "Not now."

"When?"

"Never, if you mean only to repeat your nonsense from before—"

Even in the darkness, I saw how Ben's eyes flashed with temper. "Peter, this is important. You must listen to me."

"I haven't time for your baseless accusations tonight. We're late enough as it is." Peter held out his hand to me, but I hesitated.

"Whatever is the matter with you two?" I asked.

Peter looked grim. Ben flashed him a glance and said uncomfortably, "Nothing really. A small argument."

It seemed a large one, but I made no comment to that. Instead I said, "I wonder what could possibly be worth jeopardizing Mr. Jourdain's 'miracle.'" When Peter frowned, I explained, "I thought spirits didn't care for disharmony."

"You've been studying spiritualism, Evie?" Ben asked in surprise.

"Well, no, but isn't that what they say?" I eased as close to my husband as I could with my wide crinolines and said with a conciliatory smile, "Come. Surely your disagreement is not so important that you must shout it on the street."

My husband barely looked at me. Instead, he said to Ben, "You're wasting your time. You won't change my mind. Why not just accept it?"

"Because I can't," Ben said. "You know I can't."

Peter's mouth tightened, and he pulled me with him up the walk to the stairs. I glanced over my shoulder at Benjamin, who merely shrugged before he fell into step beside us. We went to the door and Peter lifted the heavy bronze knocker, which was very ornate, with its fashioning of leaves and berries. He rapped it hard once, and then twice, and then the door was opened by a butler, an imperious man who intimidated me immediately, though I thought I hid it well enough.

"Mr. and Mrs. Atherton, Mr. Rampling," he said, stepping aside. "Please come in."

"Good evening, Lambert," my husband said, drawing me inside with the quiet authority of one who had never in his life doubted his place. No one would have known how angry he'd been only moments before. "How is Mrs. Bennett tonight?"

"Quite well, sir," Lambert said, ushering us into a hallway crowded with paintings and gilded furniture, and then closing the door and holding out his hands for scarves and top hats and cloaks. "She's waiting for you in the upstairs parlor."

Peter did not wait to be shown the way but led me up stairs so deeply polished they wavered in the flickering gaslight, as if the surface were water. Benjamin followed closely and silently behind. On the second floor, Peter paused in the hallway before one of many closed doors. He was sweating, I noticed. The house was very warm; even in the hallway I felt the blast from the central heating vents laid in the floor. The wasteful rich, to heat even the hallways, I thought, before I remembered I was one of them. For three years I had been one of them, and still the habit of envy had never quite left me.

Peter opened the door with a flourish, gesturing for me to go before him.

I stepped in, hesitating just beyond the door. Dorothy Bennett's parlor was overwhelming even by Astor standards. It was quite large—my guess was that it spanned the depth of the house—and it had the appearance of being two rooms joined together without thought or concern for whether they matched. The carpet at one end was huge cabbage roses, at the other a geometric pattern. The furniture consisted of many lovely pieces that did not seem to belong together—a mix of gilt and heavy carving and delicacy. Paintings hung from gold cords to cover nearly every square inch of the rose-patterned wallpaper; some I recognized as old masters, though I hadn't the eye to know if they were originals or copies. Every surface was covered with knickknacks, and there was statuary throughout, some marble, some bronze, one or two standing freely while the others resided on tabletops or shelves set into the walls.

Despite all this decoration, my eye was caught by a large round table in the middle of the room. It was pedestaled and heavy, and in its center, two large hands of candles were already burning, sending smoke into the glowing jets of the gasolier above—a huge thing itself, styled as a many-leaved vine, its sconces lily-shaped glass.

"There you are," said a voice, and I turned to see our hostess reclining on a sofa of mahogany and gilt, its arms carved to look like the tail of a great leaping fish, while the legs finished the body, ending in a mouth open and gasping for breath. It was a great, ugly thing, and upon it Dorothy Bennett was a mound of pillows and silk and ribbons and lace, her plump face peering out from it all like that of a wizened china doll. She was surrounded by a cadre of young men. I realized they were her nurses when I saw how they fussed with her pillows and tried to urge her to sip at a bright green liqueur. She waved them all away and motioned us over, saying, "Come, come! My dear Evelyn, how glad I am that Peter's brought you at last, though I must admit I'm surprised."

I reached her and took her fat little hands, decked as they were with rings that had long since grown too small, so her fingers puffed around them like unevenly stuffed sausages. "Surprised? Why is that?"

She shot a glance at my husband. "I'd thought Peter had grown a bit disenchanted with us lately."

"Not disenchanted, no," Peter said quietly.

I laughed. "Oh, hardly. He's talked of nothing but your Mr. Jourdain."

"Well now . . . that's good. That's very good to hear."

"I've never said I don't admire him," Peter said.

I said, "There were never truer words spoken. The way Peter talks, one would think the sun rises and sets upon this medium of yours. I confess I'm a bit nervous to meet such a personage."

Dorothy smiled. "But you mustn't be nervous, child. Michel will put you at ease."

"He's quite a charmer," Ben said as he stepped up beside us. His thick and impeccably macassared hair gleamed darkly in the reflected gaslight. "God knows I've not yet met anyone who wasn't taken with him."

I could not help myself; Ben's comment made me want to be contrary, to be the one person not impressed by this Mr. Jourdain. I had to remind myself that I was here to be persuaded by him, that Peter wanted to share this with me, and for him I had promised to be—what had he said?—*open to the possibilities.*

"You've told Evelyn of our philosophy, I imagine?" Dorothy asked my husband.

Peter looked shamefaced. I supposed he had no wish to tell her that he'd refused to tell me much at all since he confessed that he'd been speaking to the spirit of his dead mother. It chagrined me still to think of how I'd laughed, how certain I'd been that he was teasing me. What I knew of spirit circles came from the articles in the newspaper about the New York Conference's Sunday meetings in Dodsworth Hall, where spirit rappings and table tiltings were all the fashion; and the summaries given of lectures by the infamous Fox sisters, who had brought spiritualism to the world's attention. I had no patience for such things, and I don't suppose I could be blamed for mocking him, but I'd spent the weeks since trying to apologize. I was thankful Peter had forgiven me enough to bring me here tonight, though I was still uncertain why.

He said, "As busy as I've been, I haven't had the time. She's a heathen still, I'm afraid."

"I see." Dorothy's gaze was uncomfortably piercing as she looked at me. "You think you can be open to the spirits, child?"

"Evelyn's promised to put aside any doubts she might have, haven't you, my dear?" Peter turned to me with a stiff smile.

I nodded obediently. "I'm fascinated by what Peter's told me. I look forward to seeing it for myself."

"I've faith Michel can convert you. Some say I'm too besotted to see, but I swear my dear boy does work miracles." Dorothy motioned to one of her nurses, a man with dark, curling hair, and said, "Charley, go fetch them, will you? Now that the Athertons and Mr. Rampling are here, we can begin." As the nurse hurried off, she turned back to us and said, "They're in the library. They'll be here directly."

The other attendants leaned in on cue, two offering Dorothy an arm, the other reaching behind to help her rise, which she did, wincing in pain, and I looked politely away, and it was then I heard the voices in the hall—high, excited voices—and the flurry of footfalls. Peter took my arm and jerked to attention; I felt the strain in him when a group of people—four men and two women—came into the parlor, and I found myself immediately drawn to one of the most arresting men I had ever seen.

He was both delicately feminine and blatantly masculine— translucent skin, long eyes, high cheekbones, and the fullest, most perfectly formed mouth I'd ever seen on a man. He wore his thick, chestnut-colored hair tied back with a riband that matched his obviously expensive deep brown frock coat. His vest was ostentatious and beautiful, embroidered with gold threads, and the extravagantly looped bow of his silk necktie was a blue that exactly matched his eyes; among its folds nestled a rather large sapphire and diamond pin.

He was not what I'd expected. I'd thought he would be more effete, or oilier, something like the wretched quacks who had lined the side streets of lower Broadway, hawking their cure-all elixirs and pawing at me as I walked past them to my father's office. But he was nothing like that, and I could only stand stupidly as Peter called, "Jourdain!" and Michel Jourdain came away from the others with a smile. As he approached, his gaze swept me with a frank and direct interest that startled me.

"My wife, Evelyn," Peter said.

Michel Jourdain reached for my hand with beringed fingers.

"*Madame* Atherton," he said—a smooth, melodious voice made hard to understand by his accent, which I couldn't place. "I see your husband didn't exaggerate when he spoke of you, though he failed to mention you had such remarkable eyes. I hope he's bought you emeralds to match them."

I wanted to laugh at such obvious flattery. I doubted Peter had spared a single word about me. But Michel Jourdain's charm and the way he looked at me, as if I were the most fascinating thing in the room, worked as he no doubt knew they would, and I was disarmed, though I knew better than to be so. I understood Ben's words immediately—it would be very difficult not to like this man, though I knew his kind well enough. He reminded me of some of the pickpockets and street boys who had paraded through my father's office, promising valuable information in return for a dollar, each able to turn a situation to his advantage with a handsome smile and abundant charisma. I saw why Peter was so taken with him—Michel Jourdain meant him to be.

"Peter's spoken of you a good deal," I said.

"Has he?"

"Yes. He believes you're a miracle worker."

Michel Jourdain laughed. The laugh turned quickly into a cough, and he muttered an apology and reached for a handkerchief, pressing it to his mouth, and I realized that the delicacy of his face was frailty, the translucence I'd seen that of illness, though there was something in his manner that put the lie to that impression as well. Some odd vitality—I thought perhaps it was of a kind I'd seen in consumptives before, that ceaseless anxiety to live a brief life fully, no matter the cost.

"You should rest," Peter said anxiously.

Michel only shrugged and tucked the handkerchief away. As if Peter had said nothing, he smiled at me and said, "A miracle worker, eh? Ah, *Madame,* I hope I can live up to such a reputation. But in spite of what my good friend says"—a smiling glance at Peter—"I'm not a miracle worker. It's only the truth you'll find here."

Benjamin said, "Peter has her well in hand, isn't that so, Evelyn? Like any good wife, she's vowed to see whatever truth her husband wishes her to see."

"Ah. This is your first time at a circle, *Madame?* Are you a skeptic?"

I glanced at Peter. "It's as Mr. Rampling says. Tonight I've promised my husband not to be."

"How you must love him then, to do as he bids you. But I shouldn't expect too much, eh? First sittings rarely produce manifestations. Of course the rest of us have met several times before, so perhaps the spirits will overlook a newcomer."

"How disappointing," I said, though his words hardly surprised me. I'd expected some excuse as to why there might be no spirit visit tonight. I expected to see through his "miracles" easily, but for Peter's benefit—and my own—I intended to say nothing of my suspicions. I would feign awe if for no other reason than my husband's wish that I be impressed.

"Do you know the rest of our party?" Michel asked me, and when I shook my head, he offered his arm and said, "Then you must allow me to introduce you."

Peter nodded his acquiescence and let Michel Jourdain lead me toward the table, where the others were gathering.

"You have a strange accent, Mr. Jourdain," I ventured. "I can't place it—"

"I'm from New Orleans," he said.

"You're a Creole?"

He smiled. "How clever of you to have guessed my secret. Now you must tell me one of your own."

"I have no secrets, Mr. Jourdain."

"*Non?* Ah, but everyone has secrets, *Madame,* hmmm? I would think it especially true of women who find themselves so quickly in a better world."

I was startled—his words were so honeyed, said with a smile, a flirtatious glance, that I wasn't certain I'd heard the intimation within them. I was suddenly off balance. I realized with discomfort that my dismissal of him had been too quick. He was more clever than I had first thought.

But then we were at the table, and he was introducing me to the rest of the party, and I noticed that they were all from the higher levels of society, all of them dressed in the best clothes and jewels, all monied. Of course they were; this was Dorothy Bennett's home, after all, and the Bennetts were one of the best families in New York City. To capture Dorothy Bennett had been quite a coup for a man like Michel Jourdain. I wondered how he had accomplished it and found myself reluctantly impressed at the feat. No one knew better than I how difficult it was to seize the interest of society—or to maintain it.

"Mr. and Mrs. Robert Dudley," he was saying as he gestured to a sandy-haired man with a sallow-faced, rather disapproving-looking wife. "Dudley's searching for his brother, who was lost in Mexico during the war. We've achieved some success in finding his spirit."

"Under Michel's expert tutelage, of course," Robert Dudley said, taking my hand. "How pleased we are to meet you at last."

His wife smiled, though it scarcely improved her dour face. But her voice was kind. "You must call me Grace, my dear. We've so looked forward to your visit. Peter is such a favorite of ours."

"Jacob Colville," a tall, darkly mustachioed man introduced himself. "Welcome, Mrs. Atherton."

"Colville lost his wife this past spring," Michel told me.

"How terrible."

"I miss her," Jacob said. "But how can I complain when she experiences such peace now?"

"You've contacted her, then?"

"Oh yes. Quite often."

I smiled. "How reassuring that must be for you, Mr. Colville."

"Very," he said. "I must say, Mrs. Atherton, I'm surprised to see you here. I'd thought you must be a doubter. I'm happy to see I'm wrong. Atherton is a lucky man indeed to have a wife with such an open mind."

I felt a twinge of guilt, but still I kept my smile. "I hope any doubts I have might be proved away."

"You've come to the right place for it," said a small, dark-haired woman with a demure prettiness whose name I learned was Sarah Grimm. The diamonds in her dangling earrings twinkled to match the light that shone in her eyes when she looked at Michel Jourdain. "Michel is the preeminent medium in the city."

Michel inclined his head humbly. "You place me too high."

"Not at all," she said, and I heard the echo of Peter's reverence in her voice. She fingered the heavy ruby brooch at the bertha of her deep rose-colored gown as if she wanted to tear it off and press it into his hands, and I had the distinct impression that it wouldn't have been unusual for her to do such a thing. "Mrs. Hardinge and Mrs. Fox cannot come close to matching you, and I've seen them both. I know."

"Sarah's right about that." A man with curling red hair set his arm around her shoulders and gave her an intimate smile. "You're in for a treat, Mrs. Atherton. The world that communicates with us through Jourdain is a remarkable one."

"It has nearly made Maull put aside his Fourierist tendencies, hasn't it?" Robert Dudley teased.

The redheaded man flushed and then raised his chin proudly. "On the contrary, Dudley. Rather it has inflamed them. To know there is a chance at a world where love is the supreme ruler—"

"Wilson," Sarah admonished quietly.

He flushed again and looked at me. "My pardon, Mrs. Atherton. Sometimes my . . . passions . . . run away with me."

"You must all call me Evelyn," I said. "And please, don't apologize. I'm exhausted with the fashion of boredom. It's refreshing to see enthusiasm, whatever the reason."

"I'm Wilson Maull," he said with a smile. "And you are indeed as charming as Atherton has always said you were."

Another surprising statement. My husband came up beside me, Benjamin in tow. Peter settled his hand rather possessively at my waist and said, "I confess it was her charm that captured me. You must watch out for Maull, my dear. He has quite a reputation for pretty women. I would hate for him to steal you away."

"Consider me on notice." Maull smiled at Peter's gentle teasing.

My husband's words were so unexpected, and the way he pulled me close so out of character, that I could only gape at him. He had ignored me for months. The Peter I was looking at now reminded me of the man I'd married, a man I'd nearly forgotten existed. My hope for this night returned with an almost painful acuity.

"Let's begin," Dorothy called out breathlessly as her attendants settled her in the large armchair that had been pushed up to the table, along with an embroidered footstool for her feet. When they hovered around her, tucking and clucking, she waved them away. Her eyes were sparkling now. The pain I'd seen in her face earlier was gone.

Michel said, "Shall we?" and motioned to the table, and they hurried to it like ants to a much-anticipated picnic. Then he turned to me. In a low voice, he said, "As our special guest, I'd be honored if you would sit beside me."

There wasn't a society event I'd ever attended that seated husbands next to wives, and usually I would not have hesitated. But Peter's mood was so strange that I looked uncertainly at him. "Well, I—"

"Yes, of course," he said, releasing me, though he was frowning, and he said nothing more as Michel led me to the table.

"We must have positive and negative influences, alternating, as in electricity," Michel said, and I noticed that the others were arranging themselves so—alternately, male, female. He pulled out a chair for me, and as I sat, he took the one beside, with Dorothy on his other side, and Peter next to her. Benjamin sat across from us. Grace Dudley went around the room, turning the gas down until it was nothing but a faint glow about the perimeter, and most of the light came from the candles on the table. Michel leaned close and said, "Is there someone in the spirit world you wish to contact?"

I laughed. "Me? No. No one."

"A pity. It would help."

"How so?"

"The spirits sense hesitation. Any unwillingness to believe—"

"I've promised not to be a doubter tonight, Mr. Jourdain."

He said nothing, only looked at me so thoughtfully I had to turn away, and then he said, "Very well. Let's begin."

He motioned to the candles, and those on either side of the table blew them out. I had not realized how blazing their light had been until it was gone. Now the room was in shadow but for the soft glowing gaslight. My uneasiness returned, though I knew that this was only a show; there was nothing true in it.

"You must take your gloves off, *Madame,*" Michel whispered to me, and when I looked at him in surprise, he explained, "The energy must flow through us, with no impediment, eh?"

When I looked around the table I saw that everyone was taking hands, and no one wore gloves. It seemed indecent, but when I caught Peter's glance, he nodded curtly, and I peeled mine off, though they fit so tightly it took some doing. Then Robert Dudley, who sat on my other side, took my hand. To touch strangers like this—skin on skin—was not done, and I found it uncomfortably intimate, though it was vaguely titillating as well. The atmosphere felt charged with anticipation, like the air before a lightning storm, and when Michel Jourdain took my other hand, I jumped—it seemed I felt that charge leap between us. He grasped my bare fingers tightly, and pressed his arm against mine in a fashion that was far too familiar.

He said, "Let us pray for divine guidance in our search tonight."

In the time it took me to understand him, there was a rustle of movement; the others bowed their heads and closed their eyes. Their lips moved silently in prayer. I bowed my head with them.

Then Dorothy began to sing, and gradually, one by one, the others joined in. Though I knew the tune—it was a familiar hymn—I didn't recognize the words.

> *"Oh, the gracious good plantation*
> *Over there!*
> *Shining like a constellation*
> *Over there,*
> *Holy with a consecration*
> *From all tears and tribulation*
> *From all crime and grief and care*
> *To all uses good and fair*
> *Over there!"*

The moment it was over, Sarah Grimm began another hymn, and so it went, the others singing and me staying silent, for at least three more songs. I glanced over at Michel Jourdain. He was not singing. His eyes were closed, and his breathing had gone deep and even, almost as if he were asleep. But there was a strange alertness about him as well, as if he were aware of everything around him.

The songs ended. Jacob Colville said, "Dear God, who watches over everything in each sphere, watch over us tonight, and bless our communications. Amen."

Michel Jourdain's fingers twitched. His eyes opened, but they were unfocused and glassy, like those of lecturers I'd seen in mesmeric trance, though his voice was strong and vibrant.

"In the name of Almighty God, I pray the spirit of Elizabeth Atherton to communicate with me."

I'd expected more elaborate exaltations, more showiness. Such directness caught me off guard. In my imaginings of spirit circles, I'd pictured them more like P. T. Barnum's entertainments, with his dramatic pronouncements: *Now, ladies and gentlemen, we view the impossible! The undeniable proof of the afterlife! Watch, as the spirit appears!*

The others were so quiet I could hear the soft hiss of gas, the rustle of a skirt, breathing. The air went taut with waiting.

But there was nothing.

Michel Jourdain said, "Almighty God, permit the spirit of Elizabeth Atherton to come to me."

Again, silence. Then one of the gaslights went out.

I jumped, startled despite myself. Michel went rigid. His fingers flattened on mine as if to hold me in place. "Is that a spirit come to talk with me?"

Silence.

"Answer me if you be a spirit."

Another light went out. Now I was amused—here was what I'd expected. The drama of the unknown, the showmanship of the trick. I was not my father's daughter for nothing. I found myself searching the darkness for Michel's confederate. Then I reminded myself of why I was here, of my promise to Peter, and I schooled my expression into one of fascinated interest and tried to see my husband's face in the dark.

He, like the others, wore an expression that was eerily blank in the half-light. I felt their collective expectation swell like a wave.

"Is this the spirit of Elizabeth Atherton?"

I was ready this time for a light to go out.

RAP RAP RAP.

I jumped again, and Dudley's hand gripped mine so tightly it hurt. The raps seemed to shake the walls. The sound was everywhere and nowhere at the same time.

"Three raps for yes," Dudley whispered to me. "The spirit of Peter's mother is among us."

I felt a reluctant admiration for Michel Jourdain's skill. He was craftier than I'd expected. Even I couldn't see the strings.

"Mama?" Peter's voice, supplicating and soft, like a child's. "Mama, are you there?"

I waited for the raps. Instead, there was silence. Then I saw a light—no, three of them. Three small balls of light that hovered on the edge of the room. I stared at them, trying to see beyond to any movement in the darkness, but I could see nothing. The balls moved closer, growing brighter, and then one flew so quickly at the table that I jerked back. It slowed and hovered just above the surface, and then it bounced against it with such a sharp rap that the table vibrated into my fingers.

I was so busy watching it that I was unnerved when Michel spoke, and my admiration turned to startled respect.

"I'm here, my dear," he said, and his voice was feminine and low, not his at all. There was no trace of an accent. When I looked at him, he seemed to change. A softening of his face, a wilting . . . whatever it was, he seemed no longer to be himself. He tilted his head as a woman does when she's pleased. The transformation was stunning. He was a man, and one with a very masculine presence, and yet at that moment, he seemed as much a woman as I knew myself to be.

Rapping, table tilting, musical instruments flying through the air, and the ephemeral touch of spirit hands . . . these things I'd thought to see. But I'd never expected anything like this. I looked around the table, at the rapt attention of the others. I did not blame them for being fooled—had I been less inclined to doubt, I might have believed him myself.

"Mama," Peter said. "I've brought Evelyn. Do you see her?"

"Indeed. I can feel her touch upon my hand."

He had captured Elizabeth Atherton's imperiousness perfectly, that superiority that had colored her voice even to her last hours, when she had leaned helplessly upon my arm, disliking that she needed me, yet unable not to. How had he known that? Had he occasion to see her before her death? Michel Jourdain and Elizabeth Atherton would hardly have moved in the same circles, but perhaps during one of her Reform Society's fashionable tours to the Five Points, or some downtrodden but morally elevating mission—

"You must say hello to her, Evie," Peter said quietly.

How desperate he was that I believe. Feeling foolish, I said, "Mother Atherton?"

"You must speak up, Evelyn. There is such a fog between us. How hard it is for me to hear you."

"She's come to see if you're happy, Mama," Peter said.

"Happy? Yes, indeed. There is no pain here, my dear. I am unencumbered at last."

Eagerly, Peter said, "I've done everything you've asked me to do, Mama."

"You are my dear, good son."

"Everything."

"Continue to do as Michel directs you, my dear. He is my servant."

"I will. I will."

"Might I touch you, my dear? Just once, before I go. . . ."

Peter said, "Yes. Yes, please"—and leaned forward, as if he could will her to materialize before him. Just as he did, the ball of light rose from the table, becoming brighter until it settled just over Peter's shoulder. He turned, as if to greet it, and it moved with agonizing slowness until it touched him. His face lit with a smile. "Mother, I can feel you."

But as he reached up to touch it, the ball lifted beyond his reach, and then it danced in the air for a moment, beguiling us with its movement before it fell to the edge of the table between Peter and Dorothy. It hit with a sharp, percussive rap. And then, suddenly, there was another flare of light, and a loud crack that hurt my ears, and then a splintering sound in the wall beyond. Michel jerked back, his hand pulled from mine.

"What was that?" Peter shouted.

I smelled something smoky and acrid.

"Grace, turn on the lights!"

There was the sound of footsteps, and then the gaslight went up, so bright after the darkness that for a moment I was blinded. Then I saw Peter race over to the wall, wrenching a painting from its hook to examine it. I was confused; I had no idea what was happening, or what he was doing. Not until Dorothy said, "Is that a hole in the wall?"

Peter looked up uneasily. "And in the painting. Someone's shot a pistol."

"A pistol?" Dudley said from beside me. "Why would the spirits do that?"

Michel frowned as he rose and walked to where Peter stood. He reached into his pocket and took out a penknife, which he worked into the wall, probing until he'd pried the ball from the plaster. It fell, round and bright, into his hand, and he rolled it between his fingers. "A real ball, eh?"

"Meant for who?" Benjamin asked.

"For Michel," Peter said grimly.

Dorothy made a sound of dismay.

Michel looked at her quickly. "Never fear, *ma chère.*" He held up his hand. "You see? I'm untouched."

"Was anyone hurt?" Peter asked.

"Why do you think it was meant for Jourdain?" Ben asked.

"Look where it lodged. It could've been you it was meant for. Or Dorothy. My God, one of you could have been killed."

I looked at my husband in horror. What had seemed a harmless trick, a show, had taken a terrible turn. "It's from a pocket pistol," Peter said. "Who among us has such a gun?"

"No doubt we all do, as you well know," Jacob Colville said impatiently. "I'll warrant even Sarah has one."

Sarah nodded, trembling. "My father gave it to me. I've never had occasion to use it."

"Perhaps someone was standing at the edges of the room— or behind the curtains," Wilson Maull suggested, rushing to investigate.

Robert Dudley said, "Sit down, Maull. If they were there, they are surely gone now. And who else is in the house but us, and Dorothy's servants?"

"They've been with me for years." Dorothy's voice was shaking.

"Enough of this," Michel said. He pocketed the ball neatly and strode to Dorothy, settling his hands on her shoulders, as if to steady her. "No doubt it was an accident, eh? Someone had a primed pistol and it went off."

"What if it wasn't an accident?" Peter asked in a low voice.

"We're all friends here, aren't we? The only new one among us is your wife." Michel's glance came to me. "What of it, *Madame*? Did you mean to murder me tonight?"

"Why would I want to kill you?" I asked in surprise.

"What a preposterous idea," Peter said.

"You see?" Michel shrugged. "Best to forget it, eh?"

Sarah looked uncertain. "Perhaps we should call the police."

"Whatever for?" Jacob Colville asked with a snort. "D'you really expect them to do anything at all without a bribe—or without exposing us to ridicule? I've enough trouble trying to persuade my family this is no passing fancy; I hardly need police gossip to make matters worse. I've my position to maintain. As does Dudley."

"Jacob's right. No police." Dorothy spoke firmly, glancing up at Michel and reaching to grab his hand.

"It was just a misfire, then—are we all agreed?" Michel asked. When no one protested, he said, "We should all go home and get some rest."

Our hostess was visibly shaking and so pale I thought she might swoon. I rose and went to my husband, taking his arm. "Perhaps we should go," I said quietly.

"Yes," Peter said. "Perhaps we should." He called out to Benjamin, "Ben, let's get our things and take our leave."

The two of them went to find Lambert, and I waited, leaning down to look at the hole in the wall, a nearly direct hit through the printed center of a drooping yellow tea rose.

"I hope you don't let this frighten you away, *Madame*."

Michel's voice was behind me; I jumped. When I glanced back I saw that Dorothy's nurses were helping her from the room. He was standing quite close, and when I turned to face him, he didn't back away. "You don't seem the least bit worried. You aren't afraid the bullet was meant for you?"

"*Non*. Who here means me harm?"

"How can you be so certain?"

"You're the only one here I don't know, *Madame*. Should I not trust you? Your husband is here quite often. Perhaps you've grown tired of being lonely."

I laughed. "I'm hardly likely to go about shooting those who displease me, Mr. Jourdain."

"Ah. So I displease you?"

"No, of course not. That's not what I—"

"Were you disappointed tonight, *Madame* Atherton?"

"On the contrary. I'm quite . . . stunned . . . at your accomplishment. I've never seen anything like it. Peter's mother . . . why, she seemed to inhabit you. How do you manage it?"

He shrugged. "I've no idea. The gift came to me early. I've never questioned the method."

I couldn't resist the urge to bait him. "The spirits just flit down from heaven to possess you? I wonder that you're not frightened of visitations from those less elevated. Or does no one make his way up from hell?"

"Evelyn," Peter called from the doorway, and I glanced up to see him waiting there, my cloak draped over his arm.

"I must go," I said. "Thank you, Mr. Jourdain. It's been an enlightening evening."

Michel took my hand. "Delighted to meet you, *Madame* Atherton. I hope to see you again, eh?" He pressed my fingers to his lips—my hand was still bare, my fine kid gloves still upon the table, and his mouth was warm and moist against my skin. It was too intimate. I drew back quickly enough that his gaze flicked to mine.

Firmly, I said, "You will take care?"

"I treasure my skin above all others, *Madame,*" he said with a small smile. "Good night."

I hurried away from him, grabbing my gloves before I went to my husband, who waited, frowning, in the doorway. As he put my cloak about my shoulders, he said, "What were you talking with him about?"

"Nothing," I said. "The spirits."

We went downstairs and out of the house, and into the fog, which had grown heavier. Now it was almost a soft, chill rain. I could barely see Cullen as he waited at the open door to the brougham. I pressed my skirts to maneuver them inside, and edged my thin-booted feet close to the brazier. When Peter sat down, and the door was shut, I said, "Dear God, to think that you might have been killed by a misfire. . . ."

Peter was silent. Then he said, "I'm going to leave you at the house tonight. I must go out."

"Tonight?" I asked in dismay. "So late?"

"When is the Reid soiree?"

"Saturday night."

"I'll meet you there."

"But that's two days away! And you've been gone so much lately—"

"The bullet wasn't a misfire," he said curtly.

I stared at him in surprise. "What?"

"It wasn't a misfire," he said. "It was meant for Michel. And I intend to find out why."

2

AN INVITATION TO MELODRAMA

TWO DAYS AFTER THE SPIRIT CIRCLE

The first time I'd laid eyes on Peter Atherton, it had been four years ago, on a February so cold that the single window in my father's office was covered with a thin sheet of ice. The tiny coal stove in the corner barely broached the chill, no matter how much fuel I piled on, and my fingers were numb as I tried to write the figures in the ledger book.

When I'd seen Peter's shadow against the wavery glass window of the office door, I thought he was one of the young men Papa often employed to help him, and I hoped it was not Clancy Owen, who fancied himself in love with me, and who exhausted me daily with his protestations of undying servitude.

But then the door opened, and Peter walked into the office, and I was struck dumb. This was not one of Papa's callow boys. This was a man, and a rich one at that. He wore a greatcoat and a top hat, but what pale blond hair peeked from beneath it seemed to be possessed of some ethereal shine. He was handsome in that way wealthy men always are, well groomed, expensively clad, cologned, and smooth skinned. He seemed a terrible aberration in the office, though my father had appointed it as well as we could afford, and we were respectable enough. But the brilliance of Peter Atherton made the silk-upholstered settee look frayed and dull and the side tables seem coarsely stained and lathed. I was suddenly aware of the soot on the ceiling from the gaslight, and the fact that the carpet on the floor was one of A. T. Stewart's more inexpensive rugs—and a popular enough pattern that no one could fail to notice it.

I felt myself flush as I put down the pencil and straightened and asked, "May I help you, sir?"

He glanced at me, and then—I noticed with satisfaction— glanced again, before he smiled and said, "Are you the new girl?"

"Both old and new. I'm Mr. Graff's daughter."

He swept off his hat and gave me a little bow. "Mr. Peter Atherton, at your service, miss. I've come to see your father. I don't have an appointment, unfortunately, but I had hoped he could spare me a few moments."

I gave him my most charming smile. "I'm sure I can persuade him to make time for you, sir."

"I've no doubt that if anyone could do it, it would be you."

I rose, wishing I'd worn one of my better gowns instead of the tartan wool, which was at least two years old, and conscious of my every move as I eased my skirts—which were not quite wide enough to be fashionable—past the table that served as my desk. I knocked briefly on my father's door. At his grunted "What is it, Evie?" I pushed it open and stepped inside, closing it firmly behind me, and said breathlessly,

"There's a Mr. Peter Atherton to see you, Papa."

He glanced up. His eyes were rheumy behind his glasses, and because of it many had been deceived—to their detriment—into thinking he had poor eyesight as well. But Joseph Charles Graff was an acutely observant man, which was why he was so much in demand as an investigator.

"Atherton?"

"Yes."

My father gave me a shrewd look. "Don't keep him waiting then, Evie. Let him in."

Peter hired Papa that day to help him investigate one of his cases, and after that, he came more and more often, and I dared to think it was due as much to me as to my father's competence. I didn't think I was imagining the sparkle in his eyes as he came through the door, and after that first time, he never failed to bring some small thing for me: a flower picked from the window box of some stoop he'd passed, a lovely bright orange, a ribbon. I dared my father's glowering looks in my attempts to make Peter smile and laugh—he had a good laugh, one that seemed to fill the very corners of the room. As time passed, I found I truly liked him, and the weeks when he didn't come filled me with terror; I began to imagine that each visit would be his last, that he would find some woman of his own class and forget all about me.

Papa sighed over me at dinner. "Our girl's got herself in a state again today."

As Mama sipped her laudanum-laced tea, she said, "Might as well try for an English duke, Evie, as that son."

I was taken aback. "Really, Mama!"

Papa grunted skeptically. "Your mama's right. You keep your distance. And keep your head. He's an Atherton."

"You talk as if we're not good enough for them," I said, stung. "The Graffs are respectable tradesmen. You've said it often yourself. You've said we have nothing to be ashamed of. It's not as if we live in the Bowery."

Papa pointed to the framed landscape on the wall. "You see that lithograph?"

"Of course."

"You know what's on his walls, Evie? The original, that's what. The Athertons are Knickerbockers—from the Faubourg St. Germain set. You stay away from what's so far beyond you. It'll only lead to misery."

"You told me the world was changing," I said. "You said I was good enough for anyone."

"The world hasn't changed that much. You keep to your place."

"My place," I said bitterly. "What's that, Papa? What were my studies for if not to use my mind for something better?"

He glanced at Mama, who would not meet his gaze. "I've come to think perhaps your mama was right about that. Perhaps I've done you a disservice."

His betrayal nearly made me cry. "Oh, I see. So I'm to marry Clancy Owen and spend my life having babies until I'm half mad with boredom like—" I broke off as my mother glanced blandly up at me.

Papa gave me a warning look.

"It's not right to want what you can't have, Evie," Mama said.

But I did want Peter. I couldn't help it. And I thought he wanted me too. He began coming to the house a few evenings a week, his eyes glittering with admiration as we discussed philosophy with my father, or, more often, played chess at the table overlooking the narrow street.

One night, as I took his white bishop, he smiled and said, "You are damnably good at this for a woman!"

I smiled back at him. "One of my many skills."

"I honestly believe you're playing to win."

"Of course I am. What other reason is there?"

He moved a pawn. "Well, most women I know would never dare to best a man. Don't you know we're supposed to be the superior chess players?"

"Should I hide my skill then? Even if it meant I was insulting you?"

"How so?"

"It would mean I thought you stupid enough to not see I was pretending. And it would mean you *were* that stupid, for believing a win was your right simply because you're a man."

He laughed. "Oh, I would love to see you among society, Miss Graff. How they would blink!"

"Somehow I don't think they'd quite appreciate me." I glanced at my father, who was across the room, supposedly acting as our chaperone, but so immersed in his book I doubted he would notice if Peter leaned across the table to kiss me, which I could not help wishing he would do. Still, I lowered my voice to keep my father from hearing. "Papa says the upper ten expect their women to be demure and unclever."

"I think most of them are. Or at least they pretend to be."

"I guess they wouldn't take to me then. I don't think I could be demure. Mama says intelligence in a woman frightens men, but I couldn't abide not being respected for my mind. It's a terrible flaw, isn't it? I suppose any man would think so." I spoke honestly, but nervously too, in the hope that I had not misjudged him, and Peter did not disappoint me. He looked at me with an expression that seemed to light a fire within me.

"If a man feels threatened by your intellect, it's his flaw, not yours. I don't think most of my fellows know how invigorating it is to have a real conversation with a woman instead of listening to her go on about gewgaws."

"I don't even know what a gewgaw is."

"You see?" Peter's smile was broad. "You are a rare creature indeed, Miss Graff. If they could only meet you! I think they'd find you as refreshing as I do."

"I hope you still feel that way after I beat you." I moved my rook into place, lifting the pawn he'd just set there. "Checkmate."

His laughter was golden and sweet, and Papa rose and put aside his book and went into the kitchen for a drink of water, and Peter put his hand on mine, and I linked my fingers with his and felt charming and beautiful and alive. Peter made me believe that my ambition and intelligence and desire to be respected were things to appreciate, instead of the faults I knew they were, and as the months passed, I fell in love with him—or at least, I fell in love with who I thought he was. I harbored dreams of him carrying me off to live uptown. I dreamed that what he said was true, that the upper ten would embrace me, that I would charm his family and they would grow to love me, and Peter and I would have children and be romantically in love for the rest of our lives.

Even clever girls can be fools sometimes. In my heart, I knew those things could never come true, but I grew more and more daring nonetheless. I would touch his hand, or brush against him. I said such outrageously suggestive things that they made me blush even as I said them. All in the hopes that he would suddenly go down on his knee and proclaim his undying love.

And then, one day, I was coming back from running an errand for my father. It was May, and the days were warm and growing hot. The spring had set my mind into a whirl—the rich perfume of flowers, bees buzzing around pollen-laden stamens, dogs mating in the streets—it seemed the world around me was consummating its love, and I felt bothered and irritable. I was short-tempered and hot as I came hurrying back to the brick building on lower Broadway that housed my father's office, and the traffic was loud and unbearable, and the stink of the street— of dust and garbage and manure—made my head ache. I reached for the lever on the cast-iron gate just as another hand did—a man's hand—and I looked up into Peter's face.

"Why, Miss Graff," he said. "How fortunate that I've run into you here."

I smiled prettily at him. "Why should it be a surprise, Mr. Atherton, when I can be counted on to be here every day?"

"I meant here, in the street. I was just on my way up to see you, as it happens. I had wondered"—he looked down at his hands, as if he were nervous, though of course he could not have been, not a man like him—"I had wondered if you'd care to accompany me on a short promenade."

"Oh," I said stupidly. "I . . . I see. Is there something you wish me to . . ."

"As it happens, I do wish to ask you a favor," he said quickly.

Of course there was some errand he needed of me. There could be no other reason. But I would have done anything to be with him—he could have asked me to swim the Hudson in midwinter and I would have agreed—and so I nodded and said, "Of course."

He crooked his arm and held it out to me, and I tucked my hand at his elbow. He glanced back at the building. "Should I tell your father I'm taking you away for a bit?"

"There's no need. He's sent me on an errand. He'll think I'm still on it."

"Then you trust me enough to see to your safety?"

I smiled at him. "You're a gentleman, Mr. Atherton, aren't you? Is there a reason I should worry?"

"None at all."

He led me away from my father's office, and farther down Broadway toward the Battery, where couples often promenaded in the summer evenings for the cool breezes coming off the bay. But making our way there was filled with peril—omnibuses and carriages and wagons were too busy dodging the dogs and pigs scavenging in the piled-high refuse gutters along the walks to care much about pedestrians, and their wheels splashed heedlessly through the slime-covered, fetid sewage. Drovers unloading merchandise clogged and blocked the sidewalks with their barrels and boxes; a load of rolled carpets forced us to abandon the sidewalk for the street, and Peter directed me courteously over the piles of garbage and back to the flagstones again, and said, "I apologize. How anyone expects a gentlewoman to get about without offense in the city, I'm at a loss to know."

How different he was from so many of the men I'd known. He seemed to be aware of every little bothersome thing—the stench of slaughterhouses and the tanneries, of manure and coal smoke, the pools of horse piss, the rush of men too busy to look about them, so one constantly had to stop suddenly to avoid a collision . . . things I had long since grown used to, that seemed hardly worthy of comment. But he spoke idly of everything, of the wretched streets and the rag-and-bone men picking through the garbage alongside the pigs, and the loud and unavoidable curses of the drovers. Even the layers of paper plastered onto every empty surface occasioned comment.

"I do wish they'd pass a law against all this . . . paper, don't you? Flyers everywhere about . . . Miss Graff, I'm horrified that you must be assaulted by such obscene details of a body's ailments."

I smiled and said, "Ah, but it restores one's hope to know a cure is available. And in only three days!"

He laughed and laid his hand over mine where it rested in the crook of his arm. "You are delightful, as always. How glad I am I ventured into your father's office that day."

How warm he made me feel. How worthy of walking beside him. As we reached the graceful stone-paved walks of Battery Park, I no longer felt like a tradesman's daughter, but like something else entirely—it felt as if all the things I'd dreamed of could somehow be possible, that I belonged not in a narrow brick house on Duane Street, but in the mansions of Upper Broadway and Union Square. He made me feel that way, with his gentle courtesy and his way of listening intently to everything I said, as if he valued my opinion above all others.

We walked among the shrubs and flowers, weaving between other couples and families with their children, and the leaves of the elms shading the walk whispered in the wind coming off the bay. Peter directed me toward the water, toward the concert hall of Castle Garden, and we stood on the edge of the huge stone wall there and looked out over the East River, Governor's Island and Staten Island, toward the rising buildings and warehouses of Brooklyn on the other side. The bay was filled with masts and sails of clipper ships and small boats, and here the wind was stronger; it blew back the dark curls I'd left dangling artfully on either side of my face and sent the waves slapping gently against the granite.

I was staring out at all this, lulled by how beautiful it was, by my own sense that I belonged here, when Peter turned to me and said, "Might I ask you my favor, Miss Graff?"

The dream that had buoyed me popped; I fell hard back into the reality of my life. The wind whipped my eyes hard enough to cause tears.

"Of course," I said in as steady a voice as I could. "Whatever you wish."

He took a deep breath. "I wonder . . . would you do me the honor of becoming my wife?"

I was hearing things. I blinked away my tears and turned to look at him. He was staring so intently at me that I faltered. "W-what did you say?"

He flushed. "I asked you to marry me."

I was becoming as mad as my mother. There was no other explanation for it. "But . . . you can't mean it. How cruel you are to tease me!"

He looked down at his hands. Stiffly, he said, "I assure you I'm not teasing. I'm quite serious. In fact, I've never been more so."

I could not help myself. Everything in me shouted: *say yes,* but I could not obey so easily. It was, my father would have said, the flaw in me. I must question everything. "But . . . but why?"

"I need a wife," he said simply. "You need someplace to blossom."

"To blossom?"

His hands came down tight on my shoulders, as if he meant to hold me in place, and there was desperation on his face. "A fine house, fine things—you'd like that, wouldn't you? To be the wife of a rich man?"

Warily, I said, "Yes, of course."

"Marry me, and it's yours."

This was not what I wanted. There was no passion, no protestation of undying love. He spoke only of need, of benefit. I said, "Do you love me, Mr. Atherton?"

Peter released my shoulders and turned to look out over the bay. Finally he said, "My mother has been nagging me to get married and produce an heir. I need someone who can keep up appearances." He laughed joylessly. "Keep up the Atherton name, so to speak."

"Why me? It seems to me you could have whatever woman you wanted. Why not marry someone from your class?"

"Because they would expect too much. And because I don't like them." His hand came to my shoulder again. "I *like* you, Miss Graff. I like how you make me laugh. It seems to me we would make a good match. And I think you'd be loyal to me. Would you be loyal?"

Weren't all wives loyal to their husbands? "Of course I would."

"So I thought." He leaned down to look directly into my face. "I can make you a success, you know. Give me two years, and no one will remember where you came from. You'll be the rich wife of Peter Atherton, that's all."

I held tight the words he'd said, that he liked me, and I thought I could turn that into love, given time.

My parents protested, of course, but in the end, what could they do but agree? It was a match so far above what they'd ever expected, and I wanted it so badly. Peter and I married two weeks later, in a little chapel on Beekman Street. Afterward, we went to the lavish St. Nicholas Hotel, where he'd procured the lovely white bridal suite, and I had my first taste of the life I was to grow accustomed to. We ordered dinner up—it was more food than I had ever seen—a salmon mousseline, stuffed squab, filet de veal, strawberries and cream and wine. I noticed he drank a great deal, but I didn't care, because that night he kissed me and took me to bed, and though he was drunk enough that his performance was graceless, I cherished it. I thought it meant that he loved me after all.

It wasn't until several weeks later I realized I had made the mistake so many had made before me, though I had made it on a grander—and therefore less sympathetic—scale. I had deluded myself into believing my marriage would be a true partnership, one of mutual respect and love. But those things had never been part of the equation on Peter's side.

I WOULD BE lying if I said I hadn't found some satisfaction in the life Peter offered me, however, and if I wished for passion and a true meeting of minds, those wishes were easy enough to banish in the wake of an emerald bracelet or a gown in the latest Parisian style. I buried my loneliness in night after night of glittering New York society—there were those among the upper ten thousand who found me charming and delightful.

Yet now, as I gratefully allowed Samuel Harrison to partner me during a Viennese waltz at Rose Reid's ball, I felt that swift pierce of loneliness that seemed always to lurk just out of sight, ready to burst upon me. I was among friends—at least two hundred of them—at one of the most anticipated suppers of the New Year of 1857, and yet I was alone.

"Atherton must be busy indeed," Samuel said as he led me back to the chairs that lined the small ballroom. "The Martin trial is all anyone talks of lately."

"He's quite busy," I said, glancing involuntarily to the door. "But he did promise to make an appearance this evening."

"Well, no doubt he's caught up in some important matter."

"No doubt." I smiled, and then my smile faded as I caught my reflection in the mirror-lined walls. How pale I looked—even the garnets at my throat and ears seemed dull. The only color in my face was my eyes, which looked like jade chips set in bone china. *"I hope he's bought you emeralds to match them."* Michel Jourdain's words flitted to me, making me feel Peter's absence all the more keenly. I did not know whether to resent him for leaving me to keep up appearances once again, or to be worried. My usual innocent flirting with the bored husbands of my society friends had been impossible tonight. I'd been unable to concentrate on any conversation, even the more spirited ones concerning the slavery question in Kansas or corrupt city politics. Dorothy Bennett's spirit circle had not left my thoughts, and though Peter had told me he would not see me again until tonight, still I'd listened for his footsteps each night since. It was foolish, I knew. It was common for my husband to disappear for days at a time without a word. As one of the most preeminent defense attorneys in the city, he was always busy with some trial or another. Or so he'd said. Now, of course, I knew that it hadn't been just criminal cases that kept him from me, but spirit circles as well.

I took a glass of wine from a black-tailed servant, glancing about the room, at its gilded mirrors reflecting the light of dozens of beeswax candles and crystal gasoliers, vases full of roses, which only grew more fragrant as the heat of two hundred dancers grew more pressing. It was as beautiful as I'd always imagined such parties to be in those days when I'd sat in my mother's parlor and daydreamed about Peter. Yet in those dreams, my husband had always been beside me. Now I was alone, and it was nearly two. Where was he?

I felt a light touch on my shoulder and turned to see Irene Cushing, resplendent in blue taffeta. She leaned close to whisper in my ear, "Evie, I've heard the most delicious story." She glanced around, as if looking for eavesdroppers. "Come with me."

She took my hand, and I put aside my wine and obediently followed her to the doors overlooking the Reids' garden, which was covered with snow. Irene drew me back into the curtains, her dark eyes twinkling. "You'll never guess what I heard."

Her blond curls shivered against her ears as she leaned forward again, and the gathered feathers in her hair dipped and tickled my temple. "Guess who was seen coming from the Astor House with William Perry? Florence Chaumont!" Her voice rose at the end, and she deadened it quickly. "Can you believe it? I heard he had rooms there, and she met him after her performance, and no one saw her leave until morning."

William Perry was one of the upper ten thousand—the very highest rung of the social ladder—and a stalwart invitee to every event. I said, "Why would he do such a thing?"

She didn't seem to hear me, so intent was she on spilling the tale. "I heard that Mrs. Astor planned to cut him, of course, and you know Mademoiselle Chaumont will be dead to everyone by the end of the day."

"But his wife—"

"Oh yes, well, she's humiliated. Simply humiliated. If you'll notice, she isn't here tonight. Nor is he."

"I hadn't noticed."

"How could you not? Didn't you wonder when he didn't ask for a dance? You're one of his favorites."

"I confess I've been a bit distracted—"

"Yes." She sighed. "I see Peter isn't here. Again."

"The trial . . ." I made a dismissive gesture, which set the candles on the nearby sideboard to flickering madly.

"Oh, who do you think you're talking to, Evie? Perhaps you can hide from the others, but I can see: you've been dull all night! Where's your legendary charm? Even Captain Post commented that you seemed peaked. Have you been having nightmares again?"

"It seems they never go away," I said. "But that's not what bothers me. The truth is that I'm worried about Peter. I know it's not *done* to confess you care about your husband, but—"

"Good Lord, I long to be rid of Daniel for a few days. You simply need to keep yourself busy. I know—we'll go shopping Monday. And have a luncheon at Taylor's."

"That should cure Monday," I said.

"You need an occupation. A hobby, perhaps."

"How many watercolors can one paint, Irene? Especially when one has as little talent as I do? I've got them littered about the house already. Even the servants wince when they go by them."

"But Peter's always been busy. I thought you liked the freedom he accorded you." She looked at me with concern and sympathy, and I knew that, unlike my other friends in this room, I could trust Irene to truly listen. And because of that, I revealed what I never would have otherwise.

I bent close to say, "It's not just that. You know he's been going to spirit circles?"

She nodded and shuddered. "I confess I don't understand it.

All this talk of ghosts and such! There's nothing a spirit could say to me that I care to hear, I can promise you."

"Yes, well, Peter believes it," I said glumly. "And he's fallen in with a new medium who makes him think he's speaking to his mother's spirit."

"Elizabeth Atherton?" Irene laughed. "I can't imagine her deigning to return through a spirit rapper. The Second Coming would be more to her liking."

I smiled weakly. "You're a philistine, Irene."

"So I've been told. I'd thought Peter too canny to get caught up in such business."

"This man is very convincing."

"A man? How odd for a medium. You've seen him?"

I nodded. "Thursday night. Peter insisted I meet him. He's been leading a circle at Dorothy Bennett's. She brought him from Boston."

"Dorothy Bennett? My Lord, spiritualism does run rampant among the upper ten! Next you'll be telling me Mrs. Astor's taken up the calling as well."

"Please, Irene."

She sobered. "How serious you are, Evie! So you saw this medium and he was very convincing. Did he convince you too?"

"Hardly. He's no more genuine than any other. But he was very charming in that way most charlatans are. And . . . attractive. I understand why people want to believe him. He makes it seem almost offensive not to."

Irene eyed me carefully. "You sound taken with him yourself."

"Dear God, no. But something happened at the circle the night I went. Something strange."

"As if speaking to spirits wasn't strange enough!"

"A gun misfired. The bullet just missed Peter."

Irene frowned. "I do wish men would take better care. Why, just last week Daniel told me someone shot his own foot while having lunch at Bodes."

"Peter seemed to think it was something more than a misfire."

Irene gave me a sharp look. "He thought it was deliberate?"

"He thought the bullet was meant for Mr. Jourdain, the medium."

Behind us, the orchestra began another waltz. Irene glanced over her shoulder. "Is that what you thought?"

"I'd thought at first it was part of Mr. Jourdain's show."

"I'm certain that's what it was. These mediums try all sorts of things, I'm told. I imagine Peter was beside himself at the thought that you might have been hurt."

"Me?" I laughed bitterly. "I don't think so. He was more concerned for Mr. Jourdain."

"Ah, Evie, you sound jealous!"

"I suppose I am. He spends so much time there. I hardly see him."

"The romance fades, you know, with time. How long have you been married? Three years? Take my advice: don't go wanting things you can't have."

The words were oddly reminiscent. It seemed I was sitting again in my parents' dining room, with the scents of mutton and my mother's violet perfume filling my nose. I felt a sudden, swift rage. Viciously, I said, "I tell you, Irene, there are times when I almost hate him."

She gave me a wry glance. "Oh, but, my dear, that's what marriage is. How have you not known that before now?"

THE ORCHESTRA AND the dancing were still going strong more than an hour later, and still Peter had not put in an appearance. I had just decided to call for my carriage when I saw Benjamin Rampling enter the ballroom. Although the room was filled with people, Ben stood out. He was a handsome man, and the darkness of his attire became him.

He paused at the doorway, searching the crowd. In relief, I hurried toward him.

He broke into a smile when he saw me. "Ah, you're still here, then. I was counting on the fact that no one leaves a Reid soiree early. Where's Peter?"

"He hasn't come with you?" I asked in dismay.

"No, of course not. Isn't he here?"

"He was to meet me here tonight, but he hasn't arrived," I said miserably. "I haven't seen him since we left Dorothy's. I thought he must be with you."

"I haven't seen him," Ben said. "In fact, that's why I stopped by. He has some papers I need. I'm heading for Albany tomorrow morning for a few days for one of my own cases. I was hoping he could save me a trip to the office before I go."

I thought again of Peter's set expression. *"I intend to find out who."*

"Dear God, where can he be?" I whispered.

Ben gave me a sympathetic look. "Come," he said, taking my arm. "Call your carriage. Let me see you home."

"But if Peter arrives——"

"It's nearly four, Evelyn. If he's not here by now, I think he won't be tonight."

Of course he was right. But I could not hide my apprehension as I made my good-byes and my apologies for Peter's absence to Rose Reid.

"Oh don't fret so, my dear," she reassured me. "Everyone knows how busy he is with the Martin trial."

Benjamin held my arm tightly as we went into the night, which was cold beyond bearing. The walk was icy, the streets snowy and abandoned, and the music echoing from the house seemed vaguely wrong in the dark quiet. Cullen was waiting by the brougham, holding the door open, and he gave me a curious look at our approach, one that made me feel faintly guilty, as if I had something to hide, and I looked away and ducked quickly inside the carriage. Ben climbed in after me.

"Cullen probably finds it strange that I'm leaving the party with you," I explained to Ben as the door closed. "He's used to my going home alone."

"You shouldn't allow such familiarity in your servants," Benjamin said. "I'm surprised you haven't learned that by now."

"Cullen's not just any servant. He's been with Peter since he was a boy."

"Peter's always been too tolerant."

"Where do you suppose he is? It's not like him to not appear when he says he will."

"I doubt there's any need to worry. He does this kind of thing all the time. He'll turn up soon enough."

"What if something's happened to him? After the other night . . ." When Ben looked at me in puzzlement, I said, "The shooting at the circle."

"The shooting?" he asked blankly. Then, as his expression cleared with understanding, he laughed. "Good God, Evelyn, how can you believe anything that happens at that table?"

I was startled. "But I thought you said you'd been to the circles with Peter before. Do you mean to tell me that you don't believe in Mr. Jourdain's spirits?"

"Not in the least."

"Then why do you go?"

"In the beginning, I went because I was the one who recommended Jourdain; oh, yes, it was me, I'm afraid. I'd heard of him when I was living in Boston, and Peter seemed in such need. Well, it wasn't long before I realized Jourdain was another mountebank, if one more talented than most. After that I went just to keep an eye on things. I didn't want Peter taken advantage of."

"I see. It seems I owe you my thanks, then."

Ben shrugged. "I would do the same for any friend."

"I imagine Peter told you of his suspicions?"

"His suspicions?"

"About the shooting that night. He thought someone had

fired deliberately. He thought the shot was meant for Mr. Jourdain, and said he was going to find out who it was, and why."

Benjamin looked troubled.

"I told Irene I thought—"

"Irene? Irene Cushing?"

"Yes. I was worried for Peter, and I—"

"It might be best if you kept such things to yourself, Evie," Ben advised soberly. "You heard what Colville said—he didn't want police gossip. I'm certain he won't look kindly on talk among the upper ten."

"There's already talk," I said. "I can't think why it matters. If one truly believes in the spirits, why not tell the world?"

"Because no one wants to be made a fool of. Imagine you're known for your shrewdness in business. Imagine you've given Jourdain gifts and money for calling the spirit of your departed beloved. Now imagine the police—or anyone else—comes in and begins to question your judgment. Do you see?"

I did. I understood too well. Reputations, family connections, gossip, these were the things that made—or ruined—one's position in society. Uncomfortably I realized what a gaffe I'd made. The story of a shooting at Dorothy Bennett's would be as irresistible a tale as William Perry's affair with Florence Chaumont.

"I didn't think," I admitted.

"There's probably no harm done, but if I were you I'd say nothing more on it."

"Of course." I paused. "What did you think about what happened that night, Ben?"

"I thought it was a trick," he said without hesitation. "I was angry that Jourdain had tried something so dangerous. What if it had hit one of us?"

"I wish I knew why Peter was so certain it had been meant for Michel. Had something happened? Had he reason to be suspicious?"

Ben shook his head slowly. "Not that I know of. Peter's always been gullible, Evie. And you heard for yourself how much he admires Jourdain. Such evenings invite melodrama. I'm certain Peter was simply caught up in the delirium."

"I expect you're right," I said.

"You were there." Benjamin leaned forward. "Did you think Jourdain looked like a man who believed he'd just been shot at?"

"No. Not the least bit."

"You see." Ben sat back again, folding his arms over his chest. "No doubt Peter's thought better of his suspicions already."

"You don't think it has anything to do with where he is now?"

"Where he is now is probably at the office, asleep on a settee, or buried in papers. He's no doubt forgotten all about the Reid soiree." Ben smiled warmly at me. "You know how he is. He'll be there until court adjourns on Monday, and then he'll be home and you'll realize how foolish you were to be concerned."

His words eased my worry. "Of course, you're right. Forgive me for being so silly."

"Never apologize," he said. "Peter should know better than to leave you this way, without a word. In fact, I'll say something to him when I return from Albany."

"I wish you wouldn't," I said quickly. "He'll only be angry that I've confided in you. And it seems he's angry enough with you already."

Again he frowned. "He is?"

"I thought so. The way you two argued that night—"

"Ah, that. That was nothing. A disagreement over how to proceed in a certain matter. Nothing more. We parted friends, as I hope you and I are."

"Of course we are."

"I'm glad to hear it," Ben said. "I wish you'd feel free to confide in me whenever you like. I must confess that it saddens me to see the way Peter neglects you. He doesn't realize what a treasure he has."

I felt myself grow hot, and I looked away. "Please, Ben."

"Forgive me. I've no wish to embarrass you. It's only that I want you to know how much I admire you. If I can serve you in any way . . . Well, you must know I would find it a privilege to do so."

The carriage stopped. I glanced up quickly to see we were on Irving Place, before my own house, and then I felt the bounce as Cullen left the driver's seat and opened the door.

I turned to Ben as I stepped out. "Thank you. For seeing me home, and for your reassurances. Cullen will take you home."

"You mustn't worry," he said again. "Good night, Evelyn."

I knew he was probably right, that Peter was no doubt holed up in his office, asleep over his trial notes. Yet I could not keep myself from listening for him as Kitty sleepily undid my hooks and laces and helped me into my nightgown.

My husband didn't come that night, nor did he return in the morning. The day was frigid, the temperature hovering near zero, so I stayed inside instead of making my usual Sunday pilgrimage to Grace Church. I spent the day practicing my embroidery, which had never been good, but I was determined to finish the cover I was making for Peter's footrest. Before long, my frustration over the sheer number of stitches I had to rip out made me put the embroidery aside and reach for a book, but it couldn't hold my attention, and I fell asleep by the fire.

By three that afternoon, I was awakened by the howling of the wind, and such a volume of swirling snow that the world beyond the windows was nothing but a dizzying void of white. Had Peter meant to come home, he certainly could not now. I doubted any carriage could move through the storm. My disappointment overwhelmed me, but then, as the hours went on, I grew angry. The next day, snow lay icy and thick on the ground, and every eave was decorated with dangerously thick long icicles that glittered in the light, and the streets were empty. Cullen came inside, dusting off snow, white with cold, to tell me the city was shut down, that no one could get about, and when I asked him if he'd heard from Peter, he shook his head and said kindly, "No, ma'am, not today."

It wasn't until the following day, when three policemen showed up at my door, that I understood I should have been very worried indeed.

3

MORBID THOUGHTS

FOUR DAYS AFTER THE SPIRIT CIRCLE

My first reaction upon hearing Kitty's announcement that the police were waiting in the parlor was a panicked urge to run; I'd grown up in a world where they were just another Irish gang with a liking for rowdyism and brutality, and their main duty was strong-arming men into voting for whichever candidate they favored on election day. Though I was now of the class that the police served, I was nervous as I went to meet them.

"Mrs. Atherton, I'm Robert Callahan, with the police department," said the tallest of the three, and the only one not wearing the customary blue wool frock coat, copper badge, and leather cap of the New York City police. He wore brown, with a frayed checked vest and a cheap top hat worn shiny in spots, which he took off to reveal shaggy brown hair. The three of them seemed clumsily out of place in the parlor, which was mostly appointed in my late mother-in-law's taste, in burgundies and Louis Seize gilt and chintz, so feminine and exquisite that even I often felt too coarse for it. He tugged nervously at his long, fuzzy sideburns as he sat, and the other two perched gingerly on the delicate settee. "Your husband never showed up in court this morning. We've been sent to see if he might still be at home."

"He didn't show up in court? But Peter would never miss a trial. Have you gone to his office?"

"Yes, ma'am," said Callahan. "No one there has seen him since after court on Thursday."

"Thursday? You mean he wasn't there Friday? Or Monday?"

Callahan frowned. "No, ma'am. Court was closed due to the storm. I understand Mr. Atherton's partner is out of town?"

"Yes. In Albany."

"Mr. Atherton didn't go with him?"

"No. Mr. Rampling is working on another case. There was no reason for Peter to go with him."

"What time did Mr. Atherton leave for court this morning?"

"I don't know." I was too worried to sit. I paced to the fire, moving the parrot-decorated fire screen away and then pushing it back again. "I didn't see him. He wasn't home."

"I see." Robert Callahan took a stub of pencil from his vest, along with a pocket notebook, and thumbed through the pages until he found what he was looking for. On the settee, one of his partners shuffled and coughed. Callahan threw him a quelling glance before he said to me, "When was the last time you saw your husband, Mrs. Atherton?"

I turned away from him and looked at the mantel, where two Parian ware dogs stared blankly back at me, their tongues hanging in perpetual greeting. "Thursday night. We were returning from a . . . social engagement . . . and he delivered me to the house and went out again."

"Was this usual for him? To go out again that way?"

"Yes, but—"

Callahan scratched at his side whiskers. "It's been four days since then, Mrs. Atherton. You didn't find it odd that he was gone so long, without leaving any word?"

"It's not uncommon for him to leave for days at a time. For his work. But on Saturday night I did grow worried. He'd promised to meet me at the Reid soiree. He never arrived."

"I see." He marked something in his notebook.

"And then there was the storm. I thought—I hoped—he was waiting it out at his office."

"Did you think that's where he went that night, Mrs. Atherton?"

I thought of the circle, the shooting. I remembered Ben's cautions. "I suppose it's obvious that he didn't."

Robert Callahan cleared his throat. "I know this is indelicate, Mrs. Atherton, but, well, it's not unusual for men to have other . . . relationships."

I stared at him in confusion.

Uneasily, he said, "I know this is painful for you, ma'am. I'm sorry, but d'you think you could check through his things? See if there're bills for jewelry or gifts? Things you don't recognize?"

He thought Peter had a mistress. The idea shook me; I had never considered it before, and I was unnerved to realize how much it explained, his frequent absences, our recent estrangement. I saw Callahan's sympathetic look, and remembered myself. I knew why Peter had been gone so often, and it had nothing to do with a mistress. He had been at the circles. And despite Ben's advice, I said, "I don't think Peter was seeing a mistress, Mr. Callahan. My husband is a spiritualist. Do you know what that is?"

"Sure. One of those rappers."

"It was where we were on Thursday night. At Dorothy Bennett's spirit circle."

He was writing, and he stopped midstroke. "Dorothy Bennett?"

"Yes. My husband was there quite often, I believe. Thursday he had asked me to go with him. He believed he'd been speaking to the spirit of his mother—she died only six months ago. He was determined I see it for myself."

Callahan glanced up from his notebook. I saw a smile play at the corner of his mouth. "Did you? See a spirit, I mean?"

"What I saw, Mr. Atherton, was a very cunning charlatan. But more important, someone fired a gun at the circle that night. It barely missed my husband."

"Someone fired a gun at a spirit circle at Dorothy Bennett's."

His tone was frankly disbelieving. "I'm sorry, Mrs. Atherton, but I don't see what this has to do with anything. Was someone hurt?"

"No."

He shrugged. "Accidents happen all the time."

"Peter didn't believe it was an accident. He thought someone was trying to hurt Mrs. Bennett's medium. That night, when he left me, he said he intended to find out why. And now he's disappeared, and I can't help thinking the shooting might have something to do with it."

"Who else was at the circle that night?"

"Besides Mrs. Bennett and Mr. Jourdain, the medium, there was Sarah Grimm and Wilson Maull. Mr. Rampling, of course. And the Robert Dudleys. Oh, and Jacob Colville."

Callahan stopped writing. "The Dudleys? Mr. Colville? Of Colville Mining?"

"The same."

"And you think one of them might have fired a gun at your husband?"

He was skeptical, and I realized suddenly that if the shooting had not been an accident or a trick, then I was suggesting that one of those at the circle had attempted murder.

I understood Callahan's skepticism—I felt it myself. It was unbelievable to me that one of them would have done such a thing. Whom should I accuse? The Dudleys? Jacob Colville? The petite Sarah Grimm or Mr. Maull or even Dorothy—or Benjamin? Of course it must have been an accident or a trick.

I glanced at Callahan's faintly amused expression and wished I'd followed Ben's advice and said nothing of this. It only served to make me look a fool. The police would not pursue this, not with the Dudleys and Dorothy Bennett and Jacob Colville involved. Not unless someone from that set specifically ordered them to.

Callahan rose and scribbled something, then tore the paper from the notebook and handed it to me. "Here's my name. I'm at police headquarters on Mulberry Street. I'd appreciate it if you could do what I said, Mrs. Atherton. Go through your husband's things. See if there's anything that don't seem right."

"You'll at least check the hospitals?"

"The hospitals?"

"Because of the storm, Mr. Callahan. If something happened to Peter, if he was caught in it—"

"I see. Yes, ma'am, we'll check the hospitals."

He jerked his head at the other two policemen, who rose quickly. One of them had been turning a wax rose in his hand, and he set it aside almost guiltily. Callahan gave me a reassuring smile. "We'll find him, don't worry. Men like Peter Atherton just don't disappear without a trace."

"I pray so, Mr. Callahan."

He looked as if he would say something else, but just then I heard a knock on the door, and Kitty's rapid footsteps, and Callahan inclined his head and said, "We'll take our leave now, ma'am. It appears you've other visitors."

I watched as they went to the front door and tipped their hats at whoever stood in the doorway, and then I heard the unmistakable voice of Pamela Burden, my sister-in-law.

"Good morning, gentlemen. Has my brother been found yet?"

Callahan murmured something and stepped hastily away, and Pamela watched them go before she came into the house. The frigid air rushed inside with her, making me shiver where I stood in the hallway.

"Shut the door, Kitty, please, before we all take cold," I said.

Pamela was dressed completely in the deep gray of half mourning, as I was, but unlike me, the color became her. Instead of looking severe, as I did, Pamela looked softly radiant, with her translucent skin and blond curls and delicate face with its even features that were nothing like my own more exotic ones. She looked fragile and malleable, but looks were deceiving, I knew. Pamela had a formidable will; I'd been lucky she'd welcomed me so readily into the family.

She stilled the bobbing black plume on her hat with a gloved hand and came hurrying toward me. "Evelyn, my dear, I see you've heard the news." Her voice was girlish and breathy, slightly lisping. She took my hands in hers—the kid of her gloves was still cold from outside—and squeezed my fingers gently. The rose scent of her perfume wafted sweet and cloying. "I came as soon as I heard."

"Thank God. I don't know where he could be. I've told them to check the hospitals."

"John was at the courthouse this morning, and sent a messenger telling me to come straight to you." John Burden was Pamela's husband. He was an attorney, as Peter was, but in civil law. He spent his days writing clever contracts and his nights gambling at his club, where his shrewdness, I understood from Peter, was legendary. "We had hoped, of course, that Peter was at home."

"He hasn't been here. Not since before the storm."

Pamela's blue-eyed gaze was piercing, so like Peter's. She squeezed my hands again before she released them and called to Kitty, "Bring us tea please." Then she said reassuringly, "Come now, Evelyn. I see your mind has leaped to all sorts of morbid thoughts. Nothing's happened to him! I'm sure it's something simple. He'll show up, and we'll all laugh about how silly it was."

She led the way into the parlor, angling her wide skirts through the doorway with that effortless Atherton confidence.

"Now tell me," she said the moment the parlor door shut behind us, "what did the police say?"

"They don't know where he is. They've asked me to check through the bills, to see if there are any strange purchases. Gifts and the like."

Her eyes lit with understanding. "They believe Peter's run off with some mistress? Good heavens, Evelyn, I can't imagine him doing such a thing. I would have heard, I assure you, or John would have." Her conviction brooked no opposition.

I was comforted that she felt as I did. "That's what I'd thought."

"What did you tell the police?"

Before I could answer, there was another knock on the door. Pamela said, "No doubt that's Penny or Paul. I've sent notes to both of them."

She went to the window. "Yes, it's Penny."

Of all of Peter's brothers and sisters, Penny was my least favorite. I tried to be charitable, but Penelope Atherton had none of the legendary Atherton charm. She was twenty-five and an avowed spinster, and the least attractive of the Athertons, having inherited all the worst qualities and none of the best. Her face had carried the long, thin nose to extremes, and her eyes were so deep set as to be almost cavernous, and were such a muddy blue they were nearly brown. Her hair, while blond, was so white, thin, and wispy that it seemed nonexistent, especially when pulled into the tight chignon she favored, so it looked like a skullcap, with thready curls framing a face that was too gaunt to take well to the girlish fashion.

She had the extra burden of a contentious personality, and one so determined to do right by her fellow man and so ill-suited for the cause that she was easily drawn into unwinnable fights and just as easily abandoned them when her naturally quarrelsome temperament offended her leaders—her latest cause being abolitionism, though I'd heard Pam remark acidly that Penny had also lent her considerable financial assets to the "woman question."

But she was no doubt here to provide support, and I was grateful for it, and so when Kitty announced her, and she swept imperiously into the room, I welcomed her with a sisterly kiss, which she barely tolerated.

"Well, I'm here," she said, taking a seat on the nearest settee. "What exactly do you intend us to do, Pam? No doubt Peter's simply been gambling and is too embarrassed to come home."

"Gambling?" Pamela had little patience for Penny as well. "Peter's far too parsimonious for that, as you well know. He's never showed the slightest inclination."

"Well, he certainly didn't just disappear into thin air."

The maid brought tea, and the two of them waited while I poured and handed them each a well-sugared cup. Pamela took a sip and said, "It's not like Peter to miss a trial. He's so *dedicated* to his profession." She said it as if it were obscene. Peter's family had never truly understood or supported his passion for criminal law. His mother had scolded him constantly for his devotion. *"Now, the kind of law John practices! That's the kind of law for a gentleman, darling. Not this hobnobbing with undesirables. . . ."*

"What have the police said?" Penny asked.

"They think he might have a mistress somewhere," Pamela answered before I could.

Penny laughed. "A mistress? I can't imagine him taking the time now he's married. Why, he's such a slave to his work it was all we could do to get him to show any interest in courting."

Pam nodded in agreement.

Penny gave me a direct look. "Evelyn? Where do you think he is?"

Peter's family didn't know of his penchant for spiritualism. Peter had felt they wouldn't approve, and he was afraid of their ridicule. Given the reaction of the police, I knew he'd been right to be afraid. But if I wanted their help, I had no choice but to tell them the truth. "Peter was going to spirit circles," I said.

Had I hit them both over the head with the teapot, I doubt their expressions would have been more surprised.

Finally, Pamela sputtered. "Spirit circles?"

"Whatever for?" Penny added.

"He wished to speak to your mother's spirit."

Penny snorted disapprovingly. "If there were such a thing as speaking to spirits, I can't imagine Mama condescending to make an appearance. Can you, Pamela?"

"Hardly," Pamela said. She set her teacup into her saucer with a definitive *clink*. "It's not dignified."

"Whatever you may think, he believed he was speaking to her." I remembered Michel Jourdain's voice, how like Peter's mother he'd sounded. I felt again a grudging admiration for his ability. "The medium he went to was very convincing."

Pamela said, "You mean you went to these circles with him?"

"I went to one."

"Where?"

"At Dorothy Bennett's house."

"Dorothy Bennett?" Penny looked horror-struck.

"She wanted to speak to her sons—"

"I'd heard she was addled," Penny said to Pamela.

"She doesn't seem so," I said. "But this medium she brought from Boston—"

"I cannot understand why you allowed Peter to do this," Penny snapped. "Of all the ridiculous things—"

"Half of your friends indulge in it, Penny," I said impatiently. "That trance lecturer you like so much, the one who speaks on women's rights—what was her name? Achsa Sprague? She's a spiritualist."

Penny lifted her chin. "I've never put any credence in such a thing. It's charlatanism."

Pamela said sharply, "You told the police this, Evelyn?"

"I'm afraid I did."

Pamela's forehead creased; she pursed her lips. "You think this circle might know something of where Peter's gone?"

I hadn't thought of that and wondered that I hadn't. What if he'd gone back to Dorothy's that night? What if someone in the circle knew where he was now?

"I don't know," I answered Pam thoughtfully. "There was an accident that night. A gun went off. Peter thought it was suspicious. I suppose he might have gone back to ask questions."

"A gun went off? Did you tell the police that as well, Evelyn?"

"Yes. I told them everything."

Pamela exhaled audibly. "Well, we must put an end to that."

Penny nodded. "Yes indeed."

"End what?" I asked in confusion.

Penny said, "I don't expect you to understand, of course, Evelyn. You can't help your upbringing. But it would be most unwise for the police to continue to pursue this."

"Peter's an Atherton, after all," Pamela added. "Why, the talk, imagine it! Peter a member of a rapping cult! Talking to Mama through a medium!"

"But shouldn't someone speak with the circle? What if they know something of Peter's whereabouts? And Dorothy Bennett—"

"People have talked about Dorothy for years. She's never been the same since her sons died. Everyone knew she was seeing rappers in Boston."

"There's certainly no need to sully the Atherton name with Dorothy's peculiarities," Penny interjected quickly. "No doubt Peter will return by tonight or tomorrow. We can keep this between us."

"There's no need to worry, now that John and Paul are involved—where *is* Paul? I sent that note an hour ago." Pamela rose again, moving quickly to the window. "In fact, Evelyn, you must let us handle everything. Please don't mention this rapper nonsense again. If the police call on you, send them to John. There's no need to upset yourself over this. We've the means to find Peter without their help."

"Of course, but—perhaps I should go to Dorothy Bennett's and make inquiries?"

"Good Lord, Evelyn, what a dreadful idea!" Penny said. "It would be best if you stayed home. That way, if Peter returns or sends word, you'll be the first to hear."

"You should stay here too, Penny." Pamela turned from the window. "It would help to have someone near, wouldn't it, Evelyn? Some family to help you through this trying time?"

"I'd be grateful for it," I said, though I didn't like how quickly they dismissed the one bit of information I had.

"And Evelyn," Pamela went on thoughtfully, "do go through his things, as the police suggested, won't you? I doubt anything will surface, but it does seem that Peter kept secrets from us after all, and I wonder"—she looked up at me, and I had the startling thought that there was smugness in her gaze—"if perhaps he kept secrets from you too."

Her words sent a frisson of unease through me. But then I banished the feeling as uncharitable. The Athertons had embraced me as family; what could I possibly have to fear from them?

4

A PRETTY THEORY

THE FOLLOWING DAY

Penny brought her trunks with her the next morning. "The roads are impassable! It took us nearly an hour to move two blocks!"

"It's not surprising, after such a storm." I stood back to allow her servants—a chambermaid and driver, and one other—entry. Penny came bustling in behind them.

"You could use more help, Evelyn. Mama always had at least an upstairs and downstairs maid."

She also brought the news that Peter's disappearance had pushed the difficulties of the snowstorm to the back of everyone's mind, and that the speculation about where he was and what might have happened to him abounded. Someone had even suggested he'd been drugged in a local opium den and abducted by white slavers—to this, the *New York Times* had responded tartly, "It appears there are those to whom Peter Atherton's disappearance gives the opportunity to indulge in childhood flights of fancy."

"Has Paul talked to the police?" I asked her. "Has John?"

Penny nodded as she directed her maid in the unpacking of her trunk. "Both of them were with the commissioners last night. The police have been told to leave Dorothy Bennett alone. They were quite relieved, I gather. I doubt they would have intruded upon her in any case, but one never knows when the police will suddenly get it into their heads to actually do something."

I found myself wishing Ben was in town, and that I could turn to him for advice. Though I understood the Atherton concerns, I wanted answers, and I'd spent the night sleepless and asking myself how it could possibly hurt to talk to Dorothy personally. Was there some reason I hadn't considered? Some little known society rule or breech of etiquette that would make everything worse? Ben would know the answer. It would relieve my mind to at least discover if Dorothy had seen my husband after Thursday night, and to ask the same question of Michel Jourdain. If no one knew of the visit, what could be the harm?

I had myself talked into it within the hour. After that, it was only a matter of waiting, of looking for an excuse to go out. When Penny told me she planned to cancel a dinner engagement with one of her abolitionist friends, I told her not to worry about me, and to go.

She frowned at me. "Are you certain, Evelyn? You'll be fine here by yourself?"

"I'm almost always here by myself."

"Very well." She wrapped a muted scarf about her throat— only Penny would have managed to find such a colorless paisley. "If the police come, you'll send for me right away, won't you? Don't speak to them yourself, Evelyn."

"I won't. I promise."

She went out into the night reassured, but the moment she was gone, I bade Kitty follow me to my room and dress me for a social call.

As I was still in half mourning for Peter's mother, I wore a deep lilac silk with a high collar and long sleeves and black lace flounces. I directed Kitty to do my hair in a simple chignon, and I wore no jewelry but for the locket around my neck that held some of Peter's hair.

In the street, Cullen was moving from foot to foot against the frigid breeze, which blew the snow about in blinding clouds, rearranging it for its pleasure. Tiny, icy flakes pricked against my cheeks. The bare-limbed trees lining the street creaked and cracked their branches against one another, and the snow crunched and squeaked beneath my boots.

"It'll be a hard journey, ma'am," Cullen warned me as he opened the door and helped me inside. "The roads're froze."

"We aren't going far. Only to Mrs. Bennett's house."

"I lit the brazier a half hour ago. You keep warm, Mrs. Atherton." Then he closed the door and mounted the driver's seat, and we were off.

We were only going a few blocks, but the roads were as impossible as Penny had warned, and it took us forty-five minutes to reach the familiar Bennett brownstone only a short distance away. Even with the brazier, I was stiff with cold when we finally arrived. The lights of the Bennett house were burning, and there were carriages lining the frozen, snowy street in front. Dorothy must be holding a circle.

I hesitated. I'd intended to speak only to Dorothy and Michel Jourdain. I had no interest in voices from beyond or eerie parlor tricks, especially now. Penny or Pamela would be horrified to discover I'd gone to another. I could turn around now, go home, and no one would be the wiser. The Athertons would find Peter without my help.

But I wanted answers. And now that I'd taken the trouble to come, I didn't want to go home with nothing. What could be the harm in asking them all my questions?

My booted feet slipped and slid on the ice-slick walk as Cullen escorted me to the stoop. I rapped sharply on the door.

It was opened by the butler. I held out my card. "I know I'm not expected, but—"

"Come in, Mrs. Atherton," he said, though he didn't take my card, nor seemingly glance at it. I was surprised that he recognized me, but I didn't question it. I stepped inside.

"They're upstairs, ma'am," he explained as he took my cloak. "They've only just arrived."

"They haven't started yet?"

"No, ma'am."

I went upstairs. The door to the second-floor parlor was open; I heard the voices beyond it. I remembered the conviction on my husband's face the last time I'd been here, and it was that memory that shored my determination. I stepped into the parlor.

Michel Jourdain stood in the middle of a group composed of Robert Dudley and Sarah Grimm, and he was talking animatedly; with every gesture, strands of his hair came loose from its riband to fall into his face. He was wearing gray today, an exquisitely tailored frock coat, and trousers of a silvery hue. As if he felt me there, he stopped speaking and turned, and looked directly at me, and I felt the full and compelling force of his gaze.

"Evelyn!" Robert Dudley had followed Michel's glance, and now he came toward me with his hands outstretched. "How wonderful that you've come! We were just speaking of you."

Sarah came hurrying over. "We've heard the news about Peter. Is there any word? Any word at all?"

I shook my head. "None at all, I'm afraid."

"I'm certain there's nothing to worry about."

I said, "I hope not. His family is looking into everything. But I thought perhaps—"

"Ah! Well, the Athertons will find him soon enough." Jacob Colville stepped from the corner, where he'd been with Grace Dudley. "You mustn't fret, Evelyn, truly. You're with friends. We can help ease your mind."

I heard a flurry behind me. I was still standing in the doorway, and down the hall now came Dorothy's nurses, two of them supporting her as she made her wheezing and difficult way toward us. She was trembling, and the green she wore today only accented the sallowness of her skin, the dark circles beneath her eyes. Ribbons from her hat dangled beside her face like loose and unruly hair, and her neck disappeared into the voluminous folds of a beribboned lace bertha.

She squinted up at me as they reached the doorway. "Evelyn? Evelyn, is that you?"

"Yes, it's me. I'm afraid I've come unforgivably uninvited."

"Nonsense. There's no such thing." As she spoke, Michel Jourdain moved past, brushing against me as he went to her. Dorothy straightened, smiling, and slapped at one of the nurses so he released her arm, and the others let her go into Michel's keeping. "There you are, my boy. Did you see our Evelyn has returned to us?"

"*Oui, ma chère.* I've barely had time to greet her myself." The moment he touched her, I witnessed a remarkable transformation. Dorothy's trembling stopped, and the pain I'd seen in her eyes disappeared. Michel again gave me his charming smile. "Did you find us irresistible after all, *Madame?*"

"I've come because of Peter," I said. "He was troubled the night we were at the circle, and—"

"Troubled?" Dorothy asked sharply. "About what?"

They were all staring at me as if they had no idea why Peter might have been disturbed. Uncomfortably, Ben's words to leave it be returned. I forced myself to forge ahead.

"Over the incident with the gun. I thought perhaps he'd come back here to ask questions."

Dorothy shook her head. The ribbons around her face shook with her. "My dear child, we've heard nothing. I'd expected him last night, but he never showed. And it seems he isn't here tonight."

I'd put more hope into this meeting than I'd realized. Still, I persisted. "Are you certain? Have none of you heard from him at all?"

"Not a word," said Dudley.

"I'm afraid not, my dear," Jacob told me.

Wilson Maull shook his head, and Sarah Grimm fingered the ruby at her throat—a little nervously, I thought—and said, "Not since that circle."

Michel Jourdain was noticeably silent.

"What about you, Mr. Jourdain?" I asked pointedly. "Did my husband visit you again that night?"

"I've not seen him, *Madame*," he said. "It seems none of us has."

I didn't disbelieve them, but I didn't quite believe them, either. "I was so certain he had returned here."

"Oh, child, I wish he had," Dorothy said with a troubled expression. "Perhaps we could have dissuaded him from pursuing this any further. Such bother over a silly misfire."

"Dissuade Peter?" Michel lifted a brow. "*Non, ma chère*, not possible."

"Of course, you're right," she agreed with a sigh. "Once Peter gets an idea in his head, it takes heaven and earth to move him."

"Didn't you find it so, *Madame*?" Michel asked.

They were both looking at me as if they expected me to agree, and so I found myself nodding, saying, "Yes, of course," though their simple observation was a revelation to me, and I realized in dismay that they were right. It was one of the reasons my husband and I were so often at odds. *"I am the husband here, Evie! God, I could strangle your father. Instead of teaching you Plato, he should have been teaching you how to be a wife."*

I winced at the memory of Peter's words, and when I looked at Michel, I saw he was watching me.

"I'm sorry we couldn't be more help," he said, but I had the impression he was not that sorry at all.

"There is one thing we could try, I suppose," Robert Dudley said thoughtfully. "With Evelyn here, we've the affinities we need."

"Oh, of course," Grace said. "Won't you stay for a circle, Evelyn?"

It was the last thing I wanted to do, but Peter had said he wanted questions answered, and who else would have answers but those who had been present? He must have talked to one of them, and I was determined to find out who it was.

"Do you really think a circle could help?" I asked.

Wilson Maull nodded so his fiery curls shook about his head. "Assuredly. The spirits care deeply for the world they've left behind. They watch over everything. I'm certain one of them could tell us Peter's whereabouts."

"You must stay, child," Dorothy said. "The spirits could ease your worries. Michel, tell her to stay."

Michel dug into his vest for a handkerchief, which he pressed to his lips, as if he would cough, though he didn't. Dorothy looked worried.

"My dear boy—"

He ignored her concern and looked at me. "Dorothy wants you to stay, *Madame*. Surely you won't disappoint her? Or me?"

I gave him a stiff smile. "I wouldn't dream of disappointing either of you."

"Excellent!" Robert Dudley said. "Shall we begin then?"

I stood back as Michel escorted Dorothy to the table. He helped her into her chair and pulled up the footstool for her feet. He leaned close to listen to her, laughing at something she said. Dorothy glowed in response. When he started to his seat, she grabbed his arm to forestall him, and then let him go with a reluctant and foolish smile.

Like a young girl in love. How easily he worked her. I could not fault him for trying. Dorothy was a grown woman. To be a fool or not was every person's prerogative.

I realized the others were sitting, and the only vacant chair was the one next to Michel Jourdain, where I'd sat before.

"Come, *Madame*," he called to me.

I made my way to the table. He took my hand, and once again, his grip was too tight, and he was too close, and I felt the deliberateness of it.

Grace Dudley dimmed the lights, and the circle began.

It progressed much as before, with prayers and singing. When Michel spoke his invocation, his voice was strong. There was no sign of his cough, or of the usual breathlessness of a consumptive. "Almighty God, we ask you to bless this meeting tonight, and ask that you send a spirit to converse with us."

The dim gaslight flickered, but did not go out. There was silence for a moment, and then the first rap sounded.

"Who is it?" Wilson Maull whispered.

There was a chorus of ssshhhh's. Michel seemed not to hear. "Is this a spirit come to speak with us?"

RAP RAP RAP.

Yes.

"Who is it? Tell us your name, spirit."

I felt a shaking through the floor. Across from me, Sarah Grimm gasped and said, "Oh, how lovely!"

Michel said, "The table is going to rise."

The shaking subsided; I felt the rise of the massive table beneath our joined hands. It held steady for a moment, and then it began to rock like a wave. There was a quick rapping, like heels dancing on a wooden floor, though there was thick carpet beneath our feet. The table rocked more slowly, as if it were tiring, and then it settled, but the rapping didn't stop. As before, I found myself searching the shadows, looking for the means.

"Who has come?" Michel called out. "Who wishes to speak with us? Is it Peter?"

I tensed, waiting for the voice to come into him the way it had before. But it did not. *RAP RAP RAP RAP RAP.*

"The alphabet," someone—I think it was Wilson Maull—called out. "It wants us to use the alphabet."

Michel said, "Who are you, spirit? Have you a name?"

RAP RAP RAP.

"Spell it out for us."

Across the table, Sarah began reciting the alphabet, slowly, "*A, B, C . . .*"

The table jerked beneath our hands.

"*C,*" Grace Dudley said excitedly.

"*A, B, C, D*"—on and on, until she reached the letter *H.*

Again, the jump of the table.

"*C, H,*" Dorothy said. "Go on, go on."

Letter by letter, the table spelled out the name *CHARLES.*

"It's my cousin," Sarah said breathlessly. "My cousin Charley!"

Robert Dudley said, "No, it's my brother Charles. Is this my brother? Charles Dudley?"

"Let Michel tell," Dorothy broke in. "Let him find out."

When they all went silent, Michel asked into the darkness, "Who have you come to speak to, Charles?"

Sarah began to spell out. "*A, B, C, D, E*—"

RAP.

"*E*," she said with a smile.

If the others did not realize the name the spirit was spelling out, I did. Who else at this table had a name that began with *E*? I glanced curiously at Michel, wondering what he was about, what he intended.

Sarah went on. The spirit rapped to *V,* and then to *I,* and then to *E.*

"*EVIE,*" Sarah said. I felt them all look at me, but Michel's gaze was the one I felt, and I thought, though he was seemingly entranced, there was something else there in his eyes, something that made me want to squirm.

"Do you know a Charles, Evelyn?" Robert asked.

"Her father," Michel said softly.

I started in surprise.

"He's the Charles you know, *mais oui?*"

I was too startled to answer. My father's Christian name was Joseph. It was what his friends and customers had called him.

But his middle name had been Charles, and that was my mother's name for him. Joseph Charles Graff. No one who knew that was now alive. No one but me. How could Michel know this? It was impossible. I was intrigued; I was also wary.

"I hear—" Michel broke off, tilting his head, as if he were listening.

I tensed. Would I now hear my father's voice coming from Michel's mouth in the same way I'd heard Elizabeth Atherton's? Uncomfortably, I anticipated it, though I made a desperate wish that it not be. I had loved my father, and I missed him. But I did not want to hear his voice; not in this way, not as part of a silly game.

But Michel did not speak as he had before. Instead, he seemingly answered a voice inaudible to the rest of us. "I see. Ah, *oui, oui.*" His gaze had been distant, but now he turned to me. "Your father begs leave to touch you. Will you allow it?"

It was too reminiscent of the other night. I wanted to say no, but more than that I wanted to know what he meant to do, and it was that curiosity that got the best of me. "Yes."

"He'll touch you upon your head," Michel said.

Then, I saw it—a glowing, flowing ball—only one this time, and faint, hardly there in the darkness. I froze, suddenly afraid. The light moved as quickly as a man might move. There was a rush of cold air, and I expected it to rap on the table as it had before, to disguise a gunshot; instead I jumped as I felt something upon my hair, the lightest of touches, something that could almost have been a breeze. But there was no breeze. I twisted in my chair; I would have reached out to touch whatever lurked there in the darkness but for the fact that both Michel and Robert Dudley held my hands fast.

"Your father says he's well now," Michel said. His expression was impassive. It was as if he didn't see me at all. "Well and strong. He says you must believe in his world. Trust your instincts."

Trust my instincts? Now I was assured of Michel's fakery. My father would never have said such words. He was a materialist, and he'd taught me to be as well. Instinct had no place in a rational world.

Michel paused, again listening. "He says your mama is there as well, and she tells you her dreams were real, as are yours. Nothing but truth now clouds her visions."

As unlike my father as the earlier words were, these from my mother took me aback. I thought of her visions, the laudanum she drank to dull them. Michel was not referring to that, was he? How could he know it?

Michel said, "And now he must go. He says good-bye."

He was already slumping forward, and I felt something slip from the air around us, as if something indefinable had been sucked away. Again, I felt the heat from the vents near the floor—no more chill from the other world, if in fact that was what it had been. I knew it could not have been real, but Michel Jourdain's ability was stunning. I was ill at ease; I didn't understand why he had chosen to do this. He hadn't known I would be here tonight, or even that I would ever come again, and yet, when the opportunity arose, he took it. How did he know these things? What did he mean to gain?

As if on cue, the gaslights went up, though there was no one there to turn them.

The talk began, excited and rushed, everyone speaking over one another.

"Did you hear what he said?"

"Wasn't it wonderful, Evelyn, how your father came to you? Has he come before?"

"How he must love you to visit you! And to give you word of your mother as well!"

Then, beside me, Michel roused. He straightened, gazing about with a blank-eyed stare that gradually became focused. The others began to rise, to talk among themselves. Dorothy's nurses gathered around her. On my right, Robert Dudley released my hand and went to join the rest. But Michel did not, though he was conscious now. Another time I might have been entertained by his ingenuity. Tonight I was only annoyed. This had not been helpful at all. I'd learned nothing. I tried to pull my fingers away, but his tightened to keep me there.

"Please, Mr. Jourdain. Release me."

He didn't. "Has your father's spirit come to you before?"

I sighed in exasperation. "Really, sir. I must tell you: I'm not what you think I am."

"What do I think you are?"

"Someone as gullible as my husband."

"Ah." His gaze was thoughtful. "You're not so easily fooled?"

"I'm afraid I'm quite above it. But thank you for refraining from gunshots tonight. The next time you might consider how at odds such exhibitions are with your philosophy. I thought spirits returned to better the world, not to kill its inhabitants."

"Did your husband not explain any of this to you, *Madame*?"

"Explain what?"

"Spirits are only the souls of men. As men are imperfect, so must their souls be, eh? Old habits aren't easily undone, and death is only a change in form, not in character. When spirits leave us, they go to one of the seven spheres, not to heaven or hell, as you've no doubt been taught. At the lowest levels are criminals and immoral spirits, true. They'll lie to you if you let them, or play tricks—sometimes quite cruel ones. But the goal in the invisible world is the same as in the visible one—to become better—and they can't go on to the next sphere until they earn the right, and for some, that takes time."

"You sound a blasphemer, sir."

"We no longer live in a world where blasphemers are beheaded, eh? And I'd say it's those preachers who teach only heaven and hell who blaspheme."

"Your spiritualism is a pretty theory—"

"But one you don't believe."

"My father was an investigator, Mr. Jourdain. I'm afraid I tend not to believe most things."

"But you attend Grace Church."

"I didn't say I wasn't a Christian."

"Does your Episcopalian God help you with your nightmares?"

I stared at him. "My nightmares?"

He coughed, pulling the handkerchief from his vest, pressing it to his mouth. As he took it away again, he said, "Your husband tells me you have them often."

The intimacy of his knowledge surprised me enough that I answered him. "Yes. I've always had them."

"Always?"

"Yes, but more so since my parents died."

"Ah," he said.

"You ascribe some importance to them?"

"*Non*. It's only that it distresses me, *Madame,* to think of you unable to sleep." His gaze said something different. It leaped quickly and directly to mine—I had no doubt he'd used such a provocative glance to his benefit many times before.

"You're very bold, Mr. Jourdain."

"Too bold, *Madame?* Or not bold enough?" He smiled at me, and though it was flirtatious, there was an edge to it. "Perhaps you're one of those who come to circles because they like the boldness of them. Above the table they're proper as a queen"—his fingers stroked my hand—"but they're pressing thighs beneath."

I stiffened and pulled my hand from his. "Are you in the habit of making advances toward married women, Mr. Jourdain?"

"Habit? *Non*. Too many husbands have tempers. Or pistols."

I rose. "Good-bye, Mr. Jourdain. I don't expect I'll be returning."

"Such a pity," he said quietly.

"What do you mean?"

"I think you aren't as unaffected as you pretend, *Madame*. Perhaps you could find what you're searching for in a circle, if you've a mind to look. I hate to see you walk away before you try."

"If I change my mind, I'll certainly call on you."

"I look forward to it," he said with a small smile. "If you'd allow me to give you a word of advice: you should listen to your nightmares. I've no doubt your father is trying to tell you something through them."

I went still. "My father?"

"Doesn't he come to you in your dreams, *Madame?*"

Again, the fact that he knew this flustered me, and I found myself lying. "N-no. No, he doesn't."

"Is that so? I would've thought otherwise. Ah, well, I'm truly mistaken then."

"Yes," I said, though I was shaken. "Good night."

He said nothing more, and I didn't look back to see if he

watched as I took my leave of the others. The night had been a waste of time. I wished I hadn't come. I was no closer to an answer about Peter's whereabouts, and I'd been caught off guard by the circle and the knowledge Michel Jourdain had of me that he shouldn't have. My father's name, the fact that I saw him in my nightmares—such intimate things, things only Peter could have told him. To think that my husband had spoken of me in such a way to Michel Jourdain was disturbing. It hurt that he felt me so insignificant that the most private details of my life were fodder for casual conversation.

The ride home was dark and silent. Penny had already retired when I arrived. As I readied for bed, I was uneasy. I left the lamp burning low, as if darkness might prevent Peter from finding his way home. I pulled the blankets up around my chin and closed my eyes, but I was too unsettled, and when the lamplight wavered, touched by a breath, my eyes flew open again. The shadows of the room seemed smoky, full of form and substance. I thought I would never sleep, but I was more exhausted than I'd realized. I closed my eyes.

And fell immediately into a dream. It was the spirit circle once again, but it was as if I were watching it through a shifting mist. The candlelight was watery, the darkness suffocating. The only real thing was the feel of Michel's hand holding tightly to mine, the sound of his voice. "Is Peter Atherton there? We wish to speak to Peter Atherton—"

"I'm here." It was Peter's voice, and it was so loud I looked at the others around the table, expecting to see their surprise, but they were still staring intently at Michel. It was as if they hadn't heard, as if they didn't know.

"Is the spirit of Peter Atherton present?"

"You can find the truth, Evie." Peter's voice filled my head, beloved and frightening at the same time.

Michel Jourdain laughed and said, "You see, he's dead after all," and Peter screamed. . . .

I woke with a start. The lamp was still burning. I was bathed in sweat, my heart pounding. It had been a dream. Just a dream, though it had seemed so real.

I sat up, pushing back the blankets. I hated these vivid and terrifying dreams; what I would give to have them disappear forever. I turned up the lamp. The light filled some of the shadows, but not all of them, and I was frightened enough that I hurried across my bedroom and lit the gas, turning it up, banishing the darkness. There was nothing there, and yet I had felt him. He had been in my head—a dream so real I could not shake it.

I was still awake, and still uneasy, early the next morning, when two solemn-faced policemen appeared on my front step to tell me that Peter's body had been found.

My husband was dead.

5

TRAGEDY ENOUGH

THURSDAY, JANUARY 22, 1857
ONE WEEK AFTER THE SPIRIT CIRCLE

When we arrived at the high brick wall of Bellevue Hospital, it felt as if I were still within a dream. As they took Penny and me down the two steps that led to a low-roofed building, past the lamp painted with black letters reading THE MORGUE, I refused to believe that it was Peter they'd found in the East River. My nightmare haunted me like an uncomfortable premonition.

Inside the morgue, there was a glass partition, and behind it a row of marble slabs, two with uncovered bodies upon them. I heard Penny's sharp inhalation. I gasped and stumbled; one of the policemen took my arm and whispered, "There, there, Mrs. Atherton. This way."

We were not to be given the comfort of distance. They took us around the partition, where a coroner waited in a stained frock coat. Despite the cold, the sweetly rotting scent of decaying flesh and blood was so strong I gagged. Water sprayed from the ceiling to cool the bodies; droplets splashed my cloak and my cheeks.

"Dear God," Penny whispered. She pressed in closer to me, clutching my arm.

The coroner said kindly, "Ladies, if you would please have a look," and motioned toward the nearest slab.

The body wore only a pair of good wool trousers and one boot. The rest had been stripped away, whether by the doctors or the river I didn't know, though the river had done its part by leeching the color from his skin. He was bloated and pale like the belly of a rotting fish. Penny began to cry and turned away.

"The eyes are gone," I heard the coroner whisper to the police. "Fish got to 'em."

My stomach lurched. Despite myself, I looked into Peter's face, his skin misted with the spray from above so it looked like sweat, his lips blue from the ice of the river—and that image washed away every good memory I had of him, guaranteeing that for the rest of my life, whenever I thought of my husband, I would see him with riverweed tangled in his hair.

"Is it him?" the coroner asked.

I could only nod. Behind me, Penny's sobs grew louder.

The coroner said, "His pockets were emptied. Nothing on him but a cuff link. A robbery, no doubt. Looks like he's been in the water more than a week. Maybe two. He was knifed. There, you see it? That wound on his side—"

"I'm going to be sick," I whispered.

One of the men grabbed a nearby bucket, and I vomited into it.

The coroner seemed impervious. He asked, "Did your husband carry a weapon, ma'am?"

I looked up from the bucket, and one of the policemen held out a handkerchief, which I took with shaking hands. "A gun," I whispered, wiping my mouth. Before I could say more, or explain, I was overcome by tears, soft at first, then heaving, choking so I couldn't stop. Through them, I heard one of the constables say, "Best get 'em outta here."

"Come along, ladies," said the other, not unkindly, and they escorted us from the morgue and back to the police wagon. We were just climbing aboard when another carriage came clattering up, a black brougham with gilt trim that I recognized through my tears as belonging to Peter's brother. The driver pulled the horses to a stop, but even before it was completely halted, Paul Atherton came hurtling out.

I felt a moment of profound shock. I knew it was Paul, but he looked so like Peter. I heard Penny's gasp of recognition, and then she was rushing toward him across the icy walk, barreling into his arms so that he nearly fell over with the force of crinoline and serge and sobbing female.

He was pale and red eyed. "I came as soon as I heard. Is it him?"

Penny nodded and buried her face in his wool greatcoat, and he closed his eyes briefly; I saw his struggle with grief and control in the moment before he said grimly to the policemen, "I'll take them home."

"As you wish, sir," said one of them, and they climbed back into the police wagon, leaving us alone before the morgue.

"I can't believe he's dead," Penny sobbed.

Paul looked across her to me. His expression was bleak. "Pam and John are at the house."

He led Penny to the carriage, where the driver waited before the open door. He helped her in, and then me, and then Paul came in beside us, sitting next to his sister, who collapsed against him despite the voluminousness of her skirts, which ballooned between them.

"I heard only that they found him in the river," Paul said.

"He was m-murdered," Penny hiccoughed. Her face was ravaged by her tears, reddened and swollen. "He was stabbed. They said it was a—a robbery. Dear God, who would have done this to him? Who would've wanted to?"

I could have told her it might have been anyone. It could have been any passing street Arab or gang boy who had seen Peter's rich clothing and sensed an opportunity. How many times had I heard of such things? How many times had my father shaken his head and said, *"You remember that, my girl. There's always someone looking to take advantage of a situation. Don't give them the chance to see an opportunity in you."*

A robbery would have been tragedy enough, but I didn't believe that was what it had been. Peter had gone out that night on a mission—I was so filled with anger toward the liars in Dorothy Bennett's circle that I could barely contain it.

Penny was sobbing again, and Paul put his arm around her shoulder, pulling her close into his side. "We'll find the monster." He looked at me, and his eyes seemed to burn with the intensity of his feeling. "I promise you, we will."

His support took my anger and brought hot tears to my own eyes, and I fumbled for a handkerchief, and then realized Paul was holding one out to me. It smelled of sandalwood—a scent Peter too had favored, and I began to sob again at the unexpected reminder.

He let me cry for a few moments, and then I felt the pressure of his hand on my leg, a too-familiar touch, though Paul had always been so, and I liked him enough that it was easy to ignore. I looked up. I saw the glassiness of his eyes, though he didn't cry. He said, "We *will* find who did this, Evelyn. Never fear. And you mustn't worry."

I blinked at him in confusion. "Worry?"

"We'll take care of you, you know. You needn't add fear over your situation to your grief."

Penny looked up from dabbing at her eyes with her own handkerchief. "You made him happy these last years," she agreed. "He spoke often of how thankful he was to have found you. He would have wanted us to see you were looked after."

"You're very kind," I managed, grateful to have family to help me through this. Now that my parents were dead, I had no one else.

Paul gave me a small, encouraging smile. "There's no need to talk of it now. Tonight, we must take comfort from one another."

My tears welled again. Paul sat back with a sigh, and Penny leaned her head on his shoulder, and I felt warm at my inclusion—how good it was to belong to them.

6

MISSING SOME ESSENTIAL THING

FRIDAY, JANUARY 23, 1857

New York Times

KNICKERBOCKER MURDER

Body Found in East River—Suspects Questioned

MANHATTAN—Thursday morning witnessed the grisly discovery of the body of Peter Atherton, New York City attorney, and youngest son of the prominent Knickerbocker family. Mr. Atherton's body was found caught by the ice floes in the East River, at the foot of the Novelty IronWorks. He was stabbed and apparently robbed.

Mr. Atherton was first noted missing on Tuesday morning, when he failed to make an appearance as the defending attorney in the notorious murder trial of Scully Martin.

Robert Callahan, of the Mulberry Street Station, has informed us that the police are questioning possible suspects now, and believe they are close to making an arrest.

I felt the blood drain from my face as I read the words, and I turned the newspaper facedown upon the table.

"Don't worry, Evie," Irene Cushing said. Her face was a study in sympathy as she leaned forward to pat my hand. "You won't have to suffer long, they'll catch who did this vile thing."

"Three paragraphs," I murmured. I put my hand to my temple—the megrim I'd been resisting all morning had turned the world into soft edges and pulsing halos. "How little it takes to describe something so devastating."

"Oh, my dear, we all feel so," Irene said. "I was relieved to see Penny's come to help you."

"Yes, it was good of her." I heard my sister-in-law moving about in the dining room beyond.

"How prescient you were to be worried for him the other night. Who could have imagined that he might have been . . ." She gave a little shudder. "I suppose you think it had something to do with your medium's trick?"

Carefully I said, "It's the reason Peter went out that night, to ask questions."

She exhaled slowly. "Poor Peter. No doubt he was simply in the wrong place at the wrong time. The paper said the police are questioning suspects. Have you any idea who?"

"They believe it was probably some vagrant. He was robbed, you know."

"So meaningless. I hope at least the police have been circumspect."

I nodded, pressing my handkerchief to my eyes. "John's made certain of it. They've really not troubled us at all."

"Well of course not. You're an Atherton!"

"Yes. Thank God for that, at least."

"Evelyn, I know how terrible you must feel, but Peter would have wished you to take care of yourself. You know that's true. Did he"—Irene picked with deliberate nonchalance at a loose thread on her cuff—"I assume he took care that you're provided for?"

"Paul has assured me of the family's support."

"Has he?" She looked surprised, and then relieved. "Thank goodness. The two of you were married such a short time, really, and . . . well, you remember Judith Duncan, don't you? Her husband left no provision for her, and everything went back to his family. God knows the Duncans never cared for her. They sent her packing almost the very day after the funeral! It was a scandal, of course, but she's certainly not the only one it's happened to. Her father gave her a considerable dowry, I understand, but once she was married—well, there was nothing she could do. I heard she was making hats now."

"Peter's family has been very good to me," I said. I was exhausted; I had been up with the Athertons nearly the entire night, preparing the house for mourning, and my headache was becoming unbearable. Softly, I said, "I am so glad you came, Irene."

"Well, you're my dear friend. I'm concerned for you. Everyone is. You know you must call on me for anything. Anything at all." She rose, her crinoline and petticoats rustling beneath the heavy gray satin of her skirt.

"Thank you." I showed her to the door, past the dozens of bouquets lining the hallway—so many that the scent of the lilies and roses was overpowering and nauseating. She kissed me goodbye and I stood in the open doorway and watched as she stepped into the frigid air—what a relief it was to smell the clean, sharp scents of ice and mud, to burn my nostrils with the cold. Irene turned to wave just before her driver helped her inside her waiting carriage.

I shut the door and turned to the china salver on the side table—it was overflowing today with cards that had their corners turned down for sympathy. Above it was a portrait of Peter as a young man that we'd moved from upstairs to hang in the hallway. He looked so innocent—that wide-eyed expression I had never seen, though I knew the smile; he'd used it often to charm me out of a difficult mood. Involuntarily, I reached up to touch it—I could not believe he was gone. The drawn curtains and the stopped clocks, the black crape that swathed the front door—surely those were meant for someone else? But no, the shrines Penny and I had erected were for him. We'd arranged childhood toys he'd loved, a lock of his hair tied with a black ribbon—so soft, so golden; how well I remembered running my fingers through it— and the lace-edged handkerchiefs that had once belonged to his mother that he always carried, all things that meant something to him and therefore to me, though what he should have left behind was nowhere to be found.

"What's the hurry?"

Peter's voice came to me, a quiet whisper of memory, and with it I remembered the two of us in the parlor. He had come home only half an hour before, and was readying to go out again, and I hurried over to him and helped him put on his frock coat, speaking quickly, before his mother had time to call me or interrupt.

"She asks me about it every day. What am I to tell her?"

"Whatever you've told her up till now."

"She makes me feel as if I'm neglecting my duty—"

"Then tell her it's me neglecting mine," he said, pulling the coat over his shoulders, shrugging the fabric into place. He stepped away from me.

"She's worried about the Atherton legacy."

"The Atherton legacy can go to hell. She's got Pam or Paul for that. Not Penny, I suppose. She'll no doubt be a spinster all her life."

"But you're her favorite, Peter, and she lives here. I can't avoid the question forever."

"No? It seems to me you've done a good job so far." He went

to the sideboard and poured himself a drink. "It's none of her business anyway."

"No," I said softly. "But what if it's not just her? What if it's what I want too?"

He stopped in the midst of taking a sip. "What you want? *You* want a child?"

"I want something. You're hardly ever here. I'm lonely—"

"You've Mama for company."

"I want a real conversation. She wants to talk about ribbons, for God's sake. Or sewing stitches."

"I doubt a child would be more scintillating," he said wryly. "Don't you find enough conversation to satisfy you at your soirees and dinners? You seem to like Tom Post enough. The two of you are always together in some corner somewhere."

"It's nothing but a game for him," I said. "A silly flirtation. It's not honest talk. None of them cares what I really think about anything."

"How your father spoiled you, Evie. It's him you want, not a child."

"I want not to be lonely," I said sharply. "If you were home more often, perhaps I wouldn't be."

He sighed, and it was long and exhausted. He put his drink aside. "Not this again."

His words stung enough that I drew back.

He must have seen that he hurt me, because he gave me a soft and rather shamefaced smile and said, "Ah, Evie, don't look so sad! Haven't you everything I promised you?" He gestured around the room. "A fine house, and a closet full of fine gowns, and your evenings as full as you'd wish them to be?"

I said deliberately, "I wish my nights were fuller."

He stiffened, and I cursed myself beneath my breath when he stepped back from me. "I'm a very busy man," he said in a stilted tone. "I'm sorry you aren't satisfied."

"That's not what I meant," I said, though it had been, and we both knew it, and my words now did nothing to soothe him.

He pulled at his cuffs and buttoned his coat. "Take up a hobby if you like, or go shopping. There's enough money that you don't have to be bored—don't give me that look. I never promised you companionship, and you know it."

He strode away from me. "Good night. Don't wait up for me."

As he went from the room, the sob that lodged in my throat turned into a bitter laugh. *"Don't wait up for me."* I'd long since learned better than to do that. I heard the close of the front door. From upstairs came his mother's voice:

"Peter? Is that you? Peter?"

I thought to let her call out forever, but then I relented, and I went into the hall. "He's gone out again, Mother Atherton," I said, and stood there waiting for her inevitable response.

"What have you done to upset him this time?"

"I took away his hobby horses," I said dryly, and then I went up to tend her, taking what solace I could from a woman who thought me a failure in every way.

Now I looked at the altars we'd erected and—suddenly—they held no comfort. How sad it was that only handkerchiefs and childhood toys remained as proof that he had lived.

I was exhausted with my thoughts, with grief and sleeplessness. I had spent the last day sending letters to Peter's friends, and I'd instructed Peter's assistant to telegraph Ben in Albany. I'd heard nothing from him as yet, and I found myself wishing for his steadying and comforting presence. The headache was quickly now becoming debilitating. I wanted nothing more than to go to bed and sleep, though I was afraid the nightmare would come again if I tried.

I heard the sound of a carriage in the street outside, the rattle of wheels over the frozen road, the screech of the brake, and I moved away from the door, not wanting any more visitors. Let Kitty take care of the well-wishers; I would look over their cards tomorrow.

But then I heard the opening of the carriage door, and a shouted voice, and I pushed aside the black draping at the small window to peek out. It was Robert and Grace Dudley coming from the carriage, and Jacob Colville, and the sight of Peter's friends surprised me. I was even more surprised when Michel Jourdain stepped from the carriage behind them, and I felt a great surge of anger. I thought of turning away, refusing their call. No one would blame me in the least if I did so, but my questions were still there. This was an opportunity to discover more of what they knew. Without giving myself time to reconsider, I opened the door, as improper as it was, to greet them.

Grace wore a heavy cloak, and she was swaddled in shawls. Her breath rose in clouds from what little showed of her face. "Oh, Evelyn!" she cried, and then she tried to hurry toward me, slipping and clumsy on the icy walk.

"Careful, darling!" Robert called out, grabbing her elbow just as it looked as if she might fall. "You'll be no help if you break a limb."

Jacob strode past them. "We came the moment we heard. Or at least, the first moment we could." He took the two steps up to the door and put his hand on my shoulder. "My dear, have you slept at all?"

Despite my suspicions, his sincere kindness and Grace's worry brought tears to my eyes. I could not help myself, and I was embarrassed. I didn't know them at all well enough for such emotion. I reminded myself of what I believed about them, composing myself as I stood back to welcome them inside.

"Don't bother with tea or anything else," Grace instructed as I helped her remove her voluminous wraps. "We haven't come to make things harder, but to pray with you."

"Yes, indeed," Jacob said, laying his top hat aside. "To help speed Peter's spirit on its way."

Michel Jourdain came inside and closed the door behind him. He took off his top hat. "*Madame* Atherton, how good it is to see you. I only regret the reason."

"It was kind of you to come," I said stiffly.

"I bring a message from Dorothy. She would've been here with us today, but she's taken poorly."

"Not too bad, I hope?"

His smile was small. "As she ever is."

When they'd divested themselves of their outer clothing, I led them into the parlor. I saw how Michel Jourdain looked about the room, and I thought his eye seemed caught by the black draping, the veiled mirrors.

He stepped to the shrine Penny had erected, and I followed him. He lifted the handkerchief there with careful fingers, bringing it to his nose. "His mother's, I take it?"

"Yes. How did you know?"

"Her perfume," he said. He laid it down again. "Her spirit often brings her scent."

I chose not to address that. "Peter always had one with him."

Michel glanced at me. "Are you sleeping, *Madame*?"

"Very little," I found myself admitting.

"Grief? Or nightmares?"

Again his question was too intimate. It reminded me of the things Peter had told him, and I couldn't answer. Instead, I said, "I find I miss him greatly. There's not much comfort in sleep, or in anything else I've found, Mr. Jourdain."

"Perhaps you're searching for comfort in the wrong places," he said quietly. He gestured to the shrine. "The world's contaminated with material things. Want more for yourself, *chère*."

When I looked at him in surprise, he began to cough. He turned away, and I was grateful for that, because I had no idea how to respond to his words, or to the guilt and sadness they raised within me, as if I'd missed some essential thing when Peter and I had married, something I should have thought to want. To my surprise, I again felt the prick of tears—I was so tender now, it seemed anything pierced.

Grace had seated herself on the settee, and now she called out, "Dear Michel, are you all right?" When he nodded, she called,

"Come, Evelyn," and I blinked away my tears and went to sit beside her. She patted my arm reassuringly. "I know it doesn't seem so now, but Peter's spirit is on his way to a better life."

"Well said, Grace," Jacob said as he sat.

Michel's coughing had ceased; he made his way to the nearest chair, which happened to be beside me.

Grace said, "The paper said the police were questioning suspects. Can you make any guess as to who?"

I met her gaze steadily, trying to divine any hint of dishonesty. "I'm afraid not. Peter's family has kept them at a distance, thankfully."

"Hopefully, they'll soon arrest the culprit."

"Not likely," Michel said. "Whoever murdered Peter has police incompetence on his side."

Dudley frowned. "Well yes, of course, but one can always hope they stumble upon something."

"They believed he'd been missing for at least ten days before his death."

We went silent. I turned to him, startled. "That's what the coroner said: that he thought he'd been in the river more than a week. But . . . that wasn't in the paper, was it?"

"I didn't read it. I spoke to the police this morning."

Jacob straightened. "What? You've been keeping secrets, man. You said nothing of this to us!"

"What was there to say?"

"Well . . . any of it," Dudley said. "What happened? Did they call on you?"

"*Non.* I went down myself. I thought I should tell them what I knew."

I said in surprise, "I didn't think you knew anything!"

"I only told them when I'd last seen your husband, *Madame,* which you knew as well. Peter couldn't have been missing for ten days when they found him, as we all saw him Thursday night."

"But I told them that already."

"Then I've only corroborated it," he said. "Whatever you said, they still believed it had been ten days when I spoke to them. You see? Incompetence. Or stupidity."

"Or perhaps both," Jacob said.

"Did you tell them what happened at the circle that night?" I asked.

Grace said, "Nothing happened but that incident with the discharge. What has that to do with Peter's death?"

"Peter believed it was important," I said. "The shooting was why he went out again that night."

"A foolish endeavor," Jacob said with a sigh.

"Why do you say that?" I asked sharply.

"Because we all know it was nothing but a misfire. I can't help but think that if Peter hadn't been so misguided, he would still be with us today."

"I wish I knew why he believed so," Grace said in distress. "To think that any of us might have . . . well, it doesn't bear thinking about. We could have reassured him if he'd only asked. Oh, I wish he *had* come back to Dorothy's instead of going into that part of town."

Robert touched her hand. "Yes. It's hard to imagine what questions he might have had that would lead him there."

"To think of him set upon that way breaks my heart." Grace gripped her husband's fingers.

They fell into silence. It seemed I heard them all thinking through the scenarios, each contemplating a different ending for my husband. For a moment I studied them. Grace's grief and dismay were real; I saw no insincerity there. Nor did I see it in Robert's tender gaze.

Grace said to me, "We mean to try to contact Peter's spirit at the next circle. Perhaps he can tell us what happened."

Michel said, "He may not remember."

Another deft excuse. I could not help myself. "How could one forget one's own murder?"

Michel shrugged—a movement as gracefully nonchalant as the rest of him. "In the great expanse of eternity, it doesn't seem so important, eh?"

"It seems very important," I disagreed. "To have one's life so callously taken away—"

"Ah, but you see it as one who's left behind, not one with paradise before him."

"I know he'll come to us," Grace reassured me.

Michel said, "Perhaps. Patience is necessary. In the beginning, when they're getting used to their changed world, the spirits are so enraptured listening to the music of their new life they forget to answer our calls."

"But eventually, he will, don't you think?" Jacob Colville asked.

"Eventually," Michel agreed. "We'll do our best, eh? But he may be lost or confused at the start. In the end, it's up to Peter to find us." He turned attentively to me, as if what I thought mattered greatly. "What do you say, *Madame*? Shall we try to find his spirit? Would it ease your grief?"

"Oh, you must take part, Evelyn," Grace said. She took my hand. "It would help you, I know, to hear the answers."

"Let her decide," Michel said softly. "Come—will you let us comfort you?"

How good he was! He almost made me forget that I didn't believe in any of this, that I thought him to be a charlatan. Again, I felt that wary appreciation for his talent. I almost forgave my husband in that moment for revealing my confidences. Peter's nature was no match for this man.

I said, "I doubt I can find comfort in a spirit circle."

If I disappointed him, he gave no sign. "Perhaps you can find it in your eulogies and your Reverend Potter, then. Once he's finished deciding who gets into your Episcopalian heaven."

Grace said, "Oh, Evelyn, I do wish you would reconsider."

"We're here for you if you change your mind," Robert said. "We hold the circles every Tuesday and Thursday—sometimes more often. You will let us know?"

I gave him a stiff smile. I had no intention of stopping my inquiries. "Yes. Of course I'll let you know."

"We'll tell you if we learn anything important," Grace said.

"And to that end, we should pray that Peter reaches the proper sphere quickly," Dudley said firmly. "Come, let's do what we came here to do."

We bowed our heads, and Robert led us in prayer. When it was over, and they took their leave, reassuring me of their constancy, I did not miss the fact that Michel was silent. Nor did I miss how thoughtfully he watched me. I wondered what it was he saw.

Less than an hour later, I received a note from Robert Callahan, asking me to come to the Mulberry Street police headquarters.

7

A GENEROUS MAN

When I arrived, it was late in the afternoon; the sun was falling, beaten into submission by the cold, and the whole city was gray and huddled into itself.

I had gone alone, leaving a note for Penny because I hadn't been able to find her, and when Cullen helped me from the carriage, he looked doubtfully at the massive stone and windowed building that extended back a block to Mott Street and said, "Should I come with you, ma'am?"

"This is police headquarters. I think I'll be safe enough."

I said the words as much to reassure myself as him. Those old habits again. I had to tell myself I should be annoyed as I went up the stone steps and into the station. Callahan's note had given me no hint as to what this meeting was about, and it was odd and presumptuous that he'd summoned me to the station instead of coming to the house as he had before. No doubt Penny would have forbidden me to come. *"An Atherton in the police station? Good Lord, Evelyn, you can't be serious."* But I was still Evelyn Graff in my heart, and I hoped they had news of Peter's killer, and for that I would have excused anything.

The inside of the station was warm and smelling of sweat, and even though the ceilings were high and the receiving area large, it seemed close and crowded. There were policemen hovering about, some accompanied by vagrants or prostitutes, whom I tried to ignore as I sailed to the high countered desk in the center of the room, where sat a heavyset man with a dark mustache.

"I'm Mrs. Peter Atherton," I told him. "Robert Callahan asked me to come."

He nodded shortly and barked, "Matson! This here's Mrs. Atherton. Can you take her up to Callahan?"

A thin, mustachioed watchman came hurrying over. "This way, ma'am," he said, and I followed him past the desk and up narrow, dimly lit stairs whose walls were covered with paper bills printed with criminal faces. Finally, he took me to a small room— an office. There was a desk, a chair, an ancient and rather threadbare settee. There were more criminal portraits on the walls here: "Lazy Jack Ives," "Bourbon Bill," and an extremely ugly woman named "French Bertha" among them. The ceiling was gray with soot from gaslights whose lamps looked as if they'd never been cleaned. There were no curtains at the window, but the glass was so filthy the daylight lent almost no illumination at all.

The officer motioned me to the settee. Just as I sat down, Robert Callahan stepped inside. He looked somber and harried.

"Good afternoon, Mrs. Atherton," he said politely. He looked at the policeman. "Would you mind staying, Matson?"

Matson nodded. He pulled out a notebook and a pencil and sat at the desk.

Robert Callahan snagged the leg of the chair with his foot and yanked it closer. Then he sat, facing me.

"Thank you for coming, Mrs. Atherton. I know it's an inconvenience."

"I assume you have something of importance to tell me?"

"Actually, I was hoping to ask you a few questions."

I frowned. I couldn't imagine why he'd thought I must come down here for that. "Of course. However I can help."

He took a deep breath and glanced over his shoulder at Matson, who lifted his pencil in readiness. Then Callahan asked, "Were you aware of the contents of your husband's will, Mrs. Atherton?"

"Peter left a will?"

"Yes, ma'am, he did."

"I had no idea. Have you told his brother of it?"

"I'm certain he knows. Mr. Burden—your brother-in-law, I believe?"—he waited for my nod—"discovered it in your husband's papers yesterday."

"He did? But . . . he said nothing of it to me."

"So you didn't know your husband left you everything? His monthly allowance? The house and everything in it? Generations of Atherton possessions?"

I was stunned, but through my surprise came a quick warmth at Peter's thoughtfulness. My husband had taken care that I would be protected. There was no chance that I would share Judith Duncan's fate. "No. I—I had no idea."

Callahan said, "Your father was Mr. Atherton's investigator, I understand?"

"Yes. Until he died."

"He must have been happy to see you so well married."

"Yes."

"Quite a stunt, wasn't it, to marry an Atherton?"

"I—I never thought of it that way."

"Was it a love match, Mrs. Atherton?"

It was then I understood. It wasn't the words themselves, but the look in his eyes, the chill of the question. I felt a sudden, numbing dread. "Are you accusing me of murdering my husband, Mr. Callahan?"

"Did you murder him?"

"No! Of course I didn't!"

"He left everything to you."

"I had everything when he was alive. Why would I want him dead?"

"I don't know," he said. His eyes were hard as agate. "Maybe you could tell me."

"I didn't kill my husband!"

Callahan sighed. He rubbed at one unruly sideburn. "Where were you on that Thursday night, Mrs. Atherton?"

Desperately, I said, "I was at Dorothy Bennett's. I've told you this already!"

"What time did you arrive home?"

"Near midnight."

"Apparently you were the last person to see your husband alive, Mrs. Atherton."

"Not the last person. His murderer would have been that."

"Exactly," he said.

"*You* said it was a robbery."

"Yes. I would have thought such a clever ruse beyond a woman, but then again, your father was an investigator. You worked for him, I understand?"

"I did his accounts," I said.

"Did you? Only that? He never spoke to you of his cases?"

"Mr. Callahan—"

"What happened that night when you and your husband returned from Mrs. Bennett's? You said he went out again—is that the truth?"

"Of course it's the truth! I told you—there was the shooting at the spirit circle—"

"The misfire?"

"Yes! Yes. If you want the truth of who murdered my husband, you should question them."

"Ah. You mean question Robert Dudley? Jacob Colville? Perhaps even Mrs. Bennett herself?"

"Peter believed—"

"Did you kill your husband when you returned home that night, Mrs. Atherton? Or was someone else there to do the job for you? A lover, perhaps?"

"No, I—how dare you! I was faithful to my husband!"

Callahan sighed. "Would you like to confess now, Mrs. Atherton? Or should we keep playing this game?"

"Am I under arrest, Mr. Callahan?"

His smile was grim. "Not yet."

I grabbed my bag. I was shaking. "Then I assume I'm free to go?"

Callahan glanced at his man and gave me a reluctant nod. "You're free to go. For now. But we ask that you don't leave the city. We'll assign a watchman to follow you, so don't try to sneak away."

"I have nothing to sneak away from."

Callahan only waved his hand dismissively. "Go home, Mrs. Atherton."

I didn't hesitate. I was afraid they would change their minds, that they would arrest me on the spot, and my fear grabbed my better sense; I fled that office and the station without a shred of dignity, panicked beyond thought or reason.

There was no carriage waiting for me. Wildly, I looked about for it. I had told Cullen to wait, hadn't I? Where could he have gone? But there was no sign of the familiar brougham, and I was too frightened to wait. I began to walk. It was impossible, of course; by the end of the block my corset pinched so cruelly into my ribs I couldn't breathe. I stepped from the curb, into the hard snow piling against it, but it wasn't hard at all, it was merely a thin and icy crust over garbage, and my thin boots sank into it, sending me off balance so I gasped and tottered, nearly falling into the street. A carriage careened around the corner—the horses' hooves threw ice into my face, the driver shouted at me to get out of the way, and I faltered back, stumbling again to the curb. I missed a step and suddenly I was falling. My crinoline bent and collapsed; I tried to catch myself, but the walk was too slippery. I fell hard against the ice, my wrist twisting beneath me.

"Dear God, Evelyn, what do you think you're doing?"

The voice was familiar. I looked up to see a man standing beside me, clad in a greatcoat and top hat. Paul.

"Oh, thank God it's you. Oh, Paul, I—"

"Not here, Evelyn," he said firmly. He put a hand on my arm and hauled me unceremoniously to my feet. He looked around impatiently. "I've been waiting for you. Penny told me you'd gone to the station. I sent your driver away. Come. This way." He raised his hand, hailing his driver, who waited with the carriage I now saw across the street.

Once we were inside, Paul said, "Everyone's waiting at the house."

"I can't tell you how grateful I am." My voice fell to a whisper. "They've accused me of murdering him. Me! I think I . . . I believe I shall need your help, Paul. And John's as well."

Paul said nothing. He moved aside the leather curtain to peer outside. "Did you know about the will, Evelyn?"

I shook my head. "I'd no idea."

He let the curtain fall again and leaned stiffly back against the seat. "You know I've always admired you, Evelyn. Just as Peter did."

"You've always been very kind."

He cleared his throat as if he were uncomfortable. "There are things the family must discuss."

"Yes, of course."

"And you should know . . . well, we'll talk of all this later."

We fell into silence that lasted until we reached the familiar brownstone on Irving Place, the house that had been the Atherton stronghold since 1835, when trade had begun to overtake the upper-class homes on lower Broadway, and their original mansion on Pearl Street had no longer been fashionable. I was relieved to see the Burden carriage waiting before it. John knew every judge and attorney in the city. If there was anyone who could help me withstand these false accusations, it was he.

Paul helped me from the brougham with patient courtesy. My

wrist was already feeling better as we made our way up the icy walk. Kitty opened the door before we even reached the stoop, and when I stepped inside, Peter's family came into the hall to greet us.

They were all dressed in black, as I was, in various measures of severity. Penny was grim, and Pamela wore the strained, sad look of someone bearing a too-great burden. Behind her, John hovered, his dark hair gray-tinged, his height and his importance seeming to expand to fill the narrow hallway, and I was reassured.

"She was sitting in the middle of the walk outside the station," Paul said as Kitty took my cloak.

"In the snow?" Pamela asked.

"Like a common match girl," he said.

"Whatever possessed you, Evelyn?" Pamela asked. She came over to me, putting her hand at my back, gently propelling me down the hall toward the parlor. "Anyone could have seen you!"

I felt a twinge of irritation. "Yes, no doubt it will be on the society page by morning. 'Evelyn Atherton Sits in the Snow!' How much better a headline than 'Evelyn Atherton Accused of Murder.'"

I saw the quick way they all exchanged glances.

Pamela said quietly, "Come, you're overwrought."

The others followed us into the parlor. There the fire was burning brightly and the tea was laid, and I felt drawn into safety—here was my family, who would protect me. Here was my home. Mine, now that Peter had left it to me. I sank into the consoling familiarity of the nearest settee.

Penny sat beside me. She poured a cup of tea and pressed it into my hands. "Drink it, Evelyn. You look ready to swoon."

"She can't swoon just yet," Pamela said as she took a seat. "We must have a family discussion."

Paul went to the fireplace and pushed back the screen. He was no longer wearing his top hat, and his blond hair shone in the glow from the fire, and I thought how like his brother he was, though Paul was chiseled where Peter had been soft, broad where

Peter was less so. He took the glass of bourbon John handed him and leaned against the mantel. His expression went thoughtful. "The house is yours," he said, gesturing to the room, glass in hand.

"Yes, the police told me," I said.

"You didn't know before then?" John asked.

"No, of course not. I would have said something."

"It must be gratifying to know he took such good care to see to you."

Somberly, I said, "I would much rather Peter were alive to see to me."

"We all would, Evelyn," Pamela said.

"We all loved Peter," Penny said.

"Yes, we all loved him," John said. "But now we must face the reality of his death."

"First we must manage the accusation the police have made against me," I said. "It's so absurd. Truly. To think that I—I hardly know what to do."

They were silent.

I looked at John in expectation. "As my lawyer, there must be something—"

"I haven't the expertise to handle a criminal trial, Evelyn," he said. "You know I deal almost exclusively with contracts and mortgages. And wills."

Before I could register this, Pamela said quietly, "I'm certain you realize how lucky you are. After all, had Peter died without a will, everything would have come to us. All these things . . . why, that clock belonged to my grandfather. And the vase was my great-grandmother's. They've been in the family for years."

"You should take them, then," I said impatiently. "Please— you must take what you love. Peter can hardly have wanted to disinherit you of those things you treasure."

"He was only seeing to your security," John said.

"Yes. Everything I had was sold when my own parents died. I've nothing else."

"Peter was a generous man," Penny murmured.

"Too generous," I agreed.

"I'm relieved to hear you say that, Evelyn," John said. He went to the small, gilded table beside the sideboard. For the first time, I noticed there was a sheaf of papers amid my gathered shells and the metal coils of the gas lamp. "It gives me hope that you can be reasonable. I confess I wasn't certain. But now I think we can come to an agreement after all."

I frowned in confusion. "An agreement? About what?"

"You said you thought Peter was too generous in leaving you everything. Would you be willing to stipulate to that—in writing?"

I looked at the others, who had gone still and silent. They were watching me carefully. As I had in the police station, I felt an increasing dread.

John picked up one of the papers and waved it at the room. "This house. These things. They don't belong to you. We would not have objected to your having something. We were preparing a yearly allowance for you. After all, you did make Peter happy for three years. But now, you must see, even that is impossible."

Pamela smiled at me, but it was cold and cutting as a razor.

"The family must be protected," John said.

"I thought I was part of this family."

Penny sighed. "Please, Evelyn, don't be difficult."

John came forward with the paper. He held it out to me. "You should read this."

I stared unseeingly at it. "What is it?"

"An order from Judge Denham. The estate is held in trust until the murder case is resolved. Everything's frozen. You can't sell or trade anything. Do you understand me, Evelyn? Nothing. The order's quite clear. It covers everything: anything that's in the house, anything Peter might have given to you—"

"You mean gifts he gave me? But those things are mine."

John looked at me calmly. "If you sell anything, you'll be arrested."

"I—I don't believe this. You can't mean this!"

They were quiet. Paul, still leaning against the mantel, sipped slowly at his bourbon.

"You can't mean this. You know I didn't kill Peter—" I turned desperately to Paul. "Please, you know I had nothing to do with it."

Paul looked away, but John said, "You must admit it looks suspicious, Evelyn. Peter writing a will that leaves everything to you, that disinherits his own brothers and sisters, the family he loved . . ."

"I didn't kill him."

"Perhaps not. Even so, we'll contest the will."

"But I was his wife."

"If you choose to fight us, it could be most unpleasant for you. Look where you came from, Evelyn. Count yourself lucky for the three years Peter gave you, and move on."

Everything I had believed about the Athertons and their acceptance of me had been a lie. I felt as if I were drowning. "I don't believe this."

"You should believe it," Penny said, as if she were discussing the weather, and not the destruction of my life.

"I need a lawyer," I said.

"I expect you'll have some trouble with that," John said. "As well liked as Peter was, I'm afraid there's no one in town who would defend you as a suspect in his murder."

"I want Benjamin Rampling."

"Peter's partner?" John laughed. "My God, do you really think he'll take your side in this, Evelyn? Against us? Defending the woman accused of murdering his partner? Perhaps there's someone in Boston. Or Philadelphia. Though how you can pay them I've no idea."

"You can't mean to leave me with nothing?"

"Not nothing. Penny's going to stay here for a while. She'll be taking inventory. In the time before you're arrested, you'll live in the comfort to which you've become accustomed." John laid the paper back upon the pile on the table. "I'll leave this here for you to read."

John motioned to Pamela. "Come, my dear. There's nothing more to be done here."

My sister-in-law rose in a cloud of perfume and black silk. She gave me a look that was malicious in its feigned sympathy. "Please cooperate, Evelyn. You don't want this to become a war. It will do you no good."

John escorted her from the parlor. Penny rose to see them out. Paul did nothing. He made no move from where he stood and merely watched them go.

Bitterly, I said, "What are you waiting for, Paul? Have you something else to wound me with?"

He set his glass on the mantel. To my surprise, he came to me, taking Penny's seat beside me on the settee. In a low voice, he said, "Only this. I told you I admired you, Evelyn." He squeezed my arm gently. "I don't think you killed my brother," he said in a rush, glancing to the doorway, as if he feared Penny's imminent return.

I felt a flare of hope. "Then you'll help me find a lawyer? You'll talk to Ben?"

"I only meant should you survive this, I'd offer you my protection."

Warily, I said, "What do you mean?"

"I can rent you a little house. Perhaps on Sixth Avenue." He licked his lips and swallowed and leaned close. I felt his breath against my cheek. "I could visit you there. I could take care of you."

I recoiled. He was asking me to become his mistress. Icily, I said, "I am your brother's widow. Not a whore."

His face twisted. What was so like Peter became like a vile caricature instead. "You'll end up in the Bowery, Evelyn," he snapped at me. "Or worse."

"It would hardly be worse than what you're proposing."

He took a deep, shuddering breath, as if he were trying to gain control. He rose in one fluid motion. "As you wish. I won't repeat my offer, as it offends you so. But neither will I rescind it. Should you find you wish to accept it after all—you must come to me." He smiled, so like Peter, and yet colder than Peter had ever been. He inclined his head in a small bow. "I'll see myself out."

8

THE WHOLE WORLD GONE MAD

TEN DAYS AFTER THE DISCOVERY OF
PETER ATHERTON'S BODY

The next week was wretched beyond imagining. The betrayal of Peter's family was devastating. To find them my enemies so suddenly was unfathomable—how had I not seen that they suffered me merely on Peter's account, that they cared nothing for me otherwise?

It only made my loss more complete, and that loss fed my nightmares, which had grown worse. When I did sleep, which was rare enough—mostly naps in the middle of the afternoon, when my weariness forced me to withdraw from the bitter chore of watching Penny compile her "inventory"—my dreams were little more than relived memories. I found myself walking again with Peter in Battery Park, listening to his proposal; feeling reassured as he smiled when I faced his mother for the first time; watching him wince and laugh at some knickknack I'd chosen. *"Not that, Evie. It's just flash. You've too great a love for the gaudy...."* I would wake with his voice in my ear, his tender tease, smiling for that tiny space of a moment before I remembered he was gone, and the memory melted into hopeless pain and fear. How was it possible he was no longer in this world? How could it be that I would never see him come through the door again?

I forgot all Peter's faults, all the things he'd done that excluded me, that wounded me, the absences that had grown more and more frequent. In the end he had done what he could to see I was taken care of. Despite the family that had sired him, Peter had been a caring man—what had happened to him was more than a crime; it was a terrible injustice. Though I knew it crucial that I somehow find a lawyer, I found myself waiting instead for some word from Benjamin. Regardless of John's words, I could not believe that Ben would forsake me so easily, though as the days passed, and I heard nothing from him, the evidence for his rejection grew more convincing. He sent no calling card, no flowers, not a single note of sympathy or condolence. I had no idea if he was even back in the city, but surely the office would have informed him of Peter's death by now. How difficult would it have been to send word from Albany?

I'd lost him as well as Peter, and I was surprised at how much that saddened and hurt me. This last year, since Ben had come into Peter's life, and therefore mine, I had grown to rely on him more than I'd realized. Though he was a newcomer to New York society, as I was, he'd moved easily within it. I'd been part of it longer, but Ben's inclusion was seamless. How many times had it been left to Ben to ease me through some prickly faux pas because Peter was busy elsewhere? How often had we laughed together over some ridiculous pretension of the upper ten when Peter failed to see the humor of it? To think that he had not felt the same toward me was hard to bear.

But I was not friendless. There were still those in New York who would support me. Irene Cushing, for one. Surely she knew of an attorney who could help me.

First, I must somehow get through Peter's funeral. The Athertons had used their influence to have his body released for burial despite the investigation into his murder, and I began to dread the thought of going, of seeing Benjamin there and knowing he was no longer my friend. I wished, frankly, that it not be necessary for me to attend, and it didn't help that I knew Peter's family felt the same way.

I prepared for the funeral as if I were going into battle. My life was falling apart around me, yet I knew that appearances were all: the appearance of restrained grief, of dignified, refined despair, and most important, the appearance of holding one's head up, and not discomfiting one's guests. As Peter's mother's death had been only six months ago, there was no need to dye any gowns—I already had a ready supply of black and the somber colors of half mourning. The taffeta I'd worn to her funeral was still stylish, the skirts properly wide, the fashion acceptably demure. With it I wore a hat and veil. My jet earrings, and the locket that held a few strands of Peter's hair, were my only jewelry.

Pamela and Penny had arranged everything. They had ignored whatever I had to say about the funeral, and so it was I found the chapel of Grace Church full of cascades of japonica and lilies, which Peter had hated, instead of the yellow tea roses he'd loved, the pews joined by obscenely and ornately ruffled drapings of black crape, and the most horrible, mournful music I'd ever heard, instead of the sweeter hymns he had favored.

The coffin held the place of honor at the altar. It was made of rosewood and covered with more long-stemmed, leaning lilies that dusted the polished wood with their pollen. I had arrived early, with the rest of the family, and was seated in the front pew with them. The funeral was well attended. Peter had been liked, and the Athertons were, of course, one of the most important society families in the city. I didn't think anyone invited would dare to stay away. Ben was nowhere to be seen. It surprised me greatly and confused me. Where was he? Why had he stayed away? It made me more uneasy than I was already.

I kept my eyes straight ahead—on the coffin, on the reverend. The rest of the family gathered tightly together, as turned away from me as they could be while in such close proximity. How different this was from the last funeral I'd attended, for Peter's mother. It seemed another lifetime ago, not simply six short months. I'd been in the midst of the family then—Penny had leaned on my shoulder, I remembered, dabbing her eyes with her black lace handkerchief while Peter held tightly to my hand, and Pam gave me a weak and tearful smile from her place farther down the pew. I had been so truly an Atherton, and they had been so solicitous—well, why not? They owed their mother's comfort those last days to me. It had not been long before her decline that I'd nursed my father, and so the care of Peter's mother had seemed second nature. Who else had brushed Elizabeth Atherton's hair, and washed her, and given her spoonfuls of broth and laudanum to ease her pain? Who had read to her for hours at a time, until my voice was hoarse with the strain? Not her daughters, who recoiled from the task. *"But you're so good at it, Evelyn, and I simply haven't the patience for it." "Mama's always thought me far too rough. . . ."*

But I had done those things out of a sense of belonging, as much an Atherton as one born to the name. I had thought I would be an Atherton forever.

How wrong I'd been. The funeral, more than any other event of the last days, lent the end of my life as an Atherton a terrible irrevocability. With every moment of the painfully long and horrible service, it seemed the world beyond my veil receded a little bit more. I was alone now. Every action of Peter's family made that more clear: how they looked away and whispered among themselves, the coldness of their demeanor toward me, their thinly veiled sufferance.

By the time the service ended, my head was pounding and my eyes burning. I rose with the others, stumbling a little against the pew, and followed Peter's family to the reception line. We stood near the coffin, and one by one, Peter's mourners made their progression. Rose Reid and her husband, Henry, approached Paul first. I heard their words, their solicitous "How sorry we are for your loss," and Paul's murmured "Thank you for coming."

Then to Pamela and John. A clasped hand, a kissed cheek.

"Oh, Pam, how heartbroken you must be!" and on to Penny, who received the same. I straightened, ready to greet them. I held out my gloved hand—

And Rose and Henry Reid sailed past me as if I were invisible.

The cut stunned me. For a moment I thought they hadn't seen me, that it couldn't have been intended. I'd been to their supper only a few weeks ago. Rose and I were friends. But she did not look back at me, and in hurt shock I realized it had been deliberate. I was too taken aback to realize what it truly meant. Not until I forced a pleasant look upon my face, and turned to the next people in line: Elizabeth and Donald DeGroon.

Not until they too spoke to Peter's family and ignored me.

I could have managed a single snub. Perhaps even two. But one after another, the people I had come to think of as my friends refused to acknowledge me, and I could do nothing but stand there and pretend not to be bothered by it, though my face felt as if it might crack from the strain. I waited in vain for some friendly face, for Irene Cushing, or any of Peter's friends from the circle, but apparently they had not come. I told myself not to cry, not to give them the satisfaction of seeing they had affected me, but the tears came to my eyes nonetheless, and it became a matter of trying to keep them from falling and hoping that no one could see them glistening through my veil. How did they do it? I wondered. How did they work so easily and efficiently in tandem without seemingly saying a word to one another? Was it in the air, somehow? Was it like electricity, passing through everything, some invisible web that never broke but only bound them more tightly together and left me more firmly outside?

I should have expected it. In retrospect, I should have known by the bouquets of flowers that no longer came, the lack of calling cards or visitors. But I had been blinded by my fear and my grief. I hadn't seen that my bereavement did the shunning for society. Properly secluded as I was, no one had to question where they stood or what they believed about my guilt or innocence; no one had to take sides. They could avoid me with impunity and call it respect for the grieving. Until today.

And then I saw a splash of color at the back of the church, along with the bustle of several men attending to a single woman. Dorothy Bennett.

She was wearing—incredibly—white, with such a profusion of fringe and lace and ribbons that it looked as if she wore a christening gown. Her attendants were dressed in coats of many hues, among them Michel Jourdain, whose frock coat was a lovely deep blue, with a vest of shot silk that glimmered like sunlight on water, his hair loose and looking almost red where the sunlight came through a stained-glass window to shine upon it.

The crowd was a river of black but for the rainbow that came toward me. Dorothy Bennett leaned heavily both on a cane and on Michel Jourdain's arm, and her walk was slow and labored. The nurses waited at a respectful distance as Michel brought Dorothy to speak to each of the Athertons in turn, though I was too numb to hear the words. I expected them to snub me as well—why wouldn't they? Dorothy was one of the upper ten. I remembered what Michel had said during his visit with the others after Peter's death. How Dorothy would have come had she not taken ill, and I realized it had only been an excuse—the first society snub, though I'd been too stupid to see it. As they approached, I stiffened, waiting for the cut. I was so well prepared that when they stopped before me, I stared dumbly and disbelievingly at them.

"All this fol-de-rol"—Dorothy motioned about when she reached me, hitting her cane against the pew, her face screwed up in distaste—"such a waste of time and tears. Much better to sing!" She battered a lily until it broke apart. "He still lives, Evelyn, you know, but in a different form. He's not gone."

It took me a moment to realize she was speaking to me, and then my relief that they hadn't ignored me was so overwhelming it was all I could do to keep from dissolving into tears.

"Flowers and sympathy . . . Hmpf! Such stupidity." Again, a flick of the cane. Another lily was reduced to tatters. Dorothy let out a bark of a laugh—a sound so foreign in this place today that I saw Pamela look up abruptly from where she was greeting Margaret Hill in the receiving line. Dorothy leaned close and took my arm, urging me away from the others. She whispered, "Look at these fools. I heard the rumors too, but I at least use the sense God gave me. Has the whole world gone mad? I suppose you held him down and stabbed him, hmmmm? A girl of your size against a strapping man like Peter."

"Thank you." My gratitude welled so it was hard to push the words past it.

"For what?"

"For believing I had nothing to do with his death, unlike the rest of my 'friends.'"

"Well, child, if they don't stand by you now, you're better off without them. But you've always a place at our circle, you know that? We're bound in spirit, all of us. These others'll see their error someday."

"Too late to save me, I think," I said.

"You never know," she said. "What we must do first is contact Peter's spirit. We've tried, of course, but he hasn't come yet. Still, I trust Michel will find him soon enough, won't you, my dear?"

Michel inclined his head. "I've already told *Madame* Atherton that some spirits lose their care of the material world. We hope he's gone to one of the higher spheres, where such things no longer matter. It'd grieve me to find him unforgiving—and it'll keep him from developing."

"We'll fetch his spirit," Dorothy said. "Michel will do so whenever you wish."

Michel nodded. Then he leaned close to her. In a low voice, he said, "You've overtired yourself, *ma chère*. I warned you, eh? And now you've need of your cordial."

I looked at him in surprise. To my eyes, Dorothy had rarely

seemed better. But the moment he said the words, I saw the change in her. She seemed to shrivel a little. Her hand began to shake on her cane. "Yes," she said in a small voice. "Yes, indeed."

Michel called over her nurses with a gesture. They swarmed around her, and she seemed suddenly on the verge of collapse. I felt the loss of my ally keenly as they took her from me and led her down the aisle toward the door.

Michel said, "You've Dorothy's support. And mine, of course, though I'm not one of your upper ten."

Just then, a man wearing police blue and bearing a copper badge moved down the aisle, and I saw another one just beyond, at the back of the church, and my concerns over Dorothy fled. They took up places, watching silently, waiting, but made no attempt to come for me. My mouth went dry. "Will it be enough, I wonder?"

He followed my gaze. "None of us can know our destiny, *Madame*," he said, but he smiled to ease his words, and in that moment I didn't care what kind of mountebank he was, or that I believed his circle might hold the secret to Peter's murder. Any friendly face was a balm. I was so vulnerable I think I might have gone into his arms if he'd opened them to me, even in front of so many people. But he only gave me a small bow and turned, and I watched him move smoothly up the aisle toward Dorothy.

After that, I was truly alone. And though I knew what was coming, it was still a shock when the funeral was over, and everyone had gone but Peter's family and the reverend, and the police watchmen who had been waiting so patiently approached me.

"Mrs. Atherton," one of them said in a low voice. "Would you come with us, please?"

I looked to Peter's family. Penny gave me a smug and satisfied smile. Desperately, I said, "This is my husband's funeral, for God's sake. How dare you come here?"

He took my arm, and his hand was firm, his fingers like manacles. "You're under arrest for the murder of Peter Atherton."

THEY TOOK ME to the holding cell in the Mulberry Street Police Headquarters, a dank and cheerless place in the basement, though they brought me in through the back door so I would not be exposed to any curious stares, one of the only concessions to my status.

The basement seemed to go on forever. Rooms with closed doors—the telegraph room, the third precinct offices—gave way to cells, which were adjacent to a large room with whitewashed stone walls. Cots were set about for those seeking shelter from the cold. Tonight, it seemed full of people, both men and women. Most were wrapped in rags and blankets; some lounged on cots while others snored on the floor. The smells of mildew and gas that had greeted me as we came down the stairs were now overpowered by those of unwashed bodies and filled chamber pots. I had to hold my handkerchief to my nose.

"Lookee there, Joe, lookit the fine lady can't stand the smell!" said one bearded, filthy man.

"She'll get used to it once she's 'ere for a while," called another.

The policeman who held my arm yelled, "Shut up, the lot of you, or you'll sleep outside tonight."

Then he firmly directed me to the holding cells.

There were two of them, each with huge, barred doors. It was so dim that I'd thrown back my veil to see, but even that didn't help much. The gaslight's glow extended only a little past the cell doors. Beyond the checkerboard pattern of light and shadow it cast on the floor inside, there was darkness, with deeper dark moving within it. It was only through the sheer dint of my will that I kept my threatening hysteria at bay. As a man's hoarse voice came from one of the cells, "Ah, Carter, you brought me somethin'!" I jerked to a frightened stop. The policeman stumbled.

When he looked at me in question, I said, "I—I thought I'd be given my own cell, at least."

He shook his head. "This ain't the Tombs, ma'am. There's no room for that. But I'll put you in with the women, anyway. Only a few whores in there tonight. An' one pickpocket, so I'd watch your jewels."

He put his key in the lock of the second cell and turned it, opening the door with a clanking grind of metal. One of the women on the bunks within came rushing up. She was skinny and her hair was dark and falling about her shoulders. "'Ave you come for me, ma'am? 'Ave you come to save yer lady's maid, arrested by mistake!"

The policeman shoved at her. "Back you go, Mary. This one ain't your savior."

"Please, ma'am, you can explain it to him. Explain I ain't no whore!"

The policeman said to me, "You might 'ave to fight 'em for a bunk, ma'am." Then he stepped away. I heard the clanging shut of the door, the turn of the key, and I spun and threw myself at the door—too late; he was walking away.

"Wait! I want a lawyer. You must send a message to Mrs. Daniel Cushing for me. Please . . ."

He didn't turn around.

The whore standing beside me looked at me assessingly. "Well, I guess you can't be too much of a lady if they put you 'ere."

My hands were gloved in black kid so tightly molded to my hand they'd had to be sewn on that morning. The taffeta gown I wore made a deep, rich swishing sound with my every step. My crinolines were so fashionably wide I could not enter a room without turning sideways and compressing them. And yet, here I was, my kid-gloved fingers gripping prison bars, my skirts shining dully in the half-light of a basement cell, listening to a prostitute tell me I wasn't much of a lady. Dear God, I shouldn't be here. I didn't belong here. I felt myself unraveling.

"Christ." One of the other women in the cell sat up from where she lolled on the bunk. She had dark hair too, but it was cut short and covered her head in springy curls. She was wearing a cheap satin gown so low cut one of her breasts peeked from her sagging bodice. "You look like you been to a funeral."

"What you in for?" The voice came from the shadows; I could just see a huddled figure uncurling from the corner, moving toward me in the darkness.

"Public drunkenness," said the short-haired one, laughing.

"Disorderly conduct," jeered Mary.

The two of them joined the other, who said, "Shopliftin'," and that sent all three of them into paroxysms of mirth.

The day had been exhausting; I was frightened and alone, and now I was bearing the insults of prostitutes. Those insults only added to the snubs I'd endured at my husband's funeral—*my husband's funeral*—and the betrayals I'd borne in these last days, and I reached the end of my endurance. As the women neared me, I jerked away from the prison bars and glared at them.

"Murder," I snapped.

I don't know what was in my face, but the women stopped laughing and halted, backing away, and I wasn't troubled by them again, not all during the night, as I sat on the thin, stinking cot that served as my bed. I drew back until I was hard against the wall. I would have said I didn't sleep.

But at some point, I must have, because I felt a weight on the end of my cot, heavy enough that the straps beneath squeaked in protest. I thought at first it was one of the women, and I jerked to attention. But then the figure shifted and leaned closer, and it seemed that movement triggered a light, though where it came from I didn't know. Suddenly appearing before me was Peter. His eyes were closed, and his hair was wet and tangled with river-weed and stinking of the foulness of the East River. He touched me; the cold of his hand pierced the taffeta of my sleeve and penetrated to my bones until I was shivering, and my own skin was goose pimpled and icy.

Then I heard his voice, though his mouth didn't open. *Don't believe him, Evie. Don't believe him. . . .*

I woke up screaming.

I heard racing footsteps, someone calling, "Come quick! Come quick!" and suddenly the barred door was clanking open, and a policeman bearing an oil lamp was kneeling beside me.

"What is it, ma'am? Did one of 'em hurt you?"

"We didn't touch her!"

It took me a moment to realize I was not still in the dream, longer still to quiet my screaming. "Oh dear God," I panted. I saw the three women who shared my cell standing bewildered beyond the police officer. "I—I was having a nightmare."

"You all right then? None of 'em hurt you? You sure?"

"I told you we didn't touch her," snapped Mary.

"Shut up, you." The guard turned back to me. "You all right?"

"Yes." I took a deep breath, trying to compose myself. "Yes, I'm fine."

"Good." He sat back on his heels. "Because I was just coming to get you. Callahan wants a word."

"I want a lawyer," I said.

"You can tell him that," the officer said. "My orders're to take you up." He grabbed my hand—before I knew it, he'd hauled me to my feet. My skirts swung madly, nearly unbalancing me. He took my elbow and drew me ungently to the door.

We went up one set of stairs and then another, past those artists' renditions of dangerous criminals—of which I was apparently one now—and the narrow stairwells with their filthy gas lamps sputtering against the dingy walls, until we were at the small office I remembered from before. My escort knocked sharply upon the door, and at a muttered "Come in," he opened it and stood back for me to enter.

Robert Callahan was alone in the office. He had laid his frock coat over the back of a chair and was only in his shirtsleeves. He looked worn and tired, his sideburns more unkempt than usual, as if he'd been tugging at them. He made no move to rise or to put on his coat as I came inside, but only adjusted a fraying suspender more firmly upon his shoulder and looked back down at the paper he was studying.

"Sit down, Mrs. Atherton," he said curtly.

"You need me?" asked my guard.

Callahan shook his head. "Just stay within shouting distance."

The policeman nodded and stepped out again, shutting the door behind him.

Wearily, Callahan said again, "Sit down." He waited pointedly until I finally surrendered and sat straight-backed and prim on the edge of the settee. "Enjoy your night in jail?"

I fought the urge to cry. I would not. Not in front of him. "I want a lawyer. If you would be so kind as to send a message to Irene Cushing for me—Mrs. Daniel Cushing, at Gramercy Park."

"You're aware you've been arrested for your husband's murder?"

I nodded.

Callahan sighed as he turned a page of the papers in his hand. "On the night of January fifteenth, you attended a spirit circle with your husband at Dorothy Bennett's where there were many other society members in attendance. During the course of the evening, a gun misfired."

I frowned at him. "I've told you all this."

"Everyone but you had been to this circle many times, isn't that right, Mrs. Atherton?"

"Yes. It was the first time I'd gone."

"Were you accused of firing the gun?"

The surprise of what he'd said made me forget Irene. "Pardon?"

He raised a brow and glanced again at the paper. "Don't you remember? Are you subject to bouts of amnesia, Mrs. Atherton?"

"I—surely you can't be serious. . . ." I trailed off as I realized how intently he was watching me.

"Was the accusation made, Mrs. Atherton?"

"Who told you this? Was it Mr. Jourdain? I know he came to talk to you—"

"I asked you a question, Mrs. Atherton. Were you accused of firing the gun in the circle that night?"

"I think the accusation was made in jest. No one could possibly have taken it seriously."

"Did the others in the circle know how much you disliked your husband?"

"Disliked him? But—but that's ridiculous!"

"Is it?" He glanced again at the paper. "You rarely attended society events with him. There were rumors that the two of you were estranged, that he was going to leave you."

"No. No, that's not true—"

"To be abandoned that way, without the money or prospects you worked so hard for . . . Well, that might have made anyone desperate, don't you think?"

"I don't know what you mean," I said faintly.

"Is it also true that you were having an affair with Michel Jourdain?"

I was stunned into silence.

Callahan leaned forward. "Is it true, Mrs. Atherton?"

Suddenly I was exhausted beyond measure. "He's hardly . . . appropriate, Mr. Callahan. And even if he were, I was devoted to my husband."

"So you weren't having an affair with him."

"I was not."

"Here, it says that at a ball at Mrs. Henry Reid's home on January seventeenth of this year, you told a witness that you were quite taken with Mr. Jourdain."

"I hardly would have said such a thing. I might have said I was impressed with him, but I meant that regarding his skill as a charlatan—"

"Did you also tell this witness that you were jealous of the attention your husband paid his friends, and that you hated him?"

"At Rose Reid's ball?" I asked in surprise. "I never said that. Not to anyone."

"Apparently you did. To Mrs. Daniel Cushing."

I gaped at him in disbelief. Then, slowly, the realization of what Irene had done, of the things I had said to her in confidence, dawned on me. She had been my dearest friend. I had thought, she, of all people, would help me. . . .

Only the hard carapace of my dress kept me from dissolving before him. My corset felt cruelly tight; I could not breathe.

"Mrs. Cushing alleges that you were certain something terrible had happened to your husband—that you thought so long before any reasonable person would. 'As if you had some superior knowledge,' she said."

"My God," I whispered—surely there was nothing more now that could be done to me; surely there was not a single other hurt to be inflicted.

But Robert Callahan, as if he knew what little reserve of strength I had left, said, "Your husband's family has alleged that you married your husband three years ago to get your hands on his fortune. That you manipulated him to write a will, and then you either murdered him yourself or had him murdered." He paused, looking up from his paper with a gaze so coolly detached I could see no humanity within it. "What say you to these charges, Mrs. Atherton?"

"I want a lawyer." Was that my voice? That thin and wispy sound?

"One will be appointed for you at your arraignment tomorrow morning."

"My arraignment," I repeated. I felt as if I were watching myself from far away, as if my body was not my own. "What time tomorrow? Where shall I present myself?"

"Present yourself? Oh, you needn't worry. One of the guards will take you there."

"They'll pick me up? At what time?"

"They'll retrieve you from the holding cell."

I frowned. "From the holding cell?"

He gave me a cold smile. "Where did you think you were going, Mrs. Atherton? Home? Not until after your arraignment. And only if you can make bail. If they even set it, of course. I have several statements here from people claiming you're likely to flee the city if you're released. It seems no one really knows where you're from."

"I'm from here," I managed. "I grew up in the city. My father . . . I was born on Duane Street. Near the market."

"Were you?"

"I've never . . . I don't know anywhere else. Where would I go?"

"I don't know, Mrs. Atherton." He sighed again. "So, is there anything you wish to say? Any response to these accusations?"

Faintly, I said, "Only that I'm innocent."

He nodded. Then he stood, and shouted, "Tyler!"

There was the sound of footsteps. The door opened, and my guard stuck his face back in. "Yes, sir?"

"Take Mrs. Atherton back to her cell."

I remember nothing of the return to the basement. The next thing I knew, the barred door was closing firmly behind me, and my three companions were looking up with wary interest, and I went numbly to my bunk and curled as best as I could upon it, and waited out another sleepless night.

9

THINGS AREN'T ALWAYS
WHAT THEY SEEM

TUESDAY, FEBRUARY 3, 1857

The next morning, after a meager breakfast of bread and weak tea, I was escorted again from my cell. This time, I was put into a Black Maria—a police wagon—and taken to one of the district courts. I was weary and listless; I could not even bring myself to look around me as they hustled me from the carriage and into the building that housed the court. I could not have told where in the city I was.

The lawyer I'd asked for had not materialized. The patrolman who escorted me was quick to say that after the arraignment, I'd probably be taken to the Tombs, the notorious Egyptian-styled Halls of Detention at Leonard and Elm Streets, where I would wait out the weeks or months until my trial date, unless I could afford to pay whatever bail was set. If indeed it were set at all.

I listened to these sentiments with only half an ear. Callahan's listing of the accusations against me had cluttered my mind all through the night. Irene Cushing's betrayal had been hard to bear; I shuddered to think of all the things I had told her, all the secrets of my marriage I'd revealed. It was the knowledge of her duplicity that had finally stolen my hope. Dorothy Bennett had pledged me her support, but I wondered now if she would even remember. And as for the rest of the circle: the Dudleys, Sarah Grimm, Jacob Colville, and Wilson Maull . . . I'd seen no sign of them at Peter's funeral. I knew they didn't believe in such ceremonies, but in my despair their absence took on a new meaning. Their lack of help implied that Peter had been right to suspect one of them. They must know something about my husband's murder, and now I was imprisoned and unlikely to discover it. I burned with resentment and anger, but it was better than my fear, and so I nurtured it.

The two patrolmen who had guard of me took me up the stone stairs to the courtroom, which was large, but stuffy and stinking even on this cold day, and ill lit, so the prisoners and policemen and lawyers moving about were cast as grotesque shadows against the wall behind the judges, who sat on a high dais flanked by large globed lamps. There was a cast-iron rail separating the audience from the judges, and between that and the dais was a step, also surrounded by a railing, at which a man stood now, conferring with a judge.

The courtroom was full; I saw reporters scribbling away in their notebooks, and family members crying into their handkerchiefs as they waited for their friends and relatives to be charged.

"Here, ma'am," said one of my guards, directing me to a bench that lined the wall perpendicular to the audience, separated again by a railing. There were others on those benches too: several men, and one other woman, who gazed with mutinous silence on the proceedings. I sat down, and my guards sat on either side of me as I waited my turn. I found myself searching the courtroom for someone I knew, a friendly face, but there was no one, although several reporters studied me with interest. In dismay, I realized my name and misfortune would be splashed all over the newspapers by tomorrow.

Then, the back door of the courtroom opened, and I started as my relatives—all clad starkly in mourning—walked in. Paul first, and then John and Pamela. Penny came last, her face as pinched and sour as I'd ever seen it. Paul did not even occasion a glance in my direction, nor did John, but Pamela and Penny darted me vicious little looks.

"Looks like they wish you dead," whispered one of my guards, chuckling. "I wouldn't count on bail set today."

The four of them took seats in the front row before the judges. It seemed clear that now the Athertons had arrived, my name would soon come before the judges, and I'd not yet seen any sign of a lawyer. Surely I'd been assigned a public defender? Anxiously I looked about, trying to catch sight of any harried, overworked young man, but the few fitting that description were in conference with other prisoners.

Then the door opened again, and into the courtroom stepped Benjamin Rampling.

He looked so confident and self-assured in his dark suit and somber vest and necktie, so competent, and though I knew he was not on my side, I could not help feeling an overwhelming relief at his presence. I know I gasped; the sound was loud enough that he turned to look, and I watched in stunned disbelief as he stepped past the Athertons without a word and crossed the courtroom to me.

"Evelyn, my dear," he said, and then surprisingly, his dark eyes went glassy with unshed tears. "How can you forgive me?"

I could not answer. I thought for a moment this must be a dream—how could he be here standing before me now? I struggled to keep what faint hope I had from rising.

He sat beside me on the bench and reached for my hand, clasping it between his. "You must have thought I'd abandoned you. Trust me when I say nothing was further from my mind."

"But—where have you been? You—you weren't at the funeral."

"In Albany. The wretched case took longer than I'd hoped. I'm afraid I was away from my hotel for some days. I didn't receive the telegram from the office until yesterday. I came as soon as I could."

"Oh, Ben," I whispered. Damnable tears filled my eyes; I could not stop them.

His hand tightened on mine. "How terrible this must have been for you. What you must have thought . . . I would have done whatever I could to prevent it. Peter would never have wanted this." He released my hand long enough to take a handkerchief from his pocket. When he offered it to me, I took it gratefully. Then I saw the avaricious way the reporters were watching, and I straightened and attempted to restore myself.

"I was afraid of what to think," I admitted quietly. "When you sent no word—"

"You must believe I didn't know. I'd assumed Peter had returned, that all was well. When I discovered what had happened . . . Dear God, Evelyn, I cannot apologize enough."

I glanced toward the Athertons, who watched with bitter animosity, and murmured, "You don't believe it then? The things they're saying of me?"

"No, I don't believe it."

"Peter's family means to see me hang."

"They've been angry since Peter's mother left him the house."

"I didn't know."

"Peter protected you from it. My dear, there is so much we must speak about. I've contacted several people in the short time I've been back. I believe I can help you. Will you allow me to do so?"

I took a deep breath. "I'd be so grateful, Benjamin. Truly. It's been so horrible! Everyone's abandoned me, I'm afraid—"

"Not everyone. You're not alone, my dear. There are still some who deplore what's happened here." His voice lowered with what seemed a fiercely contained anger, and he glanced quickly over his shoulder at Peter's family. "This time, they shan't get their way."

I whispered, "Are you certain, Ben? Peter's family can be formidable—"

"Peter would have wanted me to do this," he told me. He

looked as if he would say something more, but just then the bailiff's voice rang out over the room.

"Mrs. Peter Atherton, approach the bench."

Benjamin gave me a reassuring smile and helped me to my feet. He directed me past the benches, to the small table on the step before the judges, who looked down from their high desk like avenging angels.

"Benjamin Rampling representing Mrs. Peter Atherton," Benjamin said, waiting while a secretary scratched his name onto a piece of paper.

One of the magistrates peered at me over the order before him. "Are you Mrs. Peter Atherton?"

I gripped the railing before me. My throat felt too dry to speak, but finally I answered, "I am, sir."

"Evelyn Graff Atherton, you are charged with first-degree murder in the death of your husband, Mr. Peter Atherton, on January fifteenth, 1857. How do you plead?"

"Not guilty, Your Honor."

Again, the scratching of the pen. I heard the whispering behind me, the furious scribbling of the newspaper reporters.

"So noted," said the judge. "We'll set the trial date for Monday, March twenty-third, 1857. Will that give you sufficient time to prepare, Mr. Rampling?"

"It would, Your Honor. Now to the subject of bail. Mrs. Atherton begs for leniency. As you will note, Mrs. Atherton is an upstanding member of society—"

"Your Honor, sir, Mrs. Atherton is hardly upstanding." The district attorney stepped forward. He motioned to Pamela and the others. "The family of Mrs. Atherton's late husband believes she murdered him for his fortune. They state that before her marriage, Mrs. Atherton was not known. They're uncertain where she came from. Surely three years of marriage is hardly enough time to solidify the ties that keep a criminal from taking flight. The crime itself was especially heinous. The state requests that bail be denied."

"Denied?" Benjamin looked at him in disbelief and then back at the magistrate. "Your Honor, Mrs. Atherton was born and raised in this city, as anyone who has taken the time to investigate would know. In her life, she has seldom set foot out of it—before the last three years, when she summered at Saratoga with her husband and his family, never so."

"Mrs. Atherton has nowhere to go," protested the district attorney. "She is not welcome to stay with her husband's family, and no one has come forward to vouch for her. We believe, Your Honor, that she may have unknown friends who would help her leave the city before the trial."

Benjamin turned to him. In exasperation, he said, "Either she has no friends and will flee the city, or she has unknown friends who will help her flee. Which is it, Hall?"

The magistrate peered over the podium. "Did you have something to add, Mr. Burden?"

I glanced back to see that John had raised his hand. Now, he stood. "I do, Your Honor. Mrs. Atherton has shown herself capable of great duplicity. She has no family; her friends have shunned her. In short, she has no reason to remain in this city. Peter Atherton's family wishes to see justice done. They would ask that Mrs. Atherton be kept safely behind bars."

"Mrs. Atherton is a lady, Your Honor," Benjamin objected. "And Mrs. Dorothy Bennett has given her word that Mrs. Atherton will be present for her trial. I myself will vouch for her as well."

I looked at Benjamin in surprise, but he didn't turn his gaze from the judge.

"Dorothy Bennett? Have you a paper to that effect, Mr. Rampling?"

"I do, sir." Ben opened the case he carried, rummaging around until he found the proper document. He stepped forward and laid it upon the bench.

The judge picked it up and read it closely. Then, with a sigh, he set it down and turned to the district attorney, who was frowning.

"Mr. Hall, have you any objection to Mrs. Bennett's promise that Mrs. Atherton will be present for her trial?"

"Only that I don't believe it, Your Honor. Mrs. Bennett has been ill these last years. I wonder if she knew what she was signing."

"Not only did she know," Benjamin responded tartly, "but she has lent her financial assets to the promise. Mrs. Bennett is willing to post bail for Mrs. Atherton."

"Then bail is set in the amount of twenty-five thousand dollars," said the magistrate. "Mr. Rampling, you may make arrangements with the bailiff."

It was over, and yet I couldn't move. I stood speechless, my hands curled about the railing until Benjamin touched my shoulder and murmured, "Come, Evelyn. You're free to go."

I turned just in time to see my in-laws rising; Penny's stare was venomous, and Pamela's face was set. John did not bother to look at me, but Paul inclined his head slightly in acknowledgment. Then the four of them left the courtroom.

It did not take long to secure my release. Benjamin took my arm, leading me from the district court and out to the street. He hailed a cab and helped me into it, spoke a few words to the driver, then climbed in to sit across from me.

"I'm so grateful to you," I told him as the carriage started off. "But I'm afraid you'll be as much a pariah in this city as I am, now that you've decided to help me."

"I've no regrets," he said.

"The Athertons have so much influence—it would have been much easier to let me face them alone."

"Peter wouldn't have wanted that," he said.

"So you said, but I doubt he would have asked you to sacrifice so much—"

"You don't think so?" His voice was quietly venomous. "Things aren't always what they seem, Evelyn. Didn't you wonder why Peter left everything to you?"

"He wanted to take care of me."

"I'm certain he did. But he could have done so by leaving you a yearly income, which would have satisfied you and soothed his brothers and sisters as well. He didn't do that. Don't think that his disinheriting them was an accident. He did it deliberately."

"But he loved his family—"

Ben snorted. "The biggest curse of Peter's life was being an Atherton! There are tensions in that family you know nothing about, Evelyn. Suffice to say that it's no sacrifice for me to oppose them. In fact, I relish the opportunity."

I was taken aback. "I had no idea."

He waved my comment away. "It's enough for you to know that I dislike the Athertons on Peter's account, but even if that weren't true, you and I are friends. I need no other reason to help you. I'll hear nothing more about it. Now there are some things we must discuss. Some changes have occurred since you were arrested."

"Changes? It's been only two days."

"More than long enough for this city," he said grimly.

I leaned back as well as I could against the seat, raising the tang of onions and sweat from the stained upholstery—still a better smell than the mildewy, stinking jail scent that clung to my skin and hair. I wanted desperately to change from these wretched clothes I'd worn since my husband's funeral.

"I'm exhausted, Ben. Can't it wait until we reach the house? I imagine Penny will throw a fit when I ask her to leave, but if you're there—"

"We're not going to the house."

"We're not?"

He gave me a sober look. "The Athertons have taken it over pending the trial."

I forgot my clothes and my exhaustion. "They can't do that. Peter left it to me."

Ben laughed shortly and bitterly. "Are you really so naive, Evie?

The Athertons have conspired to have you arrested since the moment they learned the contents of Peter's will. A few bribes, one or two discussions with police commissioners . . . No, the house is theirs. You won't be able to dislodge them, and you'll be arrested again if you show up on the doorstep."

I stared at him in disbelief. My rage over the injustice was so overwhelming it was all I could do to keep still. "They'd have me on the street? I won't let them do this!"

"Come, Evie. You've lived among the upper ten long enough to know how things work. You've no power here. However, you do have other options. Dorothy Bennett's been quite a friend—she asked that you stay with her, but I've taken lodgings for you at a boardinghouse near mine. Very respectable, though it will be quite a comedown in circumstance for you, I'm afraid. The court has approved it on the condition that a watchman be posted out front to make certain you don't flee."

My anger grew, and along with it came a desperate powerlessness. "I want to fight them. The house is mine. Why should I stay in a boardinghouse when I've a perfectly satisfactory home of my own?"

"It would be a pointless battle. You must know that. Let them have the house for now. It doesn't matter. What matters is what you're facing. You could hang if you're found guilty. The evidence against you is quite intimidating."

I felt myself pale. "But how could it be, when I didn't kill him?"

"Circumstantial evidence has weight, and it's not as if the police will investigate beyond it. The commissioners have told them what to think, and the commissioners are in the Athertons' pockets. This case will be tried on hearsay and rumor, and it will be admissible because the Athertons want it to be. Society is on their side; they'll crawl out of the woodwork to offer proof against you, especially now that Irene Cushing has been so very obliging."

Until that moment, I had not truly realized the horror of my situation.

"In any case, this trial will be very difficult. I would have wished you'd said nothing of the shooting incident to Irene or the police—"

"How could I not? Peter thought it important enough that he went out that night to ask questions."

Ben gave me an odd look. Then he turned to glance out the window, and I had the distinct impression he was keeping something from me.

"What is it?" I asked anxiously, and then, when he said nothing, "Ben?"

"This is what I want you to do, Evelyn. I want you to go to that boardinghouse. Forget about what Peter said that night. Let me take care of everything."

"But why?"

"I'm asking you to do this. Not just as your attorney, but as your friend. What happened to Peter . . ."

I was shaken by a quick dread, a terrible apprehension. "What *did* happen to Peter, Ben? What is it you're not telling me?"

He was quiet.

I made a sound of dismay. "I can't just be silent. You tell me to do nothing, but you must know that's impossible. My life is at stake. To just sit quietly—you must understand—I can't."

He sighed. "There are times I wish you were truly just another society wife, Evie."

"I've no doubt Peter wished that as well," I said wryly.

"Peter didn't want you to worry." He paused. "The shooting was no accident."

"So Peter was right! Someone meant to kill Michel!"

Ben shook his head. "He told you that to protect you. The truth is he felt the bullet had been meant for him."

I was stunned. "But—you told me it was nothing, a trick only. You told me not to take it seriously."

"I know. Forgive me. I was only doing what Peter asked me to do. He didn't want you to worry, and he most assuredly did not want you involved. But that was before he ended up dead, with you accused of his murder."

"So the shooting did have something to do with his death?"

Ben nodded heavily. "I believe someone meant to kill Peter that night, and when they failed at the circle, they followed him."

"I knew it!" I was vindicated. My suspicions had been valid ones. "I knew it had to be one of them. But who? I've seen all of them since, you know. I doubt it was one of the Dudleys—they seem so sincerely to want to pass the word of the spirits on, but as for the others—"

"It wasn't the Dudleys," Ben said quietly. "They're innocents in all this."

"Then who? Do you think it could be Jacob? Or perhaps Wilson Maull? Which of them had a reason to want Peter dead?"

He looked at me. "Neither. I believe it was Michel Jourdain."

"Michel Jourdain?" I stared at him in disbelief, and then I laughed. "Why, he's nothing but a charlatan. I mean really, Ben, he's very clever, but I'd say Dorothy has more to fear from him than any, and only because she's in love with him, but for now he seems to make her happy enough—"

"He's taking money from her," Ben said sharply. "Peter was determined to stop it."

"Dorothy's not a child, and she's not addled. If she wants to make a fool of herself over him and give him a few dollars, why should Peter have objected?"

"She's not in her right mind. She's old and she's sick. And it's not just a few dollars, it's thousands. She's been completely taken in by Jourdain. He's not just any flimflam man. He's a dangerous one. Once Peter realized how much control he had over her, he was bound to expose him. It became . . . an obsession. He couldn't concentrate on anything else."

Ben's words confused me. I thought of the reverence I'd heard in Peter's voice on our way to the Bennett house. "But Peter nearly worshipped him, and it was clear he believed. The way he spoke to his mother's spirit—"

"It was an act. He was working hard to convince Dorothy to put Jourdain aside. But he didn't want Jourdain becoming suspicious. Peter was afraid, and he was right to be so. I think Jourdain discovered what Peter was trying to do. I think he set up the shooting that night to kill him."

"It seems rather extreme, doesn't it? And the two of them were sitting so close—only Dorothy was between them. The angle was impossible."

Ben was grim. "Did you think the rapping real? Or the balls of light? The man has a hundred ways to fool the eye. I've no doubt he set up some mechanism. I'm certain that, had we searched the room that night, we would have found it suspended in some corner somewhere, or even hidden by drapes."

"It seems rather elaborate," I said dubiously.

"The best of these tricks are, and he has a great deal to lose. I don't know what's going on in that house, Evelyn, but it's clear he has some kind of hold on Dorothy. I wish I knew what it was. My guess is that he's found a way to control her fortune, and Peter either discovered how or was close to discovering it."

"Yes, but murder . . ."

"Who else in the circle had such a motive? Jourdain's charming, I'll admit, but charming men can be liars, and he's the best of them. Do you really doubt he's capable of such an act?"

I thought of Peter's funeral, how Michel had managed Dorothy, how she'd changed at his word to a trembling invalid. I remembered the circle I'd stumbled upon, how he'd seized the opportunity to deceive me as he had the others, and my sense that he'd had something to gain. One by one, every moment I'd spent with Michel gathered to indict him. His flirtation, the way he'd wormed information about me from my husband, the way he'd gone to the police himself to talk to them about Peter—so he could tell them what he'd known of Peter's disappearance? Or to discover whether they suspected him? I thought of my father's informants. Appealing and charismatic and handsome, yes, but had I ever doubted they would cut someone's throat if they felt the need?

Yet those men were petty criminals with nothing to lose. Michel Jourdain was Dorothy Bennett's houseguest, and a well-taken-care-of one at that, and the others in the circle were of the upper ten. To take the risk of killing Peter—an Atherton, no less—was foolish indeed, and I did not believe he was a fool. My father had taught me to look carefully at every situation, to ask the right questions. Now I meant to do so.

"Stop the carriage," I said.

"What?"

"Stop the carriage. You said Dorothy asked me to stay with her. That's where I want to go. I want you to arrange it."

Ben looked startled, and then alarmed. "I will not. I told you, I don't want you involved."

"I'm already involved, wouldn't you say?" I asked. "You're right when you say I can't fight Peter's family, but this is something I *can* do. Would you really keep me from trying to save myself?"

"This is not a game, Evelyn."

"No, it's not." I met his firm tone with one of my own. "I'm an investigator's daughter. If I'm at Dorothy's, I'll be right in the midst of things."

"That's exactly why I can't allow it. Jourdain is a dangerous man. Peter would never—"

"Peter is dead," I said harshly. At Ben's stricken look, I softened. "Perhaps he wouldn't have allowed it. But he would not have wanted me to hang for his murder, either."

"Your father was the investigator, not you. You did his books—"

"He taught me a great deal."

Ben leaned forward. He looked as if he might take my hand, but then stopped just short of doing so. "You are a dear, dear friend, Evie, and I want to help you—but Jourdain's already killed Peter. I don't think he would hesitate to kill you, and that I could not bear. Please don't ask it of me. This is real, not some game you must win at all costs. Let me handle this."

I drew back, stung. "You don't believe I can find proof that he murdered Peter?"

"It's not a matter of believing or not. My conscience will not allow me to let you try."

"Will your conscience rest easier when I'm swinging from a scaffold?" I demanded harshly. "When the Athertons are congratulating themselves for getting rid of me so neatly?"

He shook his head in frustration. "You must believe I won't let that happen!"

"You've said yourself we're dealing with the power of the upper ten. All of the city is against me but for you and Dorothy Bennett and that circle. If you and I both believe the secret to Peter's death is in that house, and she's offered me a way in—how can I refuse it?"

"I'll continue to go to the circles," he insisted. "We'll discover it that way."

"Not if you're right, and Michel is Peter's killer," I pointed out. "He lives in that house. How much better would it be for me to be able to watch what he does all day long?"

"I don't think—"

"I'll know where he is every moment. I can discover what his hold is on Dorothy. I can search his room for evidence. How would you be able to do that just attending a circle?"

I saw him hesitate. I knew I'd swayed him and pushed ahead. "I know to be careful. But I must tell you, Ben, that if you don't join me in this, I'll find a way to do it without you."

I never took my gaze from his face, and so I saw when his surprise changed into an expression of admiration. It was the expression I'd seen many times on my father's face, and I knew what it meant: I had won.

Then, slowly, Ben said, "By God, I'll bet you would."

I said nothing. I waited.

"Very well," he said finally. "We'll try it your way. But only for a time, Evie. If I feel things have grown too dangerous, I shall want you to leave."

"When that happens, I'll consider it," I said.

"You'll promise it now," he said.

I nodded. I could always persuade him otherwise if I needed to. "Very well."

"Then I'll make the arrangements," he said, pounding on the roof of the carriage to tell the driver to stop.

10

EVERYONE HAS SECRETS

THE BENNETT MANSION

When we arrived at Dorothy's that evening, Benjamin let me go with a comforting reminder. "If you need me, you've only to send a message."

In the hours it had taken Ben to make the arrangements with the court and with Dorothy, we had contrived a plan: I was to question Dorothy and Michel and the others, but subtly, so Michel especially would not think he was a suspect. If I learned anything, I was to contact Ben immediately.

The task was not difficult, and I was certain of my ability to manage it. Hadn't Papa always said I had a discerning eye? But once I stepped foot on Dorothy Bennett's porch, my uncertainty returned. It was one thing to resolve to find proof of Michel Jourdain's perfidy; it was quite another to be in the same room with his charm and ease and not be swayed. The fact that I had admired his ingeniousness worked against me now. I found myself equivocating—Ben's belief in Michel's guilt was unshakable, and I knew without a doubt Michel's ability to take advantage of people. Yet that was hardly the same thing as murder.

I would have to keep my head if I wanted to find the truth, and the last days had left me so exhausted and battered that I determined to start nothing until I'd had a decent night's sleep to restore me. I hoped, in fact, to keep from seeing either Dorothy or Michel until then, as Dorothy had been kind enough to cancel tonight's circle so I could get settled in.

Lambert was warmly polite when he greeted me at the door—as if it were an everyday occurrence that a newly accused murderess came to take refuge in his mistress's house.

"Mrs. Bennett asks you to excuse her, but says you must make yourself at home," he said. Then he called Molly, the upstairs maid, to lead me to my room on the third floor.

The hallway was lined with closed doors but for the end, where huge double doors were open to reveal finely polished bookcases laden with books—a library. At the other end, two nurses lounged on a settee outside a closed door.

"That's Mrs. Bennett's room," Molly told me as she took me to the second door on the right. "An' this one's yours, ma'am."

I stepped inside. The room itself had hardly registered—blue and white, elegant and beautiful—before I saw that Kitty and my trunks had preceded me.

"Mrs. Bennett asked me to pack your things," my maid said with a short curtsey and a worried look, "and told me to come along. I tried to bring as many things as I could, ma'am, but there weren't much time."

It was a thoughtfulness I had not expected. "Thank you. I'm so grateful you decided to come . . . despite everything."

"Oh, ma'am, I was glad to. They turned us all out. Miss Atherton says she's no need of us. She only kept Cook."

"They did what?"

"Turned us all out, ma'am. Cullen too." Kitty's eyes filled with tears. "And him being with Mr. Atherton since he was a boy and all—just let him go without even a warning."

I was stunned, and angry—and angrier still at the impotence of my rage. I wanted to do something for them—but what? I had no money to give them; my references would mean nothing. "I'm so sorry. As you can see, there's nothing I can do. No doubt you heard the rumors—"

"Yes, ma'am. But no one believes them."

"Thank you," I whispered, moved more than I could say.

Kitty nodded with an embarrassed little smile and helped me change from the black taffeta I now thought of as my jail gown. I shuddered as I stepped from the folds of the wrinkled fabric, and as Kitty moved to hang it up in the armoire, I opened my mouth to tell her to burn it, and then swallowed the words before they were said. Though I doubted I would wear it again, my future was not assured enough to destroy a perfectly good gown—how I wished it was. How I wished I could burn it to ashes and never be reminded of these last two days again.

Yet things were too unsettled, so I let it be and went to the china basin and washed myself as best I could. My hair was thick and abundant—it would need more water than the basin could hold to wash it, and so I resolved to bear it for the time being and let Kitty do what she could with it.

"There now, ma'am," she said, when at last I was changed and recoiffed. "You look yourself again."

It was only then that I allowed myself to relax and to look about the room, to see the luxury Dorothy accorded her guests. The pale blue silk damask that covered the walls seemed to shimmer in the gaslight. An armoire and desk and bureau were of white trimmed with gold, as were the settee and two chairs that stood before the Italian white marble fireplace, all with deep blue velvet cushions that echoed the colors in the velvet tapestry carpet. The bed was large and canopied, draped in blue with gold tassels. Dorothy's kindness in offering me this place, in settling me so comfortably, touched me deeply. It also made me feel a bit guilty. I was here, after all, to disrupt her life. I consoled myself with the thought that if it was indeed true that the man she trusted was a murderer, she would thank me for it in the end.

I went to the window, pushing aside the layers of curtains—

brocade and velvet and silk—to look out. The view from this window was of the side yard, and the snow-crusted windows of the brownstone next door, but it was angled just enough that I could see to Fifth Avenue, to the tree-shrouded grounds of the First Presbyterian Church across the street, with its high tower and Gothic architecture. I leaned into the window, pressing my cheek against the glass to see better, as curious as any child peeking into a shop window. It was then I saw the police watchman on the corner. He seemed idle enough, but I froze—I knew he was there for me.

The world I'd once belonged to—the world of women who promenaded the Avenue in sarcenets and bombazines and velvets, who spent the hours in idle chatter, in meaningless shopping, in receiving boxes delivered to the house that held fans and hats and veils that were soon forgotten and seldom if ever worn—had slipped away. It didn't matter that I'd always felt as if I were playacting; I had wanted it and embraced it, though I'd never been able to rid myself of the sense that those women knew some secret I had not been privy to, that if they would only share it, I would be happy too. . . .

I remembered saying as much to Benjamin not so long ago— only a few months, really, though it seemed a longer time than that. It had been late summer, after dinner, and the two of us sat at the chessboard, an elaborate and beautiful set whose carved marble pieces were usually a pleasure to touch. But I was halfhearted; I could not keep my mind on the game. Peter was at the pianoforte, running his fingers idly over the keys. The notes were discordant and melancholy. I'd felt his strange mood all through dinner, and any attempt I'd made to draw him into conversation had resulted in his snapping at me to leave him be. *"It's nothing to do with you, Evie, can't you see that?"*

Ben had done his best to lighten things. He'd been the one to suggest a game of chess, but tonight I watched without much interest as he took my last bishop, and he looked up in surprise. "What? No protest? Are you ill?"

I smiled weakly at his tease. I would have replied in kind, but Peter said from the piano, "I don't know how you can play with her. I won't do it anymore. It's unnatural for a woman to want to win so much."

I felt my face burn at his criticism, but Benjamin looked at him and said, "Unnatural? That's quite a condemnation, my friend. I'm surprised to hear such words from you."

His tone was even, but I saw the way Peter scowled and glanced away. The room filled with tension, and I looked out the parlor window and said in a low voice, "Perhaps he's right. Perhaps I am unnatural. Certainly I can't seem to be the wife he wants."

Benjamin's voice was equally quiet. "He's unhappy. His mother's death . . ."

"Yes. His mother's death." I sighed. "Sometimes it seems so unfair—why should everyone else be so happy when we're not?"

"I don't think everyone else is," Ben mused. "I think everyone feels as you do—if others are so happy, why should they confess the truth of their lives and be found lacking?"

"Perhaps." I looked back outside. A couple I didn't know walked in the twilight. He took her hand and tucked it into the crook of his arm, pulling her close to his side, and she leaned her head on his shoulder and smiled; it seemed they'd been put there just at that moment to underscore my words. "Look at them. It looks as if they have everything."

Peter brought his hand down hard on the keys. I jumped a little, and Benjamin glanced at my husband. "It only seems that way. Everyone is hiding something, Evelyn. Happiness is just another mask we wear."

Now, as I stared out the window at the policeman on Fifth Avenue, Ben's words spurred an odd and troubling echo. *"Everyone has secrets, Madame, hmmm? I would think it especially true of women who find themselves so quickly in a better world."*

I drew back, letting the curtain fall again into place. And then, as if I had summoned him, I heard Michel's voice at the doorway.

"I see you've arrived."

Startled, I turned to see him. His smile was so disarming that I found myself smiling back. I had to remind myself of the fact that this man might be responsible for my husband's death. We all had secrets, indeed.

I schooled my expression to careful pleasantness. "Yes, I arrived just now."

"I think you'll be comfortable here, eh?" He stepped inside the room. "Mine is just across the hall, should you need anything."

There was nothing in his voice, no innuendo. But his charm allowed one to read whatever they wished into his words, and implied that he would accommodate. "I can't imagine I will. But thank you."

"I've come to escort you to supper."

"Oh, I—"

"It's early, I know. But it must be if we've any hope of Dorothy joining us. Her cordial dictates her hours." He began to cough, motioning for me to wait while he grabbed his handkerchief, coughing so hard it seemed to wrack his body. When the spell finally ended, he tucked away the handkerchief with an apologetic smile.

I said, "New York is a terrible place to be in the winter. Perhaps a drier climate—"

"*Non, non,* it's a cold, nothing more."

"Then, perhaps you should rest."

"One can't rest one's life away, eh?"

"Perhaps not, but a few hours . . . In fact, I thought I might rest myself, and take supper in my room. I'm really very tired."

"How disappointed Dorothy'll be."

I was excruciatingly aware of how much I owed my hostess. My resolve to wait until morning faltered. If she took the trouble to come to supper, I could not stay away. "I suppose I could make the effort, if she decides to join us."

"And leave me to myself if she doesn't?"

"You hardly seem in need of a companion."

"You think not?" He made an expression of feigned hurt. "Is it my lack of necessity that makes you say that, or your lack of desire to dine with me?"

"I owe Dorothy a great deal," I said. "So I would make the sacrifice for her. But truly, I doubt I could be an interesting dinner companion tonight."

"Perhaps you should leave that verdict to me, eh?" He smiled and crossed the room to where I stood.

I had managed him at a distance, but when he was close, he was really quite overwhelming. I was aware of him in a way that unsettled me, and I had the uncomfortable sense that he knew it. If we were to live in the same house together, I must find a way to come to terms with him—at least until I found some evidence of his guilt, or the lack of it. For now, it seemed, simple friendliness—and wariness—was easiest. I gave him a small smile. "As you wish then. But I doubt I can entertain you."

The moment I said the words, I realized that nothing about Michel Jourdain was destined to be simple. The smile that crossed his face was provocative and knowing. "*Madame,* Dorothy's feeling that you can entertain me, as you say, is one of the reasons you're here. She worries that I've no one to talk with. She's very much the invalid, *ma pauvre chère.* Abed all day. I visit her when she's awake, but she fears I might become bored."

"Perhaps you should do some reading. I saw the library down the hall."

"*Oui.* Books're fine ways to pass the time. But Dorothy gets these notions in her head. Ah, *Madame,* I'm sure you understand."

"I'm afraid I won't have much time to be convivial. Surely Dorothy knows I've a trial to prepare for."

"So I reminded her. Sometimes, her potions"—he touched his temple with a slender, ringed finger—"she doesn't always think clearly. I had to remind her of the Doctrine of Affinities."

"I'm afraid I don't know what that is."

"Swedenborg told us that everything in the spirit world corresponds to the same thing in the material one. It's true for men and women as well. We all have a spiritual affinity, *oui*? Someone who understands our soul."

I frowned at him. "What has that to do with it?"

"Well, any companion won't do, eh? One tends to know, doesn't one, whether there's an affinity? I confess I'm not interested anymore in wasting time with those who don't . . . understand. To find the right companion, well, it's worth waiting for. But I'm sure you found that to be so yourself."

I stared at him blankly.

"In your marriage," he explained.

"Oh. Yes."

His gaze was too intimate, as if he knew something I didn't. He held out his arm, crooking his elbow. "Will you come to supper, *Madame* Atherton, and entertain me?"

It would be churlish now to refuse. I took his arm and allowed him to lead me from the bedroom and down the stairs.

The dining room was warm and inviting, with its gold-flocked red wallpaper and a fire burning in the grate. A sideboard held china tureens and silver platters and a vase filled with bold red dahlias and white roses—fresh flowers in the dead of winter, a luxury I had never thought to take advantage of even when I could, so bred was I to frugality. A rosewood table gleamed in the gaslight, one end set elaborately for three, decorated with an ornately cast bronze epergne that overflowed with apples and greenery. Jeweled rings held gold damask napkins; thick beeswax candles flickered, scenting the room with their honeyed fragrance, sending dancing shadows across the walls.

"Ah, how fortunate we are," Michel said. "It seems Dorothy will join us after all." He motioned for me to take the seat on Dorothy's right, as he took the left. There was wine already decanted and ready to pour, and this he did without asking if I would have any, and then lifted his glass to me. "To success, *Madame,* in finding the true villain in Peter's murder."

His words took me aback; for a moment I thought he knew why I was here, and then I realized he could not know, that it was what anyone might say. I took a sip and said, "Shouldn't we wait for Dorothy?"

He shook his head. "Sometimes her intentions change, eh? She asks us to start without her."

"Oh, but—"

"Please, *Madame*. She would be troubled to know you waited."

I clenched the stem of my wineglass and said as casually as I could, "How well you seem to know her. And yet, you met such a short time ago."

"Not so short," he said. "We met last June."

"In Boston?"

"Oui."

"Peter said it was Dorothy's sister who brought you and Dorothy together?"

Michel took another sip of wine. "You know my history well."

"Only that part of it. How did you meet Sally Bayley?"

"She'd heard of me and asked me to come. She's dedicated her life to investigating spirits. It was she who first asked me to contact Dorothy's sons."

"And when you did, Dorothy brought you to New York?"

He inclined his head modestly. *"Oui.* She invited me to stay with her here. It gave her such comfort, I couldn't refuse."

"What about Peter? When did you first meet him?"

"Soon after his mother died, I believe. It was . . . in August, I think."

"How long did it take to contact his mother?"

Michel smiled. "So many questions!"

I could not smile back. "Forgive me. It's just that . . . Peter was murdered. I feel there's so much I must know."

"Oui, of course. I'm happy to help you any way I can."

I watched him carefully in an attempt to measure his sincerity as he drained his wine and poured another glass, and then poured more into my own.

"What did Peter wish to know from her?" I asked.

"That she was happy, of course."

"And was she?"

"*Oui*. But she was troubled."

"Why?"

Michel looked at me. "Because of you, *Madame*."

"She wished better for her son," I murmured.

He said, "All mamas are like that, eh? What matters is that Peter loved you more."

"Than his mother?" I laughed bitterly. "No."

"He married you, didn't he? Either he loved you, *Madame,* or you bewitched him."

The words held an uncomfortable familiarity. I thought of the Athertons, the will. "Bewitched him? Who told you that?"

"No one. But where men and women are concerned, there're only the two ways, eh? He said he loved you. It seemed true to me."

But his smile seemed feigned—or perhaps it was simply that I saw through it.

Just then, I heard a commotion in the hall, and I looked up to see Dorothy entering, supported by three of her attendants.

"Ah, Evelyn, child! I was told you'd arrived—how glad I am to see you!"

Michel rose, hurrying over to her, and one of the nurses relinquished his position so that Michel might take her arm. The moment he did, I saw again an incredible transformation—it was as if she regained her strength, as if the years and pain dropped away. She waved away the others and let Michel alone guide her to her seat at the head of the table.

She sat in a flurry of exhalations and fussy reorderings, and then she gripped Michel's arm and said, "Thank you, dear boy," with such heartfelt gratitude that it was faintly embarrassing to watch. He smiled at her and took his seat.

"*Madame* Atherton and I were just toasting to success," he said.

"Oh yes, oh yes." Dorothy reached for her own wineglass, which Michel had already filled. "I hear Benjamin's got things well in hand—how happy I was to hear of his involvement."

"I'm grateful for yours," I said quietly. "What you've done for me, Dorothy—I can hardly repay it."

"I don't need repayment. To let such stupidity stand, well, it isn't in my nature." She reached over to pat my hand. "You know, child, in some ways you remind me of me. Oh, I was born a Van Rycker, and I married a Bennett, but I never had much patience for all these airs everyone puts on. You'd think Caroline Astor didn't use a chamber pot like other people. It's why I don't pay any attention to their talk. They'd gossip about dust if given the chance. You think I don't hear what they say about me and Michel?" She looked to Michel, as if she were waiting for him to approve of what she'd said, and when he took her hand, she tittered like a girl in the throes of calf-love.

The maid brought in a tureen and began to ladle a lovely smooth and fragrant turtle soup into our bowls. Once it was steaming before us, and the servant was gone again, Dorothy said to Michel, "When should we make another effort to reach Peter's spirit?"

"As soon as *Madame* Atherton wishes."

"I thought you told me it would avail me nothing." When he looked at me in question, I explained, "You said Peter wouldn't remember, that he would have moved on."

"*Non.* I said I hoped he'd moved on."

Dorothy said, "I know he's found joy and peace, child. But that doesn't mean his spirit won't help you. The spirits have so much knowledge. They understand the meaning of life in ways we can't hope to. They want to help us."

"If they can," Michel amended.

"When I think of your poor father's visit to our circle, and how much he wanted to reassure you . . ." Dorothy sighed. "I wonder how long he'd been searching for a way to contact you before Michel came along and provided the path? When did your father join the spirit world, Evelyn?"

"A year ago. He and my mother died of the cholera."

"Cholera?" She seemed to pale. "How terrible you must have felt not to be able to go to them."

"Oh, I went to them," I said softly. "I insisted upon nursing them, though Peter didn't like it."

Dorothy frowned. "Thank God you escaped it."

"I didn't escape it. I survived it."

Her spoon dropped with a clank into her bowl. "You caught it? You survived it? How?"

"I don't know."

Her eyes became suddenly watery. She picked up her napkin and dabbed at them, and Michel leaned over solicitously, saying, "It's no cause for sadness."

She nodded and tried to smile. "It's what took my oldest boy, Everett, you know. Cholera. Terrible thing. Horrible. He's at peace now, of course, but I hadn't the heart to ask his spirit if he'd been in pain." Her gaze was suddenly sharp. "Were you in pain?"

"I was feverish, mostly. I'm afraid I don't remember much of it."

My words seemed to comfort her. She sagged a little in her chair and grasped Michel's hand convulsively. "I shouldn't care, you know. He's in a better place. He's happy, but . . . ah, it's silly. Pardon a silly old woman, will you, child?"

"I don't think it's silly," I soothed. "Had I a child, I wouldn't want him to die in pain, no matter how lovely the spheres beyond are."

"I miss them terribly, you know—seeing they're happy helps but doesn't ease the days without them. That's why I'm so grateful for Michel."

"Ssshhh, *ma chère,*" he said. "You know I won't leave you."

"I know." She nodded, and then again, more vigorously, as if his words strengthened some inner resolve. "I know you won't.

Especially not now." She gave him a coy and flirtatious look—coming from such an old woman, it made my skin crawl. But Michel showed no such revulsion. As if I weren't at the table, he leaned close to her—I could not tell if he whispered in her ear or nuzzled it; all I saw was the way she flushed and giggled and turned to kiss him fully on the mouth. She lingered overlong, not simply a friendly kiss, and I thought of what Ben had said about Michel's manipulation of Dorothy and his influence over her purse. *"I don't know what's going on in that household, or how he's controlling Dorothy. . . ."* No, perhaps Ben did not know, but I was beginning to understand, and I was sickened by it.

I pushed my bowl away, no longer hungry. Dorothy drew back from Michel and looked at me as if she'd forgotten I was there, and then she motioned to the girl standing near the dining room door. "Bella, bring the lamb, please." To me, she said, "Thursday night, we'll call a circle. We'll find Peter's spirit, my dear. Michel will find him."

As the maid brought the rest of the courses, I watched him. He did not cough once during dinner, which I found to be faintly ominous, and he ate heartily, though with a casual grace that bespoke entitlement. I saw how Dorothy seemed mesmerized by him. I watched how he served her, how he controlled even what she ate, and I marveled at how comfortable he was, like a man without secrets. He was so good at manipulating her; there was not a seam that showed. He maneuvered everything to get what he wanted—even the maids seemed to race to do his bidding.

And then, suddenly and uncomfortably, I realized that I too was only here because he wanted me to be. How easily he could have convinced Dorothy to leave me to my fate. A single word from him, and I would be in the Tombs now.

The thought was troubling. I didn't think Michel Jourdain was in the habit of being altruistic—whatever he did, he did for his benefit, of that I had no doubt. So what benefit was my being here to him? If he had killed Peter, why not just leave me in the

Tombs to hang—as long as I took the blame, no one would come looking for the real culprit. And if he had not killed Peter . . . I didn't fool myself into thinking he had some noble motive in helping me. I was here for a reason, and somehow I had already played into his hands.

11

THE DREAM

That night, I had the dream again. I was in the spirit circle, but it was very dark, and the only light in the room was a halo about the table, a dim glow like the press of streetlamps against the night. I could not see where the light was coming from, but we were bathed in it, and there was nothing beyond but darkness. I felt the touch of Michel's hand on mine, his fingers pressed flat, almost caressing, as if to soothe me, and then he began to chant in a language I didn't understand—French, I thought, as it slipped over me. I felt his breath on my skin, and it was seductive and strange and seemed to say, *Close your eyes and dream of me,* and I felt myself swaying, relaxing.

And then I heard Peter's voice: *Find the truth.* I felt his hand on my shoulder. *You can't stop looking, Evie. You must never stop. You can find the truth. I know you can.*

I woke sweating and frightened in a strange room. It was a moment before I remembered where I was. And then I climbed from bed and went to the small desk near the door, rifling through it until I found some notepaper, a pen. I scrawled a note to Benjamin Rampling telling him of the circle tomorrow night—in that moment, I did not know if I could manage it without him.

When I was finished, I sealed the note and put it aside to wait for morning. But sleep eluded me, and when dawn broke, I was haggard and hollow-eyed.

I listened to the clanking through the heating vents as one of the servants stoked the furnace. I had no idea of the workings of this house, whether or not Dorothy truly stayed in bed all day, or what Michel did with his time. What I did know was that, after my haunting dream, I had no wish to find him soon, even though I knew that eventually I must.

There was a soft knock on the door, and Kitty peeked in. "Oh, ma'am, you're awake already. D'you need me now?"

I was sitting at the dressing table, brushing out my hair, and I nodded. As she came in and closed the door behind her, I said, "How is the household? I hope they've made you comfortable."

"Oh, as can be, ma'am." She went to the armoire and began going through my gowns. "Will it be the serge today, ma'am? It's cold out, that's for sure."

"The serge is fine. Where have they put you?"

"The servants' quarters are upstairs, at the ends of the ball-room, which ain't nothing but an empty room. I've never seen such a thing as that, and it's kept that way but for a few nights a year."

"Probably not even that, now," I said.

"That's what Mr. Lambert says. He says it's been years since Mrs. Bennett used it, and it's all full of cobwebs and such."

I looked in the mirror, pausing midbrush. "What does Mr. Lambert say about Mrs. Bennett's invalidism?"

"That it's a pity, poor thing, and that she's better than she thinks she is, if she'd only get up and walk about now and then." Kitty pulled the serge from the armoire and laid it upon the bed before she turned to the bureau and took out my underthings. "What with all them boy nurses she has, I guess I'd stay abed too. That Charley, ain't he a comely one? And sweet too."

"You'd best keep your distance from that sort, Kitty."

She flushed. "Oh, that's not what I mean, ma'am. Truly. You know I got my own Sean, and I'd never—"

"What about Michel Jourdain?"

"Oh, *that* one," Kitty said disapprovingly. "Well, they don't say nothing of him but nice. The house runs so much smoother now he's here. Miz Bennett is so happy. . . . But he's too fair by half. Reminds me of my brother Conan—that boy could talk the wings off a butterfly and wouldn't give no thought to smashing it after." She shook her head. "Ah well, what do I know? The rest of the house like him well enough. Mr. Lambert even calls him the master."

"The master? How odd."

"They talk about him like he's royal or something." Kitty lifted my chemise. "Here now, ma'am."

Obediently I came over to her, letting her slip my dressing gown from my shoulders and slide the chemise over my head. "Did they have anything to say about his habits?"

"His habits?" Kitty held out the corset for me. As I put it on and hooked the front fastenings, she said, "Well, I don't know as to that. He takes to visiting Miz Bennett a couple times a day—always at least once, no matter how poorly she says she's feeling. Can you hold in your breath a minute, ma'am?"

I did so, and she tightened the laces. Then she went on, "He's a learned one too, he is. Spends most of his time in the library, I guess. Agnes—that's the downstairs maid—says sometimes she sees him wandering alone in the yard. She thinks he's lonely. They're all glad you're here to keep him company."

"I'm hardly here for that."

"Oh, that's what I told them, ma'am. But I think they wish you would. They want him to be happy. No one wants him to leave—not on his account or Miz Bennett's."

I thought of Michel's intimacy with Dorothy, her obvious infatuation. "Mrs. Bennett doesn't keep him happy enough?"

"Well, she's a sick old lady, ma'am."

"Yes, but . . . is there any talk of . . . does anyone think their relationship odd?"

"Odd? Not that I've heard, ma'am."

I was silent as she continued to dress me, thinking of what she'd said. Surely, if his relationship with Dorothy was uncomfortably intimate, the servants would have spoken of it. It bordered on scandalous—Dorothy was in her late sixties, and Michel? Well, I had no idea how old he was, but certainly not much more than I. Perhaps I hadn't seen what I thought I had.

Then again, perhaps the servants simply chose not to see it. Michel had so obviously charmed them—hadn't I seen evidence of that last night at dinner? How easily he commanded them, how the maids nearly fell over themselves to serve him. Even so, the fact that Lambert referred to him as the master surprised me. Servants knew the true inner workings of a house. To call him master implied ownership—did they really think he would stay so long?

Kitty's conversation did not answer any of my questions. The one thing I learned was that Michel spent most of his time simply lazing about the house. It would be difficult to avoid him. And, I supposed, if I meant to find answers, I must ask the questions.

It was an hour later, when I was fully dressed, as Kitty was putting the finishing touches on my chignon, that there was another knock on my door. I swallowed and summoned my courage. "Come in."

The door opened, and Molly, the upstairs maid, peeked in, and I felt a moment of relief that it was not Michel. The moment was short-lived. She said, "There's a Mrs. Burden downstairs, ma'am."

Pamela. I should have known the Athertons would not be content to let me be. For a moment, I considered not seeing her, but my curiosity over what she might want won out, and I rose, bracing myself for what was sure to be an unpleasant encounter.

I went slowly down the stairs, making her wait, and when I saw her pacing the parlor impatiently, I felt a stab of satisfaction.

"Pamela," I said.

She turned. "Evelyn." She was as lovely and delicate as ever, the black she wore as unrelieved and flattering. But her voice was clipped and hard, and her eyes were little flints of blue stone. "I don't know what you think you're doing. If you think Dorothy Bennett can save you from these accusations—"

"Have you come only to insult me, Pam? If so, I've other things to occupy me."

"I've come to talk some sense into your patroness. And to tell you that I intend to do so. To take advantage of her the way you have—"

"She believes I had nothing to do with Peter's death."

"Oh, you've convinced her of it, I've no doubt, but I'll soon put things right. You'd best start packing. John's with Elisha Capron right now. I expect they'll have you in the Tombs by nightfall."

Elisha Capron was one of the police commissioners, and the mention of his name did shake me, as Pamela no doubt intended. But the Bennetts still held power in the city, and I didn't think Judge Capron would dismiss that so easily.

"I don't know what they would use as cause. I've fulfilled all their requirements. Bail's been set. I haven't left the city, and Dorothy's lent her protection."

"Yes," Pam said with a smug smile. "But what would happen, do you suppose, if Dorothy were to withdraw?"

"She won't," I said, with more conviction than I felt; I didn't underestimate Pam's powers of persuasion.

"No? Come, Evelyn, can you really think the woman sane? She speaks to her dead sons."

"I hardly think mocking a woman in her own home will do much to win her support, Pam."

Pamela snorted a laugh. "How pious you sound. What have you done, Evelyn? Persuaded that poor deluded woman that you're a rapper yourself? How clever of you. I suppose next you'll be telling me you plan to talk to Peter's spirit."

"I think Dorothy intends to."

Her look was piercing. "What will he say, do you think? Will he forgive you for killing him? You can't think it will matter much to the police department. Or to my family, for that matter. I suppose I shouldn't have put it past you to try to fool Dorothy, given how you fooled Peter, but don't you dare think that the rest of us can be taken in so easily."

Pamela glanced up suddenly, looking past me, and the meanness of her expression changed to bland politeness. The transformation was so complete and seamless that I stared at her for a moment before I thought to see who had caused it.

Then I heard the coughing, and I knew before I turned who it was. Michel was standing in the doorway, as elegant-looking as ever, clad in a silvery-gray frock coat that made his blue eyes seem paler—even strangely transparent—and a vest in a blue tartan. The sapphire and diamond pin sparkled in the folds of his dark blue necktie. He made a little bow and tucked the handkerchief away, smiling. "*Madame* Atherton, forgive me for intruding. I wasn't aware you had a guest."

"My sister-in-law," I said brusquely. "Mrs. John Burden. Pamela, this is Michel Jourdain."

"Peter's sister?"

"You knew my brother, Mr. Jourdain?" Pamela asked.

Michel came into the room, moving past me to take Pamela's hand. "Yes, *Madame*. I miss him greatly."

"As do we all." Pamela gave him her best grief-struck smile.

I couldn't keep from needling her. "Mr. Jourdain is Dorothy's medium. You remember—I told you about him. She brought him from Boston to head the spirit circles."

Pamela's expression went politely rigid. "A medium?"

"Yes, indeed. It was Mr. Jourdain who contacted your mother's spirit for Peter."

"Your *maman* is as lovely a spirit in the spheres as her children are in the corporeal world," Michel said. "You take after her, *Madame* Burden."

The flattery only partially appeased Pamela. She obviously had no idea what to say. "Thank you."

"Perhaps you'd care to attend a circle, *Madame?* To hear your *maman's* voice for yourself?"

Pamela looked flabbergasted at the very idea. "I think not."

"Are you sure you wouldn't?" I asked. "Mr. Jourdain is quite renowned. A miracle worker, some say."

Pamela glared at me. Her lips pressed tightly together. Just then, Lambert appeared at the door. "Mrs. Bennett will see you now, Mrs. Burden."

"At last," Pamela said. She swept past me, saying, "A pleasure to meet you, Mr. Jourdain," and then she was in the hallway, leaving nothing behind but the cloying scent of her rose perfume and a scornful distaste that seemed to linger in the air with it.

"She's not much like her brother," Michel noted. "Why'd she come?"

"She hopes to persuade Dorothy to withdraw her support. She'd like nothing better than to see me in the Tombs."

"You've no worry on that score," he told me. He went to the fire, spreading his hands before it, even though the parlor was so warm the barren trees outside seemed incongruous.

He spoke with such confidence, such assurance, and I remembered last night, my belief that he had somehow engineered my staying here, my sense that he wanted me here for some reason I did not yet understand.

"You seem so certain," I said.

"*Oui.* I am."

"How can you be?"

He turned to look over his shoulder, and his gaze was uncomfortably sharp, as if he could see through me. "Don't question the fates, *Madame* Atherton, lest you tempt them to change their minds."

It was a threat; I felt the danger in his words, and I stared at him in surprise. I remembered what Kitty had said about her brother: *"He could talk the wings off a butterfly and wouldn't give no thought to smashing it after."* Michel *was* like those men in my father's office, with their magnetic attraction and vicious immorality, and suddenly I was afraid. I was here by his sufferance—yet he must realize I would try to save myself, and how I would do so. I had not fooled him for a moment. I heard Michel's warning, and I understood: he would be watching me.

I didn't see Pamela leave. Nor did I know how her meeting with Dorothy had gone. Not until later that afternoon, when Dorothy sent for me.

Dorothy's room was large, divided by lacquered Japanese screens into a sitting room and bedroom. On the sitting room side was a long, low table crowded with bottles of amber and clear and green, holding powders or liquids, along with medicine cups, a pitcher of water, an empty hot water bottle and a well-used mortar and pestle. Beside it was a settee, where one nurse lounged reading the *Herald* while another organized towels on a shelf.

Beyond the screen was a large, lace-festooned bed, where Dorothy Bennett rested in a nest of satin and lace-edged pillows that were so plumped around her that she was sitting straight up. A bedside table was littered with bottles and spoons. The room smelled of laudanum and orris root and musty, unwashed skin, but the pale chintz drapes covering the window beyond were open, which was not what I would have expected from an invalid. The room was bright with overcast light from outside.

"Ah, Evelyn," Dorothy said when she saw me. She motioned me to a chair beside the bed, and as I sat she said, "Your sister-in-law isn't fond of you, child, that's for sure."

"Not anymore," I said. "I suppose . . . not ever."

"You know why she was here?"

"To tell you I'm a ruthless schemer, I imagine."

"She expected me to be asylum bound. The way she talked! As if I were too addled to see what was in front of me. She's convinced you murdered Peter and that you're fooling me."

I met her gaze. "What do you think?"

"That she wants you in prison and she thinks I'll help send you there."

"What did you tell her?"

"To stay the hell out of my business." She sighed and reached for my hand. Her skin was dry and rough, as thin and frail as onionskin over her plumpness. Her nails were yellowed, too long, a little clawlike, and they dug into my fingers. "I told Pamela not to set foot again in my house. I told her to leave you be."

"It may not be so easy as that. She said her husband was talking to Elisha Capron."

"Elisha?" She chuckled quietly. "Oh, he won't side against me."

"Dorothy, I don't want to bring trouble upon you—"

"You're no trouble, Evelyn."

"But I might become so."

She squeezed my hand again. "We'll fight them all. As long as I have Michel to give me strength, I can do it."

Her words made me uncomfortable. It was the opening I'd looked for, but now that it was here I hesitated. I remembered Michel's unspoken warning, and I knew to be careful. "Dorothy, about Michel . . ."

She frowned at me. "What about him?"

"What exactly do you know of him?"

My words seemed to have a remarkable effect on her. She dropped my hand and fell back against the pillows as if she were suddenly exhausted. In a voice so soft I had to lean close to hear, she said, "You know, it's hard to be old, Evelyn. People forget that old women were young once, but d'you think we old women forget? In my heart, I'm still thirty. But these bones of mine . . . I can't move so fast, you know, and you start getting . . . left behind. It's as if I've become invisible. But Michel saw me. He looked right at me. He listens to me. I'm just a sick old woman to everyone else."

"No. Not just that," I said quietly.

Her eyes were rheumy-looking, shiny with unshed tears. "My life wasn't worth living until I met him, child."

And it was those words that quieted me. I understood what she meant about someone truly seeing her, listening to her. I'd had that once, with my father. I also knew that, regardless of Michel's manipulations, I couldn't take this away from her. Not unless I had irrefutable proof. Until then, she wouldn't believe me anyway. She had chosen not to.

"I understand," I said. "I hope you're right."

"Oh, I am," she whispered. "If you only knew, child. If you knew . . ." She smiled, her gaze distant, as if she were recalling some particularly pleasurable memory, and I had to look away.

12

THE VOICES OF THE DEAD

THURSDAY, FEBRUARY 5, 1857

I was not looking forward to Thursday night's circle. I knew Michel would know the truth of my participation, and that meant he would guard himself even more carefully, but there was no help for that. My biggest concern was in being careful not to offend him. Now that I'd seen the power he bore here, it was crucial I not get myself banished before I determined the truth.

Benjamin arrived early, before the others, and I was relieved to see him.

"You got my note," I said as I greeted him in the foyer. "I wasn't certain you knew there was to be a circle tonight."

"As it happens, I did," he said, unwrapping his fine gray wool scarf from about his neck and handing it and his top hat to a waiting Lambert. "I'd already received word from Dorothy. We're to attempt to reach Peter's spirit, I understand?"

"Yes. To see if we can discover the truth of his murder."

"Now that you're here, my dear, perhaps the affinities will be enough to lure Peter's spirit." With a glance at the hovering Lambert, Ben took my arm, directing me gently down the hall toward the parlor. In a low voice, he asked, "Where's Jourdain?"

"In the upstairs parlor," I answered him, equally quietly.

He motioned for me to follow him across the room to the corner, out of earshot of the open parlor doorway. "Tell me quickly, before the others arrive—you've been here three days; have you noticed anything? How is Jourdain toward you?"

"I think he knows why I'm here."

"What makes you think so?"

"He warned me—in so many words—that I'm here only because he allows me to be—and that he would be quick to move against me if I displeased him."

Ben frowned. "Do you think he could convince Dorothy to abandon you?"

"Oh, I think certainly he could. His control of her is uncanny. It's almost as if . . ." I trailed off, reluctant even to voice the thought. "As if there's an unseemly affection between them."

Ben raised his brows. "You mean he's seduced her?"

I felt myself grow hot at the image his words raised. "I don't know. I suspect it."

"My God." The flash of anger in his eyes was quick and hard. "To debase an invalid woman—"

"'Allo, Rampling." Michel's voice startled us both.

I turned to see him coming into the parlor, his movements languid, his smile welcoming, as if he hadn't noticed how huddled Ben and I were in the corner, how private we meant our conversation to be.

I forced a bright smile of my own. "There you are. Benjamin's arrived a bit early. I thought to offer him a brandy."

"It's good to see you, Rampling," Michel said. "But I've a special liqueur waiting for us—perhaps you'd rather have that?"

"As you wish." Benjamin bowed his head, his anger banked now, as if it had never been. "Evelyn tells me we're to contact Peter's spirit this evening."

"We plan to try," Michel said smoothly. "Though the spirits are sometimes capricious."

"Yes, of course." Ben turned back to me with a knowing smile, and I felt warm at his complicity. "We must hope for the best."

The others arrived then, red-faced from the cold, breathing clouds of steam. In the too-warm foyer, the icy ghost of frigid air dissipated from their cloaks and scarves like magic.

"Evelyn!" Robert Dudley held out his arms to me, holding me close for a moment before he released me again. "Grace and I have been praying for a good result tonight. Surely Peter must be in the spheres by now."

Sarah Grimm said, "I've had the strongest feeling all day. I feel so certain we'll find him."

"Atherton's been squirrelly, but I feel as Sarah does," Wilson Maull agreed.

Jacob Colville leaned down to kiss my cheek in greeting. "We'll find him, Evie, never worry."

Sarah Grimm's dark eyes grew somber as she looked at Benjamin. She took his arm and leaned tearfully into him. "I'm so used to seeing you with Peter that it seems quite strange to see you without him."

"He's not really without him," Maull reassured. "Peter's spirit is watching over all of us. Why, he's no doubt bending over Rampling's shoulder this very moment. It only requires our own ecstasy to connect us."

"We should go upstairs," Michel said. "Dorothy'll be waiting."

We made the trek upward, and as we drew closer to the parlor with its pedestaled table, the talk began to fade, almost as if there were a sort of holiness attributed to the room that required the same reverence as a chapel. Dorothy was indeed waiting, settled upon the fish-monstrosity of a sofa, surrounded by her nurses. Michel made his way directly to her, and she moved to accommodate him as he sat beside her, and leaned into him as if he held her strength. He whispered something to one of her nurses, who went to the sideboard, where a row of decanters stood, and poured into a group of small glasses some kind of liqueur that glowed a pretty green. He took the first to Dorothy, who swallowed it with gusto, and then brought the tray of glasses to offer to the rest of us, explaining, "In anticipation of success, Mr. Jourdain said."

"Success in what?" I asked.

"In finding Peter's spirit, of course," Dudley said. He took a glass and held it out in a toast. "To Peter!" We all followed suit, and he downed his in a single gulp, smacking his lips after. "Delicious. Such things can be quite efficacious when it comes to the spirits, Evelyn. Try it."

I watched Benjamin drink the liqueur without care before I sipped suspiciously at my own. My reservations dissolved at my first taste. It was lovely: sweet and perfumey and herbal, though I couldn't place the flavor. I'd never had anything like it, but the others obviously had. After they drank, the conversation became more animated and philosophical.

"—and then Lewis said the laws of nature were constant, that they could not be set aside simply because tables rose. But my lovely Sarah"—Wilson gave her an affectionate glance—"asked him how a spirit lifting a table was different from a man doing so in the material world."

"I had to be simplistic," Sarah demurred. "Lewis is so literal. I didn't think he would understand the idea that spirits don't lift the table so much as they inhabit it."

Robert Dudley nodded. "The material world is simply an expression of the mind; that's what so many fail to see. We're so dependent on what is before us that we discount our intuition. Yet if one dismisses instinct, how can one understand or believe in a world that exists beyond one's sight?"

His words made me uncomfortable. I thought of my mother, how instinct guided her every move—a dead bird could send her into a superstitious terror of bad luck for days, and dreams became maps to read the future by. I remembered a morning long before she'd died, when I'd come to breakfast and she'd glanced at me and said, "You didn't sleep last night," and thrown a frightened look at Papa. "Charles, she didn't sleep."

Papa glanced up from his coffee.

"It was nothing. Another nightmare, that's all," I told her.

"You must try to fight them, my dear," Mama said, her voice hushed. "You must not let them speak to you."

Her words frightened me, as they always did. "My dreams are not like yours," I snapped.

She reached for the brown bottle on the table, her fingers trembling so much that the glass dropper clinked against the rim. I watched as she put the drops in her tea, and I knew Papa did too, each of us silently counting. Fifteen drops—more than last week. She replaced the dropper and brought the cup to her lips, taking quick, deep sips, even though it steamed and must have burned.

"They're only dreams," I insisted, as I had a hundred times before.

Her cup clattered into the saucer. She and my father exchanged a glance, and I saw again her fear, and heard it in her voice when she said, "Of course they are, Evie. Of course."

I hated it when she spoke that way. I watched as she went into the kitchen, her step a bit staggered from the effects of the laudanum, and then I turned angrily to my father. "Why don't you reason with her? Why don't you ever tell her that there are no spirits?"

He set down his cup and said softly, "I don't know that there aren't."

"Papa!"

"We can't know everything, Evie, though I would wish we could. Logic only tells us what's there; it can't really address what isn't. Even the most devoted empiricist must admit that we have no hope of understanding the universe. Some things are unknowable."

"How can they be real? What if it's—" I couldn't say the word. "What if I'm like her?"

"Then you would be special indeed."

His words did not reassure me. "*She* doesn't feel special, Papa. You must see how it frightens her. She's taking more medicine than ever."

"Her trial is that no one else believes it, Evie. So she has no choice but to doubt it herself. If anything would drive one mad, I think that would be it."

"I don't want to be mad," I whispered.

"Then you must do what everyone must do. We can only trust in what little we know. Put your faith in that. Trying to justify a world we don't hold all the answers to is what bedevils the best of us. Sometimes it's better just to accept that things are as we see them." He sighed and looked toward the kitchen. "I think it would help if she could believe that. So I try to believe it for her."

I tried to blink the memory away, but the liqueur I'd drunk crept up on me; I felt a strange lassitude, an easing of reticence that made me ask sharply, "Isn't that what sends people into asylums? Belief in a world one can't see, that might not even exist?"

"I think perhaps the mad are misunderstood," Grace said gently. "How can we condemn them when most of us refuse to see any world beyond the material one? How much happier we would be if we all accepted Divine Love without question and admitted that it's our destiny to join with it!"

"Hear hear," Wilson Maull said, taking another glass of the liqueur and lifting it in a toast. "To the invisible world—the only real one!"

He drained his glass and the others looked on approvingly. I heard the rustle of movement—Dorothy's nurses were helping her rise. She called out, "Let's begin!" and I was relieved at the ending of a conversation that troubled me. As I turned to go to the table, I saw that Michel was watching me with a thoughtful expression. When I caught his gaze he glanced quickly away, and I felt a puzzling disquiet that had nothing to do with the conversation.

"This should be interesting," Ben murmured as he came up beside me.

I had thought that, as Benjamin was here, I might sit beside him and change the composition of the seating, but that was not to be. Sarah motioned him to the chair beside hers, and Grace took the seat on his other side, and I stood there hesitantly until only the chair beside Michel was empty.

He sat down and looked at me questioningly until I took my place. Then he said in a low voice, "Are you ready, *Madame?*"

"I hardly know. Can one ever be ready to hear the voices of the dead?"

He took my hand, and Robert Dudley took the other, and the lights were lowered, the room cast in a dim gloom. Silence descended. Michel's hand opened slightly on mine, his fingers pressed flat, almost caressing, and his touch brought back the dream I'd had and I began to feel strange, too sensitive and yet distant at the same time, as if I were falling into sleep. I started when Jacob began the prayer—I had expected instead Michel's voice, the lulling French chant.

Quickly I looked across the table at Benjamin. I could see only the shadows of his eyes in the stripe of pale skin above the darkness of his beard. I could not see his expression.

Dudley said, "Almighty God, let us talk with the spirits tonight. Let us speak to Peter Atherton."

There was quiet.

"If there are spirits present, let them be heard. Let them direct us to the spirit of our friend and husband Peter Atherton."

I felt the tension as we all waited. I heard hushed breathing, the faint rustle of silk. Michel's hand tightened on mine; I felt his sudden rigidity in the moment before Sarah burst out, "Is there a spirit here?"

"I am here," Michel said, and I was surprised that it wasn't Peter's voice he'd chosen, but one soft and light, not that of a grown man, but of a child.

"Atherton?" Dudley asked. "Is this the spirit of Peter Atherton who speaks through Jourdain?"

"I miss you, Mama."

Dorothy gasped. "Johnny!" she called out; it was almost a sob.

"Johnny, my dear, dear boy, how glad I am you're here. What do you say tonight, my son?"

"You must take better care of yourself, Mama. As much as I want to have you with me, there are still things on earth you must do."

"Yes, yes," she said eagerly. "I'm doing them, just as you said."

"I know. May I touch you again, Mama? Upon your shoulder? I miss you so."

"Of course, of course." Dorothy was like an excited girl; her need and pleasure were embarrassingly transparent. She waited, and then after a moment she seemed to sag beneath a touch only she could feel. "Oh, Johnny . . . Is Everett there? Is he with you?"

Whatever lassitude the liqueur had inspired in me disappeared. The obviousness of Michel's manipulation annoyed me, for the way he fooled her was almost pathetic in its simplicity. Michel said, "I must go, Mama. There're other spirits here, waiting to talk."

"Atherton?" Jacob Colville spoke. "Is Peter Atherton's spirit among you?"

There was a pause, but the rigidity in Michel's body did not ease. His thigh, beneath the table, pressed closer, into my skirts, moving with me even as I instinctively moved away. "Peter's spirit is not yet strong," he said, still in the youthful voice of Johnny Bennett. "He will come to Michel in dreams—"

"For God's sake, he comes to *me* in dreams," I burst out, impatient at his lack of deftness. "That's hardly enough."

The moment I said it, I knew I'd erred. I felt their sudden attention, their confusion and surprise. And betrayal too, from somewhere, I felt betrayal. The cacophony was so startling and strange that I was bewildered. When Benjamin asked quietly, "What did you say?" I felt Michel's sudden absence. He sagged, as if the spirit of Johnny Bennett had been physically holding him upright; his fingers went lax upon mine.

"Turn up the lights!" Grace called in a high, nervous voice. "Look at Michel—the spirits are gone."

He had collapsed; his head lolled on the table like one asleep. Robert Dudley loosed my hand to rush to him. Dudley grabbed Michel's shoulders, pulling him back against the chair. Sarah ran to turn up the lights—one by one they went bright, but Michel did not rouse, and the tension in the room did not abate. Slowly, I realized they were all staring at me.

"What is it?" I asked. "Why are you looking at me that way?"

Jacob Colville roused, as if he'd just been awakened from a deep sleep. "Did you say Peter came to you in dreams, Evelyn?"

"I'm simply pointing out—"

"How does Peter's spirit manifest itself?"

"It isn't like that." I looked at Benjamin, who was frowning. "It's more like . . . nightmares."

"What happens in these nightmares?" Grace asked.

I glanced at her in confusion. "I dream I'm in the circle and then I hear Peter's voice. Or sometimes, it seems I'm awake, and he's there beside me. But I'm really asleep."

"But those aren't just nightmares, Evie, surely you see that? Why, Peter's been communicating with you all this time and you never said a word!"

"Because they're only—"

"What does he say?"

"Nothing. He says nothing. 'Find the truth. Don't believe him' . . . Things like that."

"Find the truth?" Grace repeated.

"It doesn't really make sense, like all dreams. Nothing really means anything."

"Few mediums believe in their gift at the start," Dorothy said. "Even Michel didn't. But once you're called, there's no turning back."

"Once I'm—" I stared at her in surprise. "What are you talking about?"

Slowly, Robert Dudley straightened, lifting his hands from Michel's shoulders. "How wonderful! We've another medium in our midst."

Wilson Maull said, "Good God."

I was incredulous. "What?"

"You've been called, Evelyn dear," Grace said. "The spirit said Peter would come to Michel in dreams, but he's already visited you—it seems clear he's chosen the medium he wishes to communicate through."

"Perhaps we should be cautious here," Ben said.

"What's there to be cautious about?" Dorothy asked sharply. There was a light in her eyes—the same kind of light I'd seen when she looked at Michel. Except this time, she was looking at me, and I felt a strange stir in my stomach. "The spirits have spoken. They've called Evelyn to attend to their mission. She's no choice in the matter."

Beside me, Michel stirred. He lifted his head, blinking, and said, "They're gone."

"Yes, yes, we know," Dudley said excitedly. "But they've left us something very valuable. They've left us a fledgling medium."

Michel frowned, as if he were confused.

Grace's sallow face was almost pretty in its animation as she said, "Peter's spirit's been visiting Evie in dreams. Isn't it wonderful?"

Michel turned slowly to me.

"We can develop her! What a gift we've been given!" Grace said.

I glanced again at Dorothy. She was smiling, and I realized suddenly that this was my opportunity. I had wanted to guarantee that Michel could not dislodge me, and the way had fallen into my hands.

Slowly I said, "Do you really think so?"

"Evelyn," Ben said sharply. "Don't be absurd."

"Ben, how can you not see? Look around you—why, look at Dorothy. We've been invigorated—can you doubt the truth of it?"

I saw the protest jump to his lips, and I tried to warn him with my eyes. His gaze went to Dorothy, as I'd intended. I knew he was seeing the rapturous excitement in her, and I was almost giddy as he turned back to me and said reluctantly, "Are you certain? Isn't it possible we're misinterpreting this?"

"The signs are all here," Sarah said. "Peter told us you had nightmares, Evelyn."

Dudley said, "Why, the spirits have been urging your development for some time!"

"Or perhaps not." Michel's voice was soft. "Perhaps they're only nightmares."

"But what of her father's visit?" Dorothy asked. "Why, he was here at our last circle."

"Was he?" Ben asked. He looked at me. "You didn't tell me that."

"I'd forgotten it in all the other . . . excitement," I said.

Sarah said, "Michel, you're the expert. How shall we develop Evelyn? What should we do?"

Michel put his fingers to his temple. "I don't know. My strength . . ."

"He's overtired, poor boy." Dorothy turned to her nurses, calling, "Fetch him some sherry!"

"You must give us a plan when you've recovered yourself," Robert said. "Who else but you can help us?"

"I'm no expert at developing others," Michel snapped—an uncharacteristic loss of control. I had to hide my smile.

"Please, let him rest. We mustn't ask more of him just now. Tomorrow will be soon enough," Dorothy said.

One of the nurses brought Michel a glass of sherry, which he swallowed in a single gulp.

"Yes, tomorrow. Perhaps we should meet again then," Jacob said.

"Perhaps." Michel set the glass onto the table hard enough that I felt its vibration through the polished wood. "Or perhaps tomorrow will bring us some other wisdom, eh?"

Dudley said, "I could talk to Mrs. Hardinge at the New York

Conference. She's such an accomplished medium herself, she may have some insight for us."

"And the *Spiritual Telegraph,* darling," Grace said. "Remember? Last spring, there was a piece on developing mediums. If I could remember where I put it . . ."

Michel coughed. It was nothing at first, but as he felt for his handkerchief it grew stronger, doubling him over, and Dudley fumbled anxiously for his own handkerchief and handed it to Michel, who pressed it to his mouth. His eyes were watering from the force of the attack.

Dorothy tried to rise, and then sank again helplessly into her chair. Anxiously, she said, "He should go to bed. Charley! Charley, for God's sake help him."

The nurse with the curling hair hurried toward Michel, but the moment he put his hand on Michel's shoulder, Michel waved him away almost violently.

"Good God, man, is there nothing you can take?" Jacob asked.

Finally, the coughing eased. I heard the wretchedness of Michel's breathing as he tried to regain himself. When he looked up again, his face was red, fading quickly to a frightening pallor. He crumpled Dudley's handkerchief into his hand. "You don't mind?" he asked weakly, holding it out for a moment before he shoved it into a pocket.

"No, of course not. Keep it," Dudley said.

Michel pulled himself from the chair. "I am overtired." His voice was hardly there. "I'll retire, if you'll excuse me."

We all made the appropriate sounds of dismay. Michel walked slowly to where Dorothy sat. He leaned over her, whispering something in her ear. She had looked desperate and afraid, but whatever he said seemed to reassure her. She reached up, cupping her hand to his cheek as a lover might, and he kissed her upon the top of her head and straightened again. Then he left us.

Dorothy herself left quickly after that, and the others lingered only a few moments before they too made their departure. Only Benjamin remained, and as I showed him to the door, he glanced warily up the stairs and said in a quiet voice, "What are you thinking?"

Before I could answer, he drew me aside, from the hallway into the parlor, which was dark but for the embers burning low in the fireplace. The light from the hallway glanced upon his face.

Excitedly, I turned to him. "Did you see the way Dorothy looked when Robert said I'd been called? She was delighted. I've become her personal quest, Ben."

His expression was still disapproving. "How exactly does that avail us?"

"She believes in all this. Wherever the spirits lead, she'll want to follow, and now she believes she was meant all along to develop me. She won't withdraw her support now, no matter how Michel tries to persuade her!"

At last, I saw understanding in Ben's eyes. "Ah. Very clever, Evie—but for one thing. You do realize that this will put you in close proximity with Jourdain?"

"No closer than I am now—"

"Much closer," he disagreed. "You heard what the others said: they believe he's the one who must lead the circle in developing you. My guess is that he'll agree to do so for Dorothy's sake, and then try to sabotage you in the process. Are you prepared for that?"

I hadn't thought of it. Still, I insisted, "I can beat him at this."

"Can you? These are people, Evie, not pawns. Jourdain won't like this. He was dangerous before, he'll be more so now." Ben took a deep breath. "If he's willing to seduce an old woman to get what he wants, in how much more danger of seduction is a young and pretty one?"

I was startled. "I hardly think—"

"Don't assume he won't try." Ben raised his hand, as if he might touch me, and then lowered it again. "You're a courageous woman, but please don't lose sight of what we're trying to accomplish here."

"I will be careful," I said. "But you must admit that this can only help us. Not just with Dorothy, but in finding out more about what Michel knows."

"If you can manage him. He's spent years developing the skills you've seen."

"But I've the advantage here. I *know* he's dangerous. I *know* what he's capable of. Didn't I tell you when you arrived this evening that I was afraid he would convince Dorothy to throw me out? Haven't I already found a way to prevent that?"

Ben looked unconvinced. "You haven't his skill at deception."

"I can learn it. You can help me. You've been to more circles than I, surely you can guess his tricks easily enough?"

"Yes," he admitted reluctantly. "I suppose that's true."

"And we have so little time. My trial is little more than six weeks away. It will be here before we know it. This is a small risk for what I might gain, Ben. I can do this. You must trust me."

He exhaled, and then he nodded slowly. "Very well. I dislike putting you in such danger, but I must admit it will secure your position with Dorothy. And if you're clever enough . . . But please, Evie, be wary. I've grown quite fond of you."

I smiled at him and touched his arm. "In this game, we'll be the victors, I promise you. I think we already have him on the defensive. Did you notice? His little coughing spell kept us from setting another date for the circle—and my development."

Benjamin looked thoughtful. "No doubt there will be many more such maneuvers. And what was that about your father visiting you in a circle? You told me nothing of it."

"You were in Albany," I said. "I'd come here to ask questions about Peter, and they were holding a circle. I was persuaded to join them."

"Jourdain called your father?"

"Just another of his tricks. It hardly seemed worth mentioning. He didn't fool me, in any case."

"Is there anything else you haven't told me?"

"There were no other visits. I'd thought I was done with the whole business until now."

"Well, as I've said before, don't underestimate Jourdain. People see what they want to see, I've found. It's their blindness to their own natures that makes them so easy to fool. Even Peter used to say to me: 'What about *this*? Surely this can't be explained!' But I think it was when Dorothy's 'son' persuaded her to give Michel carte blanche over the servants that Peter began to see the ways Jourdain's studied how to use others. You'd be wise not to forget it."

"Oh, I won't forget," I said. "Believe me, I won't."

"I hope not, Evie." He cleared his throat. "Now, I fear I must take my leave." He stepped back into the hallway. I followed him. He took his greatcoat from the hooks behind the stairs, and settled his top hat upon his head. At the door, he paused. His eyes were dark with concern as he turned to me. "The merest word, Evie. Remember that. If you need me, I can be here at a moment's notice."

Then he was gone, into a night heavy with clouds and snow beginning to swirl in a bitter wind. I stood there, watching after him, feeling suddenly bereft. It wasn't until his carriage clattered away that I closed the door and turned back to the stairs.

And saw Michel waiting at the landing.

13

LOST

How long had he been there? My mind leaped through my conversation with Benjamin, trying to think of what he could have heard. Michel came down the stairs, as graceful and deliberate as a cat.

"Everyone gone?" he asked when he reached me.

"I—I thought you were abed."

"Non."

"But your cough—"

"I'm quite recovered," he said. He took my arm. He was not rough, nor cruel. His strength was easy; evidenced, but not displayed. "I thought you and me should have a talk, eh, *chère?*"

When he took me down the hall, I didn't protest. Best to play along, I thought, not to seem nervous, though I could not help throwing a glance at the door, or sending Benjamin a silent plea that I knew had no hope of answer. Michel released me when we reached the parlor. He turned to close the doors, plunging us into darkness. I heard fumbling, the strike of a match, the hiss, and he was lighting the gas, his face weirdly illuminated for a moment, frightening in the depth of its shadows. The jet caught; he turned the key, and the lamp blazed to life, and he was himself again, but no less frightening.

He came toward me, and I found myself backing away like some wretched coward. It was that thought that rallied me. He would hardly do me physical harm here—not here in this house. I forced myself to face him as he came to me, too close, and I made myself remain still as his fingers traced my cheekbone.

"You're a pretty woman, *chère,*" he breathed. "But, I begin to think, a stupid one. This little game of yours . . . What are you about, I wonder?"

I wanted nothing more than to look away, to jerk away. My skin felt charged where he touched me. "I don't know what you mean."

His fingers moved nonchalantly to the corner of my mouth. His thumb swept my lower lip, and his gaze followed the movement of his hand. For a terrifying moment, I thought he would kiss me. "*C'est bon comme la vie,* eh? Ah, but *non,* I think not."

I wrenched away. "I don't understand what you're saying."

"You're no medium," he said.

I was here by his sufferance. I could not risk antagonizing him until I knew for certain the strength of my position with Dorothy. "I'm not the one who said I was." I took a step back.

He followed. "D'you know how long I've been here, *chère?*"

The change in subject confused me. "You—you said eight months."

"*Oui.* Eight months." He moved away from me as he spoke, and though I felt nothing but relief at his distance, somehow it seemed even more dangerous. He was so deliberate; he went slowly about the room, his fingers skimming the surface of a heavy rosewood sideboard, the carved back of the settee. At the fireplace he paused. He picked up a Sevres vase from the mantel, turning it in his hands as if considering its best use. "Eight months. D'you know what she was like when I met her?"

"Dorothy?"

"She was hardly alive. Her doctors had her sleepwalking. I've given her back a reason to live, and now you want to come between us. I have to ask myself: why is that, hmmm? What does she want? Money? Ah, perhaps. She's lost everything. Power? Perhaps. But then I think, *non*. She's accused of killing her husband. What's money or power if she hangs?"

He set the vase back upon the mantel. "But she wants something, eh? What could it be?"

"I don't know what you're talking about."

He sauntered away from the fireplace, making his circuitous way back to me. "Don't you? Because I think you do." He was there again, beside me. "You and me, we've much in common, hmmm? I understand you, *chère*. I know what you're about. Don't think you can fool me."

"We—we've nothing in common."

He raised a brow, and I immediately flushed, feeling the full weight of my fear, and hating myself for being so weak as to reveal it, and he leaned close.

"The circle doesn't need two mediums," he said quietly, and I did not mistake the menace in his words. His voice was a hot breath against my skin. I lurched back, and then wished I'd held my ground when he smiled. How easily he'd got beneath my skin. How easily I'd let him. I'd been too confident, after all, and he was so good. . . .

Michel stepped away, as if he hadn't been threatening me only moments before, and made me an elegant bow and said with benign politeness, "Now our talk is over, *chère*. I must admit, I'm ready for bed. So I'll leave you—unless you'd care to join me?"

It took me a moment to respond, and when I found my voice it was weaker than I would have wished. "I can't imagine why I would."

"Can't you?" Again, that wretched, knowing smile. "Ah, well then. *Bon soir.*"

After he was gone, I stayed for a while in the parlor. I was afraid to go up the stairs to my room, where his was across the hall. He'd let me be for now; what if he changed his mind? So I stayed. I listened to his footsteps up the stairs, one landing, then the second, and then the fading resonance of the third. I imagined him going down the hall, pausing at my door, considering, before he moved on. Then the twist of the key in his lock, the stepping inside. I thought I heard the faint, hollow thud of the closing door.

And then I realized I was standing in a darkness that pulsed with the flame of the single gaslight, that the shadows beyond still held the feel of him, as if his spirit lingered, and I picked up my skirts and fled the parlor, not stopping to turn down the gas, nearly running up the stairs, my skirts swinging like a bell. When I reached the safety of my room, I closed the door tightly behind me, leaning back against it, too shaken to do anything more, and angry with myself for being so rattled. Finally, I rang for Kitty, who was there in minutes, and who set to undressing me with a comforting familiarity.

"You look pale, ma'am," she said with concern as she undid the crinoline. "Are you ill?"

I shook my head. "Just overset."

"Perhaps a sip to calm you then? There's a bottle over there on the desk. I saw it just yesterday."

I glanced to the desk. I could not think how I'd missed it before, but there it was, a crystal decanter that was dark with some liquid, with two glasses turned upside down beside it. Sherry, I thought. I was tense with nerves; it would relax me, and so I nodded, and Kitty went to get it. I heard the gentle clink of the stopper as she lifted it, and then she brought a glass to me, and I took it and drank, surprised to find that it wasn't sherry at all, but the same green liqueur I'd had earlier that evening. I liked it better than sherry, in any case, and I finished it quickly. Its effect was nearly immediate. I closed my eyes, sighing at the warmth that stole over me. When Kitty finished undressing me, and left, I poured another.

I was feeling better now, not so unnerved, but still Michel's threat resisted the palliative, and I didn't feel completely safe until

I had locked my bedroom door from the inside and put the key beneath my pillow.

No one would think to search for it there, I thought with satisfaction, but with that thought came another—the very briefest, most ethereal of notions, the echo of his words: *Can't you?*—and I took the key from its hiding place and put it in the drawer of the desk. And refused to think of it again.

The drink had relaxed me enough that I fell immediately into sleep, but my dreams were scattered and strange, and when they finally did coalesce, it was into the now familiar darkness lit slowly and inexorably by the glow in the very center of it, a glow that illuminated the table and the people around it. Dorothy, and Wilson Maull, the Dudleys, Sarah Grimm, Jacob Colville, and finally, myself and Michel. He was holding my hand tightly, speaking in a voice I didn't recognize, that song he'd chanted to me before in another place, another dream time, and it bound me as easily and as well, and I knew I must somehow break the hold.

Before I could, I felt his hand against my skirts. Impossible, how could it be his hand—his hand was clasping mine—but it was there nonetheless, pressing, trailing down my leg, though he sat straight at the table; I didn't see him move at all. But I felt his hands—both of them now—beneath my skirts, stroking up my legs to my garters. His fingers easing beneath the ribbons, moving ever upward. I felt his warm breath on my skin, and my own breath suspended, waiting, and I heard myself asking, *"What was that song?"*

I heard his answer like a whisper in my head. *"A nun's lament. An old Creole tune."*

"What does it mean?"

"She's longing for love, and can't find it."

"A nun? Longing for love?"

His lips pressed against my inner thigh; I felt them move on my skin, I felt his kiss, though I heard his voice as if he were sitting beside me, and when I looked over, he was.

"*For God's love,* chère," he said.

I woke abruptly and sat up in bed, my sweat chilling in the cold night air. I'd kicked the blankets down about my feet, and my nightgown was twisted around my thighs. I tugged my gown into place and pulled the blankets up again about my shoulders and sat there staring into the room, too alert, every little sound— the *ssshhh* of the sheet against my skin, my own breathing, the creak of the house settling—seemed to set my nerves jangling. I was wide awake, my emotions a jumbled confusion I could not set straight.

I looked at the door. I had locked it, but suddenly I was unsure. Before I knew it, I was out of bed, unreasonably panicked, though I knew logically that I was being foolish. I put my hand on the knob and turned, thinking it would not unlatch—how could it? But when I pulled, the door creaked and opened, and I stared at it without comprehension. All I could think was that it couldn't be so. I had locked it.

I closed the door and went to the desk, pulling out the drawer, fumbling about for the key I'd put there earlier.

I couldn't find it. I went through the drawer, pulling out everything inside in my haste to find it. Notepaper and a notebook, a penknife, scattered pen nibs, the printed card of a ferry schedule. I pressed my fingers flat and felt along every inch of the inside, clear into the cracks, thinking it had fallen into a crevice. . . . Nothing.

I opened the other drawers, doing the same to them, until there was a pile of papers and such on the top of the desk, and dusty pen nibs and pencils scattered across the floor. The key was gone. I lit the candle beside my bed and brought it to the desk, bending to send its light into the very corners of the drawers, but they were empty.

Weakly, I went back to my bed and sagged upon it, and though I knew the key was not there, though I remembered moving it, I felt beneath the pillow. My fingers touched something—paper, and I stopped short, my breath too fast and too

loud in my ears. Carefully, I pulled it out. It was an envelope—
fine stock, very thick and expensive. I'd never seen it before. But
I knew unmistakably what was in it. I felt the weight and the
outlines, the flat round head, the cylinder of the rod, the flat,
short bars.

My fingers were trembling. The urge to throw it from me was
great, but I didn't. Almost despite myself, I opened the envelope.
I drew out the key, and with it, a note. A few words only, in a
hand I didn't know, but one I recognized just the same. Elegant.
Flourished.

You lost this. M

There was no thought of going back to sleep now.

IN THE MORNING, even Kitty noticed my exhaustion.

"You look ready to fall over, ma'am," she said, peering at me
with worry as I sat in a chair by the fire. "The missus was askin'
for you, but I could tell her you're still asleep."

It was a moment before I realized she was waiting for my answer. I roused myself, shaking my head. "No. I'm fine. Just help
me dress."

Kitty clucked her tongue, but she did as I asked, and she was
mostly silent about it. I refused breakfast, taking only a cup of
strong tea with milk and sugar as she dressed me. The vestiges of
my nightmare clung, and as the hours of the night had drifted
into morning, I'd wondered if I were quite sane. Perhaps I hadn't
locked the door. Perhaps I'd lost the key after all, and Michel's re-
placement of it was not the threat I saw it as.

But then I remembered my dream, and I knew he'd been in
my room, and that he meant me to know it. What was real
about the dream, what was not, that was what I didn't know.
Uncomfortably, I remembered the feel of his hands, his lips,
against my skin. I remembered my disarray when I'd awakened. While I slept, had he . . . ? I was too distressed to finish the

thought. *"I know what you're about. . . . The circle doesn't need two mediums. . . ."*

Ben's warning that Michel would try to seduce me had not frightened me; I realized now it should have. I'd placed too much faith in my own sharp-wittedness.

How quickly I'd lost the upper hand. I'd thought I'd put him on the defensive, but he knew this game, and now my only hope was to strategize as well as he did. I must play Michel's weaknesses as he had played mine. I was here to save myself; I could not let my fear get in the way.

"The missus is waitin', ma'am," Kitty reminded me.

Dorothy was leaning back upon her pillows when I arrived in her room, and the curtains were closed, though the morning was bright, the sun sparkling on a thin layer of newly fallen snow. The gaslight was burning high; the close room stuffy with its smell, along with the usual scents of medicine and potpourri. It was hot too, with the furnace blasting up my skirts and the fire stoked. Dorothy herself was huddled in the blankets as if she were freezing.

She turned her head on the pillow, obviously too tired to do more. "Evelyn."

I hesitated. "They told me you wished to see me. Perhaps I should come back."

"No, no," she said. She fluttered her hand weakly at the chair. "I haven't seen Michel yet this morning is all. He has my elixir."

"Then I don't want to delay him. You should call him; I can wait until later."

"No, child, now's when I wish to speak to you." There was a touch of imperiousness in her tone, and obediently I sat down.

Dorothy sighed and looked at the ceiling. After a few moments, she closed her eyes. I waited for her to speak; when she didn't, I thought she had fallen asleep. But just when I had decided it was definitely so, and began to rise, she said weakly, without opening her eyes, "Are you going to do it, child?"

The question could have had a hundred different meanings. I leaned forward in my chair. "Pardon?"

She looked at me then. "Are you going to let the circle develop you?"

I was very careful. "Is that what you want?"

"The decision isn't mine."

"I think it is," I said. "You've got Michel already. I don't wish to overstep. I ... are you certain you'd care to see another medium in the circle?"

"I don't have a choice, Evelyn. Neither do you. The spirits have chosen you. To have such a gift and do nothing with it, why, it would be a crime. The spirits have reasons for everything. I'd thought to speak to Michel about it today."

"Michel?"

"I want him to tutor you, child."

It was what I'd expected. But I had hoped for a little more time. Michel's threat still resonated; my dream left me uneasy. It was best to play cautiously. "I doubt I'll have much time for tutoring. I've the trial to prepare for."

"Ben's taking care of all that. What've you to do?"

"I don't want to impose. Won't it take away from Michel's time with you?"

She sighed again. "Good God, Evelyn, I'm asleep half the time. What's he to do all day? Read? It's half the reason I brought you here, you know. I reckon he needs someone to talk to. A friend. Someone I can trust."

Her last words caught me off guard. I thought of what I was trying to do and felt guilty. I owed her so much, after all. But Michel was taking advantage of her, he was stealing from her. If he was a murderer too, wouldn't it be better if, in saving myself, I could save her as well?

Dorothy was talking again. "Without him, I would've swallowed laudanum long ago." She looked at me. "So much pain. He's eased it, you know. The spirits come through his hands. He's a healing touch. It's why I want to reward him. I've no sons left. No one to carry on the Bennett legacy."

"I don't understand."

"What am I to do with everything? Give it to some charity I don't believe in when I owe so much to him?"

I stared at her, certain I'd misheard. "You mean to leave everything to him?"

"I do. I'm adopting him."

"But . . . can you do that? He's a grown man!"

"His parents are long dead."

"But he—he's . . . who is he? Where did he come from? What do you really know about him, Dorothy?"

"I know everything I need to know. And my sons have told me it's right. They like him. They trust him."

"Yes, but what if—what if you've been misled?" I stepped as warily as I could, though I wanted to say more.

She frowned. "You sound like Peter now."

I was startled. "Peter knew of this?"

"Of course he did. He was my lawyer."

"And he didn't approve."

"No, he did not." She snapped out each word as if its taste offended her, and I realized she was still angry with him. "He made things very difficult."

"He did? How?"

"I tell you, child, I loved that boy, but he tried my patience. He was ready enough to speak to his mother's spirit when Michel brought her. And he didn't hesitate to give my boy gifts himself, but he didn't want me to adopt Michel, and he did everything he could to get me to stop it."

I was stunned at how casually she revealed a motive for murder. As if Peter's protestations added up to nothing, as if it had been only a simple disagreement. But a fortune was in the balance, and I understood—better than ever now, given my experience with Peter's family—how fortunes changed everything. I'd had doubts about Michel being Peter's murderer, but now those doubts wavered. This was not just Peter trying to convince Dorothy of Michel's dishonesty, as Ben had said, but something much different. How Michel must have felt, sensing a fortune was about to fall into his hands, playing the game so very carefully, and then, suddenly, seeing a threat that could take it all away.

I had not truly understood. I had thought Michel no better than the flimflam men I'd known, but they would never have had such grand aspirations; picking a pocket, fooling a few customers with a patent medicine, selling counterfeit stock certificates—these were the extent of their ambitions, and I had not had imagination enough to look beyond what I knew. But this . . . Ben couldn't have known how close Michel was to having everything, or he would have told me. An adoption that made Michel Dorothy's legal heir!

Motive was everything, my father had always said. Now I had it. Now, the possibility that Michel had killed my husband loomed very large, and very real.

I tried to keep my voice even as I said to Dorothy, "Gifts are not the same thing as a generations-old fortune. I'm certain Peter only meant to protect you."

"In the end he treated me like a confused old woman, just like everyone else does." She gave me a frank look. "Are you going to be like them too, Evelyn?"

I chose my words carefully. "I only wonder if you should trust Michel so readily."

"I trust him. And I'm surprised you disapprove, given your own circumstances." Her words were sharp, her expression slyly astute. "You and Michel have plenty in common."

The echo of Michel's statement was too surprising to ignore. "Did he tell you that?"

"He doesn't need to. It's plain as day. Even the spirits think so. After all, they chose you, just as they chose him."

There was a knock on the outside door; I heard Dorothy's

nurses scurry to answer it, and then one of them peeked around the screen to say, "Mr. Jourdain, ma'am."

Dorothy sat up quickly, preening, adjusting the lace of her dressing jacket, straightening the ribbons of her cap. "Tell him to come in."

The nurse disappeared. I heard voices, then his footsteps. Instinctively, I stiffened.

When he came around the screen he gave me a quick nod of acknowledgment before he went around the other side of the bed. Dorothy put out her arms to him and pulled him close, pressing her lips to his for a brief moment before she released him with a sigh.

"I've been waiting for you," she said, a little querulously. "You're late."

"I saw *Madame* Atherton come in. I thought I would let the two of you speak alone." He glanced at me. "Good morning, *Madame*. I trust you slept well?"

His pale eyes glittered. The motive, last night's threat, my dream, the key . . . now I truly understood how precarious was my position. There was so much at stake for him—it was all I could do to sit there, to keep my composure, when all I wanted to do was run with this information to Benjamin. "I slept well enough, thank you."

"Did you get my message?"

He knew just what to say. A frisson of fear brushed my skin, and I knew by his small half smile that he saw it. "I did," I said quietly.

Dorothy said, "What message?"

"I wondered if she might dine with me this morning when we're finished." He bent to brush her cheek with his finger. The full force of his charm was directed at her, and I saw the reflection of it in her face, like the sun glancing off a diamond.

"It's a kind invitation, but I'm afraid I can't," I said. "I— thought I would catch up on my correspondence."

Dorothy told him, "I've told Evelyn I want you to tutor her. For her development, you know."

"Ah." Michel's glance was unreadable. "She's decided to heed the call, then?"

"Who better to teach her? When one looks at the affinities between you, it's clear the spirits chose her for a reason." She grasped his fingers, as if she could not bring him close enough. "And I've told Evelyn of my plans."

"Oh? What plans're those?"

"The adoption, my dear boy. What else?"

He smiled down at her. "What other secrets are you sharing, *ma chère*?"

Dorothy didn't seem to hear the dangerous silkiness in his tone, but I did.

"I've told her how Peter objected."

"It's one thing to be good enough to call a spirit, and another to be good enough to hand a fortune, eh?" Michel said, looking at me as he spoke.

Suddenly I understood what Dorothy had meant when she said my circumstances and Michel's were the same. The similarities *were* startling. I, like Michel, was a newcomer to the upper ten. My own reward was deemed too great by those who claimed to care about Peter, just as everyone close to Dorothy objected to the reward she planned for Michel.

But Peter had known exactly what I was when he married me. Michel Jourdain was a liar who had set out to cheat her.

Yet didn't the Athertons think the same of me?

"You and me, we've much in common."

Dorothy gazed at Michel in adoration, and I felt uncomfortably like an intruder. Michel brushed aside a loose hair that had fallen from Dorothy's cap, cupping her cheek in his hand as he did so, and she leaned her face into his palm. Without looking at me, he said, "I'm afraid *Madame* Atherton's time is up, *ma chère*. You need your elixir."

She didn't turn; it was as if she were loath to lose his touch. "Good-bye, child. It's time for my rest."

She had to say no more; I was anxious to leave. But as I went past the screen, and to the door, I saw a movement from the corner of my eye, and I glanced back to see that Michel was taking off his frock coat, loosening his necktie. I saw how Dorothy watched him, how hungry was her gaze.

Shocked by the intimacy of his movements, I fled.

14

Other Hopes for Your Future

Friday, February 6, 1857

I was in the midst of composing a note to Ben, telling him what I'd discovered, when there was a knock at my door. I jumped— I had left Dorothy's room only moments before, and so it didn't make sense that it could be Michel, but still I panicked at the thought.

Then Kitty called, "Ma'am?" and pushed open the door, and I sighed in relief.

"What is it, Kitty?"

"Mr. Rampling's waiting in the parlor for you, ma'am."

He'd said nothing last night of calling again today. But it seemed prescient of him to visit now, when I most wanted to see him, and I crumpled up the note I'd penned and threw it in the fire, and then I hurried past Kitty and downstairs to the parlor.

He was standing at the window, and when I came into the room, he turned with a smile and said, "Forgive me for arriving unannounced."

"I'm just so thankful you're here," I told him, though it seemed not enough; what I wanted to say was how much I depended upon him, how much seeing him reassured me.

"I meant to come earlier, but they discovered a murder over on Bond Street. A doctor in a rooming house, stabbed to death."

"How terrible."

"It's had the fortunate effect of distracting the city from Peter—and you, I might add. But it did delay the appointment I had with the prosecutor."

His expression was so somber that I felt again the anxiety his presence had eased. "You've news?"

He nodded shortly. "There are some developments we must discuss."

"I've something to tell you as well."

"Oh?" His eyes brightened, and then he looked past me to the parlor door. "Then we should talk more privately, I think. Perhaps . . . would you care to walk with me? The sun has disappeared, I fear, but there's no snow as yet."

I nodded. "Let me get my cloak."

I told Lambert I was going for a short stroll, and then Benjamin and I stepped out into the cold winter day. The sky was overcast, and Fifth Avenue looked bleak and barren, the trees colorless and stark. The snow that had covered the narrow lawn this morning was already melting to reveal the mud and brown grass beneath. What remained was gray with the soot from coal smoke and dust. In the street it had been turned to muddy slush by carriage wheels and the hooves of tired and dirty horses, splashed into icy brown piles that mounded against the walks.

"You'll note our escort," Ben said to me quietly, glancing across the street as he took my hand and tucked it into the crook of his arm to help me down the steps. I followed his glance to the police watchman, who straightened to attention, and then turned to follow as we reached the flagstone walk.

Ben released me, and I felt a little disappointment and a wish that he had kept me close. I pushed my gloved hands farther into the black wool muff I carried—though it was not as cold as it had been, our breath still raised clouds of steam on the air, and the light breeze chafed at my exposed cheeks and nose.

It was too cold and dreary for promenading, and the sidewalks were nearly empty. There were no men about now, in the middle of a business day, and what women there were hurried quickly to their destinations. I supposed most of my friends were ensconced in warm places—huddled in their parlors taking tea or drinking weak lemonade and cocoa in the cavernous cacophony that was Taylor's Restaurant during its ladies' luncheons. I felt a wistful regret at the thought that I was no longer welcome among them.

"Keep your voice down," Ben advised as we passed the house and moved farther down Fifth Avenue, "I've no idea how well your watchman can hear us. Now tell me: what have you discovered?"

I spoke in a rush. "This morning I learned that Dorothy means to adopt Michel and leave him her fortune."

He looked as surprised as I had been. "Who told you this?"

"Dorothy. And she said Peter didn't approve. She's quite angry with him, even now. I don't know what he meant to do to stop it—"

"Whatever it was, he was killed before he could." Benjamin stroked his beard thoughtfully with gloved fingers. "Do you think Jourdain knew of Peter's objections?"

"I know he did. He said Peter thought he wasn't good enough to inherit a fortune." I laughed shortly. "I wonder that Peter didn't think the same of me."

Ben gave me a quick look. "You weren't out to cheat him, my dear. And you were his choice. He was like anyone else in the upper ten—he wanted to guard the door and admit only those of his own choosing. Did Jourdain seem angry when he told you this?"

I hesitated. "He's a chameleon. It's difficult to know what he thinks."

"Exactly what makes him so dangerous."

"He threatened me last night, after you left," I admitted. "He told me the circle didn't need two mediums."

Ben cursed quietly. "What did I tell you? What did he threaten you with?"

"Nothing overt," I said. "But it's very clear he doesn't want me to interfere with Dorothy."

"We must get you out of there. I'll talk to the judge tomorrow—"

"No!" I had spoken too loudly. Quickly I lowered my voice and put my hand on Ben's arm. "No, not yet."

"Then when?" he asked grimly. "When you disappear as well?"

"I'm not going to disappear. Dorothy wants me here, remember? He won't risk her disapproval."

"I don't want you taking the chance."

"I won't. Not if you can tell me that what I've told you is enough. If you think we can go to the police now with evidence of a motive, and they'll listen, then I'll leave Dorothy's."

He hesitated, and then grimaced. "It's hearsay, unless Dorothy testifies against him."

"She won't."

He sighed. "Your word isn't enough. Not when you have motive yourself."

"Then I've no choice but to stay."

He took my arm, drawing me close again, close enough that I caught a whiff of the macassar oil on his hair. "Does he frighten you, Evie?"

I looked away. "Of course he does. He means to. But that's only emotion, not reason."

"Sometimes emotion can be a shrewder judge."

"No. Logic tells me he won't hurt me. At least not yet."

Ben glanced at the police watchman across the street. "What makes you think so?"

"He seems more interested in making me uncomfortable. I think he hopes I'll leave of my own accord."

"I don't like this, Evie. Not at all." Ben's eyes had gone nearly black in distress.

"Tell me what I must find for the court to consider him a suspect."

He considered for a moment. "The adoption papers themselves.

That would be evidence powerful enough to sway them. You must discover if the papers were drawn up, and if they were, where they are now."

"I could find if they were drawn up easily enough. But to actually find them . . ."

"You may have to go through Dorothy's things. Or"—he glanced at me—"or even Michel's."

The thought of going through Dorothy's things, or of going into Michel's room at all, was anathema to me, but I nodded. "I'll search his room, and I'll see what I can do about searching Dorothy's, though she's nearly always in it."

Ben said, "The sooner the better. The Athertons have wasted no time in helping the city build a case against you. Irene Cushing has met three times with John Burden and the prosecutor."

"Three times? What more can she find to say about me?"

"That's what I must ask you, my dear. I know it's difficult, but any conversation you can remember having with her could be important. What have you told her?"

"She was my closest friend," I said bitterly. "I trusted her. What didn't I tell her?"

"Perhaps you trust too easily. Did you say you thought Peter was avoiding you?"

"I—I may have. I don't remember. I suppose I did. It was very difficult, you know. He was so busy, and he seemed to grow busier with every month, and well, he was never home. I did wonder, sometimes. . . ."

"I must—" Benjamin cleared his throat. A carriage went by, splashing dirty slush upon the walk. When it passed, he glanced about, as if searching for eavesdroppers on the empty sidewalk. "I must ask you some deeply intimate questions, Evelyn."

"I understand."

"Were you . . . were you and Peter sharing a bed?"

My face went hot; I looked down at my mud-spattered boots. "Not often."

"When was the last time?"

"I—I don't remember. Is it important?"

"It could be."

"Oh, I don't know. Months, I suppose."

"Did you confide this to Mrs. Cushing?"

"I was unhappy. I felt alone." I laughed ruefully. "How silly it seems now."

His face went soft with compassion. "It's not silly, my dear. Peter was gone a great deal of the time. I don't wonder you felt lonely. Is that what you told Mrs. Cushing?"

"I'm sure it was."

"Did you also tell her that you were angry with Peter for not being around long enough to produce a child?"

I flushed again. "I suppose I must have. It was true."

"When she suggested that you take a lover, did you tell her that you would start looking—and that she must help you find someone with dark hair and brown eyes so that whatever child you had would obviously not be Peter's?"

"But I was teasing—"

"Did you also say that this was because you wanted to torment him with the knowledge that you'd been unfaithful?"

I pulled away from him and stopped abruptly. "Oh dear God."

"Did you say those things, Evelyn?"

"Yes. Yes, I did, but I didn't mean them! I was angry with him. I thought . . . he was so busy; he didn't even look at me, and I told her it might take something like that to get his attention. But I didn't mean it."

I felt Benjamin's hand on my shoulder. "Ssshhh. My dear, my dear . . ."

I looked up at him. His expression was stricken, and I longed for him to understand. "I'm not a terrible woman. I'm not. I never . . . I was faithful to Peter. But I didn't realize. . . ."

I couldn't say the words. I felt disloyal to even think them. I had admitted those things to no one but Irene—not even my father knew them, though he had suspected. In those last months before he died, he had taken to watching me carefully whenever I visited, as if he could somehow discern the truth of my marriage from my movements.

I remembered the last time I'd seen him before he contracted the cholera. It had been after my mother died, and I'd gone to visit him, and he'd prepared supper for me, slicing ham with such careful precision, buttering my bread as if I were still a child, urging me to try the pickles—the last that my mother had put up. He'd seemed so old suddenly, and though I'd always thought of Mama as little more than an adjunct to him, even an impediment, I could not fail to miss his loneliness now that she was gone. He was restless with it, like an old dog who padded about constantly looking for a dead companion, unable to figure out where she'd gone, or why, inspecting every turn of the corner, as if it might hold the mystery of her disappearance, or as if she might suddenly appear. . . .

"The jam is here somewhere," he told me as he rose from the table for the tenth time to go to the pantry. "Strawberry preserves. Can't abide them myself, but she knew you loved them." He leaned into the cupboard, rooting around.

"You should bring in someone to help you, Papa," I said.

He rummaged a bit more, emerging with an "Aha! Here they are," and a jar of jam. He set it down on the table and eased slowly into his chair. "Now why should I get someone, Evie? Look around you—does it look as if I need some busybody housekeeper?"

It didn't; Papa had always had a genius for organization and a need for cleanliness. The house was as spotless now as it had been when Mama was alive.

"It's not that," I said, biting into my bread. "It's—"

"For God's sake, eat the jam. I went to all that trouble to find it."

Obediently, I put down the bread and reached for the preserves. The lid was stiff; I couldn't pry it open. "It's not the house-keeping. I hate to see you alone so much."

"How is that different from your own life, Evie?"

I was taken aback. "Why, I'm busy nearly every moment. You've no idea what it requires to be an Atherton."

"Doing's not the same," he said quietly. He took the jar from my hands and opened it with little effort. "I read the papers. Atherton's got case after case. Half the time you show up in the society page 'sans husband.' Your mama and I wondered from the start—"

"Wondered what?" I asked.

But he only looked at me. "Does he still listen to you the way you said he did? Does he value your thoughts? Is he really the true companion you thought him to be?"

"He's very busy—"

"Ah." The sound was knowing and sad. "Your mama always said he was hiding something. She said she felt it—"

"Or did her dreams tell her?" I asked sarcastically.

My father gave me a chiding look that shamed me. "Your mama was afraid for you. I told her you were a smart girl, that you knew what you wanted. But now I wonder if maybe she wasn't right to be afraid."

I looked down at my plate. His words made me want to cry. "It's all right," I said—as much for myself as him.

"It's not," he disagreed. "It never was. I don't know what he really wanted from you, but it wasn't companionship, and now I see: two years and no grandchildren—not even a false hope."

"I think children would be a burden—"

He silenced me with a look. "I'll let it all go. I won't say an-other word about how strange it is if you just tell me: are you happy?"

I didn't know what he would do if I told him no, if I told him all the things I suspected, that Peter didn't truly love me. That his mother had insisted he take a wife, and I always thought Peter had chosen me because he thought I wouldn't complain, and I didn't, at least not to him. But what could my father do? What could anyone do?

So I looked my father in the eye and lied. "Yes. Yes, I'm happy."

Now, I looked at Benjamin, with his compassionate eyes, and I wanted to tell him everything. But the habit of the last three years was hard to break, and I'd burdened him enough since I'd met him, in spite of the etiquette dictating that one not tax friends with the details of one's situation. What appeared to be the truth was the truth, and to reveal it as anything else was simply a lack of courtesy. Had I not learned that well enough before now, my experience with Irene assured I would remember.

I glanced away from Benjamin, focusing instead on the pattern of vines and leaves on the cast-iron fence bordering a yard. "I was the wife I thought Peter wanted. I was not unfaithful."

"But you were lonely," he said.

I turned back to him. "Yes. You knew that already. But it was my fault, I know. I could not quite ... I couldn't quite change enough for him." I tried to laugh it away. The sound fell flat. "Well, perhaps you couldn't know. You're a man, after all. I don't imagine you've ever felt that way."

His voice was very soft as he said, "I wouldn't be so certain of that."

The admission arrested me. Ben had always seemed so sure of himself; I didn't know whether to believe him, or whether he was merely trying to sympathize with me. But before I could say anything, he took my hand again, curling his fingers over mine.

"Forgive me," he said.

"For what?"

"For doing nothing about your unhappiness."

"Oh, Ben, what could you have done? You knew how dedicated Peter was to his work. Could anything have changed that?"

He was quiet for a moment. Then he said, "Things were complicated. Men live in a different world, Evie. The things we must do . . . there are many you wouldn't understand."

"Perhaps not," I said, but my bitterness seemed larger than ever. "But would it have been so difficult for Peter to spend a single evening a week with me? Or was I so unimportant that even that was too much?"

"I know he thought about your happiness."

"Did he? How often? An hour a day? Once a week? Or whenever he happened to drive past his home and remember I was there?"

Benjamin sighed. "This will not help your case, Evelyn."

I drew my hand gently from his, immediately contrite.

Ben said, "You told these things to Mrs. Cushing. Did you ever speak so to any of the Athertons?"

I looked up in horror. "Heavens, no! Peter's brothers and sisters are very close. They wouldn't hear of any flaw of Peter's."

"That's one less thing to worry about then. But your in-laws are working tirelessly. They've filed a motion challenging Peter's will, and they've gathered several witnesses against you. Not just Mrs. Cushing, but Rose Reid and her husband, and Captain Post, who says you seemed preoccupied and short-tempered in the days before Peter disappeared. He also says you spoke to him often of free love, which he found distasteful, as he felt you were asking him to partake of it with you—"

"That's ridiculous," I snapped. "Thomas Post is a flirt and an idiot. I danced with him, and he was the one who brought up free love!"

"It's all most damning, Evie."

"But none of it's true."

"Nonetheless, the furor against you grows. People liked Peter, and you're an outsider."

"There are witnesses you can call on my behalf," I said. "Everyone at the circle would speak for me. Not just Dorothy, but the Dudleys, and Jacob Colville is very respected. Wilson Maull,

do you think he could help? Or would his Fourierist beliefs offend? He's spent time at Brook Farm, but I think—"

"What about Jourdain?"

I frowned in confusion. "You think it would help to have him
speak for me?"

Benjamin shook his head. He glanced around again, waiting
until a shivering and silent couple hurried by, and lowered his
voice. "No. There's only one thing that will help you, and that's
finding the evidence against him. Don't let him distract you with
his 'tutoring.' Please. I confess I had other hopes for your future
than the Tombs."

I heard something in his words, some faint promise, and when
I looked at him, his expression was so sincere and sympathetic
that I realized our relationship had changed in the last days—perhaps it had started even before then, during those weeks of Peter's
all-consuming grief and distraction, when it fell to Ben and me
to fill the silences during our companionable suppers for three,
when the two of us had challenged each other so ruthlessly during
our chess games after.

I could love him, I thought. Benjamin Rampling would make a
good husband, and one more appropriate for me than Peter had
been. With him, I could have a stable, solid existence like that of
my parents. I wished suddenly that I had met Benjamin before
Peter.

But then I realized that Benjamin would not have considered
me then—and would not in the future if the Athertons had their
way. Even should I be acquitted, there was the matter of Peter's
will. Men like Benjamin Rampling could not both support a wife
and move in the circles he required to make a living. He must
marry a woman with an allowance of her own. I would have been
a woman like that, had all gone as I expected, with the Athertons
providing the allowance they'd promised. Without it, my fate
would be no better than Judith Duncan's, making hats or tatting
lace until my fingers were stiff with rheumatism—or worse: liv-

ing penniless in a city as unforgiving as this one. The uncertainty of living as a woman without prospects, without money, was terrifying. To always be alone, to know that despair might lead one to a life of degradation and shame, where each day one only wished for the strength to end it—

"Evelyn?"

Benjamin's voice brought me to myself. I realized he was peering at me with concern. I looked past him, to the police watchman who now stood across the street.

"It will all work out," I whispered, as much for myself as for him.

15

THROUGH A CLOUDY GLASS

MONDAY, FEBRUARY 9, 1857

The task Benjamin had set for me loomed impossibly. To go through Dorothy's private effects meant gaining access to her room when she or her nurses weren't there—such a rare occurrence I could not imagine how I might accomplish it. And though there was no such impediment to any search of Michel's room, there was my own reticence to master.

The pressure of Ben's expectation pressed heavily, and I dreamed of Peter every night now. The little sleep I managed was haunted by visions of him, eyeless and dripping wet, touching me with that chill hand. *Don't believe him, Evie. You must not believe him.* I knew who he meant, and I knew I could not afford to be idle. But I could not bring myself to search Michel's room. I was afraid to try.

Then, three days after my meeting with Ben, I woke at three-thirty, terrified, from my dream of Peter. As always, I could not go back to sleep, but this time I did not just lie in bed, staring at the ceiling. I drew on my dressing gown and lit a candle and went to the fireplace, where I started a fire and sat in a chair before it, afraid to move beyond the nimbus of its glow, the comforting flames. But the minutes dragged and the thought that I might sit there and stare at every passing minute until I went mad seemed so possible that I decided I must find something to read. I thought to go to the library, but I didn't want to leave the safety of my room. Instead, I went to the desk. The mess I'd created had long since been cleaned up by Kitty. Everything was back in its proper drawer, the pen nibs, the papers, the gold-chased penknife. The decanter with its liqueur glowed green and tempting, and I remembered how it had relaxed me, and poured myself a glass. Then I took one of the notebooks and the nubbin of a pencil from a drawer, though I wasn't sure what I meant to do with it. Write down my thoughts, perhaps, or draw—something to pass the time. I took the drink and the notebook back to the chair before the fire, and as I sipped the comforting liqueur, I flipped through the pages.

There were scrawlings within, the beginnings of a letter to someone named Percy, what looked like the times for the train. I finished the drink and set the glass aside, reading without interest until I came to the first blank page, and then I paused, staring down at the white paper that glowed dimly in the firelight. The blankness seemed to mock me, as if the paper itself existed solely to be infinite, and had only disdain for the limits my writing would impose upon it, the littleness of my efforts, the very humanness of them. I could not possibly write words profound enough to do justice to it, just as I could never understand the world beyond my own, the one Peter's spirit now supposedly inhabited. Whether it was heaven or hell or one of spiritualism's spheres didn't matter. One could sit in church every Sunday or a circle every Tuesday and Thursday and ask God—or the spirits—for guidance, but in the end it was like viewing something through a cloudy glass—every attempt to see more clearly only narrowed one's vision, until what was understood was only a moment in a vast and unknowable universe, in which the only absolute was how much was unknown.

I started at a sound, and looked down to find the pencil had fallen from my fingers to the floor. I was so tired, and I felt a bit woozy as well—no doubt due to the liqueur. Perhaps it was better to put the notebook aside, to try again for sleep. I picked up the pencil and glanced down to close the notebook—

—and saw words upon the page.

I bent closer, puzzled. The words were pale, as if written with a dull pencil, but pressed into the page so hard it dented the paper. But there had been no words there, pale or otherwise. I had turned to a blank page. Or had I? I was exhausted, after all, and the light was dim. There must have been words there already that I hadn't seen. I slapped the book shut and rose to take it back to the desk, glancing at the clock as I did so.

It read five o'clock.

Impossible. It couldn't be five o'clock. I had got the notebook at about three-forty. I'd been sitting here no more than ten minutes, if that. I looked again, thinking I must have made a mistake, but no, the hands were clear, there was no mistake. Where had the hour and twenty minutes gone?

My skin prickled; I felt suddenly as if I were being watched, and I spun around, staring hard into the shadows about my bed. I saw nothing, but the dread that came upon me was inescapable. I was clutching the pencil, and this time I dropped it purposefully and kicked it away. It rolled across the floor until it caught against the leg of the desk. And then it was as if something outside of me took my hand; I felt an urge I couldn't deny, directing me to open the notebook I still held. The leaves separated neatly, opening exactly to where I'd last been, to the pale but heavily penciled words.

I moved closer to the fire, to the candle, and brought the book to the light to see. The penmanship was terrible, the words difficult to make out:

You are not listning and you SHD. There are those in the material world who WLD keep you from us and those who WLD use decepton. Do not let them. Yer world is lies and DEATH.

Secrets and danger suround you. Hear from those who know, who have felt the knife of betrayal. The way for you is dark and cold, but you must find the truth and soon or be damned. Can you hear us call? We ask for justis. We CNT affect it from here, so you must do so for us. To understand is to AXCEPT, to AXCEPT is to KNOW. Heed those who WLD warn you. DNT deny those who will come to you. Go further than you will and be satisfyd. The truth is there for you to find if you will but trust a guide.

I stared at the words in bewilderment. I had no idea what they meant. But it seemed clear that they were meant for me. And what seemed clearer still was that I had written them. It was not my handwriting, but it was. I recognized the *t*, the little flourish I always put on the *s*. My handwriting, but I remembered nothing of writing it. Reluctantly, I thought of the newspaper articles I'd read, of invisible and mysterious hands guiding one who wrote, of obscure messages meant to show the way to God. I knew what the circle would call this: a message from the spirits.

I didn't believe that, but neither did I know how I could have been made to do this thing, and that frightened me. I thought of my mother, who had spent the last months of her life staring into space, drawn into herself by her addiction to laudanum. Her habituation had been painful to witness. She had tried to dispense with it many times, but to no avail. I remembered my father sitting over her in bed as she shook, feeble and sweating, screaming for relief. Finally, he had determined she was happier with the laudanum than without, and I supposed that was true, though I often found myself wondering what happiness she saw as she stared numbly into space, watching a world beyond the one I knew, one that had shaped itself into some fascinating story for her alone.

I had wondered if it was the laudanum that caused her growing madness, or the other way around. Had the medicine been the cause—or the cure? She had claimed to hear otherworldly voices since I was small; how often had I been made to suffer some wretched and foul poultice because of her belief that it would banish the "bad spirits" she saw lingering about me? I'd been afraid of the things she heard and the nightmares that were as vivid as my own, and so I was relieved when her laudanum dosage began to dull them both—but the relief it offered from ennui and night-mares had come at too great a price. I'd hoped that by denying my nightmares, they would go away. I had refused to admit that per-haps I'd inherited her propensity, and I'd been relieved that at least voices did not speak to or through me.

At least, they never had before.

The thought that her madness might be in me was terrifying. There must be a logical reason for this, a rational cause. There had to be some trick in it. I sank into the chair before the fire and stared into the flames and tried to determine the ways. I couldn't deny it was my handwriting. How had Michel manipulated me? Was he a mesmerist, could he put me in a trance and make me do this? And if he had, when? Had he drugged me? Had he put something in my food or drink—

I looked at the decanter on the desk, glowing with an almost sinister incandescence in the faint light. I rose and went to it, pulling off the stopper, leaning down to breathe deeply of it. I knew the scent of laudanum very well, and I smelled nothing of it here. Only a clean scent, rather grassy, a little bitter, very smooth.

I put the stopper back into place with a trembling hand and went back to the chair, staring down at the notebook I'd aban-doned on the floor. I grabbed it up and closed it. I did not want to look at it again, and until I understood what it meant, or how it had happened, I would say nothing.

I put the notebook beneath my bed, where I thought no one would find it, and then I settled myself in bed and looked to the window, waiting for the dawn.

By the time Kitty came to dress me, I was well and truly afraid. I'd never anticipated that Michel might have the power to do such things to me. Ben was right; I must escape this house as quickly as I could. I was determined to do what I could to clear my name today.

While Kitty did my hair, I said, "The house is so quiet this morning. Where is Mr. Jourdain?"

With quick ease, she twisted my hair into a chignon. "I don't know where he is just now, ma'am. But it's nearly eleven, and he usually goes to see Miz Bennett around this time."

"Does he?"

"Oh yes. And don't the rest of 'em just love him for it too. That Agnes never stops talking about it." Her voice rose in imitation. "'The way he takes care of Miz Bennett—why, he's such a gentleman! We mayn't ever fear for her with him around!'"

I couldn't help smiling at her mockery. I glanced at the clock. It was eleven now, and I found myself tensing, waiting for the sound of his boot steps along the hallway.

Kitty finished my hair, and while she straightened up the dressing table, I rose, going as nonchalantly as I could to the door. Again, I looked at the clock. Ten minutes after eleven. Surely he would go there now. I listened, and then I heard the opening of his door, and, before I had time to talk myself out of it, I opened my own, stepping back as I saw him, putting my hand to my heart in feigned surprise.

He stopped. "*Madame* Atherton. Good morning."

"To you as well, Mr. Jourdain. Do you go to breakfast?"

"Is that an invitation?"

I cursed myself inwardly. "Well, I—I'm afraid—"

"As it happens, I've already eaten," he said smoothly. "I was going to Dorothy."

I tried to hide my relief. "I would hate to disrupt her schedule."

"Perhaps you'd care to join me for tea this afternoon? I've some things to discuss with you."

"Of course," I said, though the moment I said the words I began thinking of excuses.

"Later then," he said. I watched him go to Dorothy's room,

the quick knock, the entry without invitation, the quiet closing of the door. He did not look back at me.

I took a deep breath and closed my own door behind me, and then I crossed the hall to his. The knob turned smoothly in my hands, and my mouth went dry with nervousness. I had expected the door to be locked, but it was open, and I had no choice but to enter before someone spotted me. With a final look down the hall, I slipped inside.

Where the guest room I inhabited was feminine with its delicate furniture, its blues and whites, his was its masculine counterpart. The dark green drapes were open to let in the overcast light of late morning, which glimmered darkly over the polished rosewood furniture. The evidence of his inhabitance was everywhere—a frock coat on the back of the chair, a tangle of ribands on the bedside table, a shaving strop hung next to a small mirror over the washbasin. The room smelled of him—sweat and something else, an herbal scent that I realized I associated with him, though I'd barely been aware of it.

As it had the other night in the parlor, the room seemed to pulse with his presence, and it made me so nervous that I stumbled in my haste. There was a desk near one wall, and instinctively I went there first. It was heavily decorated, inlaid with mosaics of what looked like ivory. Above it hung a painting of a couple caressing each other before a great bed—the woman had masses of curling hair, the youth was darkly handsome. A calla lily sprung tall and upright from a vase next to them. It was uncomfortably hedonistic, and I tried to ignore it.

His desktop was clean, unlike that of any other man I'd known. There was a single ledger pushed beneath a row of cubbyholes beside an ink bottle and scattered pen nibs, a well-used penwipe, and a cloisonné box. On the shelf above was a decanter, very like the one in my room, and I lifted the stopper and realized it held the same liqueur. My suspicions about the drink solidified, and I put the stopper carefully into place, and approached the desktop again more zealously.

First I lifted the lid of the cloisonné box. Inside was the diamond and sapphire pin I'd seen him wear, along with a pile of rings—different stones, different settings, all expensive—a jeweled watch chain, a single cuff link set with an opal, along with four other sets of different design, and two other brooches, one of garnets and one decorated with diamonds and blue topaz. A fortune in jewelry, but that alone was not evidence.

The desk had two large drawers; I tried them both, but they were locked, and I pawed through the cubbyholes, searching for a key—there was one, but it didn't fit, and it looked so old and rusty I doubted it had any use at all. I opened the ledger, a listing of accounts and expenses, and glanced over the numbers, looking for anything suspicious, though I was aware of the foolishness of this—how would I know? It looked like the usual things: payments to Madison Clothiers and Jacques Larouche, tailor; Ball, Black and Company; and a perfumer's in Union Square. He obviously had a liking for fine things; beyond these, he had so few expenses, there was not much to see.

But the amounts listed under income were impressive. Payments—gifts, no doubt—of five thousand dollars, another six, two of four—just in the last six months alone. I wondered angrily how much of it had come from Peter, but none were itemized; he was clever enough to explain nothing. Michel Jourdain was a wealthy man. In the last year he'd amassed an income of nearly fifty thousand dollars.

I closed the ledger and shoved it back into its place, and then I glanced about the room for where he might have hidden a desk key. There was a nightstand with a drawer by the bed, but when I opened it I saw nothing but handkerchiefs, and I was just bending to go through them when I heard footsteps in the hallway.

I froze, but the footsteps passed—the maid, thank God. I closed the nightstand drawer softly and took a deep breath to calm my nerves. I glanced toward the door, and as I did, my eye was caught by a flash of light. I turned back quickly, trying to find it again, and then saw the way the window light slanted across the nightstand, glancing across a half-drunk glass of water, shimmering on the ribands—how many colors he had! More than any woman . . .

Then I saw what I hadn't before. The flash of a jewel hidden beneath the ribands. I thrust my fingers into the silks until I grabbed what felt like a chain, and pulled it loose.

My heart seemed to stop. It *was* a chain, a watch chain, and one I knew. It was made of fine gold, adorned with pale sapphires to match his eyes, dangling with a charm—a tiny fish, with scales made of the smallest diamonds—in answer to a joke he used to make about fishing for me in muddy waters. *"Who knew there was such an exotic thing there among the eels?"*

Peter's watch chain. A gift from me in the first year of our marriage. He'd worn it since, but it had not been found on him when he died. It had been taken, either in a robbery or in the semblance of one. . . .

I dropped the chain into my palm, where it sent cats of light about the room. To have found this . . . to have found it here, where it should not have been, where it could not have been unless Michel Jourdain had taken it himself . . . I clasped the chain tightly. This was what I needed. It was not the adoption papers, but surely it was evidence enough. How ironic that it was to be something of Peter's that would save me!

Again I heard the footsteps of the maid. I looked toward the door, seeing her shadow pass beneath it. I knew I could not tarry. Michel's appointment with Dorothy could not last that long, regardless of what he did there. I looked back at the watch chain pooled in my hand. I wanted to take it with me—it should be mine, now that Peter was gone, and it was so precious—but I knew I could not. Michel would know someone had been in his room, and I could not afford to keep something that might prove to be evidence in Peter's murder. I must leave it here where I found it and tell Benjamin. He would know what to do about it.

But I was reluctant to put it back. I curled my fingers around it, squeezing as if I could imprint it into my hand, and then I pressed it to my lips. Only then did I let it slide from my fingers, hiding it again in the pile of ribands where it coiled like a snake. Then I went to the door, pausing to listen before I opened it slowly. The hallway was empty. I eased out, closing the door tightly behind me.

LATER THAT AFTERNOON, Molly knocked on my door and said, "Mr. Jourdain's waiting for you in the parlor, ma'am. He says you're to have tea."

I had forgotten all about it, but finding Peter's watch chain had removed my fear of Michel. Now that I knew he'd killed Peter, now that I knew he had manipulated me, I felt a hard triumph. And though I realized I must be cautious, I went into the parlor believing I had the advantage again.

He was sitting with long-limbed elegance upon the settee, with the tea set before him, along with a platter of tiny lemon tarts and sandwiches of biscuits and thinly sliced ham.

He rose when he saw me, and that set off a spate of coughing. I waited politely until it ended, and then I sat across from him in a silk-upholstered chair.

He motioned toward the teapot and said, "Would you do the honors, *Madame*? I'm sure you've more grace than I."

I perched on the edge of my seat and poured, and handed him his cup, though I was careful not to do so much as brush his fingers when I gave it to him.

"Would you care for a lemon tart? They're Cook's specialty, and my favorite."

"I'm not hungry," I told him. "You have things to discuss with me?"

"Ah, so this is how it's to be? No friendly comment on the weather? Not even a 'Will it be as cold today, d'you think?' A pity. I'd so hoped for diversion. I'm sorely in need of it."

"I'm sorry I can't oblige you. I find I'm not much in the mood to be diverting." I looked down into my tea.

He said, "Life's a trial in itself, eh? Fortunately, you've one thing to look forward to."

I glanced up. "What would that be?"

"Why, your development, of course." Idly, he ran a finger around the rim of his cup, and I found myself drawn by the motion, almost mesmerized by it. "Dorothy's quite insistent that I tutor you."

Now I heard the danger in his voice; my sense of having the advantage over him weakened. "What did you tell her?"

"That I would, of course. I obey her every whim."

I thought I heard a slight mockery, even self-deprecation, but I wasn't certain. "I release you from your duty," I said, putting the cup aside. "Especially as you seem so opposed to it."

"Ah, but I don't have to be." He too set down his cup, stretching out his legs, leaning forward. "I think you'll find I can be very accommodating."

I rose abruptly, without thinking, wishing only to put space between us. I went to the window and pulled aside the drapes to look outside. "Mr. Jourdain, you made yourself perfectly clear. As I told Dorothy, I've no wish to inconvenience you."

"But you've inconvenienced me already, *Madame*. Whether you like it or no, I'm bound by my promise to Dorothy. She'd be unhappy if I ignored it."

"God forbid you make her unhappy."

"You've the grasp of it, it seems."

I heard the creak of the settee as he rose, and I focused on the scene outside—the watchman across the street, the muddy lawn, the last vestiges of snow in the lee of the house, the slushy, icy brown of it in the gutters. Still, I was sensitive to his every move. I made myself remember Peter's watch chain tangled in with his ribands, and tried to raise anger; instead I felt only panic as Michel drew closer. Then I felt him standing behind me.

"It'll be spring soon," he said casually. Then, softly, "You wear a distinctive perfume, *Madame*—what is it? Lily, I think, with something . . . ah, what is that? Something sharp—ginger, perhaps? Why, I think I'd know it anywhere. It lingers . . . even after you leave a room."

He knew.

He leaned closer. "It's quite unusual. Very like you."

"P-Peter chose it."

"Did he? That surprises me. I don't believe he would've spent time choosing a scent for a woman he neglected."

It was meant to inflame me; I knew this, but I was unable to stop myself from reacting. "He did not neglect me." I turned quickly to face him—only to find he was much closer than I'd thought. I stepped back and nearly lost my balance, and as I reached to regain it, he grabbed my elbow, steadying me and at the same time pulling me closer, so there was only the width of my skirts between us.

"Come, *Madame,* why lie? He was here most every night, 'til very late. Where were you? Lying alone in your big bed, waiting for his step upon the stair—"

I pulled away from him. "You go too far, Mr. Jourdain."

"Did you never wonder where he was? What he was doing?"

"He told me he was working."

He smiled. His expression confused me. He was wry, and sarcastic, but there was something else there too, something that made me hesitate, that took my fear and replaced it with curiosity. "Is there a reason I shouldn't believe it?"

"You didn't know your husband very well. But I wonder, did he know you at all?"

I couldn't abide how he looked at me. I would have backed away from him, but I was already against the window, and he was standing so close I could not dodge him easily.

"Do you wonder why I have it?"

"Have what?" My voice was nothing, barely a sound.

"He told me a story. About a girl he found in an office on Lower Broadway. 'A pretty fish,' he called her. 'Like an angelfish. An angelfish in muddy water.'"

Peter's words. The story was always the same. "He told you?"

"Just before he gave it to me. She was an angel, he said, 'but you're something grander, Michel. You're my savior.'"

"He didn't give it to you—he wouldn't have! You stole it from him."

"Before I murdered him, *chère*? Ah, that's what you think? That I took him down there and knifed him and took his watch chain to make it seem like a robbery—"

"You seem to have the grasp of it," I mocked. "I won't go to prison for you. I won't hang."

"I hope not. Such a waste of a pretty face."

"I know what you are."

He touched my chin. I turned my face away, but still his fingers lingered. "I know what you are too, *Madame*. Tell me: have you ever made love with one who's your affinity?"

"My husband—"

"Another lie." He sighed. "Come, can we move beyond such disguises? Must we still pretend your husband loved you?"

I opened my mouth to tell him it was no lie, but Michel's face blurred before me; I realized with horror that I was crying.

"Dear God, I despise you." I pushed at him, and he stepped back. I raced past him to the doorway, blind through my tears, but I heard his final words even as I fled, a whisper that was more frightening than anything he'd said to me before.

"Do you, Evie? Do you really?"

16

THE WAYS WE DELUDE
OURSELVES

THE OFFICES OF ATHERTON AND RAMPLING

I fled to the kitchen, where I startled the cook and the scullery maid, and Lambert, who did not show any surprise, but merely looked up from packing tobacco into his pipe. I asked him to call me a carriage. Then, to the discomfort of the cook and the maid, I waited there, a place I was fairly certain Michel would not follow.

When Lambert returned with my cloak and the message that the driver was in front, I hurried from the kitchen.

"Will you be home for supper, ma'am?" he asked as he followed me to the door.

"No. Please give my apologies to Mrs. Bennett."

I rushed outside. It was growing late into the afternoon, and the sky was darkening, the air growing colder. Dorothy's driver bundled me into the carriage and asked politely, "Where to, ma'am?"

"Pearl Street," I told him. "To the offices of Atherton and Rampling."

I had no idea if Benjamin would be at the office, but my rush was to be away, to be safe, and I could think of no one safer than he.

The nightly exodus out of downtown had not yet begun; as we made our way into the business district, the sidewalks were not yet crowded with men hastening to catch the omnibuses and horse cars uptown. Carriages for hire waited along the side of the street, the horses dipping their heads in tired resignation, the drivers smoking as they waited for their fares. Merchants rolled barrels back into their stores. Boys sweeping the walks with more vigor than efficiency raised dust that only added to the constant cloud already raised by the city's building boom. Like fog, it grayed everything, and fell again like dew on the bruised apples of the pushcart peddlers on the corners, who were beginning to appear now with the ending of the day, lighting their oil lamps to show off the produce that hadn't sold at market.

The city was changing so quickly that parts of it seemed to become unrecognizable overnight, and it had been a long time since I had made the journey to Peter's office. I was disoriented until the driver pulled up before an old Federal-style stone mansion that, like many in this area, had been converted into counting-houses. The driver opened the door and helped me out, holding securely to my elbow as he directed me past the refuse and sewage until we were safely on the flagstone walk, where he left me to make my own way into the building.

Atherton and Rampling was on the second floor, up a wide and winding staircase that had once displayed women floating down it in silk and satin splendor, but now held only black-suited clerks and accountants who were oblivious both to its elegance and to me as I went past them to the door of my husband's office.

I paused at the sight of Peter's name still stenciled on the glass in black and gold. Then I pushed open the door and went forward so hastily I nearly collided with the desk just inside, where a handsome young man wearing glasses looked up curiously.

"Ma'am? May I help you?"

"I'm here to see Mr. Rampling," I said.

He looked down at the ledger on the desk and frowned. "Have you an appointment? I don't see—"

"I'm Mrs. Peter Atherton."

He nodded and looked down again, as if the name meant nothing to him, and then he froze, and looked up again quickly, rising. "Mrs. Atherton, forgive me. I didn't recognize you—"

"I didn't expect you to. I don't think I've set foot here in more than a year."

"Let me just say how sorry I am for Mr. Atherton's death. He was a good man. Mr. Rampling told me he had taken on your case."

"Thank you," I said sincerely. "Mr. Rampling's been very kind."

"I wish I could say he was here to meet you, Mrs. Atherton, but I'm afraid he's gone home for the day."

My disappointment was keen. "Do you—might you have the address? I'm afraid I've misplaced it, and I'm not good with directions."

He nodded, reaching for a piece of paper and scrawling upon it. He handed it to me. "It's not far from here, actually."

"Thank you." I tucked the paper into my palm. "You've been very helpful."

"Not at all, Mrs. Atherton."

I left quickly. I handed the piece of paper to the driver, who waited for me in the street, and said, "Please, take me there."

The clerk was right; it seemed only moments before the carriage was pulled to a stop in front of brick row houses only a few blocks over. These too had once been the homes of the upper ten, abandoned for more desirable real estate higher up Broadway or over on Fifth Avenue. They now served as some of the better boardinghouses in the city, or were owned by modest business-men like my father. I hesitated only a moment before I took hold of the iron rail and went up the narrow steps to the door. I knocked, softly at first, and then, when I heard nothing, more loudly. I heard a shuffling behind the door, a call: "Just a minute, just a minute! I'm coming!"

The door opened to a striking woman with dark eyes and un-blemished skin. She was wearing blue with jet trim, and her hair was dark and smooth and shining. I knew a moment of profound dismay. I tightened my hand on my bag and said, "Excuse me. I'm looking for Mr. Rampling?"

"Of course," she said. She stood back, ushering me inside, into a hallway hung with framed lithographs and smelling strongly of roasted mutton. "Is he expecting you?"

"I don't think so. I'm Mrs. Peter Atherton."

If the name meant anything to her, she showed no sign. She took me to an open doorway just past the stairway. "Well, you're a step up from most of his visitors, I'll tell you that. I think you must be the first lady who's called. The parlor's empty just now, but if someone comes in, you tell them you've private business and to get out. Too many undesirables coming around here lately."

"Is this—a boardinghouse, then?"

"Yes, ma'am," she said. "I'm Mrs. Harris. I'll go get him, then," she said, and disappeared, leaving me alone.

The room was nicely appointed, with two horsehair-upholstered settees and sturdy maple tables that looked very like the ones in the house I'd grown up in. The carpet too was one of Stewart's ready-mades, but it was a good one, and showed little wear. A fire burned in the fireplace, but the house lacked central heating—the room was chill beyond the reach of the flames, and the windows were thin. The cold air from outside emanated from them, easing through cracked, warped sills. On the walls were hung two portraits by obviously mediocre artists, and a few other lithographs of paintings with classical themes: the fall of Rome, the Battle of Troy, along with a copy of Holman Hunt's ubiquitous *Light of the World* hanging beside a carved and polished wooden crucifix.

I went to stand near the fire, glancing idly down at the books lined upon the mantel—a few farming journals, and a book of Shakespeare whose pages looked uncut—and I heard rapid footsteps coming down the hallway outside the room. I turned just as a young man entered. He was fair and slight, almost delicate, with gleaming hair, and eyes that seemed too large for his face. His style of dress was elaborate—a complicated necktie, a fancy green-checkered vest.

He stopped short when he saw me. "Oh. Pardon me. I didn't realize anyone was here. Are you new? I haven't seen you before."

"I'm waiting for Mr. Rampling."

"Why?"

His bluntness took me aback. "I—I'm afraid that's none of your concern."

He looked as if my answer surprised him, and then he stepped farther into the room and rubbed his hand nervously against his vest. "I'm sorry. That was rude of me. I haven't introduced myself. I'm Willie Chesney. I'm Benny's assistant."

Benny? "His assistant? I wasn't aware he had one."

"Oh yes. I'm actually quite indispensable to him."

"Really? He's never mentioned you."

"Should he have?" He gave me a frank look. "I mean, who are you?"

He was very young, and obviously very proud, and it was hard to take offense at his impertinence, though I had to curb the urge to scold him like a child. "I'm Mrs. Peter Atherton."

His pale skin turned ruddy. "Oh . . . there, I've done it again, haven't I? I thought you were nobody, or at least, well, a seamstress or something. But I see now you don't look anything like that."

I was amused. "Thank God for that."

"I—Benny's always telling me to be more circumspect, but I'm afraid I'm not very good at it."

"He must be quite a taskmaster."

"Oh, I don't mind. He pays me well enough." He glanced away with a small smile.

"Have you been working for him long?"

"A few months."

"Then you must have known my husband."

"Oh . . ." Mr. Chesney looked away, as if the thought of Peter was painful for him, and I decided I liked him, despite his bluntness. "Yes. I was sorry when he was found that way. But I suppose, given how often he went down there——"

"Willie?"

Benjamin's voice came from the doorway, and the young man started and turned.

"What are you doing here?" Ben's tone was harsh—unduly so, I thought.

"Mr. Chesney's been amusing me," I said.

Ben barely glanced at me. His jaw was tight. "He has work to do."

"I—I left my case in here." Mr. Chesney glanced about the room, and I saw the black case on the settee at the same moment he did. He rushed over to it, shoving it beneath his arm. He turned to me, making a quick bow. "Mrs. Atherton . . ." then scurried from the parlor.

Benjamin closed the door firmly and said, "I apologize, Evelyn. I hope he didn't disturb you unduly."

"What did he mean about Peter going often down to the river?"

"Peter often visited clients in that area. The lad's a bit of an idiot, actually. I'm not sure why I keep him around. I suppose he has potential, but only just. He is, however, eager to please." He came quickly over to where I stood. "I was concerned when Mrs. Harris told me you were here. Has something happened? Are you hurt?"

"Yes, something happened. I did what you asked. I searched Michel's room."

He went very still. "And did you find something?"

I took a deep breath. "Peter's watch chain."

"His watch chain? Evelyn——"

"The watch chain he wore all the time. It was in Michel's room. On his bed stand. It was the watch chain *I* gave to him,

Benjamin. It had some meaning for him—or at least I thought it did."

"Peter gave Jourdain a great deal of money. Are you certain he would not have given him a gift like that as well?"

Miserably, I said, "That's what Michel said. That it was a gift. I didn't believe it. Or I suppose I did believe it. I just didn't want to."

"You told him you'd found it?" Benjamin's voice was raw with shock. "You told him you'd been in his room?"

"He *knew* I'd been in his room. He knew I'd found the chain. He said he smelled my perfume. I was so careful, but he knew. Dear God, he knew just what to say—"

Gently Benjamin took my arm, leading me to the settee. "What do you mean?"

"He knew the story of the watch chain. But he wouldn't have known it unless Peter had told him. And everything he said . . ." Despite my best intentions, I felt tears coming to my eyes, and impatiently I brushed them away. "It was *our* story. About me being an angelfish. Peter had no right to tell it. It belonged to us."

"I'm certain, if he'd known how strongly you felt—"

"Michel said I didn't know him. That I didn't know my own husband."

I felt Benjamin stiffen. "Ridiculous. Who would know a man better than his wife?"

"But he was right." I opened my bag, searching for my handkerchief. "We've talked of this already. He was simply never there—"

"He was dedicated to his work."

"You needn't bother with that story," I said sharply. "Michel told me that Peter was at Dorothy's nearly every night. I suppose you were as well."

"We were there often." Benjamin's voice was consoling. "But not so often as he says. Evie, don't you think it serves Jourdain's purpose to tell you such a thing? He doesn't want to be caught—

he would have known from the start that you might find the watch chain. He would have had his story perfectly rehearsed. Think of it: what was your reaction when he told you?"

"I was hurt that Peter would have told him."

"And the rest? When he told you that you didn't know your husband?"

"Disconcerted," I whispered. "Distressed."

"Disconcerted people don't push for answers, my dear," Benjamin said. "Do you see how he's manipulating you?"

I did. How easily he'd managed me. How stupid I'd been—I'd forgotten every lesson my father ever taught me: to listen, to school one's responses and one's emotions.

"You mustn't let him distract you with his talk. It's what he does. How do you think he makes the spirits appear? He distracts with words, he tells you what you should expect to see; why then are you so surprised that you see it?"

I was angry now. "I saw his ledger. He's made a great deal of money this year."

"And like every mountebank, he won't be happy until he has more. Until he owns the Bennett name, and everything that goes along with it. Remember, Evie, Peter believed Michel was a fraud. He meant to expose him. You know he protested Dorothy's adoption. He was there so often for those reasons."

"I'm sorry," I said, and I was. I hated that I'd disappointed him.

Benjamin shook his head, as if it didn't matter, and took my hand. "Don't be. But as long as you've decided to go along with this mediumship foolishness, you must truly make it work for us. You must be especially convincing at the next circle. Jourdain knows all the tricks; therefore you must do what he does. Listening is imperative. The things people want, the things they expect—they say it all either in words or in movements. That's the genius of it. While you're 'listening' to the spirits, you're really listening to the things people are saying, the things they don't realize they're saying."

It was a kind of shrewdness I hadn't expected of him. "How do you know this?"

"I'm an attorney. What a client says and what he means are two different things. So it is with those at a circle. Someone is saying: 'The spirit is my brother Harry!' and Jourdain's watching the way they move; he knows how they feel about that brother simply by the way they sit. Are they leaning forward? Do they look eager? Or are they pulling back in their chair, as if they would rather be anywhere else? Jourdain does his research too—don't forget that. He goes to the newspaper office. He checks the society pages. Birth and death records. Marriage records. He talks to servants. It's a complicated business, setting up such a flimflam. One can find anything, but it takes a great deal of work. He's so successful because he takes the time."

I remembered the touch of my "father's" spirit, my fruitless search for a confederate in the darkness. "The other night, Dorothy felt her son's hand. How does he accomplish that?"

Benjamin smiled thinly. "Do you remember what occurred just before it happened?"

"Michel said her son wished to touch her."

"You see? He suggested that she would feel her son's hand. Then he watches, and she follows his gaze, as does everyone. She 'sees' her son's hand because Michel pretends to see it. She feels it touch her. But in reality she will feel only what Jourdain has suggested."

"I can't believe that works."

"Well, I've seen it happen in court—or under police questioning. I've seen people confess to crimes they didn't commit simply because they'd been made to believe they must have done it."

I thought uncomfortably of the spirit writing hidden in my room. "You believe it's all fakery?"

He sighed. "Don't you? I've never yet seen a medium who changed my mind. Do you think the spirits truly deign to speak with us once they're gone? I tend to think they have bigger tasks than communicating with those left behind."

I looked down at our hands, clasped together, and I could not resist asking him, "How do you explain spirit writing, then?"

"Oh, the ways we delude ourselves! I suppose, if one sits long enough staring at a blank piece of paper, one is likely to write anything and believe it came from outside of oneself."

"It's a hallucination, then? Or could it be made to happen by some . . . some drug?"

"Probably. Many hallucinations are the product of such habits. I confess I haven't seen enough of it to wonder. Or to care." He took a deep breath and released my hand. "It's getting late. I suppose they'll wonder where you got to."

"Forgive me for interrupting your work."

"You *are* my work, my dear," he said, smiling. "Shall I call you a carriage?"

"I've Dorothy's waiting outside." I started to the door and he followed me; when I got there, I paused, turning to face him. "These people have attended many circles. I hope I can fool them."

"Where's the confidence you had the other night?"

"A bit shaken, I suppose," I confessed.

He stepped close, and his eyes were deep with an admiration that left me breathless. "Then I shall have enough for the both of us. I *know* you can do this."

I looked down, feeling myself flush with embarrassed pleasure. "I shall trust in your judgment, then."

"I think you'll find I'm right. And, Evelyn, remember that Jourdain's goal is to discomfort you. If you let him succeed, we will have lost."

"Thank you, Benjamin. You've greatly reassured me."

"As I hoped." He smiled. "I'll see you at the circle, my dear."

I stepped outside. The late afternoon had slid to twilight in the time I'd spent with Benjamin. The lamplighters were making their rounds, their torches blazing, and I felt like any woman might who was leaving a prospective suitor.

Then I saw Dorothy's driver waiting in the street, hurrying toward me. Beyond him, there was a movement—another man mounting a horse—and I went cold at the sight of him. It was my watchman, sent to make certain I did not leave the city.

I wasn't just a simple woman leaving a suitor.

I would never be that woman again.

17

THE WOLF OR THE RABBIT

AFTER FINDING PETER'S WATCH CHAIN

I t was two days later that Lambert appeared in the doorway of the dining room to announce, "The master asks that you join him in the library when you've finished your breakfast, ma'am. He would like to start your lessons."

I glanced up from my eggs and toast. "My lessons?"

"At Mrs. Bennett's request," Lambert said.

The breakfast I'd just eaten seemed to curdle in my stomach. I pushed aside my plate. "Thank you, Lambert," I managed.

The very last thing I wanted was to be alone with Michel, but I knew I had to play this charade out to the end. I tried to gather my composure, to tell myself this was the opportunity I needed to discover what Michel knew of my husband. I thought also of the spirit writing, and I was determined to find out how he had engineered it. Those convictions restored my courage. Still, my steps were slow as I made my way up the stairs to the third floor. I had not yet been inside the library in my time here, and now, as I looked upon the giant open double doors and the bookshelves laden with books within, it seemed absurd that I had not. My father's passion had been books, and they had cluttered nearly every surface of our small house and cost enough that he was often sheepish about their purchase—especially on those nights when we could afford nothing for supper but bean soup and bread. I hadn't realized Dorothy shared his affection for reading.

The library ran the entire width of the house; on the opposite wall was a mullioned window as tall as a man and at least that wide overlooking the backyard, banked by a seat cushioned in a moss green velvet that matched the wallpaper gilded with fleurs-de-lis. At one end of the room was a fireplace framed in elaborately carved mahogany, flanked by two wingback chairs and a settee. At the other end was a desk—also mahogany, and near it stood a small round table that held a book too small to be a dictionary, but one that was obviously treasured, set as it was under glass.

"Ah, there you are."

I turned to see Michel leaning around the edge of one of the wingback chairs before the fire. He said, "I trust you had a pleasant breakfast?"

"Lambert said you wished to see me."

He rose, coming smoothly toward me. "I thought perhaps we could start developing you today. I'm quite at liberty, so you have me all to yourself." He smiled intimately as he said it.

I chose not to acknowledge the smile or the insinuation. "How shall we begin?"

He motioned to the settee, near the fire. "Please. Take a seat."

I went to the settee, and Michel sat beside me. He leaned back against the arm of the settee, twisting to look at me, and I was uncomfortable at his half smile and the frankness of his gaze.

I looked away, toward the fire. *Don't let him disconcert you.* "Please. Could we proceed?"

He straightened and his voice became businesslike. "To call the spirits requires a passive mind. Our first task will be to teach you how to cultivate it."

Warily, I said, "A passive mind? What does that mean?"

"A term of art," he explained. "A good medium is like an instrument that can be played by any hand."

How indecent he made the words sound. The images he conjured . . . I felt myself flush.

He continued as if he hadn't seen, which was odd—he'd never before missed an opportunity to needle me. "There're many who believe strong-minded people don't make good mediums. Too unwilling to be played, eh? Some feel only women and children have the skill."

"Why is that?" I asked.

"Because their minds aren't as developed. They're easily influenced."

I felt a twinge of irritation. "Is that what you believe?"

"How could I? I'm a medium—do I appear weak willed to you, *Madame*?"

"I'm not sure I could say. Are you immoral, Mr. Jourdain? Or a sinner?"

"Does it matter?"

"I was taught that immorality and sin were indications of a weak will."

He steepled his hands, pressing his fingers against his lips, as if to suppress the smile that teased them. "I've never felt a woman's mind was inferior, but I may have to rethink that now—at least about yours. How easily influenced you must be to allow the church to lead your thinking."

Again, I was irritated. "What else can show us the path to righteousness?"

"How about one's own conscience?"

"Not everyone follows his conscience. Not everyone would choose to be righteous."

"True, but I'd rather trust each man's conscience than church dictates, eh? Especially when it isn't God who gains by our obedience."

I scowled at him. "What do you mean?"

"What was the rent you paid on your pew this year, *Madame* Atherton? Did you tithe?"

"That money's given to the poor and needy."

"Ah, *oui*. But who decides who's poor and needy? I think it'd take an unusual reverend indeed not to find God's will in his purchase of new velvet drapes when his old ones are out of fashion."

"How cynical you are."

He shook his head. "*Non*. It's only that I don't believe any man has the right to decide who deserves salvation and who doesn't."

"Who else should do so?" I asked.

"When a wolf kills a rabbit, don't you think the rabbit believes the wolf is evil? Should the rabbit be allowed to decide the wolf must be condemned?"

"A rabbit is an animal, not a man. A rabbit can't reason, nor has it the faculties for higher thinking."

"*Non,* but would you agree it's a natural creature, put on earth by God? Or that the wolf was only doing what it was meant to do when it killed the rabbit?"

"Of course," I said.

"Would you question God's wisdom in giving the wolf the things that make him a wolf? Sharp teeth? Claws? The sense of smell that tells him where the rabbit hides? Or do you think the wolf is evil, as the rabbit does?"

"Evil? No. I would say the wolf is perfectly made to be a wolf—as God intends."

"So then you wouldn't deny that each of us is perfectly made as well—to be what we are?"

"I wouldn't deny it, no," I said. "God has made us what we are for a reason."

"Then why question God's intentions by trying to diminish what we don't like? Why not just accept that each man is here to do as he must? That we were each given certain gifts to take advantage of?"

Intrigued despite myself, I said, "I don't think God would consider immorality—or evil—a gift to be taken advantage of."

Michel leaned forward, his eyes mesmerizing in their intensity. "How would you know? How would any of us?"

"The Bible tells us—"

"The Bible was written by man to serve his own ends. The idea of immorality is an artificial construct. Like society. Like the church. We use such things to control one another, but what right have we to do so? Wasn't your intelligence God given? Weren't you meant to do something with it? Why then should I—or anyone else—have control of it or say you can't use it because you're a woman? It's yours, isn't it? To do with as you will. To be the wolf"—he grinned—"or the rabbit."

I stared at him, speechless. His ideas were stirring, and I found myself leaning toward him, wanting to spin those ideas out, to search for the flaws I knew must exist in his logic.

"Now then, shall we try?" he asked.

I blinked. I had been so caught up in his words that I had forgotten entirely why I was there. "Try what?"

"To cultivate a passive mind," he said. "The idea's simple enough. You must close your eyes and think of nothing. Don't resist when you feel another consciousness enter yours."

Reluctantly, but obediently, I closed my eyes. "Do all lecturers and mediums begin this way?"

"All the ones I've seen."

"What of spirit writers?"

"The same. They allow the spirits to enter their mind, to guide their hand."

His voice was his greatest tool—smooth, seductive, changeable, it seemed to wind through me.

"Are you a mesmerist, Mr. Jourdain?"

"I know something of animal magnetism, *oui*. It's what allows the spirits to come to us."

"Mr. Dudley said it was like electricity."

"*Oui*. Think of it as a fluid, eh? It moves through us and around us and animates the spirits as well. It informs the universe, both our world and the unseen one."

"Could such fluid be used to control another person, the way mesmerists do? To make them do spirit writing?"

"What would be the point?"

I opened my eyes and looked directly at him. "That's what I'd like to know. What *would* be the point?"

His gaze was considering, and I forced myself to hold it, determined not to be the first to look away.

But neither was he. He said, "Imagine you come upon a house painted brown. What color would you say the house was?"

"Why brown, of course."

"But what if I came upon it from the other side, and found it to be white?"

"That would be absurd. Who would paint a house two colors?"

He ignored my question. "You say it's brown, and I say it's white. Who's right?"

"We're both right."

"*Non,*" he said. "We're both wrong. The house isn't brown or white. It's both. You and I only see one side. But that doesn't mean the other side doesn't exist. To not see the whole is to not see the truth."

"And what is the whole in your spiritualism, Mr. Jourdain? Invisible levers? Silver paint? Stagecraft?"

He smiled. "It seems all spirits need theatrics, eh? Even Christ himself requires incense and holy water. We're a skeptical people. We need convincing."

"What if I said you've simply found a clever way to explain what's nothing more than trickery?"

He shrugged elegantly. "All of life's a trick. Nothing can be believed."

"Some things can be. What one sees with one's own eyes—"

"Sight is one of the most easily deceived senses. I could make a coin disappear and your eyes would believe it gone, even if it were merely up my sleeve."

"You're speaking of illusion, Mr. Jourdain, but not everything is that. Most of the time life is exactly what we see before us."

Michel laughed. "Is that so? Like the brown house you come upon?"

"In the absence of any other information, I would have to believe what I saw."

"Even if it weren't the truth? If we believe only what we see—"

"—we'll never know that the house is brown *and* white," I finished. "And I would say we can never know the whole truth, and perhaps we aren't meant to. This is the world we must live in, whether it's an illusion or no. To make our peace with partial truths is the only possibility for happiness."

He looked surprised, and I could not help but smile. Our conversation reminded me of the many I'd had with my father, the twists, the rapid turns. How often had we sat before the fire, debating philosophy and literature for hours, so caught in the words that whole pots of tea disappeared without our being aware we'd drunk it?

In that moment, my mind felt cleaner and brighter than it had since my father had died. Those times with him had been the best of my life, and I had not expected to find their echo here, in this library, with this man.

I looked at Michel in astonishment, and he smiled, and I realized what this was, what he had meant to do.

He had known what I most wanted—a listening ear, a balm for loneliness, a mental challenge—and he had fulfilled it. He was manipulating me, and I had let him.

I rose quickly, angry and humiliated at the disappointment I felt. "I think that's enough for today, Mr. Jourdain."

He rose as well. "As you wish, *Madame*."

"I'M SO EXCITED!" Sarah said as she came inside the next evening, her eyes sparkling. She took both my hands in her gloved ones. "I've never helped develop anyone before."

"I've done some reading on it since we last met," Dudley announced. He unwound the scarf from his neck and took off his top hat, handing them both to a waiting Lambert. "The *Spiritual Telegraph,* you know, has been most helpful. And I spoke to Mrs. Hardinge. In her time at the Conference, she's helped develop several new mediums. Thankfully, we have a stable company from which to embark. Mrs. Hardinge says it requires careful preparation under a skilled and benevolent eye."

"We've Michel for that," his wife said.

Dudley looked at me. "One must discipline the mind to harness the spirits without enslaving them—or allowing oneself to be enslaved."

I nodded sympathetically, but I was perspiring, and it had nothing to do with the warmth of the rooms. I cast a glance at Benjamin. He had come in only moments before the others, and there had been no time for anything more than his hasty and whispered "You can do this, Evelyn."

When Wilson Maull and Jacob Colville arrived, we adjourned to the upstairs parlor where Dorothy waited—already seated at the table. Again, they passed around the liqueur, but this time I drank none. I was too suspicious of it now.

"You look lovely, my dear," Ben said, drawing near. He touched my shoulder reassuringly and said in a low voice, "Remember what I told you: the key is in *listening.*"

"Yes, " I said, then leaned close to his ear to say, "I had a 'lesson' with Michel yesterday."

His eyes flared in interest. "Oh? And how was it?"

"He's very good."

"Yes, he is," he agreed. "But you aren't fooled by him. And you've a weapon he knows nothing of."

"A weapon?"

"Me." He smiled. "I am on your side, remember. Your confederate."

"Thank God for that."

"Just hold to your purpose. Dorothy's the one you must impress."

I felt better at his words and the warmth in his eyes, but then

Dorothy called me, and when I went over to her, she took my arm, pulling me down to hear. "Michel said your lesson went well, child. You're a good girl. You let him lead you."

She looked across the room to him, and despite myself I followed her gaze and saw Michel was watching us. His expression was closely veiled, and my nervousness returned as Dorothy called for us to begin, and everyone made their way to the table. I sat in my accustomed place beside him.

Michel took my hand. "You look pale."

I swallowed—agitated already—and looked away. "Shall we begin?"

Robert Dudley took my other hand. The lights were lowered.

Michel said, "Tonight we'll attempt to see if the spirits truly do speak through *Madame* Atherton, and to that end, *Madame,* you must empty your mind."

"A passive mind, remember, Evelyn," Dudley said.

"Just so," Michel agreed. "I'll call them. When they've arrived, *Madame* might take over."

I looked to Benjamin. His gaze was intent, reassuring.

I closed my eyes and the prayers began, the singing, the invocations. Michel finally spoke to call the spirits. His hand opened slightly; the tips of his fingers caressed mine.

"Almighty God, let us talk with the spirits tonight."

I kept my eyes closed; I felt the tension of the others as the silence grew.

"Is there a spirit present?" Michel asked.

His fingers stroked my hand, and I was too tired to protest. I was unthinking, cocooned, numbed. Moments passed.

"If there is a spirit present, would it answer me?"

His words were like buzzing in my ear, quiet at first, and then slowly the buzzing grew until I could no longer hear his words, until the sound filled my head, louder and louder until I felt I couldn't stand it another moment, until I nearly opened my eyes to ask what it was, and to make it stop—but I couldn't make myself open my eyes. I was so tired. Why was no one talking about that sound?

Then, just when it became unbearable, it changed. It became a whisper, drawing me toward it, beckoning, pulling me. It was like falling into a dream. *Come. . . .*

But I couldn't move to follow it, and then there was a clatter, a sudden movement, and I felt a pressure beneath my hands, lifting them.

I heard Michel speaking, garbled, nonsensical talk. He stirred beside me. His speech became a kind of chant inside my head, a song I could almost recognize. I'd heard it before. I knew it. *A Creole song about a nun longing for love . . .*

Finally, he was silent, and I opened my eyes.

They were all staring at me as if I'd gone mad.

I realized two things: the circle had been broken, though I hadn't been conscious of releasing anyone's hand, and I was holding a pen so tightly my fingers cramped around it.

I looked down in confusion. Before me was a bottle of ink, an open notebook whose page was filled with a nearly indecipherable scrawl. My hand was smudged with ink; there were blots and stains everywhere, as if someone had been writing very fast, meaning to get thoughts down before they leapt away. With a sick dread, I realized that someone had been me.

Robert Dudley said, "Evelyn? Are you back with us?"

I dropped the pen so quickly it sent ink flying, and I backed away from the table. But when I tried to rise, my head spun and I crashed back down again, too dizzy to move.

"Is she all right?" Sarah's voice seemed to echo as if it came from a very far place.

"Evelyn?" Benjamin's voice was equally distant. "Evelyn, are you all right?"

"Anyone can see she's not." Dorothy now, brittle and loud. "Get her to a sofa."

Hands were on me, lifting me, and I tried to struggle away.

"I'm fine. I'm fine. If I could just—" But the truth was, I did not feel fine. I wanted nothing more than to lie down somewhere, and so I stopped fighting them. I let them carry me to the settee. When I tried to open my eyes, the dim light seared into my head. I closed them again in pain.

"We went too fast." Jacob's voice was a murmur.

"No one suspected she would do this," Grace Dudley protested.

Benjamin said from beside me, "Good God, can't you see she's done in? She should be in bed."

I tried to protest, but no one was listening, and I was so tired. It was easier just to let them do as they would. It was easier to fall into darkness.

PETER WAS WAITING for me in my dreams, his skin cold and clammy when he touched me. River water dripped upon my face as he leaned over me. *"You know he's lying, Evie."* He was so intent, almost vehement. *"He's trying to fool you. He's trying to fool everyone—"*

I lurched awake. It took me a moment to remember where I was, and what had happened. It came back to me slowly: I had done spirit writing, and I had swooned. I didn't understand. I'd had nothing to drink; I'd refused the liqueur. I'd eaten nothing. If Michel had somehow caused it, I didn't see how. But what else could explain it? It had felt so real, but it could not be, could it? If it had been a hallucination, then the delusion was so overwhelming I must indeed be mad—but I could not think that. I refused to think it.

It was simply that I was exhausted. Lack of sleep could do this to a person, couldn't it? I hadn't slept a full night through since before Peter had died, and that, along with the strain of the upcoming trial, and the effort of my pretense, left me exhausted. I felt myself slowly unraveling, and I was afraid, and all I could think was that I must try to understand what was happening to me before I ended up like my mother.

Perhaps there was something in the words I'd written, some clue, some way to divine the truth of how it had been accomplished. There must be a rational explanation. Michel had mesmerized me; the writing was not mine; something. Once I saw it, I would know. I was certain of it. It was *not* madness.

I climbed from bed and pulled on my dressing gown, driven by the compulsion to see the words, by my hope of an answer.

I went to the door and pressed against it, listening. I had no idea what time it was, or how long I'd slept, but the hallway was silent, and it felt late. I opened the door, stepping out, shutting it quietly behind me. It was very dark, and a bit cold—I had grown used to Dorothy's jungle temperatures, and the central heating had been banked for the night. I gathered my dressing gown more tightly about me and went as quickly and quietly as I could to the stairs. I meant to go to the second-floor parlor first, to see if the notebook had been left there. If it had not . . . if it had not I did not want to think about where it might be.

I grabbed the banister and tried to make out the stairs in the darkness. Cautiously I felt for the step.

The door to Dorothy's room opened.

I froze, holding my breath, cursing inwardly when I saw him come out. I had some notion that if I were still enough, quiet enough, he would not see me in the darkness, even though I was only a few feet away.

But, of course, he was canny, almost preternaturally so. I wasn't surprised when he stopped, when he turned toward me, when he said, "Looking for something, *chère?*"

Nervously, I said, "I—I was hungry. I thought I'd go to the kitchen—"

He took a few steps and put both hands on the railing opposite from the one I clutched. "A good idea. Perhaps I'll join you."

I noticed he wore a dressing gown, and that his feet were bare, his hair loose. It was only then that I registered where he had come from. Dorothy's room. In repulsed dismay, I said, "I wouldn't want to interrupt your assignation."

He glanced over his shoulder at the door. "She's asleep now."

"Won't she miss you when she wakes?"

"Jealous, *chère?*"

I ignored him and began going down the stairs.

He was beside me in a moment. "Having nightmares again? Spirits haunting you in your dreams?"

Steadfastly, I kept going.

"What do they say to you, these spirits? Do they tell you how to get an old woman to trust you? How to pretend to hear their voices so you can write their words?"

I stopped, turning on the stair to face him. "I leave such manipulations to you."

"How clever you are. I'm embarrassed to admit I didn't see it, though I should have after what you said at our lesson. Spirit writing . . . ah, very smart. To say what you want without taking the blame—how could a woman think such things, after all? It isn't you who plants doubts against me; it's the spirits who malign me—"

"It's not so very hard to do," I snapped. "Given that you deserve to be maligned."

"You would take from a dying woman her last comfort?"

"If that comfort were a lie, yes."

"And then what? What does it leave her?"

"Isn't it enough not to be thought a fool?"

He shrugged. "Not everyone cares what others think."

"Maybe not. But I must live within the world of those who do."

"Even if it blinds you?"

"Blinds me? To what?"

"To the lie of your own life."

"What can you possibly know of my life?"

He leaned close. We were in darkness, but his expression was plain to me: the sharp caginess, the small, mean smile. "Look at where you are, *chère,* the things that are left you. Do you think he didn't plan all this?"

It was not what I had expected. In bewilderment, I said, "Who? Plan what?"

"Your husband. He left you the house, knowing his family would oppose it. Do you really think he didn't plan on leaving you destitute?"

Ben had said much the same thing, but that Peter meant to disinherit his family, not to leave me with nothing. The idea was horrible. Its very meanness was so unsettling I couldn't fathom it. "Of course he didn't. The house is worth a great deal of money. He left me everything."

"What'd you do to him, Evie, hmmm? How did you disappoint him?"

"I never disappointed him. I was the wife he wanted—"

"But he resented you." Michel's voice was only a whisper. "In a way, he even hated you. You loved him and he didn't return your love. With your eyes you never let him forget it. Do you think that didn't fester?"

"That's not true." I pushed past him, and he stopped my flight with a hand on my arm. For a moment, we stood, staring at each other, and I thought he would kiss me, and I was stunned by a terrible longing—

But he only said, in a voice so low I could hear it only because of our proximity, "If you're really seeking the truth, you need to see him for who he was, Evie. Just as you need to see yourself. And me."

"I see you clearly enough."

"You think I murdered Peter."

"Didn't you?" I twisted away from him. "You have Dorothy wrapped around your finger. My God, you're even her . . . her—" I swallowed, unable to say the word. "Peter was going to spoil everything. It's a great deal of money to lose."

"I think you've been blind a long time, *chère*. I'm wondering, when will you open your eyes?"

"You speak in riddles, and I'm not some mad old woman to fall for them—"

A door opened. Both Michel and I went still on the stair. From above came the creak of a footstep, a quiet "Mr. Jourdain, sir? Is that you?"

Michel said, "I'm here—what is it?"

"It's Mrs. Bennett, sir. She's awake again, and calling for you. She's in a bad way."

"I'm coming." Michel glanced at me, and then he was moving quickly again up the stairs. I heard him murmur something to the nurse, and the two of them went into Dorothy's room. I heard the door click shut.

I stood there on the stair, shaken and angry, strangely disappointed that he was gone, and dismayed that I felt so. I was truly losing my mind to be so affected by him, to believe anything he said at all. I nearly raced down the remaining stairs to the closed doors of the second-floor parlor. I pushed them open and went inside, closing them again behind me.

The room was dark and full of shadows. The drapes were open, and though there was no moon, the streetlamps on Fifth Avenue lent a dim and unearthly glow. As I moved toward the table, I thought I saw a movement at the corner of my eye, and I stopped, gasping, until I realized it was the statuary looming like men in the pale darkness. I was alone except for the ghosts of the spirits who visited us here, the lingering echo of their visits. What seemed benign and amusing during the circle suddenly felt creepy and a bit threatening.

I hoped that during the confusion of my fainting spell, the notebook had been forgotten. I went to the table, and though I had doubted I'd find it, I saw its shadowed rectangle on the table-cloth, with the inkwell beside it, and an abandoned pen.

I stared at it incredulously—how easy this was. Too easy. I

could not believe that Michel had forgotten it if it truly maligned him as he'd said. But I grabbed it, and in my haste, I knocked over the inkwell and the pen fell to the floor. Quickly I righted the bottle, breathing a sigh of relief that it had been capped, and set the notebook down again so I could recover the pen, which had rolled beneath the table. I knelt, then went down on my hands and knees, feeling along the carpet, crawling beneath the table while the tassels fringing the tablecloth caught in my hair. My fingers brushed against crumbs, and then I felt the pen—

RAP.

I started, jerking up so I banged my head against the bottom of the table. I bit my lip to keep from crying out in pain, and froze, apprehensive, waiting.

It seemed I waited forever.

"Is someone there?" I whispered, but all I heard was my own breathing in answer. I grabbed the pen and began to crawl out—

RAP.

I sat up again, careful this time not to hit my head. "Is someone there?" I asked again. And then, in a quavering voice that did not sound like mine: "Is there a spirit come to speak with me?"

Nothing.

I gathered myself in tighter, turning so I could peer out into the room from beneath the fringe. I put my hand down and leaned to look beyond the chair leg.

RAP.

This time, I felt the give beneath my hand, as if there were a spring in the floorboard. I lifted my hand, frowning, and then, deliberately and hard, I pressed down again.

RAP.

And again.

RAP RAP.

And I knew: this was one of Michel's tricks, the lever he used to make the raps during the circle. I crawled from underneath the table. I wondered what else he had hidden in the walls and the floors. What other ways had he thought to delude decent people? To delude me?

I got to my feet, setting the pen back onto the table. Ben had been right—Michel was more than capable of creating some mechanism to shoot that gun during the first circle I'd attended. No doubt the "misfire" had happened exactly as Ben suspected. I glanced up into the corners of the ceiling, searching the shadows for some evidence of where such a mechanism might have been, though I guessed whatever trick he'd used had been removed long ago. It was too dark now to do much exploring, but it was clear this room should be the focus of my next search.

I grabbed up the notebook, unbuttoned the bodice of my dressing gown, and shoved the notebook beneath it, pressing it to my breasts as I left the parlor and started back to my room.

This time, I paused at the landing, listening for any steps, any movement at all on the third floor. When I knew it was quiet, I sped up the stairs on the balls of my feet, trying to make as little noise as possible. Then, once I made the hallway, I raced to my room, closing my eyes in relief as soon as I was inside.

I went to my bed and lit the candle on the bedside table. Then I pulled the notebook from my bodice and opened it.

The pages were blank except for the first few, and those held the writing I remembered, the hasty scrawl, words abbreviated, blotted out. In some places, the nib had torn through the paper.

You are running from what you know to be true. Liars lead you astray—do not be tempted. The truth is not alwys what you want to believe. Those who say they know the truth seek to blind you. There is nothing but darkness ahed of you & folly all around. Follow yer path heedlssly & death will be your guide & you will feel the hands about your throat, the knife in your side. Will you be a fool or wise?

You have forgotten yer skill & you will be lost without it. Close your eyes to our cries for vengeance & you will be swal-

lowed by them. The truth waits & you must tell it to all & beleve it. Trust those sent to guide you. Know the others or be condemned forever.

I stared at the pages for a long time. *Liars lead you astray. Do not be tempted.* These words were more pointed than before, and frankly threatening. Whoever had written this grew angry with my incompetence. That was hardly a surprise; I was frustrated with myself. Surely that was an argument for the writing being simply a product of my own mind, my own disappointments made manifest, as it were. There was no divine knowledge here, was there? I remembered Michel's words upon the stairs, his protest that the words had maligned him. They did seem to do so, and he had been truly angry with me tonight—I had not imagined that. If he'd engineered the spirit writing, surely he would not paint himself in such a compromising light? If he had caused it to be done, why not make himself the hero he had already convinced Dorothy he was?

But if he had not done it, then how had it been done?

18

A STRANGER TO MYSELF

FRIDAY, FEBRUARY 13, 1857

The next morning one of Dorothy's nurses came to tell me that Dorothy wished to see me.

My mind felt muddy and unsubtle after my sleepless night, but I followed Charley down the hall to Dorothy's room. When I went inside, it was to find her sitting up, though the curtains were drawn and the gaslight low. She looked as pale and haggard as I felt.

"Child," she said as I sat in the chair next to the bed. She reached limply across the coverlet, grabbing my fingers, squeezing feebly. "I'm afraid it's not one of my best mornings."

"I understand you passed a sleepless night."

"Sometimes the pain is worse than others," she said. "If not for Michel's hands . . ."

I resisted the urge to pull away. "His hands?"

"I told you, child, he has the hands of a healer. If he ever left me, I don't imagine I'd want to continue on."

"I doubt he'll leave. Not with the reward that's waiting for him."

She turned on the pillow, frowning at me. "Don't you lecture me, Evelyn. I told you, if that's what it takes to keep him, it's little enough."

"I wonder"—I took a deep breath— "I wonder if perhaps he's worse for you than you think."

"I don't want—"

"The schedule he keeps you on for your cordial, for example."

"Evelyn."

I ignored the warning in her voice. "And though I've no doubt he's very good with his 'hands,' as you say, I wonder if perhaps you don't need him as much as he tells you you do. They say such . . . physical . . . habits can weaken our moral resolve. It can even lead to madness—"

She tore her hand from mine. "This isn't why you're here. I wanted to talk to you about the spirit writing."

"It's the spirit writing that makes me speak to you this way. Last night, I found—"

"I don't care," she said.

I stared at her. "What?"

"If he's taking advantage of me, I say: go ahead. He makes me happy. I told you that already. I don't want to talk about it any-more. I wanted you and Michel to be friends." She leaned back heavily into the cushions, the thin gray braid of her hair trailing over her shoulder. "It disappoints me that you don't like him as much as he seems to like you."

I laughed. "I hardly think *like* is the proper word. I don't think he's interested in friendship so much as other things."

She turned to me with a frown. "What other things?"

Her rheumy eyes were suddenly sharply focused, uncomfort-ably so. I realized I'd misstepped. My life now depended on her generosity; I could not afford to give her cause for jealousy.

Quickly, I said, "It doesn't matter. It's as you say, there's no point in discussing him if we can't agree. And you said you wanted to talk with me about the spirit writing."

She relaxed somewhat, and then sighed, and I was relieved. "Yes. We read it last night, and we agreed: you could be a power-ful medium, Evelyn. The spirits want to communicate with you, but the writing is a poor vehicle. Such mystery! At the next circle, you should attempt to allow them to speak through you as Michel does. He's agreed to show you how it's done. But perhaps it would be best if he tutored you within the circle rather than outside it. Or here, with me."

The comment was lightly made, but I knew it was deliberately so. I had raised her suspicions. She preferred Michel and I not be alone together.

"The others believe Peter's spirit hasn't appeared to Michel because he's waiting for you to gain the skill. Time goes so fast. Benjamin reminded us that your trial's only five and a half weeks away. Best to speed things up, don't you agree? For your sake, of course."

Reluctantly I agreed. "I suppose it would be best."

"I know I can trust you, child."

I heard what she didn't say. "Of course you can."

I LEFT DOROTHY's room feeling the weight of her expectation. I was aware now of having to walk a fine line—she cared nothing for whether or not Michel was a mountebank, but the particulars of my relationship with him mattered greatly to her. I had raised an alarm—I prayed I'd not lost too much of her trust.

I had taken to locking my door and keeping the key with me, though I knew it was worthless—the door had been locked the night Michel stole the key as well, and he had managed it easily. But it made me feel safer, especially now that I had the two notebooks with the spirit writing in them. The one was my own secret, the other I preferred to keep in my possession. When I next saw him, I meant to tell Ben that I'd done the writing before, to show him the pages. There was a logical explanation for this. Ben and I could find it together. The hope was even more powerful than my wish to tell him of the lever I'd found beneath the table. I could hardly wait to see him.

I unlocked the door and stepped inside, closing it carefully behind me.

"There you are."

I jumped.

Michel lounged upon my bed, playing with the hairpins I'd piled on the table beside, a solitary game of pick-up-sticks. He sat up, leaning against my pillow. "Ah, did I frighten you? Forgive me."

"W-what are you doing here?"

"You searched my room. I'm only returning the favor."

I tried to conceal how badly he'd disconcerted me. "The difference is that I'm not hiding anything."

"*Non?*" He pulled from behind him the two journals—the one from last night, and the one I'd hidden beneath my bed. "Look at this—a treasure trove."

"You knew about that," I managed. "You saw me do the writing last night."

"*Oui,* the one. But the other . . ." He shook his finger at me, *tsking.* "You've been keeping secrets from me, *chère.* I thought last night was the first time, but you've done this before."

"Only once."

"'Only once,'" he mocked. "When was this? Before we decided to develop you?"

"Does it matter?"

He put his legs over the side of the bed, rising. "You see, I decided you were a bit of a charlatan yourself. You can see why I might've thought so, eh? You claim to have nightmares, we decide to develop you, and suddenly—*voilà!*—the spirits are writing through your hand. And not only that, they're telling you someone is lying, and you think that someone is me. Perhaps you even go to Dorothy and tell her that."

He stepped toward me. "And now I find that you've done this other writing on your own. You've told no one. You have it hidden away. Why is that? I ask myself. Could it be that she doesn't trust it? Or maybe she's afraid. But why would she be afraid? It falls into her plans to discredit me. Why not show it to everyone? Why not say: I know what this means; Michel is a liar. But she doesn't do that. Why not?" He stopped just before me. "Why not? Why, because she thinks it's real. That's why she's afraid. She thinks the spirits are really writing through her. Do I have it right, *chère?*"

I was stunned. "It wasn't you?"

Michel frowned. "Do I look like a spirit?"

"But I thought—"

"You may steal from me all you like, *chère,*" he said. "Just give me something in return."

Nervously, I said, "I have nothing. What could I possibly give you?"

"Work with me," he said.

"I thought you said we didn't need two mediums."

"That was before I realized your talent."

"My talent? But you can't—you think this writing is real?"

"Isn't it?"

Such simple words, but their implication was astonishing. I was dazed—both with an odd relief and a profound dismay. He thought it was real, which meant he'd had no hand in it, which meant one of two things: either I *was* going mad, or he was right, and it was real.

Or did it mean that? *Liars will lead you astray.* Wouldn't he tempt me to believe it was real? Wouldn't he try to either lead me into madness or try to win me to his side?

"Come, *chère,*" he whispered. "Think what we could do together, eh?"

I knew he had murdered my husband. I knew he was trying to use me. But I was afraid, and that fear made me vulnerable, and I knew he understood that too, and knew just how to turn it to his purpose. *Liars will lead you astray.*

"No," I said faintly. I half turned to take the doorknob. "If you would please leave me—"

He reached around me, wrapping his hand about my own, holding both the knob and me fast. "Evie, use your sense. Look at

Dorothy—don't you see how much better she is with me? She wanted to die, her life was a misery. Isn't she happier now?"

"She's in thrall to you," I snapped. "That's not happiness. It's enslavement."

"Who're you to say? We each choose how we want to live. Look at yourself: were you happy with Peter? You had everything you could've wanted."

"Not everything," I protested.

"*Non.* Not love. Some would say love is enslavement, yet you—"

"Love is not unkindness, or . . . or selfishness."

He laughed. "You can't be so naive."

"The love Dorothy feels for you is based on lies. She doesn't know you."

His gaze seemed to go right through me. "And you do."

"Yes. Yes, I do."

His one hand was still on mine, still clasped to the doorknob, but he raised his other. He touched my lips with his finger, and then he touched his own, and it made me shiver; it was like a kiss, like a promise, and he said, "We're the same. I'm right, eh? You feel it too. We could conquer the world, Evie."

"I don't want to conquer the world," I said desperately. "I only want my old life back. I want my house. I want a good husband. I don't care about money or anything else, as long as we're happy."

"You sound as if you've someone in mind."

"Don't be absurd—"

"It isn't me, it seems, so perhaps . . . Dudley's got Grace. Maull's a Free Lover, and that doesn't seem your style. Colville's still mourning his wife, so that leaves . . . Rampling. Ah, is that who you've set your sights on, *chère*? Rampling? Or am I wrong?"

"It's none of your business," I said tightly.

He smiled, and it was mean and knowing at the same time. "Such a common choice. I'd thought you'd more ambition than that. But I guess better the devil you know."

"I don't take your meaning."

"*Non*. More's the pity." He released the doorknob and my hand and stepped back. "My offer's still open. 'Come live with me, and be my love, and we will all the pleasures prove. . . .' Ah, but you want less than that."

"I want honesty."

"Is that so? I'd never have thought it, given your past. But people change, eh?" He gestured to the doorknob. "Now, if you don't mind, Dorothy's waiting for me."

And then he was gone, slipping out, sauntering down the hallway toward Dorothy's room. Almost as if by magic, the door opened; Charley came anxiously into the hall. The moment he saw Michel, his expression sagged into relief. The two of them disappeared into the room. The door closed.

I was left standing alone, feeling oddly battered and undone, as if I'd been caught in an inexorable tide, swept onto the shore of my own life, which was suddenly a foreign land where I didn't speak the language. How did Michel do that? How did he so effortlessly make me feel a stranger to myself?

I stepped inside and saw the notebooks where he'd left them, on the bed. Michel Jourdain was a master of illusion, a man who knew how to bend words, who had lived his life manipulating others. I should not be surprised that he understood how to manipulate me.

He was a liar. That was all I had to remember.

19

AMBITION AND FACULTY

Dorothy's jealousy and Michel's denial that he had anything to do with the spirit writing only unnerved me more. It was time to speak with Ben about it, I knew, and so I had penned a note to him and given it to Kitty to deliver. The next day I waited in the library for him to arrive. Michel had gone to Dorothy, and I had no fear I would encounter him in the next hour or so. I chose a book at random from the shelves—I could hardly have said what it was—and then I found myself drawn to the huge window.

It was Valentine's Day, but there would be no heavily embossed card from Peter this year, nothing to raise the false hopes that every other February had brought. I felt a sad relief over that now as I stared out at the backyard. Statuary and urns and stone benches dotted the narrow expanse, overlooking flower beds made invisible by the snow. A cast-iron gate marked the boundary and kept out whatever riffraff traveled the alley behind, and beyond that were the brownstone and brick walls of other houses, their windows glinting dim and empty in the overcast light, their chimneys belching smoke that grayed the snow crusting their windowsills.

My own yard on Irving Street—the Atherton yard, I should have said—was smaller than this. Elizabeth Atherton had cared little for gardens and had preferred to take her children to Union Square Park to play, though by the time they'd built the house, her youngest son had already been moving quickly into adulthood. I couldn't imagine what it would be like to have such a luxury as a yard to play in as a child. My yard had been the busy streets, my games dodging traffic, tripping through the mounds of garbage and splashing through sewage, chasing the pigs and cows on their way to the slaughterhouse while their drovers hollered curses. But this—to climb the benches and race through the grass, to play hide-and-seek among the statuary, darting from Apollo and Mercury, to build snowmen to match Michelangelo's *David*—here clad discreetly in a fig leaf so as not to offend decency. Or had he a fig leaf in Italy too? I tried to remember the drawings I'd seen, because I'd never seen it for myself, as much as I'd wanted to. . . .

"You mean to tell me you haven't been there? Dear God, Peter, never tell me you didn't take a wedding tour?"

The words came from a not-so-distant memory, and I was flung back in time, remembering how Duncan Granger had looked up from his nesselrode pudding with an expression of exaggerated shock, and how I tried not to show the disappointment that still felt too sharp.

Peter had paused, his own spoon poised halfway to his mouth. "I couldn't take the time."

Duncan laughed. He'd been one of Peter's latest fast friends, a young man with dark hair and hazel eyes that were so heavily lashed they should have been a woman's, though his laugh was at odds with all that—it was blustery and deep. "You couldn't take the time? For a *wedding* tour?"

Across the table, Peter's mother dabbed a napkin to her mouth. "It truly would have been a waste, I'm afraid. Evelyn hasn't the eye to appreciate such things. Not to offend you, dear—you know

I think only the best of you, but it's the rare person indeed who can rise above one's upbringing."

Though Elizabeth Atherton smiled—a habit of hers, to cloak a cutting remark with what seemed to be sympathy—the remark still burned. I could not keep myself from responding in kind. "Oh yes, indeed. I see it myself every day."

Peter's mother frowned.

Peter explained to Duncan, "Evelyn received an uncommon education."

"Her father tutored her in philosophy and science, among other things." Elizabeth Atherton shuddered. "Why, I continue to be appalled at what he exposed her to! I know he meant well, Evelyn, and I suppose I'm old-fashioned, but I do think girls should be brought up learning French and the finer arts. What use has a woman for Latin, after all?"

"None at all," I agreed. "If one doesn't read."

"Well, I believe everyone can benefit from experiencing beauty," Duncan said. "To not take the opportunity to see it first-hand—why, I should say it was criminal!"

His enthusiasm was contagious, and I opened my mouth to agree when I saw he wasn't looking at me. He was smiling at my husband, who met his gaze and said almost wistfully, "What use have I for European beauty, when there's so much to be had here?" Peter hesitated only a moment before he turned to me and raised his glass, but I felt the perfunctoriness of his flattery. One complimented one's wife; it meant nothing more than that.

Peter's mother cleared her throat. "Have you a wife yourself, Mr. Granger?"

"Oh no, I'm afraid not," Duncan said, turning to her. "Though I expect it's my duty to find one someday."

Elizabeth Atherton frowned. "I see."

Peter set aside his spoon with a declarative clank. "Well, Duncan and I must be off."

"Oh, not so soon," I protested.

"Unfortunately so."

"You've been out every night this week," his mother said pointedly. "I'm certain Mr. Granger would excuse you to spend a quiet evening with your wife."

"Of course, I would hate to take you from such a pleasant diversion," Duncan said quickly and too politely. "If you'd rather—"

"Not tonight," Peter said firmly, though he, like his mother, softened his words with a smile.

Elizabeth wasn't cowed. To Duncan, she said, "Forgive my plain speaking, Mr. Granger, but my son has obligations to his family."

"Of course I understand," Duncan said gamely.

She turned back to Peter. "How you expect to get a child on your wife when you're never home is beyond me—"

"Mother Atherton, please," I said quickly. My face was burning.

"I'm only stating the obvious." Elizabeth's blue eyes were guileless as she looked at her son. I saw Duncan's pale skin turning ruddier by the moment, and I was embarrassed both for myself and for him, though I should have been used to such comments. God knew I heard them often enough. "You can't blame me for wanting to see the Atherton name passed on."

"We'll talk of this later." Peter sounded strangled.

"I hope so," she said. "I'm not getting younger, you know. I doubt I'll survive another winter—"

"Shall we go, Duncan?" Peter buttoned his frock coat. He bent to kiss his mother, then stepped over to me, brushing his lips hastily over my cheek. "I'll see you in the morning. Duncan may be here for breakfast."

"Has Mr. Granger no home of his own to tend to?"

"He's serving as my assistant, Mama. Until I find a law partner, I've need of him." Peter waved his hand at Duncan, and the two of them nearly ran from the dining room, leaving me alone at the table with Peter's mother.

"Would you care to retire to your room, Mother Atherton?" I

asked, rising to help her to her feet, but she only gave me a look so full of bitterness and scorn that I stopped cold.

"Don't you care that your husband keeps no hours at his own home?" she asked sharply. "What happened to your voice, girl?"

"Apparently I've no need of it," I said. "You say quite enough for the both of us."

She turned away abruptly, as if she could not bear to look at me, and her voice was low and sorrowful as she said, "I had hoped for more from you, Evelyn. I had hoped . . . well, what can one expect from such an uneven match, I suppose?"

Her question had stung then, and the memory of it did still. Elizabeth Atherton was dead, but the words she'd spoken haunted me, and with them returned the things Michel had said to me upon the stair, about Peter's resentment of me.

Perhaps it was true what Michel had said, that Peter meant to punish me from beyond the grave, but I hoped not. It seemed impossible that he had hated me that much.

But I'd been wrong about other things. I'd been wrong about the Athertons. I supposed I could be wrong about Peter too—but that would mean everything in my life had been a lie. Could I have been that blind?

"I'm wondering . . . when will you open your eyes?"

"Mrs. Atherton?"

The voice intruded into my thoughts so completely that I was confused—was I hearing things now too? Then I realized it was Kitty, hovering in the doorway.

"Mr. Rampling is here to see you, ma'am."

Benjamin. My troubled thoughts eased, and I said, "Tell him I'll be right down."

When Kitty left, I hurried to my bedroom, grabbing the two notebooks to show him, and then I went downstairs to the parlor, where Ben waited, still wearing his fur-trimmed coat and his top hat.

"I've only a little more than an hour," he said apologetically as

I came into the room. "I'm afraid I have appointments this afternoon that couldn't be changed."

I clutched the notebooks tightly. "I only need a few minutes of your time."

He glanced beyond me to the doorway. "Perhaps another walk, then?"

I nodded. "I'll get my cloak."

Lambert retrieved it quickly, along with my gloves and my hat, and I fetched a bag and slid the notebooks inside to carry with me. Ben and I had just gone to the door when Michel came down the stairs.

"What a fine couple you make," he said, though I caught the glint of mockery in his eyes. "A bit cold for a promenade, isn't it?"

Benjamin said, "I've things to discuss with Evelyn, and I'm afraid she's feeling a bit cooped up."

"No doubt, without her soirees and her opera to distract her." Michel leaned against the railing. "*Madame* Atherton, I find myself unexpectedly free this afternoon. Shall we plan another lesson when you return?"

I was in a hurry to leave, and I didn't like the way he watched me, how predatory his gaze was, and so I said quickly, "I don't know how long I'll be gone."

"I'll wait," he said with a smile.

"Come along, Evelyn." Benjamin took my arm, and Lambert opened the door to see us out. The moment the door was closed behind us, I could breathe again. I shivered in relief.

Benjamin looked at me curiously. "Cold, my dear?"

"Just glad to be away," I said.

He glanced across the street to the police watchman, who'd gone suddenly attentive at our presence. He patted my hand where it lay upon his arm. "This will soon be over, and you can go back to your old life."

"Can I? I wonder."

"We've reason to be more hopeful now, I think. With the discoveries you've made—well, it's just a matter of time until we have what we need, isn't it? Though I wouldn't expect to jump back into society quickly. A slow and circumspect return would be best; perhaps a short tour of the Continent would be in order first."

It was an uncomfortable reminder of my earlier thoughts. "I had always hoped to see it with Peter. He couldn't take the time away for a wedding tour. I think I'll always regret that I didn't insist upon it, though I wonder now if he would have taken me even if I had." Across the street, the watchman fell into step with us, not bothering to hide that he followed.

Ben gave me a curious look. "Why do you say that?"

"He can't have wanted to show me off," I said, looking down at my gloved hands. "And I'm certain his mother didn't wish him to take me. She was so disappointed in his choice—the thought of parading me through their friends' homes must have rankled her."

"You only know one side of things, Evie, you must remember that."

I was reminded uncomfortably of Michel's brown and white house, of my own assertion that it was best to accept partial truths. I could not obey my own words, it seemed.

The wind had come up, and it rippled the dark, thick fur at the collar of Ben's coat—a bit of an ostentatious touch, and one I liked, though when I'd first seen the coat I'd been surprised. Ben was normally so stolid and respectable. No doubt it was Peter's influence. My husband had liked those little, unusual touches.

Ben sighed. "I think there was a part of Peter that resented his mother greatly. Perhaps he even chose you to spite her."

"A good reason for a marriage," I said sarcastically.

Ben's glance was quick. "You made him happy, Evie."

"Did I? He didn't seem happy to me."

"You couldn't have affected that," he said, and there was something wistful in the tone of his voice, in the way he looked away from me, out toward the street, with its passing carriages. "Peter was melancholy. He had to make peace with who he was."

"I didn't realize being an Atherton was so difficult for him."

Ben smiled. "To step to the Atherton drums was not his way."

There was a man hurrying toward us, and I pressed closer to Ben to let him pass.

"I think Peter did you a great disservice," Ben said quietly. "Had you been my wife, well . . . ah, never mind. It's easy enough to say in retrospect. You've a good heart, Evie. Having had some dealings with those who don't, I would've said Peter was very lucky to have you."

I blinked away sudden tears. "That was a generous thing to say."

"But I believe it—don't you know that?"

"Yes, I—" I wiped at my eyes, laughing a little in embarrassment. "Of course I know it. I can't tell you how much I value our friendship. It's been an anchor for me. Almost since we first met. Do you remember?"

"How could I not? It isn't every society wife who greets guests wearing an apron and carrying a dust bucket."

I grimaced. "Peter didn't warn me. It was cleaning day."

"You were very gracious," Ben teased. "And when I thought to ease your embarrassment by letting you win at chess, you beat me soundly."

"I can't abide being patronized."

"You think I don't know it?"

We laughed together, and the sound was warm enough that I no longer felt cold, though the wind still stung my cheeks.

"Someday, we'll play again," I promised him. "When I'm back in my own home." Or, I thought—though I didn't say it—*the one we might one day share.*

Ben turned to me. Our eyes met. I saw something flash through his; was it sorrow? He turned away and sighed, and my good mood slipped away as quickly as it had come. He looked so sad that I had to curb the urge to take him in my arms to comfort him.

"Ben, what is it? What makes you look that way?" I asked.

"Nothing," he said, shaking his head and giving me a weak

smile. "Regrets of my own, I suppose. They tend to creep up on one at the oddest moments."

"I know what you mean," I said. "There are so many things I should have said to Peter, but I thought we had time. Now I suppose I'm left only with dreams of him."

"Dreams. Yes, I suppose we all have those."

"What do you regret?" I asked gently.

"I'm afraid there are too many to list."

"Tell me one. Come, I've told you."

"Ah, only one?" He stared up at the overcast sky as if he were too shy to look at me. "I suppose I'm sorry it took me so long to find my heart's desire. I wasted so many years. . . . Well, I suppose we all do."

I felt a funny little lurch, a pleasing heat, and I prompted, "Your heart's desire?"

His face reddened with the cold. "What I have. Or rather, what I *had* before Peter died. A good law practice. A good friend. I regret that we fought before. . . ." He took a deep breath and turned to me. "He was a good man, Evelyn, and I doubt we'll find his like again."

My disappointment—and humiliation that I'd mistaken his meaning—made me look away. "Yes, I know."

He said, "I can't help thinking, had it not been for—" He bit off abruptly. I saw the clenching of his gloved fist, and for a moment I sensed something a little desperate in him, but it was gone so quickly I was uncertain, and his voice was tightly controlled when he continued. "Had it not been for Jourdain, Peter would still be alive today."

My fingers curved around the hard edges of the notebooks in my bag. "Ben, I—"

"Which reminds me: I wanted to congratulate you for the other night. I must admit, you surprised even me. You've the makings of an actress about you, my dear. Your trance looked so very real."

"Yes. I wished to speak with you about that."

"Dorothy was enthralled. You were right to pursue this mediumship. A few more performances like that, and I doubt even Jourdain's silver tongue could convince Dorothy to release you."

"But the spirit writing—"

"Absolutely riveting." His eyes brightened with praise. "A brilliant touch, Evie, to cast doubt upon Jourdain. But you must be careful. Perhaps you should be less overt the next time. More vague. A few words about how the spirits would prefer to speak through you, things like that."

Carefully, I said, "The truth is, I'm not certain how much control I have over it. The trance itself—"

"It's very convincing. You looked quite done in. In fact, I would say you've seemed pale lately. Are you sleeping?"

"Not well," I admitted. "My nightmares keep me awake every night now." The notebooks seemed to burn into my hand. "Do you suppose there could be anything real in it? Anything at all?"

Ben frowned. "You aren't being swayed by his nonsense, are you?"

I licked my lips, feeling foolish.

"I wish I could be there with you all the time," Ben said. "I wish I could protect you better."

The wind was cold again now. I shivered and huddled into myself.

"Benjamin, the way he thinks . . . in some ways he reminds me of my father. He can be very interesting."

"Interesting?" Ben's frown broadened. "Be careful, Evelyn."

"I am careful," I said rather edgily. "I found something else. I found the lever."

"The lever?"

"The one Michel uses to make the raps. He's built it into the floor beneath the table, under the carpet. All he needs do is press on it with his foot. I suppose I could use it myself easily enough."

His laugh was delighted. "To use his own tricks against him— yes, yes, we must! Tuesday night, let him call the spirits, as he does, but then you must take over. When Dorothy realizes you can do the same things he can I shan't worry any longer about Jourdain convincing her to set you out. The only question is what he'll do once he realizes how much power he's lost." Ben took my hand into his own and squeezed it, and the worry I saw come into his eyes was so potent the thought of a future with him gained a dizzying hold. "You must be wary, Evie. I cannot warn you enough. Please. I don't want you to be one of my regrets."

"I won't be," I said, smiling at him, squeezing his hand back. "I promise."

BENJAMIN LEFT ME at the Bennett door, and I stood there, watching until he boarded his carriage and rode away. I felt bereft and alone, the notebooks a heavy weight beneath my cloak. I pressed them close, reproaching myself for not sharing the writing of the first one as I'd intended. I wanted to believe Michel had engineered it all . . . but I could not lose my niggling sense that he hadn't, and my fear that Ben would think me mad had kept me silent. I could not bear to face the dismay and disappointment I knew I would see in his eyes.

The wind brought an icy dusting of snow that brushed my face and brought me back to myself, and I shivered and opened the door.

It had no sooner swung open than Michel stood before me. At the unexpected sight of him, a strange heat flooded me, and with it came a sharp stab of guilt. The feeling so confused me that I stood dumbfounded.

He said, "Ah, there you are. Did you have a pleasant walk?"

"Quite pleasant," I said, recovering myself, pushing by him into the foyer.

He glanced outside. "Where's your erstwhile suitor?"

"If you mean Benjamin, he had to return."

"Ah, a pity," he said, though it was clear he thought it anything but. He closed the door. When I unclasped my cloak, he was there, lifting it from my shoulders. He laid it over the stair railing while I fumbled with the bag.

"What's that?" he asked as I put it on the hall table.

"Nothing." I reached for it again, but he was too fast, leaning past me, pulling the bag so that it fell against his thigh before he had the strap hard within his hand.

He opened it and glanced inside. "The notebooks? You showed them to Rampling?"

"As it happens, no," I said.

"He wouldn't believe you, you know," he said, handing the bag back to me. "He'd think you asylum bound if you told him the truth."

"I don't know what the truth is," I said, turning away from him. I was surprised to find my hands were trembling as I pulled out my hatpin, and I closed my eyes for a moment, trying to steady them. My fingers would not obey me. The pin tangled in my hair, and in frustration I cursed beneath my breath.

"Wait," Michel said quietly, and then he was beside me. His fingers brushed my cheek, and then, quickly, he loosed the pin and lifted my hat from my hair, setting it carefully on the side table, laying the hatpin beside it.

"Thank you," I said nervously.

"Come to the parlor with me," he said. "It's time for a lesson."

"Dorothy didn't want us to do that."

"Do what?" His brow lifted, there was an undeniable suggestion in his tone. I felt my face go hot again.

"Take lessons without her there. Or without the circle."

"Dorothy's sleeping. She'll never know."

I met his gaze directly. "I think it's better to follow her wishes in this, don't you?"

"Ah. Perhaps. But then we'll never discover what your *maman* might think of all this, would we?"

I was too startled to speak. I forgot Dorothy's jealousy; when he began to walk toward the parlor, I followed, and once we were inside, and he shut the door behind us, I demanded, "What did you mean by that? What do you know of my mother?"

He made his way to the settee and sat down, and without thinking, I sat beside him.

He said, "Tell me about your dreams."

"I want to know—"

"We'll get to your *maman*. Tell me first about your dreams."

I sighed. "They became worse after my father died. I caught the cholera, and I was . . . I was very sick. They told me I was delirious. The dreams were . . . I remember the dreams."

"What happened in them?"

"I was walking in a wood that grew deeper with every step. Papa kept appearing behind trees, farther and farther away, and I was . . . I was chasing him. Then I caught him. I ran into his arms, and he told me to go home. Just to . . . go home." The unbearable sadness I'd felt in the dream was a memory that never left me.

"Is it the same dream you have now?" Michel asked.

I looked down at the sheen of light upon the black bombazine of my gown. "No. Now they change all the time. I never know who I'll see. Lately, there's been Peter and—"

I stopped myself just before I confessed that Michel had been in them too.

"Does Peter speak to you?"

I nodded and looked up. I forced myself to meet his gaze boldly. "He tells me that someone is lying to me, and not to believe him. He says that I can find the truth."

Michel's expression was impassive. "Like your *maman,* you've the gift for talking to spirits, *chère*."

I disagreed. "I'm not talking to them. They're only nightmares."

"If you don't let them in other ways, they visit how they can."

"I would have thought you could come up with something better than that."

"The answers are what they are. Just because you don't like them doesn't mean they aren't true."

"I suppose now you'll say my mother was a medium too."

"Wasn't she?"

"She was mad," I said firmly. "In her last days she took lau-danum, but she never stopped hearing voices—spirit voices, she called them."

"But you didn't believe it?"

"How could I?"

Michel made a clucking sound. "Calling it lunacy makes it easier to explain away the things we don't understand."

"A pretty answer," I said coldly.

He shrugged. "Science discovers something new every day. Twenty years ago, what would you have said to someone who told you we'd be sending messages to each other over a piece of wire?"

"An invention is not the same as hearing voices no one else can hear," I protested.

"Doesn't electricity seem like magic? You can't see it, how can it be real? How do you know spiritualism isn't science too—per-haps it's a fact of nature not yet discovered."

"I know it's not."

"How?" The word was fast and blunt. He leaned forward. "You've a rational soul, Evie, but you can't continue to ignore the nonmaterial world. You said before that if you couldn't see some-thing, you didn't believe it. You can't see intuition, or feeling. Does that make them imaginary? What about instinct? What does yours say?"

"To stay away from you," I said.

"Does it? Or does it tell you to let me come closer?"

"I—"

"Admit what you are. You're an intuitive creature, you always have been, eh?"

I shook my head fiercely. "Not me."

"*Non?* You didn't daydream? You didn't tell yourself stories or play with imaginary friends? Your papa never told you your head was in the clouds?"

How did he know these things? "I was a child then."

"You learned to run from what you feel, and that's why you have nightmares. To deny is to invite madness. To accept is to control. The spirits work through the intuitive world, whether you will or no. You can invite them in and share their knowledge, or deny them and live in fear of madness."

He paused, but his eyes never left mine. Just as I began to feel uncomfortable beneath his gaze, he said, "I'd feel sorry for you, *chère,* if your situation weren't so much your own doing. All that ambition and faculty, and no idea what to do."

I was taken aback and unsettled at the truth he saw. "Don't you see what you could be, Evie? Are you the rabbit after all? And all this time I thought there was a wolf within you."

"I don't want to be your kind of wolf," I said.

He laughed. His hand, so near my shoulder, moved to my collarbone. I was safe beneath the heavy ruching of bombazine. I should not have felt his warmth, though I did. His voice was slow and urgent as he said, "But you already are my kind of wolf. Ah, we could be something together, *chère.* Why not try?"

He was looking at me as if he knew me, and I knew too what an illusion that was. I was not what he thought I was. I did not want what he offered.

I pulled away, rising abruptly. "That's not who I am," I said, and my voice was breathless enough that it seemed to give the lie to my words.

He only smiled, but it was cold and mocking.

"Go and hide, then, little rabbit," he said.

20

A MASTER STROKE

We were in the second-floor parlor, and Benjamin had drawn me away from the others on the pretext of needing a drink. We stood by the sideboard while the others talked among themselves, waiting for the circle to begin.

I hesitated, my hand upon the crystal stopper of the decanter. My anxiety over tonight's circle had grown as the hour for it approached. I was afraid. I had no idea what would happen. "I can't do the voices."

"Then do the writing again," he said. "But remember your task; Dorothy's what's important now. The more support she shows you, the more freedom you have to search. Those adoption papers must be found."

I twisted out the stopper. It was the green liqueur, and I restoppered it quickly, still uncertain, and reached for the brandy instead, pouring it into a glass, handing it to him. The tips of our fingers touched. I thought he lingered for a moment before he pulled away. The wavering gaslight shimmered on the fine fabric of his brown frock coat and shone in his eyes.

The urge to tell him the truth about the spirit words and my fears was nearly overwhelming. "Ben—"

"Perhaps you could do something with the writing that might

lead Dorothy to say where the papers are kept." Ben sipped his brandy thoughtfully. "Yes, that might be the best idea."

The moment was gone already. "I don't know. I could try."

"Well, see what feels best to you. Will you use the lever?"

I glanced past him, to where Michel sat near Dorothy on the sofa. He was watching us. Softly, I said, "I think so."

Ben took another sip of his brandy and set it on the sideboard. "I'll follow your lead then. Together, we can make this work."

Michel rose. He clapped his hands together, calling us all to attention. Benjamin glanced over his shoulder and then said to me, "I'm certain you can make this seem real enough." He took my arm, pulling me for a moment close into his side. His lips brushed my hair as he whispered, "You aren't alone, Evie."

He led me to the table as the others were taking their seats. Michel was at his place; Benjamin surrendered me with a smile. "I trust you to take care of her, Jourdain."

Michel's answering smile was thin. "She seems to do well enough on her own."

As I sat, Michel leaned close. "You can do so much better, *chère*."

When I turned to glare at him, he was leaning back in his chair, his expression bland.

Dudley said, "You're our leader, Jourdain. How do we ask the spirits to come to Evelyn?"

They all turned to him, rapt as subjects before a beloved king. I noted Dorothy's expression especially—it was alert and expectant, as if she had no doubt that Michel would do as she'd asked and lead me seamlessly into mediumship.

Michel steepled his fingers. "Women's muscles are weak, but their nerves are very sensitive. It's what makes them prone to illness and madness, eh?—but it also makes them good mediums. Passivity. Susceptibility. Impressionability. To call the spirits means you must empty your mind to them. *Madame* Atherton must find the thing that calms her enough to allow her to do that."

"How is she to know what that is?" Wilson Maull complained.

"For me, it's the songs. For others"—Michel shrugged—"some

close their eyes and pray, some merely ask the spirits to come, others think of peaceful scenes, like a forest in springtime. *Madame* will find her own way, I'm certain, as she did the other night."

The lights were lowered. We took hands. Jacob Colville began a prayer. His voice was loud and forceful. Michel bent his head to mine. Beneath the prayer, he murmured, "Shall we see what you can truly do, *chère*? Listen to me, eh? Don't think. You're nothing, no one. Only a vessel." His words were a chant; his thumb began a slow, relentless stroking upon my hand. I wanted him to stop, but the touch was like an opiate; I felt myself falling into it.

He whispered, "Close your eyes."

I obeyed him. This was the act Benjamin expected from me. The spirits were supposed to possess me. I must make it look real. The others began to sing.

Michel continued. "You want filling as a glass needs water. Your mind is empty. Your thoughts are not your own."

As he spoke, it was as if a fog filled me, an inexorable, seeking mist that obscured my own thoughts, making my skin sensitive to every movement in the air. I felt as if I would soon fall deeply asleep, and I told myself to stretch out my foot, to find the lever. It was time for the rapping to start. I needed to make the sound.

But I couldn't move. I felt electrified, strangely glowing, receptive. I heard my pulse, and then that pulse began to change—no longer a constant, steady beat, but that buzzing I'd known before, that sound that grew until I nearly screamed at it to stop, and then, suddenly, it bent and changed again, no longer a buzz but a voice that whispered in my ear—no, not in my ear, in my head. A voice inside my head. A voice disembodied and strange that said, *Are you listening?*

I heard myself say, "Yes," but my own voice was far away too; it came to me as a wind through a narrow street—everywhere and yet concentrated. The other voice answered, *Surrender to me,* and I felt myself open up, and the voice seemed to grow inside me, to beat in my own heart and fill my lungs, and I felt myself arch to meet it.

It flowed through me, and the things it said were not words, but some knowing that seemed to seep into my muscles and bones. I saw images in my head: a woman, with brown hair and vibrantly dark eyes. She told me to watch, though she didn't speak the words, I simply knew them, and then she stepped aside, and I saw two boys, both in short pants, scampering down a riverbank, racing each other, one screaming: "You said you'd wait for me!" while the other yelled back, "I did not! You're too slow!"

They dashed down the bank, raising the brown mulch of fallen leaves rotting into dirt, stumbling over bushes, and then they were jumping from the bank into the river, an eddied pool close to the shore and deep, with fishes watching from the bottom, and flies hovering lazily overhead, and they broke the silence and the laziness, and the fish shimmied away, and the flies. Two dark heads went under, and then emerged, one at a time, both laughing, splashing, and then there was a voice from the bank, calling, "You boys! Your papa's going to have your heads—and mine too!—for getting your clothes all muddy." But she was laughing as she came, and she wore a big straw hat with poppies on it, and carried a basket, which she set down on the edge of the river. "Don't tell him, but I brought cherry tarts." She sat down beside the basket, and leaned forward, watching them play, and the summer was peaceful and contented, the threat of punishment very far away. . . .

Then suddenly, the image was gone, and the haze dissipated, and I felt myself move again into my body. I felt my lungs fill, and they were mine again. I opened my eyes, blinking, and the room spun, whirling about me like a carousel, and my head felt so heavy I could not keep it upright.

And then there was nothing at all.

I JERKED AWAKE at a noxious, acrid smell to find myself lying on the chaise against the wall. My head was pounding, and my mouth was dry. The others were crowded around me. Sarah held a bottle of smelling salts in her hand. "There she is," she said with satisfaction.

"Don't crowd her." Jacob motioned for the others to step back. "Give her some air. What she's been through is taxing."

"Yes, of course," Grace said. She leaned down, touching my arm before she backed away. "How exhausted you must be, Evelyn. But so very, very blessed."

"She has such a rare gift," Wilson Maull said reverently. His expression was uncomfortably worshipful.

Benjamin sat beside me. His expression was a study in concern, though I thought his eyes were gleaming oddly. "Evie, my dear—"

"I'm fine," I said. I tried to sit up, and then lay back again when my temples throbbed.

Benjamin said, "You're better than fine. You are simply the most brilliant woman alive."

"I was successful then? Where's the spirit writing?"

There was silence. I saw Robert Dudley glance at his wife, and in confusion I looked at Benjamin. "What did I write?"

"Don't you remember, Evie?" he said quickly. "You called the spirits of Dorothy's sons."

I frowned and tried again to sit up, searching the room for Dorothy, for Michel. They were nowhere to be seen. "Dorothy's sons?"

"Let me speak with her a moment," Benjamin said to the others.

"Of course," said Jacob, and they drew respectfully away.

"Where's Dorothy?" I asked. "Where's Michel?"

Benjamin glanced at the rest, waiting until they were talking among themselves before he said quietly, "As you can imagine, Dorothy was very moved. Jourdain's taken her to bed."

"I don't wonder," I said acidly.

He gave me a warning glance.

I heard snippets of conversation from the others.

"Did you ever see such thing . . ."

"Michel never . . ."

". . . a miracle."

"You should have seen Jourdain's face. He went white as Dorothy when you began to speak in Johnny's voice. How *did* you do it? You sounded just like a little boy."

I stared at him in stunned surprise. "I did?"

"How did you know about that day? Did Dorothy tell you of it? Then again, I suppose every child has a summer memory of swimming in the river. It was a masterstroke, Evie."

I closed my eyes, suddenly too tired to try to explain, either to myself or to him. How could I? What could I say to this man who believed I was in control of this? That I'd heard a voice in my head I didn't recognize? I'd seen a woman who brought me the memory? That I didn't remember speaking? My head was pounding.

"I'm so tired," I said.

"Of course." He kissed me gently on the forehead. I felt him back away and rise from the chaise. I heard him say to the others, "She's quite done in. But what a find she is! She may be one of the most talented mediums of her time!"

"We should present her to Mrs. Hardinge," said someone else—Jacob, I thought.

"Perhaps we should wait before we do that," Grace counseled. "Until we've held another circle or two. Just to be certain."

Benjamin said, "I agree. Another attempt is what we need."

"Will this help, do you think, with her trial?" Sarah's voice was full of concern.

"Will it help?" Benjamin was vibrant; I heard his smile. "Oh, my dear Miss Grimm, I don't see how it can't. If she can contact the spirits of Dorothy's sons—"

"They were so elusive until Michel found them!"

"Yes indeed, but Evelyn brought them so easily! How long can it be before Peter's spirit decides to make an appearance?"

The others laughed, congratulating themselves, and I grew tight with anxiety and turned my head away, saying weakly, "Leave me be. Please leave me," throwing my hand over my eyes to keep the gaslight from pulsing against my eyelids. Soon, their talk turned faint, like music playing at a ball when the conversation was too scintillating to dance.

I woke to a noise. It took me a moment to realize that I'd fallen asleep on the chaise, and that I was still in the parlor. The lights had been turned low, and I lay in shadow, though I heard footsteps, a *swooshing* sound that had me turning my head. My companions had obeyed me better than I'd intended and gone. The sound I heard was that of Agnes, the maid, cleaning the room. I had no idea what time it was, only that it was late.

I lifted my head, and then, when it didn't spin or ache, I raised myself up. The maid started, whirling around, her hand to her chest. "Oh, Mrs. Atherton, I'm sorry. I didn't realize anyone was here."

"Don't fret, please," I said. "There's no harm done."

The boning of my corset cut into my skin, as did the ribs of my crinoline, and I was stiff from the strange position I'd been forced to lie in. My chignon was slipping. I drew out the pins one by one, gathering them in my hand and letting my thick hair fall to my waist. I laid them on the small rococo table by the chaise. And then, exhausted and aching, I rose and made my way from the parlor and up the stairs.

The lights in the hall were lit, though the house was quiet and full of that strangeness that came with late night and exhaustion and illness, with people still about, maids cleaning after an evening gathering, nurses tending—the sounds hushed, like mice scurrying over carpet, where one was aware more that there was a presence when there should not be, movement when stillness was the rule.

When I reached the third floor, I paused. My bedroom door

was closed, as was Michel's. But Dorothy's was open, and two of her nurses were inside, folding towels and mixing potions with the stiff, weary motions of those who wished for sleep. I went to her door, pausing just outside, knocking softly so that Charley turned to see me.

"Is she awake?" I asked. "Might I see her?"

He glanced over his shoulder toward the screen that hid Dorothy's bed. "I suppose there's no harm in it. I don't guess she'll get much sleep tonight, ma'am. Nor will any of us, I'll warrant."

"Is she alone?"

"For now. Mr. Jourdain's due back shortly."

I stepped into the room. "Where did he go?"

"To mix more of her cordial." Charley stepped ahead of me, poking his head around the screen to say, "Mrs. Atherton's here, ma'am, if you'd care to see her."

"Yes." Dorothy's voice was more of a moan. When Charley stepped back and I went to her, I was startled at how ill she looked, how tiny and drawn, her plump cheeks fallen, her skin gray. Her hair straggled about her head in wispy flyaway tendrils.

I went to her, sitting on the side of the bed. "Please forgive me. I didn't mean to distress you."

She twisted, raising her hips from the mattress, as if she could not get comfortable. "No, no, no," she said. I wasn't certain if she was moaning or answering me.

I put my hand on her shoulder. "Dorothy, what can I do?"

"It was a miracle." Her voice was crackly and strained. She moved beneath my hand, shrugging, as if my touch hurt, but when I pulled away, she grabbed me back again, whimpering. "You gave me memory. Doesn't . . . it . . . amaze—" Her breath came fast. Her fingers entwined in mine, and she made a little mewing sound of pain. "They keep the smallest things."

Then she cried out, releasing my hand, and I turned anxiously to see Charley watching from the screen. "What is it?" I asked. "What's wrong with her? What can I do?"

"Just talk to her, ma'am, until Mr. Jourdain gets here. There's nothing else to do."

"I've never seen her this way."

"Sometimes she gets like this when she's overexcited."

Dorothy was keening softly and tossing her head. "Johnny, oh my Johnny . . ."

In distress, I reached for her hand, trying to still her restlessness, but she slapped at my fingers and jerked away.

"Where are they? Where are my boys?"

"I'm right here, Dorothy," I said. I touched her face; her skin was moist with sweat. "Their voices . . ." She moaned again, and began to cry, and I had no idea what to do, how to soothe her.

"I'm so sorry," I whispered uselessly.

There was the sound of hurried footsteps behind me, a bustle behind the screen, and Michel came into the room. He looked exhausted, and he was in his shirtsleeves, his shirt mostly unfastened to reveal his under vest, his hair tousled, as if he'd run his hands through it. He carried a glass half full of liquid. He barely spared me a glance as he rushed to Dorothy's side.

"It was too much," he said. "I could've told you."

"I didn't—"

He silenced me with a glance. Dorothy turned to him, reaching out her hand as one blind, feeling in the air. "Michel? Is it you?"

"*Oui, chère,* it's me." He spoke soothingly. He bent close, holding the glass in one hand while he slipped his arm beneath her, lifting her. "Come now. I've your medicine."

She pressed her hand against his chest. "I want to hear my sons."

"Your sons have gone to sleep," he said calmly. He tried to bring the cordial to her, but she turned her head away.

"I want to hear them again."

"Not tonight," he said firmly. "*Madame* Atherton was just leaving."

She cried out in dismay.

I said, "I can stay—"

"*Non.* Look what you've done already." He was clipped and angry, but then he turned back to Dorothy, and his voice became soothing again and quiet. "Come, come, *ma chère,* you must drink."

Dorothy's fingers clawed at the wool flannel of his under vest. He hefted her again, pressing the glass to her lips, and when she drank, he soothed, "Ah, that's the way, *ma pauvre chère,* drink it up."

When she was finished, he reached over her to put the glass on the bedside table. Her head fell back, and she sighed, but her fingers still moved ceaselessly against his chest, trying at the buttons, failing. Breathlessly, she said, "I want to touch," and impatiently he brushed her hand aside, slipping the buttons free to bare his chest, and then he took her hand—gently now—and pressed it to his skin, where she flattened her palm and stretched out her fingers, sighing with relief and pleasure.

He looked up at me. His eyes were harder than I'd ever seen them. "It's time for you to go, *Madame.*"

The look he gave me was so cold. I had not realized how used I was to his too intimate warmth until it was gone. This was worse. Much worse.

21

An Angelfish Among the Eels

The strangeness of the night seeped into my skin like poison, and I did not understand what had happened to me. I could tell myself all I wanted that the spirit writing was only a manifestation of my own thoughts, and so explain it as some strange delusion brought on by strain or lack of sleep. But I couldn't say the same for tonight. I'd had no knowledge of the things I'd seen. Where had it all come from? Who was I?

I felt vulnerable and undone and frightened. Because whether or not the visions were real, Dorothy thought they were, and Peter had lost his life attempting to break Michel's bond with her. What now would happen to me? I paced my room, unable to be still, agitated beyond measure.

The quick, sharp rap on my door stopped my step. I glanced at the clock on the mantel. Four A.M. It seemed suddenly inevitable that he would come, that I would let him in, and I was well aware of the irony of the fact that the man I was most afraid of had the power to ease my fears. To help me or to hurt me was his choice. I did not know which he would make.

"Come in," I called. "It's not locked. Not that it would matter to you if it were."

The door opened. He stepped inside, closing it softly again behind him. He looked much the same as he had when I'd left him in Dorothy's room. His under vest was still unbuttoned to show his skin, which seemed to gleam golden in the light.

"I heard you pacing," he said. "Nightmares?"

I laughed, and had to look away when the laugh turned into a sob. "I think I must be going mad."

"Non," he said, and the calm assurance in his voice made me look at him again. "Remember what I told you before. Let them in so you can control them."

Desperately, I said, "How can it be real? How do you know I'm not losing my mind?"

"Tell me what you saw tonight. In the circle, what did you see?"

"I . . . there was a voice. It was your voice, and then it wasn't. It was a woman's. I didn't know her. But she asked me to listen. And then it was like a memory, but not my own."

"The boys swimming?"

"Yes. They were laughing. And then she came down the bank—"

"The woman who told you to watch?"

"No. No. This was their mother. Dorothy. She was younger. She had cherry tarts."

"And that was how it was? Just a memory? You don't remember speaking?"

"No. I was watching. It was as if I were far away, but everything was so clear. Like a dream."

"Or a nightmare?" He came toward me, and it was very like that evening in the parlor, when he'd first threatened me. The slow pace, the way he let his fingers dangle to caress the furniture, as if he owned it, and I felt again that same fear, but this time, there was something that made me wait for him to reach me.

"Did you know any of these things before you came here?" he asked gently.

"I knew Dorothy had two sons who died."

"You never investigated her? Not with your *papa*?"

"No. No, I knew of the Bennetts, of course, everyone does. But nothing else. Not until I married Peter."

"What did you know then?"

"Only that she was an invalid," I said.

"What about the things Peter told you?"

"He told me nothing."

"Ah." He was right there, just before me. "You aren't lying to me about how the visions come? Did you eat something? Drink something? Laudanum, like your *maman,* perhaps?"

I shook my head. "There was the liqueur you gave me. I drank it each time before the spirit writing—"

"That was just a liqueur, nothing more."

"Then no."

His expression went thoughtful. He murmured, "Unbelievable. How strange to find you here. I hardly expected it. Peter was right, eh? An angelfish among the eels."

I felt a sad tug at the familiar words, but I said nothing, and he went on, "I think you are that very rare thing, *chère*. A real medium. I confess I'd not thought one existed. I've seen some that made me wonder, but in the end, they were just clever women."

"The way you're clever."

"*Oui.* But it doesn't matter whether you're real or not. You know I'll do everything I can to discredit you? I'll fight you, and you can't win. Not with Dorothy. Not against me."

His honesty took me aback.

"You want to take from me what I've spent months working for. You want to prove that I'm guilty of murdering your *beloved* husband. You want to save yourself by ruining me. Should I not fight back, Evie?"

I took a deep, shuddering breath. "I'm not going to jail."

His gaze did not leave mine. "Work with me, *chère*. Work with me and I'll teach you everything I know."

Then he kissed me.

I pressed my palms flat against his bare chest. I knew I should push him away. But I didn't. Instead, I curled my fingers, and he pressed closer, putting his arms around me, trapping me against him, and suddenly, we were breathless and fumbling. I felt his fingers at my back, slipping each of the tiny buttons of my gown from their loops, and I was pulling his shirt from his trousers, pushing it off his shoulders, yanking at his under vest, pulling back only long enough for him to peel my sleeves from my arms, long enough so I could undo the hooks at the front of my corset while he loosened the ties of my crinoline. I was impatient, and so was he—our movements were hasty, jerking, our breaths coming in hard little gasps as we removed the layers of our armor: my gown, his trousers, my petticoats and chemise, his underclothes, and then we were naked, and he was pulling me down onto the floor, and I writhed beneath him until I was no longer myself.

WHEN IT WAS over, it took only a moment for the world to return to me, to remember who he was. I felt his silky hair against my shoulder, the rise and fall of his breathing against my breasts, and I was chagrined and furious with myself.

"Ah, not yet, *chère,*" he whispered against my throat. The movement of his lips tickled. "Don't banish me yet."

I pushed at his shoulders. I felt near tears. "I want you to leave."

He sighed and rolled off me. I scrambled away from him, hiding myself as best I could until I reached my gown, which I held to my breasts.

He watched me with a rueful expression. Then he got to his feet. With no care for his nakedness, he came to where I sat, surrounded by our clothing, and with a patience that made me want to scream, he separated out his own. He said nothing as he pulled on his trousers, and then he bent to retrieve his shirt and his underwear, balling them in his hand.

I buried my face in my gown so I wouldn't have to look at him. I saw him in a succession of images—bending close to Dorothy, unbuttoning his vest for her, pressing the laudanum to her lips. I heard Benjamin—*Benjamin!*—saying, *"I think he killed Peter."* How easily Michel had worked me, with the skill not of hands or kisses or charm, but of challenge and conversation, of *answers*. I heard him cross the room, and then the soft click of the door as it opened, his little hesitation before he went out, and then I was alone.

I sat there for some time, my face buried in my gown. I wanted to cry, but the tears wouldn't come, there was just a terrible heaviness behind my eyes that wouldn't go away. Then, finally, I looked up. The dawn light was creeping around the edges of the curtains.

I rose. I was sticky, and I ached. I went to the washbasin and poured water from the pitcher into it. The water was cold, but I dipped a cloth into it anyway and washed myself everywhere he had touched. My skin pimpled with gooseflesh, but I kept at it until I was certain every vestige of his presence was gone. Then I pulled on my dressing gown and collapsed upon my bed, too exhausted and sick at heart to even crawl beneath the blankets, though the fire had long since died. To sleep—even for an hour to find my way into dreams instead of nightmares, to find solace . . . I longed for it. I closed my eyes, and for a moment my mind was empty, and I was certain I would sleep at last. I felt my body relaxing, fading, giving. . . .

Then I felt the sagging of the mattress, as if someone had just sat upon it. I opened my eyes quickly and saw a shadow there, the figure of a man, but before I could move or exclaim, a light flared and suddenly he was illuminated, but it was an odd kind of light, as if it came from within him and not without, and the rest of the room was in abject darkness, even though moments before it had been dawn.

"Peter," I gasped.

My husband was sitting there, his hair matted and wet, his face pale, his lips blue. His eyes were closed. When I spoke his name, he opened them, and I saw they were gone, eaten away by fishes and eels, and he reached out to touch me, my name upon his lips, and I found myself scrambling away, falling off the bed in my haste, screaming so the sound seemed to spiral in my head—

I woke on the floor, the scream caught in my throat. I was losing my mind. I reached out in the darkness; it was a moment before I realized it was the comfort of Michel I'd been reaching for, and I drew back again, shaking, and there was a knocking on the door that raised panic within me. "No!" I called, my voice hoarse. "Go away!"

"Ma'am? Ma'am, it's Kitty. Are you all right? I heard a noise—"

Kitty. I brushed back the hair that had fallen in my face and made myself rise. "I'm fine," I called.

"Are you ready for breakfast, ma'am? Or to dress?"

I glanced about my room, at the still-made bed, the clothes piled in the middle of the floor. Clothes that I could not have removed myself and which any maid would have put away. "Could you bring me some tea, please?"

"Yes, ma'am."

I listened for her footsteps to recede, and then I picked up my clothing, the gown and corset, the crinolines, my chemise. I hung them all in the armoire, and then I crawled into bed and leaned back on the pillows and waited for her to return. When she did only a few minutes later, I took the tea from her and held it to my lips, letting the steam bathe my face. If Kitty noticed anything wrong, she said nothing.

"Charley gave me a message from Miz Bennett," she said as she went to the armoire. "She's coming to supper tonight, and she asks you to be there."

"She does?" I'd scarcely expected her to be well enough to rise from bed, much less preside over a supper.

"Mr. Lambert said the mistress was in a poor way last night," Kitty said, as if she read my thoughts. "Molly said she heard her moanin' and groanin' 'til nearly morning—what happened to this bombazine? It's all wrinkled up—" She took the gown I'd hung up and shook it out, beating at the wrinkles in the skirt before she hung it back again. "But I guess Mr. Jourdain worked his miracles. She was calling for her sons, I heard. Poor thing. And them gone now twenty years or more."

I was amazed at how easily I could answer her. "I don't suppose one ever stops missing one's children."

"I suppose not, ma'am. But not having any myself, I can't say. Noisy and selfish little things, from what I can see. Will it be the silk or the wool today?"

"I'll wear the silk. This house is too hot for wool."

But once I was dressed, three-quarters of an hour later, I didn't leave my room. I could not bear to think of last night, yet it was impossible not to. I tried to read, but I found myself too distracted even for Elisha Kane's *Arctic Explorations,* which I'd taken from the library. The book had been all the talk of the upper ten this year, but I would no more read a sentence about ice-covered landscapes and men burdened to the breaking point than I would remember the play of Michel's muscles beneath my hands. I cast aside the book, only to feel the ache of my thighs as I turned, only to catch my breath at the sudden image of his mouth on my breast.

This had never happened with Peter. Not these kinds of memories, never the visceral reaction to them after he'd gone from my bed. Peter had never made me feel as if my body was a source of endless fascination. I had never felt alive beneath his hands. I knew it was wrong to feel this way, and to feel it for my husband's murderer—what kind of woman was I? To yearn for him, even knowing how he'd played me, even knowing this was a game for him, some way to keep me from finding the truth. I could not do this, I could not think of him, and yet I couldn't stop myself either. Most women dreamed of chaste kisses, of romantic glances across the room. Of men like Benjamin. I remembered the affectionate kiss Ben had given me the night before. Respectful, fond, so different from Michel's.

I thought of Dorothy crying out to touch him, and I understood it and knew he had somehow bewitched us both. And I knew that I must put an end to it.

I went to the window, where I stared out over the barren side yard and the small bit of Fifth Avenue I could see. There, on the corner of the First Presbyterian Church grounds, stood my police watchman. He seemed so idle, watching the people walk by on their way to wherever it was they meant to pass the time. How I envied them, those people for whom a policeman on Fifth Avenue meant nothing, for whom the sight of a blue coat and copper badge flashing in the light was not a subtle reminder of what terrible turns a life could take. I had been one of them only a month ago, yet how far away that world felt now.

I must gain hold of myself. I must remember what Michel no doubt never forgot—to not lose sight of my plan. I could not let him distract me. I could not afford to fail.

THE DAY PASSED slowly, and when it was finally time to ready for supper, I was strung taut with nerves. In the first months of my marriage, I had faced the most formidable dragons of society. Now what I faced chilled me more than had my introduction to Caroline Astor. I didn't want to be alone with him. I was too vulnerable. I lingered in my room a long time. Then, when I felt I could wait no longer, I made my way downstairs to the dining room. I paused for a moment outside the doorway, gathering my strength, and then I stepped inside.

He was there, his back to me as he stood by the fireplace leafing through a book. At the sight of him, I said too sharply, "Dorothy still intends to join us, I hope."

He turned. His frock coat tonight was a deep green. I remembered how large his tailor bill had been; I didn't think I'd seen him in the same coat twice. *"Madame,"* he said with a small bow and a mocking tone. "I wondered if you'd left us. You've been scarce all day."

"I've been forbidden to leave the city," I said.

"But not this house."

"I believe the prosecutor would disagree with you. I either live here or I go to the Tombs. The terms of my bail were quite explicit."

He put aside the book. "The way you talked this morning—"

"I'd rather not speak of it."

"Ah. You'd rather ignore that it happened?"

"Exactly."

"No doubt it's become a habit for you."

"I've never done *anything* like that—"

"I meant ignoring things," he said. He moved to the table, which was set for three, and motioned to the decanted wine in its elaborately cut crystal. "Would you care for some?"

"I think I'd prefer to wait for Dorothy."

"Then you won't mind if I do?" When I shook my head, he poured the wine into his glass and drank it quickly, and then poured another. He raised his glass to me, smiling wickedly.

I heard a commotion on the stairs, the bustle that normally accompanied Dorothy's every move. Michel heard it too; he set the wineglass on the table and strode past me to the door.

I hardly saw Dorothy at first, so surrounded was she by her nurses, not until Michel took her arm and she flapped her hands at the others and told them to leave, and then I was amazed at her transformation. Her eyes were shining, and she wore a deep plum gown that made her hair seem beautifully white. Instead of her usual beribboned cap, someone had swept her hair up, catching it in a gold clasp that sparkled with garnets and peridot and topaz. She was looking into Michel's face adoringly, but when he brought her to the table, she went from his arms to me, pressing her dry, powdered cheek against mine, saying, "Here she is. My miracle."

"Indeed," Michel said dryly. "Come, *ma chère*. Sit before you tire yourself out."

"I feel reborn," she said, but she obeyed him, settling herself in the chair at the head of the table, where he waited to seat her.

"For a few hours, at least." He smiled, coming to pull out the chair for me, and I sat on Dorothy's right, ignoring the brush of his hand against my shoulder. The maid came almost immediately, ladling out a soup for which I had no appetite.

"You look wonderfully rested," I told Dorothy.

"It isn't rest, child, it's hope. The hope that soon I'll hear my sons again."

"You've heard them at nearly every circle," Michel said, reaching for the wine.

"Yes, and don't think I'm not grateful, dear boy. But last night it was like sitting down to supper with them, remembering old times." Her eyes shone. "Did you see them, child? Did you see my boys?"

I nodded.

"Describe them to me."

"They were young, maybe eight and ten. Dark haired. Very sweet. You were there too. You wore a big straw hat with poppies—"

"Yes, I remember it!"

"They were playing in the river. They ran into it wearing their clothes. They were dressed as if they'd just come from church."

"A family dinner," she corrected me dreamily. "With Edward's parents. Oh, they were a pair, stiff as deacons, and Edward obeyed them like a, well, I suppose some would say a good son. I never cared for them much. The boys had to be so proper when they were around. But Johnny and Everett! Those two weren't much for sitting still."

I smiled. "I could see that."

She closed her eyes, as if lingering with the memory. "Michel's brought them to me, but never like that."

"Perhaps they come differently through a man," I said carefully.

"Not that much different, I think," he said sharply. "But it doesn't do to tire you, *ma chère*. So much excitement! I only mean to protect you from it. I didn't want you to pass a terrible night, as you did last night."

The light in her eyes dimmed. "Yes, I know. I fear I'm not as strong as I used to be."

Politely, I said, "It must have been a shock to have them come like that, through me."

"A shock." She nodded. When Michel poured her wine, she reached for the glass almost convulsively. "Yes, it was. It surely was. Frankly, child, we were expecting Peter."

I thought of my nightmare this morning with a shudder. "He seems content to haunt my dreams instead."

"Why is that, I wonder?" Dorothy mused. The jewels in her rings sparkled in the candlelight as she clutched the stem of her glass. "Why not come to the circle? We were all his friends."

"I don't know." I glanced up, catching Michel's gaze. "Perhaps someone in the circle knows why. Perhaps there's some secret."

"What secret would that be?"

Michel took a sip of wine. His expression was inscrutable as he said, "*Madame* believes one of us might hold the answer to Peter's murder."

Dorothy turned to me with a frown. "But, my dear, why would you think so?"

"The spirit writing," I said, referring to the one thing I knew she would believe. "It tells me there are liars among us."

Michel said, "To understand spirit writing needs great skill. You're a novice. How can you be sure you're reading it correctly?"

"Michel may be right, child," Dorothy said.

"It isn't always so easy to discern intentions, *Madame*. Swedenborg says that the spirits who come will be the ones we have an affinity with. New mediums can't always tell the difference between lying spirits and those who tell the truth. They need a guide." Michel smiled contritely and curled his hand around Dorothy's, clasping her fingers. "*Madame* is like most developing mediums. Depending too much on reason, when one should trust instinct instead."

"I don't need instinct to tell me the spirits are right."

"If you believe them so well, why aren't you doing what they ask?"

"I am!"

"Non, Madame," he said. "They're telling you to ask the right questions. Why don't you? Tell me something: have you ever asked yourself why Peter was down near the river that night?"

The words held an uncomfortable echo. I remembered Benjamin's assistant. *"I was sorry when he was found that way. But I suppose, given how often he went down there ..."*

The last time I'd seen Peter flashed through my mind. His insistence on going out again, his determination to find answers about the attempt on Michel's life. Or, had it been, as Ben speculated, because he'd believed he was the target, because he meant to question Michel?

I met Michel's gaze. "He was concerned for you."

He looked surprised. "For me?"

"I told you he believed the shooting in the circle that night was not a misfire. What I didn't say was that he told me he thought the target was you. He also told me he meant to find out why." I watched him, waiting for his expression to confirm either Peter's suspicions or Ben's and my own.

Michel didn't look at me. Instead, he and Dorothy exchanged a glance, and I felt their sudden tension.

The maid took away the soup bowls, which had been almost untouched, and brought a roast bedecked with rosemary and onions. As she served it, Dorothy sighed. "There's much more to this than you've been told, child." Then, as Michel began to protest— "No, dear boy, it's time she knew. The night before that circle, Peter and I argued."

"There's no need to speak of this," Michel said in a tight voice.

She ignored him. "You know he didn't like the idea of the adoption."

"Yes, I knew that."

"Well, child"—she paused in the midst of cutting her beef—"Peter came to tell me he meant to file commitment papers."

"I don't understand. Commitment of what?"

"Of Dorothy to an asylum," Michel said. He put his hand on her shoulder, as if to comfort her. "He was going to have her put away."

The information was startling; what it meant for me was more startling still. "Because of the adoption?"

"*Oui*. He tried to convince her I meant to cheat her. When she wouldn't believe him—"

"How could I believe him? How could he believe it himself?" Dorothy held Michel's hand tight to her shoulder. "It troubles me to say it, but I lost my love for him in that moment. I thought we were confidants. He was much more than my lawyer—he was nearly another son to me. Well, I admit I was beside myself. He asked me not to tell Michel, and I obliged—until after the circle the next night." Dorothy looked at me, her gaze direct. "I was afraid he'd gone mad. In fact, I suspected him of trying to hurt my dear boy. I told Michel everything and kept him near me all night."

"A long night, *oui*," Michel agreed.

I should have been glad. It was exactly the kind of information Benjamin had told me to find, and I knew it would help my case immensely. Though I believed Dorothy when she said she had been afraid for Michel, I knew Peter would not have hurt him. And I didn't believe Dorothy's alibi for Michel—she would lie for him without even knowing it.

But I was troubled too. Committing Dorothy to an asylum was a grossly final step. It would have caused a scandal. Though it was true that no adoption of Michel would stand after, and that Michel would lose everything he'd worked for, it seemed out of character for Peter to do something that so lacked finesse and discretion. He had cared a great deal for society's opinion, and the Bennetts had been friends of the Athertons for generations. To commit Dorothy would have destroyed her. I could not think why Peter would do it.

"It doesn't seem like him," I said doubtfully.

"Ah, the supportive wife," Michel taunted. "You knew him so well, then?"

Dorothy said, "I thought the same thing. I was shocked, child, but later, I realized, well, Peter had not seemed himself those last months."

"Perhaps it was only a harmless threat—"

"He said he'd drawn up the papers," Dorothy said.

"Did you see them?" I asked.

She shook her head.

Michel took a bite of his roast. "He could've been lying, eh?"

"Peter didn't lie," I said.

"*Non?* What a fairy tale you must live in, *Madame,* to believe such a thing."

Dorothy said, "I suppose it doesn't matter now. He's gone; we'll never know what he intended. But in a way, it turned out well. His death brought you to us, Evelyn. And how much good you've done! To bring me my sons in the way you have! And look at Michel. He's much better too. He isn't coughing as much."

Or at all, I thought. I looked at him in surprise. Consumptives didn't just stop coughing, did they?

He caught my gaze, as if he knew what I was thinking. With his fork, he pointed to the window. "It isn't her. It's the weather. It's turned."

"Yes, how warm and dry it's become," I said sarcastically.

"You should have seen him when I found him," Dorothy said. She leaned toward him, stroking from his shoulder to his back, fixing upon him a gaze so tender I was amazed he didn't melt away beneath it. "So thin. So very ill. We were a pair, my dear boy, were we not?"

He took a gulp of wine. I thought he was careful not to meet my gaze. *"Oui."*

"Look at him now, that bloom upon his cheeks. Between the two of you, my life has changed in ways I never expected." She set aside her knife eagerly, pushing her plate away. "I know there's no circle, so perhaps it won't do, but it used to with Michel—do you remember, dear boy? How we used to see the boys together, just the two of us?"

"Oui. I remember. But *Madame* is too newly chosen, *ma chère.* Who knows if she can bring them without the circle?"

I frowned. "You mean now?"

"If you feel you can. I wish to hear them again," Dorothy said.

"Remember what happened last night," Michel said softly.

"I'm willing to try," I said, not because I wanted to, or because I thought I could—in fact, I was afraid—but because I felt the sway he had over her, and I knew how irresistible it was, and I wanted to weaken it.

"Wonderful!" Dorothy clapped her hands, jubilant as a child. She twisted in her chair, motioning impatiently to the maid who stood in the doorway. "Bella, come and clear, please."

"Leave the wine," Michel directed.

The table was quickly cleared but for the glasses and the decanter. Michel did not look the least bit happy, and I was glad for that, to be thwarting him at least in this one thing.

Dorothy turned to him. "We should be alternating."

He shoved his chair back and rose, helping Dorothy from her seat with grace and charm, though I felt the impatience in his movements. When they'd switched seats so that he was at the head of the table between us, he dragged his wineglass closer.

"You should direct us, dear boy," she said.

He took Dorothy's hand and reached for mine. Involuntarily, I drew back, and he said, "What's wrong, *Madame?* Are you afraid?"

I shook my head, and let him take my hand.

"You're tense, *Madame,*" he said. "One can't call the spirits that way."

I closed my eyes, trying to ignore his touch. "Will you say a prayer?"

Dorothy obliged, and I tried to clear my mind, but it was obstinate, it wanted only to remember last night, to polish each image like a gem. I heard Dorothy's words like the sound of a droning bee; I felt the caress of Michel's thumb, and my body seemed to leap toward him, as if he tuned me to his pleasure, and I was dropping deep, deep into the memory of those last predawn hours.

There you are. The words came from inside my head. I felt the push of her through my longing, almost as if my yearning for him were her own. She seemed to swell within me until the voice and I were one. There was no separating us, and I—Evelyn Atherton— seemed to disappear, to fade. I became someone else, though it was as if I watched from a far distance. I saw myself stir. My eyes opened, but I saw only vapor, and wavering forms within it. *Do you know me?*

"We're calling the spirits of John and Everett Bennett. Are they here to speak with us?"

Not today. Today I'm the one who's come. You would do well to heed me.

The voice rang in my head. I saw Michel's slow and constant caress upon my hand, and I felt the spirit within me watching as well. An avid stare. A hungry one. She was uncomfortable in my body. She longed to break free.

"Johnny? Johnny, my darling, is that you?"

He is not here. I am here now. Tell him I am here.

My voice seemed not to be mine. It came from a far distance, and yet it was loud, and I was watching myself speak. "He's not here. I am here now."

I saw Michel's polish slip in surprise. I felt her satisfaction as she waited for him to regain himself.

"Who is here? Who speaks to us through *Madame* Atherton?"

Dorothy said, "Who are you? Tell us, spirit. Who are you?"
My body smiled.

"Who are you, spirit?" Michel demanded again.

I saw my own mouth open. I felt the struggle of the spirit within me, the urge to answer, and I said—not in my own voice, not me at all—"One who knows you."

"What's your errand? Who are you?"

I felt I was being sucked like wind through a tunnel. I felt my body shudder. I felt myself pulled back—or, it was more as if the door opened again and called me to enter. I began to feel myself again—the blood in my veins, the flex of my fingers held tight in other hands, the drawing of my breath. But I could not gain the strength to open my eyes. The vision was fading.

"Child?" Dorothy's voice, soft and urgent, calling me back. "Evelyn?"

I opened my eyes, blinking in the glare of gaslight. Dorothy was staring at me, concerned, and I knew vaguely that it had something to do with what had just happened, like a dream whose color you remember upon waking, though the details escape, impossible to put together again.

Michel released my hand. He seemed disconcerted as he shoved my wineglass toward me. Roughly, he said, "Drink. It'll clear your head."

I made no move to take it, and he pushed the glass into my hand. I took a sip. The drink was warm on my tongue, and he was right; it did seem to clear my head. The blurry edges of my mind began to sharpen, and I began to remember. No boys at all, but a voice, a woman's voice. I remembered what she said. One who knows you. Then I looked at Dorothy. Her face had gone slack with disappointment.

"They didn't come."

"Non. She needs more experience. She doesn't know how to call." Michel looked at me. "You've done enough tonight."

22

ONE WHO KNOWS YOU

After he took Dorothy from the room, I put down the wine-glass and went upstairs, calling for Kitty along the way.

I let her chatter as she undressed me, but I heard little of what she said, and when she finally left me, I sat in the chair near the fire, clad in my nightgown and robe, and stared into the flames, glad for the silence, for the opportunity to think.

Yet logic or reason escaped me, and the night wavered uncomfortably before me, a mix of sensations rather than images. The way the spirit had felt within me, her restlessness, the way she had watched Michel, the words she'd said. *One who knows you.* How real it had seemed—but dreams felt real too. And I had no doubt that those in the throes of madness believed their own delusions. I thought of my mother, of her laudanum-induced stupor, her effort to silence the voices in her head, and I felt her terror in a way I never had.

Yet Michel had said to let them in, to learn to control them. It meant admitting the spirits were real. Could it be, as he'd said, that it was like telegraph lines or electricity—simply something science had not yet discovered? Did he really believe that, or were his assurances meant only to lure me into trusting him? Into madness?

I was so weary. What had I accomplished in my time here? The only evidence I'd discovered was a watch chain that Peter had supposedly given to Michel, and a possible adoption, and the bewildering fact of Peter's attempt to commit Dorothy to an asylum—the latter two of which I needed papers to prove. Worse yet, I had allowed myself into a tryst with a man I believed was a killer. I was a failure in every way. I wanted myself back, the Evelyn who did not hear voices and did not have wicked, perverse longings. I heard the footsteps down the hall, and my body recognized them before my mind did. I stiffened. I heard the pause at my door, and I waited for the knock, the turn of the knob.

The footsteps moved on.

The disappointment that came over me was so sharp I nearly cried aloud with it. What had he done to me, that I should feel this way? I felt I was vibrating, a string plucked by invisible hands, his hands, and I was so repulsed and furious that it should be so that I could scarcely contain myself. I did not want him. I wanted nothing to do with him. I wanted him in jail. Hanged. Buried in some dark place far away from me. When he was gone, I would be sure the whole world knew of his villainy. *"He was a mountebank, a charlatan who killed my husband for the basest of reasons, for money. He was the worst kind of criminal,"* I would say.

"Did you never wonder what Peter was doing down by the river that night?"

I frowned, staring into the fire, at the flames leaping and dancing before my eyes.

"No doubt it's become a habit with you. Ignoring things."

He was so confident that I would not find the evidence against him. He thought he was so wily.

I rose, restless, my mind turning, Peter's face wavering before me. *"Don't believe him. Don't trust him."* No, I did not. But I remembered how I'd reached for him after my nightmare, drawn to the comfort he offered. *"You are that rare thing, chère. A real medium."*

I felt I was drowning. I went to the window, pulling aside the drapes, staring out at the brightly colored globes of the carriage lamps gimbeling like stars in the darkness, people moving in and out of the streetlights' glow—present one moment, the next gone, as if they'd never existed, as if only the light gave them material-ity. I let the curtains fall. I paced back to the fire. I wanted an-swers. Not taunting hints, not manipulation, but real answers. Not just about Peter, but about my ability to hear spirits.

Before I could talk myself out of it, I was out of my bedroom, down the hall. It wasn't until I was before his door that I paused, and only then because the craving moved over me like a rising tide. The spirits' words mocked me. *Do not give in to temptation.* Like the Ten Commandments. *Thou shalt not steal. Thou shalt not covet thy neighbor's wife. Thou shalt not murder the husband and let the wife take the blame.*

No, I thought. *Don't do it.* There would be a better time. It was stupid to confront him now, tonight, when my yearnings were still so strong, when I doubted I could resist him.

His door opened.

"Why, *allô, chère.*" His hair was loose. He wore only a dressing gown, which opened indecently to reveal his naked chest. He leaned against the doorjamb. "Looking for me?"

My hunger rooted me. I wished I could disappear.

He said, "Why not admit what you want?"

He held out his hand.

And I, like the fool I was, took it.

He pulled me into his room, and closed the door, and then he pushed me up against it. I felt his hands at my dressing gown, jerking it from my shoulders, down my arms, until it fell in a pool around my feet, and then he was pulling the ribbon at the neck of my nightgown so it gaped open, and plunging his hands into it, pushing and twisting until the fabric gathered at my waist and I was naked above it. His mouth was everywhere—on mine, then at my throat, my breasts. My own hands crept beneath his robe, clutching at his narrow hips, pulling him close. I wanted him so badly I did not seem myself.

Then he was drawing up the skirt of my nightgown, lifting me as he plunged into me, and I curled my legs around him and moved with him. He caught my cries with his mouth, and the world dissolved—my questions and my doubts—in the force of my climax. And then, when he was spent himself, and the pleasure left us so we sagged exhausted and sweating against the door, our breathing ragged and heavy, he murmured against my shoulder, "We can't keep doing this, *chère*."

I felt sick at the words, especially when I believed them myself. "Of course," I said stiffly. "If you would just let—"

"Next time, we should use the bed."

I made a sound—I hardly knew what it was, a gulp, a cry of dismay, a laugh. I buried my face in him. "I can't be here. I shouldn't be here. I don't even like you."

"I think you like me well enough."

"No." I shook my head against him. I felt my own hair tangle with his. "This isn't what I want."

"You don't know what you want."

"Yes I do. I do."

"Ah, your safe life. Your Rampling." He infused the words with such scorn. "That isn't you, *chère*. When will you see it?"

My legs were still wrapped around him, my hands clutching him. Our sweat was cooling and slick between us. I felt the movement of his lips against my shoulder like a burn.

He lifted his head and moved so that my legs slid down his and my feet touched the ground. He pushed me a little with his shoulder, pressing me more firmly to the door, lodging his hip against mine. The posture had changed just enough: we were no longer tangled together, but I couldn't move. I was his prisoner.

He stared into my eyes, and a chill came into his that frightened me. I think I made a sound, I know I made a motion, an attempt to escape, and he pushed me back again until I stilled. His hand moved up my body, up my thigh, skating past the bunching of my nightgown at my waist, and then up the swell of my breast, to my neck, curving around, his fingers spanning my throat. "If I killed Peter, what makes you think I wouldn't kill you? Why not now, when no one's here to see?" He pressed—it was a small pressure, but I felt the constriction of air. How foolish I'd been, how stupid—

The pressure stopped. His fingers loosened. I gasped.

"You work against me when what you really want is to be right here." He let his hand fall, the backs of his fingers traced down the tendon of my throat, across my collarbone. "Why fight what's meant to be? Take what you want. I don't object."

Gooseflesh rose on my skin. My breath came fast. "It won't work, you know. This, this distraction. It doesn't change my mind about you."

He lifted his head, and the look I saw in his eyes stole my reason. I had trouble remembering what I'd said. His lips grazed mine. When I would have kissed him, he stepped away and took my hand, pulling me away from the door, into his arms. "Come to bed. Let's do this properly, eh?"

IT WAS VERY late when we were finally sated. I was aching and woozy, and as I heard his quiet, even breathing beside me, I dreaded the coming of morning and the return to myself which would inevitably bring with it recriminations and doubt. He made it easy to accept the perversity within me, the darkness made it easy. In the morning, would that Evelyn be the one who remained? Or would she shiver away, hiding in the shadows until the night brought her out again, ravenous and aching? Would I be able to admit the truth I knew: that I wanted him, and that wanting had no conscience and no morality—it made excuses, it equivocated, it asked questions like: Can you be certain he was the one who killed Peter? What if he was not?

I pushed the thoughts away. From somewhere, I heard a whisper. My eyes had been half closed, now I opened them, staring into the darkness. There was nothing.

Then I heard it again. *Listen.*

I raised myself slightly up on my elbow. Michel's arm, which was curled about me, slipped limply to my waist.

It felt as if something were lifting the top of my head. A sound beat between my ears.

Listen to me.

I fell back to the pillow with a little gasp. For a moment it was as if I were in the trance again, as if something were pulling at my soul, the prelude to the fog. But that was impossible. We weren't in the circle; no one had called a spirit—

"Ssshhh, *chère,*" Michel whispered, half asleep. His arm tightened around me again, and suddenly the feeling was gone. I closed my eyes. And then, without warning or preamble, I fell into a deep sleep—one without nightmares.

I WOKE WITH a start to a loud, pounding noise. It took me a moment to realize the sound was a knock, and another moment still to realize that I was not in my own bed, but Michel's, and that it was morning, and I should have gone before now, before the household began to rouse. There were no worse gossips than the help, and the last thing I wanted was gossip.

Beside me, Michel cursed some Creole imprecation beneath his breath, and sat up, pushing back his hair, calling, "What is it?"

"Miz Bennett, sir," called back a voice. "It's past nine—"

Another curse. "I'll be there in a moment."

"Very well, sir. But if you'd hurry."

He shoved back the blankets, rising from the bed in one fluid motion, without a single look at me. I wondered if he even remembered I was there, but the same moment I had the thought, he said, "I've got to tend to Dorothy, but I'll be back. Don't go anywhere."

"I can't stay here," I protested. "Kitty will be coming to dress me, if she hasn't already—"

"Not yet." He twisted around, coming onto the bed again, leaning down to kiss me. "I'll tell her you were ill last night and to let you sleep."

"She knows I wasn't."

"Trust me to convince her." He gave me a wry smile, and then he rose again, quickly, striding to where his dressing gown lay on the floor, next to mine. He kicked everything else aside and picked up his robe, shrugging into it. Then he went out the door. I heard his quick stride down the hall, and I was alone. I rose and went to the pile of scattered clothing. I left my nightgown there, but I put on my dressing gown. I was alone in his room, with his permission, by his insistence—this was the perfect opportunity to search it once more. But I was reluctant. I was suddenly afraid of what I might find, I was afraid of his secrets. The truth was I no longer wanted to know.

He's directing you. The thought came unbidden. *He's seduced you to keep you from looking, to keep you on his side.*

That was the truth, I knew it.

I looked at the desk, at the drawers I knew were locked. No, I thought. He'll be back any moment. I sat on the bed. I put my hands in my lap, meaning to wait. But then I was looking at the pile of ribands on the bedside table, the watch chain I knew was buried within them, and remembering how I'd meant to open the drawer to search for the key, and suddenly I was doing it.

Inside there were handkerchiefs—there must have been twenty or more, shoved about haphazardly, some of them stained with dark spots, spatterings. Blood, I thought in dismay, but then I lifted one out and I realized that blood would not have left such a stain as this—still bright, undiminished by washing. It was ink, or . . . or paint. Meant to look like blood, but not blood at all. I drew them out, one by one, and realized that they'd been deliberately marked, some with only small spots, others with more. Handkerchiefs devised to show he was consumptive.

I remembered Dorothy's words. *"When I found him, he was so thin and ill."* Her compassionate concern, her fear. He had appealed to her maternal instincts first, knowing, of course, that it was what would capture her—oh, he was shrewd.

Mulishly, I pulled out the last handkerchief, dropping it into my lap, and when I did, I heard another sound, a soft but heavy *plop* onto the carpet, and I looked down. There, lying beside my foot, was a key.

I shoved the handkerchiefs back into the drawer, and then I picked it up.

I went to the desk and fit the key within the lock, turning it until I heard the click. The drawer slid easily open.

Inside was a pile of notebooks, some leather bound, some bound in cardboard. I reached for the one on top, tooled leather, much finer than the others. I took it out and sank to the floor, leaning back against the bed, cradling the book in my lap, and then I turned over the cover to reveal pages scrawled with Michel's handwriting. It began with a date—January of last year—and then it was all notes, names I didn't recognize. Men's names, women's names, lists of their accomplishments, their children, their families. A compendium of the research he'd done on each one. I thought about what Benjamin had told me, about how Michel would have investigated Peter, and me. I turned the pages, knowing what I was looking for but afraid to find it. I turned until I came to August of last year.

Peter Atherton, it said.

I inhaled sharply.

Criminal attorney. Son of Paul and Elizabeth Atherton, née Van Ressauler, Knickerbockers. Wealth from real estate. Siblings: Paul Jr., Pamela, Penelope. Favorite son of his mother, who lived with him and his wife until dying in July of a wasting illness. Wore perfume of tuberoses and bergamot. Her favorite stones were rubies. Atherton wants above all things to speak to his mother again.

Was tutored at home. At eleven, tutored by Samuel Mason, who was abruptly fired one year later amid rumors of inappropriate behavior. Was sent away to relatives in Cambridge. Attended Harvard. Received law degree. Family attempted to match him with Ella Bishop, to no avail. Atherton apparently devoted to his work.

May 1854, after a brief and secret courtship, married Evelyn Graff, daughter of Joseph Charles Graff, investigator (called Charles by his family) and Martha (known as Mimi). Office on Lower Broadway. Mimi died of opiate overdose, though it was advertised as cholera. Graff died genuinely of cholera six months later—in early 1856. Atherton's family against the marriage initially for obvious reasons, until he insisted upon it. There are no children. Evelyn apparently accepted by society, though Atherton is usually without her, and v.versa. Is she dissatisfied? Has a lover or wants one?—something to pursue? Or is she one of those sexless women?

The notes on me and Peter ended there, and I sat staring at them. The things he knew, the ways he'd studied us. He'd reduced us to only words—such a little amount required to capture a life, a relationship. Some of it I had not known. Not Peter's tutor, nor the banishment to Cambridge, and not the courtship of Ella Bishop.

I heard a step in the hallway. I looked up just as the door opened and he came inside.

There was a moment of hesitation, and then he closed the door behind him and said, "Well. I confess you surprise me, *chère*. I'd thought it would take you more time than this."

"You're not consumptive," I said unnecessarily.

He shook his head and stepped over to me. He glanced down at the book I held, and then he sighed and went to the bed, lying down, pulling the pillow beneath his head, stretching out.

"You knew everything about me. Before I even stepped through Dorothy's door, you knew."

"Not everything," he said. "I didn't know how you moan when—"

"Don't."

He made a sound of impatience. "Come, Evie, how did you think I do it?"

"I never expected this kind of detail."

"It's the details that matter."

"You even knew Peter's mother's perfume—"

"Ah, very useful, that. At the right moment, a few drops on the tablecloth"—he acted it out in a gesture—"and *voilà*—the spirit is come."

"Does it never trouble you?"

"Does what trouble me?"

"The fact that it's not real."

"Grief is a terrible thing, eh? People are looking for comfort. If I can give it to them, what's the harm?"

"They give you things—they give you money—because they believe, but it's a lie."

He rose up on one elbow to look down on me. "Is that what worries you, *chère*? The fate of my immortal soul? You could change that, you know. You could save me. With one simple thing, you could do so."

"What's that?" I asked dully.

"Help me." He leaned over the edge of the bed, his hair falling forward to narrow his face. "It doesn't have to be a lie. It wouldn't be, if you were there, would it? Think of it: people would be comforted by their loved ones, and we would be rich. What's wrong with charging for such a service, hmmm?"

How he turned things, how he appealed to the part of me that wanted to justify my hunger for him.

"You planned all this. You planned to seduce me—"

"*Oui,* I planned to seduce you. But that was before I knew you, Evie. I didn't know then what you were—or what we are to each other."

I stared blindly at the notebook in my hands. "What we are to each other?"

"Come, you know it. You feel it. Why else are you here? We've an affinity with each other."

"You would lie about anything. No doubt you're lying about my—my *talent* as well. You've found some way to get into my mind, but it's only some kind of trick—"

"Ah, *chère,* I'm no miracle worker. How would I do that?"

"I don't know. I don't know! But you must have. What other explanation can there be, except that I'm insane?"

"How about that it's real?" He stroked my shoulder. "Why are you so afraid? You aren't your *maman.* You're stronger. You've her talent and your papa's brains and your own cunning. Think what you could do."

"I don't even believe in spirits."

"Maybe you should, since they're speaking in your head. You've let the world push you about, *chère.* Isn't it time to push back?"

I twisted to look at him. His eyes glittered in the light easing past the crack in the curtains like those of a mesmerist, a sorcerer. "Think of it," he whispered. "You could beat them all if you chose. The Athertons, the city, everyone. Take your life back. Make your own future."

His words tempted and cajoled. How easy it would be to believe, to enter into his game. *"Will you be the wolf? Or the rabbit?"*

"Let me help you. We can save each other, eh? You from hanging and me from certain damnation."

"I don't think I can trust you."

"All life's a risk, that's what makes it interesting." His hand fell to my breast. I felt the warmth of his fingers through the lawn of my robe. "In the end, there's only one thing you can believe. Bodies are honest; they don't lie."

"Jourdain's watching the way they move; he knows how they feel about that brother simply by the way they sit. . . ."

"Believe what's between us." Michel leaned closer and kissed me. When he pulled away again, leaving me breathless, he said, "At the next circle, I want you to bring Dorothy her sons."

"I can't control them that way—"

"You can," he said. His long fingers went to the buttons on my robe. I watched him unfasten them, one by one; I could not move my gaze, and I felt the heated deliberation of his touch. "You can do whatever you please, *chère,* don't you know it yet?"

23

A GUIDING SPIRIT

Forgive me for coming so early, my dear," Benjamin said as Lambert showed him into the parlor. He glanced at Michel, who was lounging on the settee, a glass of bourbon dangling from his hand. "I'd hoped to go over a few things about your case. Briefly, of course."

"Such dedication," Michel said. "*Madame* is lucky to have such a loyal servant."

Benjamin looked at me. "Is there somewhere private we might go?"

Michel rose, saying, "Never fear, I'll remove myself. The others should be arriving soon. I'll see to Dorothy."

"Your own dedication, sir, is admirable," Benjamin said.

"*Oui,* I am the best of sons." Michel made a little bow, and his glance slid to me for just a moment. My stomach jumped, and he smiled as if he knew it, and then he left.

I took a steadying breath and turned to Benjamin. In his presence, I regained my footing—I was the Evelyn I felt I should be, calm, reasoned, with moral compass firmly in place. He took my arm, leading me from the doorway to the French doors at the far wall. "You look different, Evie. Are you well?"

I could not hold his gaze. "Better now that you're here."

"Is something troubling you?"

His concern only made me feel guilty. I knew I could not explain to him what I'd done with Michel; I could barely explain it to myself.

"Evelyn?"

I glanced out at the side yard, at the marble urns flanking the doors. Pale green shoots poked from the dirt beside them. Snowdrops, or crocuses. "I *am* troubled," I admitted finally. "Dorothy told me that Peter meant to file papers committing her to an asylum. It was his way of stopping the adoption when Dorothy wouldn't listen to him."

"*Commitment* papers? When did he tell her this?"

"The night before he died. Michel said he thought Peter might be bluffing, but—"

"Jourdain knows you know this?"

"He was there when she told me. I couldn't avoid it."

"I see. Why does this trouble you, Evie?"

"Why would Peter punish Dorothy that way, when what he meant to do was prove Michel was a charlatan?"

Benjamin shrugged. "He would have done a great deal, I think, to keep Dorothy from adopting Jourdain, and bringing such a man into society. I wonder if Peter had those papers with him when he died?"

"I don't know. Dorothy said he never showed them to her."

Ben glanced behind us, and then he leaned close to me, saying, "If he did, then Jourdain may have them now. Can you get into his room again?"

I kept my expression as impassive as I could. "I think so."

"I received discovery from the prosecutor this morning. The police report says Peter's gun is missing. He carried it everywhere, but it wasn't on him when they pulled him from the river. Nor was a cuff link. He was wearing only one. It was gold, about this big"—Benjamin rounded his fingers to show me the size—"with an opal. Quite distinctive."

I didn't remember such a set. "I've never seen those."

"He hadn't had them long. They were a gift."

"A gift? From who?"

"Why, from me." Benjamin's expression became sorrowful. "He'd admired them in a shop window one day as we walked past. We'd just won the Ferguson case. It seems so long ago now." He roused himself. "I'll search the office to see if the commitment papers are there. I feel certain that if we find any of those things, we'll have found the truth of Peter's death."

"You don't think Peter was bluffing, then?"

"No, I don't. But it's to Jourdain's advantage to convince you the papers were a figment of Peter's imagination. They're another motive; he knows what he's about. The man fleeced half of New Orleans before he was run out."

"He was run out?"

Benjamin nodded. "He went through the Creoles there like a house afire, but the crowning touch was when he tried to swindle Andre Bizot, one of the most ruthless men in the city. He took over ten thousand dollars from him before Bizot realized it wasn't his wife's spirit he was talking to, but a maid Jourdain had seduced into speaking through a hole in the wall."

"How do you know this?"

"I've done some research of my own these last weeks. I wish I'd thought to do it before I urged Peter to go to him. I'd trusted what others said. . . ."

"You mustn't blame yourself," I said quietly, feeling more guilty and torn than ever.

Ben spoke bitterly. "Who else should I blame? I introduced them. Peter believed I was sending him to a reputable medium. My God, we'd known each other at Harvard, and the first thing I do when I see him again after so many years is lead him to this—" His voice broke. He paused, as if to recover himself. "All I can hope is that I haven't led you equally wrongly."

He took my arms and said urgently, "In the end, it doesn't

matter what Peter meant to do about Dorothy. He was killed. Now we must prove Jourdain did it."

As he'd spoken, his voice had grown both softer and more venomous, until his fingers tightened painfully on my arms. I tried to pull away.

"Ben, please. You're hurting me."

He inhaled deeply, dropping his hold, stepping back, passing his hand over his face. "Forgive me. I'm afraid I'm not myself when it comes to this case. I've put you here, into Jourdain's hands, just as I put Peter. . . . The days are passing quickly. You will hang if we don't prove that Michel is the true villain, Evie. Don't forget that."

"Believe me, I can't forget it," I said.

The others arrived. I heard Michel greeting them in the hall, and soon Benjamin and I went upstairs to meet them in the parlor. Dorothy looked wan and tired, but when I walked into the room I saw the way her eyes riveted to me, I saw the hunger on her face, and I understood Michel's directive to find her sons tonight. She was starving for them.

"Evelyn's here," she said in a loud voice. "Let's start. It's past time."

Benjamin pressed my arm and gave me a conspiratorial smile as we separated to go to our respective places. Then the lights were lowered, and we joined hands.

"Her sons," Michel reminded me in a whisper. Then he raised his voice to begin the prayers and the invocations. As the hymns started, his fingers moved on mine, a subtle stroking, and it was that touch that brought me back to his bed, and I found myself falling into that rhythm again—the rhythm of lovemaking, the soft, drowsy satisfaction of afterward, the surrender of my will.

The dream was easy to bring. I felt the call, the *shooshing* pull of myself into the fog, the peace it brought, the sense that everything was as it should be, that the present and the past and the future were all combined, and that I was one with all of it.

But then the peace was gone. I heard her voice in my head. *Didn't you feel me before? You must let me in when I ask.*

"Spirit, are you with us?"

I felt the stirring, the force against my throat, and then the satisfaction. "Yes."

Dorothy's voice, too eager. "Is this Johnny? Or Everett?"

The spirit was angry. I felt her impatience in the way she pressed against my skin, as if she meant to feel everything my body felt—the press of Michel's thigh against my skirts, the warm moist curl of fingers.

"They are not my errand. Why do you care for such trivial things?"

"Trivial?" The gasp came from Dorothy.

I felt as if I were floating, watching from a distance, from above, as Michel gave Dorothy a warning glance.

Soothingly, he said, "We wish to speak to Johnny or Everett Bennett. Bring them to us, and we'll hear your errand after."

I felt her twist with anger, pounding against the frame of my bones. I saw the things that came into her mind as if they belonged to me. I saw Michel leaning over her. Kissing her, touching her. I felt her longing and her anger. But she obeyed him. I felt the change within me, as if she'd stepped back to make room for another. A boy—no, a young man. He was not strong, but once inside he gasped, "Mama?"

I saw Dorothy pale and clutch her throat. "Everett?"

"We're here, Mama. Johnny and me. He tells me to remind you of the gray scarf."

"The gray scarf?"

"You remember it? He wants you to look for it."

"Oh, my dear boy—"

"There's something there. He won't tell me what. Look for it, Mama."

"I will. Oh, I promise I will."

"Don't forget."

"No. Of course not. Oh, my darling . . ."

"We worry over you, Mama."

"Are you well, Everett? Are you and Johnny well?"

The young man's power was wavering. I felt his weakness. He could not keep my heart beating, or my lungs filling. I felt his distress. "I must go. I'm happy, Mama. It's so beautiful. . . ."

I saw my head sag forward. My breath stopped, my heart faltered, but from where I watched, it all seemed so unimportant, so distant. I saw Michel lean forward, frowning.

The other spirit, the woman, gained control again. My head snapped up. My breath came in a whoosh.

"I brought you your son. Are you satisfied now?"

There was so much rage in the voice. And something else: smug satisfaction. "Who are you, spirit?" Robert Dudley burst out.

Her laughter was harsh and bubbling in my chest. "Don't you want to know my errand?"

"What is your errand?" Michel asked.

"Why, to see you again." The spirit bent my body toward him. The voice was flirtatious and angry at the same time.

You see? He did not expect this. You see how he starts? How he pales? He knows who I am. He knows what he's done. He played to your weakness, didn't he? He's done it before. He did it with me.

"To see Jourdain?" Wilson Maull asked. "Why?"

"It's nothing to do with you."

"Why are you here, spirit?" Dudley's voice again. Sterner, a little angry. "Who are you?"

"Quiet," Michel said softly.

And then her memory danced again before my eyes. It was dark—night, late—and she was running and breathless, racing through streets in a city I didn't know, though she did. She knew her way and was unerring even in her panic, past the gaslit part of town into the darker warren of wharves and storehouses where the smell of the river—ice and stinking mud and rotting fish— was strong, past drunken men who tried to catch her with tar-stained, rope-burned hands and who called out as she went by, "Hey, girlie, don't run away! Care for a fuck?"

She cursed them because they gave him a trail to follow. The street was narrow, rutted and slippery with frozen mud and snow, and she lost her footing in her thin boots, falling hard enough to jar her breath. The satchel she held went flying, skidding across the road, and she lost precious time battling her skirts to climb again to her feet, slipping to grab the bag again with fingers too numb with cold to curl around its handle. She turned to look over her shoulder, and there he was—dear God, she had not lost him after all; she had not escaped him, and he was still so angry, so much angrier than she'd imagined. She had never expected to be afraid of him, but now she knew she'd pushed him too far at last. Her fear filled me until I would have screamed to ease it. But she did not scream. Before her was a light, a tavern. If she could just reach it before he reached her . . .

You see now, don't you? Don't forget. Never forget.

"Spirit, will you answer us?"

"Don't you know who I am?" The voice—my voice—was colder, more needling. I felt the danger of her. I started across the divide; I wanted to stop her.

Grace Dudley's voice was high. "No, spirit, we don't know. Please, you must tell us. Why have you come to us? Who are you?"

The mist grew thicker, the veil stronger. She was trying to keep me out. She was laughing.

I was past the veil. I was pushing in.

Not yet. Not yet.

"Spirit, are you there?"

"I am here," said my voice, but it was thin as I tried to wrest control from her.

Let me speak. Listen to me. You are my errand.

She was taking up too much room. I could not get past her. And yet the danger I felt was increasing every moment.

"Who *are* you, spirit?"

Too late. Too late.

"My name is Adele."

I saw Michel's shock in the moment before all thought left me.

When I opened my eyes, I was myself again, and they were all staring at me as if something astounding had just happened. I felt as if I'd struggled loose from a dream, still hazy, loopy, too groggy to think. From somewhere, I heard a quiet sobbing.

"She's back," Dudley said. "Evelyn, is it you?"

"Yes, I'm here."

Michel was not beside me. He was kneeling at Dorothy's side, and she was clutching him, crying softly into his shoulder while he comforted her.

"Who is Adele?" Wilson asked.

"You must know, don't you, Michel?" Sarah asked. "She said she'd come to see you."

He lifted his head to look at us. "*Madame* Atherton seems ready to swoon."

The echo of the spirit's voice was still in my head; I felt her enmity toward Michel—an enmity colored with longing. I thought I heard a whisper. I jerked around to see who stood behind me, but there was no one, and I pressed my hand against my temple in sudden wooziness.

"Evelyn?" Robert asked. "Evelyn, what's wrong?"

"Let's get her to a chaise," Benjamin said.

I heard a chair scoot back. I felt a hand on my shoulder. "Come, Evelyn, you should rest. You look ready to fall over."

But even as Robert Dudley helped me rise, Benjamin was there, grabbing my arm, saying, "Allow me."

I felt a *whoosh* through my head, as if she had gone in one side and out the other, and I gasped. Benjamin pulled me close into his side. Dorothy's crying seemed a country away. I thought I smelled a strange perfume, something citrusy and woody, like orange blossoms mixed with sandalwood. Who wore such a perfume? Not Dorothy, and Grace eschewed scent. Sarah favored jasmine. I'd never smelled it before.

"Come along, my dear," Benjamin whispered. He led me to the chaise, and when I sank down upon it, I looked into his eyes.

"What is it?" I asked, confused. "Why are you angry?"

He glanced about, as if to make certain the others couldn't hear. Then he whispered, "How did you know?"

My head was pounding. "Know what?"

"I thought we understood each other, Evelyn. We're partners. But you said nothing of this! Did he tell you those things? Did he put you up to it?"

I pressed at my temple again, closing my eyes. "Tell me what? Put me up to what?"

"Did Jourdain tell you what to say during the spirit visit?"

"No. No." I shook my head—even that motion exhausted me. "I don't know. She's been coming to me. She's in my head. I can't keep her out."

"Evelyn, for God's sake. No one's near enough to hear. You don't need to pretend."

"I'm not pretending. She's been coming for days now. I meant to tell you. I—I thought I was going mad, but Michel says it's real and—"

"*Michel* says?"

"During our lessons," I explained weakly.

"Is that so? What else does he say?"

I felt nauseated. "That I inherited this from my mother. My dreams—"

"Are just dreams. You know not to believe him. We've spoken of this!"

"I don't . . . I can't . . . I see things I couldn't know otherwise."

"Things you couldn't know?" he repeated slowly. "Like what?"

"Things about Dorothy's sons."

A little roughly, he said, "Evie, you must tell me the truth.

What has Jourdain done to you? Has he given you something? Some drink, some—"

"Nothing. He's done nothing. He's given me nothing." I opened my eyes. The light made the pain flare, but I ignored it and grabbed his hand. "It doesn't make sense for him to do so. Why would he wish me to come between him and Dorothy?"

Ben's face was pale, his expression strained. He pulled his hand away impatiently. "I don't understand. What trick are you using? Why won't you tell me?"

His distress was real, but I could not think. I hurt, and I hadn't the strength to lie or dodge. With a sigh, I said, "I don't know how to explain it. I don't understand it myself."

Benjamin sat back thoughtfully. I heard the voices of the others swirling around me. Dorothy was no longer crying, and they were speaking in excited whispers.

"She could lecture," Sarah said eagerly. "She could fill the entire hall. If Kate Fox can with only rapping, think what Evelyn could accomplish!"

"Once the trial is over, we should take her to the conference, to the Sunday meetings—"

"And there's the spiritualist meeting in May!"

"If she's not in prison."

"The spirits won't allow that. I know they've come to help her."

Benjamin said quietly, "Grief does strange things to people. Peter hasn't been gone six weeks. Can you not admit that perhaps you aren't seeing things as clearly as you might?"

His voice sounded stiff, not like my Benjamin at all. This was what I'd been afraid of. I was losing him. Quickly I grasped at the excuse he offered. "Yes. I can admit that."

He leaned close. "We will save you, Evie. I promise it."

I closed my eyes. Eventually, I felt him ease away. Then, one by one, I heard the others go, tiptoeing past me, as if they thought I was asleep, and I was tired enough that I let them think it. I heard Dorothy's nurses lead her away; I heard her pause beside me.

"Evelyn, child," she said, and there was a reverence in her voice that seemed to vibrate, though I didn't open my eyes, and soon I heard her go too.

Still, I waited. Until she must be back in her room. Until I was truly alone.

"She's gone," he said. "They've all gone."

I opened my eyes. Michel stood at the table, his back to me. He was pinching out the candles; their thin gray smoke curled into the bronze leaves of the gasolier above.

"Who is she?" I asked.

He didn't pretend to misunderstand. "She's an affinity with you, it seems. She wishes to—"

"Don't lie to me. Why does she hate you?"

"She's dead. Why does it matter?"

"Because she's in my head. Because I want to know why."

He sighed. "I met her in Charlestown. She was a medium too, but not so talented as you, eh? She knew people, and I'd just come from New Orleans. She offered to help me, we became lovers. She had a husband who couldn't satisfy her, and I did."

"She fell in love with you," I said.

"She never said so, but I guessed it."

"And then?"

"I began to gain patrons. They liked me, and she grew jealous. There was no future for us. She was unhappy. I was sorry. In the end, she went back to her old life, and a few months later I heard she died."

"How?"

"She was killed."

"Killed? By whom?"

"I never knew. I guessed it was her husband. She left some of her things with me, and I kept them for the police, but they never came."

But his gaze had slid from mine, and I thought: *bodies don't lie.* He was not telling me the truth. Something about her frightened him. That, more than anything else, told me he wasn't lying when he said he believed these visitations were real. *He knows who I am,* she'd said. *He knows what he's done.* And I began to believe that maybe my visions were true. And if they were true, it meant she was here to guide me—hadn't the spirit writing told me to expect her?—and Michel knew it. If someone else had killed her, why did she not haunt that person? Why was she still so angry with him?

He came toward me. When he sat down beside me and caught my arm, holding me in place, I was afraid of him. But still his touch made me tremble; still, I wanted him so badly it was like a poison. When he kissed me I remembered the way he'd put his hand around my throat, and I knew I was a fool, but I could not resist him.

"I must check in on Dorothy," he whispered, drawing away. "I'll come to you after. Will you wait for me?"

I told myself to say no. I meant to say no. But my body leaped to his words as he must have known it would do.

"Don't be long," I told him.

It was as if the door between worlds, once open, could not be completely closed. She was there, in my head, vibrant and pretty, with hair lighter than mine and deep brown eyes. But her face was sharper, and there was a greediness to her that was avid and unpleasant. Her memories unspooled in my dreams as if they were mine: I saw a small room; a boardinghouse room. Ill furnished. A poorly sprung bed creaking with the rhythm of love-making. I heard her moans, and his deeper ones, whispered words in a Creole accent. Michel. And then it was quiet, and he was rising from the bed, distracted, dismissive, stumbling over the chamber pot so that it slopped on the floor, cursing beneath his breath. He went to the basin on a nearby table and poured water into it.

"Tell me about the woman again," he said. He bent over the

basin, splashing water into his face, and grabbed a cloth to wash himself. Then I saw her come from the bed. She went up to him, pressing her naked breasts against his back, wrapping her arms around him.

She kissed his shoulder. "Come back to bed. We can talk of her later."

He dropped the rag and turned, prying her hands loose, holding her from him. "*Non*. I want to be prepared. Tell me."

She tried to touch him. "We don't need her, dear heart. She's just an old woman. We could do six others in the time it would take to convince her."

He dropped her hands and stepped away from her with a sound of frustration, muttering, *"C'est une charrette à trois roues."*

"I don't understand."

He looked at her, tapping his finger against his temple. "You think too small, *chère*. Why do six circles for pennies when we could do one for so much more? You said she was rich, *oui*?"

"Yes. Yes, she's rich. But it would take so much time. You said you wanted to leave this place." She went to him, grabbing his arm. "He'll find us here. The longer we stay—"

"Why would he follow you if you were both as miserable as you say?"

"*I* was miserable. He's a fool, but if he came for me . . . Please, dear heart—"

"Just a few more weeks," Michel said.

"It's too long."

"Is this all you want?" He raised his hands, gesturing around the room in frustration. "Only this? You'd ask for no more? *Chère,* we can leave here with everything—or nothing. Which seems better to you?"

"It wouldn't be with nothing. We'd have each other."

His eyes narrowed. "I'm staying. Stay with me or not, as you like."

Her desperation was terrible. To leave without him, or to stay and risk everything. I felt her struggle. He walked away from her to where his clothes hung on a hook. His indifference chilled the room.

With a little cry, she ran to him. She grabbed him about the waist, forcing him to turn around, kissing his chest, his throat. "I'll stay. Of course I'll stay. Tell me what to do. Tell me what to say. Whatever you want. Please, Michel, I'm so sorry. What should I wear? The dressing gown again?"

His smile was cold and calculated. "For a group of women? *Non, chère,* tonight you must be as respectable as my wife."

I WOKE, AND it was deep in the night, so dark I could see nothing. Had I not heard Michel's deep, even breathing beside me, I would not have known where I was, or even who I was. The dream left a lingering taste, one too sour to simply swallow or spit away.

I remembered the words in the spirit writing—*To accept is to know. To know is to understand*—and Michel's advice: *trust your instincts.* And those instincts told me that if I found what had happened between Adele and Michel, I would discover the truth about Peter.

I turned my head on the pillow to look at Michel. He was sleeping on his stomach, one arm thrown over my hips, as if he meant to imprison me even in his sleep.

The desperation Adele had felt in the dream did not leave me for a long time, nor did the coldness of his smile.

24

A Very Old Scarf

WEDNESDAY, FEBRUARY 25, 1857

Late the next morning, Kitty brought word that Dorothy wished to see me, along with a note that had come from Benjamin.

When she was gone, I drew back into my bedroom and stood at the fire, fingering the note, remembering Ben's distress, and his anger that I might be keeping things from him. Then I noticed the stationery, which was printed with the law firm's name and address. This was an official missive. What new revelation would there be about my case this morning? And why had he not come to tell me himself?

My mouth was dry as I slit the envelope with my fingernail and opened the note. The writing was pinched and difficult to read—I had never seen Ben's handwriting before that I could remember, and I assumed this must be it, though it seemed at odds with his generous nature, and then, when I read the first words, I realized two things: he had penned it hastily, and it had little to do with my case.

My dear Evelyn,

Forgive my hurry—I'm on the way to a hearing—but I must talk with you this afternoon. I will call on you near one—it would please me greatly if you could meet with me, and if we could speak privately and candidly with each other. I am very worried for you, and disturbed at what is obviously Jourdain's growing influence. In short, I think it best that we find you other lodgings. I will speak to Judge Denham and Hall about it today.

With affection,
Ben

I stared down at the writing in dismay. I should never have told him the mediumship was not in my control. In a burst of irritation, I threw the letter into the fire and watched it burn. He would be here at one. I had that long to think of a way to relieve his suspicions, to convince him I should stay here. How was I to save myself if I did not have access to Michel? How could I possibly leave now?

The paper curled to ashes, and Dorothy waited for me, so I hurried out of my room and down the hall. Last night's visit of her sons had left her crying, and I had no real hope that I hadn't sent her into the same distress she'd experienced with their first visit. But neither had she called for Michel last night—early that morning, he'd returned to his room, but to save us from servants' gossip, not because Dorothy had sent for him.

I was relieved when I saw her smiling. She was sitting up in bed, and the curtains were open to let in the light, her cap tied neatly about her plump face. I could smell the faint taint of laudanum about her—no doubt Michel had dosed her well, though she did not seem the worse for it.

"Good morning, child," she said as I went to the usual chair. "I hope you slept well."

"It looks as if you did," I told her.

"They were with me," she said simply. "You are a miracle, Evelyn."

"I'm glad I could comfort you."

"You did more than that." She reached for a bundle that lay at her side, half hidden by the coverlet, and pulled it into her lap. It was a gray wool scarf, unraveling and stiff with what looked like mildew, and when she lifted it I could smell the mold and the dust. But she held it reverently in her hands, teary-eyed. "I sent Charley to find it this morning. Do you know what it is?"

"It looks to be a very old scarf."

"You don't remember what my boy said last night?"

It took a moment for me to remember and then it came to me like a distant memory.

"He told me to look for this scarf," Dorothy went on, and I was startled. I had just begun to believe my visions might be true, and this material proof of them shocked me into silence. I told myself it was just a scarf, but the sight of it raised a strange and frightening conviction within me.

Dorothy didn't lift her gaze from it; she twisted a loose, crinkled strand of yarn about her finger. "When Everett died, so soon after Johnny, I couldn't bear to go into the schoolroom. I just locked the door and walked away. I kept thinking I'd go there someday, but I never did, and then I got to be so old and feeble—such an old woman. Ah, well, you see how impossible it would be now."

She sighed. I said nothing, waiting.

"I made Johnny this scarf. I wasn't much of a knitter, and he never liked it. Too itchy, he used to say. But I made him wear it, and then one day, he said he lost it. Oh, I was so angry with him. I'd taken such trouble with it too—look here, see these tassels?" She held it out to me. "Took me all day to knot the dratted things, and then I didn't do it right, so the damn thing kept coming apart. But I was determined that he wear it. I repaired and repaired it. Stupid, isn't it? I could've bought a hundred cashmere ones, and he would've liked them better."

"When I was young," I confided, "my mother used to embroider handkerchiefs for me. But she was never content to just make borders or fancy corners. She turned them into tapestry—there was so much thread on them I couldn't use them." I smiled, re-membering, and then melancholy came over me. "There was a time later when I would have given anything for her to make me one of those handkerchiefs."

Dorothy nodded. "You see how it is, then, child. But you know, I'd forgotten all about the scarf until last night. It took Charley a couple hours to find it—it was shoved into the win-dowsill—there was a crack in the pane that one of the boys must have made and was trying to hide from me."

"No doubt they felt guilty over it," I offered. What else could I say?

"Oh, it wasn't the crack that mattered. It was what was on the scarf." She reached over to the bedside table, curving her gnarled fingers about something. "It was this."

She opened her hand to me, and lying on her palm was a brooch. It was obviously old, and quite expensive gold filigree, beautifully done, surrounding a huge square-cut emerald bor-dered with small diamonds. The stones were dulled from their years trapped within a molding scarf, but it would be a stunning piece once cleaned.

"It was my mother's. Johnny loved it. He would sit there sometimes while I dressed and beg me to put it on, and then he would say: 'Mama, it looks like mysteries in there,' and he would lean close, as if he could peer inside it." Dorothy shook her head, laughing a little. "He was the most inventive child."

"Why was it with the scarf?"

"It went missing one day. I couldn't find it anywhere. Of course, I thought Johnny had taken it, but he denied it over and over again." She sighed. "Of course he had. He'd pinned it to the scarf and forgot all about it, I suppose. Until you called him from the spheres." She looked up at me and held out the brooch. "I want you to have it, Evelyn."

For a moment, I thought I hadn't heard her correctly. I stared down at the jewel in her hand. "You can't mean that. It was your mother's. It's no doubt worth a fortune."

"It's worth a great deal, yes. But what you've brought me is priceless. The boys want you to have it. Why else would they have sent the message?"

I shook my head. "I owe you so much already. I can't possibly—"

"Child, I've lived a long time. I don't care anymore for material things, and I want to reward you. You could use it too, I think. It'd be yours alone. You can keep it or sell it, as you wish. I expect you could live on it for a year if you had to."

How potent her words were. I stared at the emerald, and suddenly I felt a great hunger for it, for the security it offered. *What's wrong with charging for such a service, hmmm?"*

"If you don't take it, it'll only go to Michel when I'm gone," Dorothy said.

I reached out. The piece still held the warmth of her hand as I took it into mine. Even through the grime, the diamonds bordering the emerald seemed to glimmer.

"If the Athertons keep on with their suit against you, you'll need more than that brooch," Dorothy said.

I glanced up at her. Her eyes were slightly narrowed, speculative, as if she were trying to take my measure.

"I can reward you handsomely, Evelyn, if you keep bringing my boys to me."

"What about Michel?"

"He won't want to share. But there's enough for both of you."

To say he wouldn't want to share was an understatement. He would be angry, and I had the sense that Dorothy not only knew that, but she was also deliberately making it so. I felt the work of her jealousy in this; she wanted to put a wedge between Michel and me.

I fingered the stone, rubbing at the dirt with the ball of my thumb. It raised an oily shine. The Athertons were trying to take everything from me, and I knew with desperate longing how

easily Dorothy's money could change that. My life could be returned to me. Another thought intruded, a small and niggling
seed of an idea that bloomed quickly into possibility. Would the
Athertons be so quick to prosecute if I were Dorothy Bennett's
heir? If Dorothy began to depend on me more than Michel, perhaps I could convince her that she no longer required him. I
needed protection, and Dorothy needed someone to leave a fortune to. Why shouldn't it be me?

"As you wish," I said finally. "You must know I'm your
servant."

"That's fine, child. That's good." She leaned her head back
against the pillow, yanking at the blankets as she did so.

I tucked the jewel into my pocket and rose, taking the blanket
from her hands, pulling it into place, tucking it securely around
her. "What a pity it is you didn't have a daughter to care for you."

"You're like a daughter to me."

"Well, I'll certainly try to be. All you need do is call, and I'll
come. I'll bring your sons whenever you wish it. But you may
have to convince Michel of the benefit. I suppose he feels they've
abandoned him for me."

She opened her eyes again, frowning. "He's said nothing like
that."

"I could be wrong. But . . . it's nothing, I suppose."

"What's nothing?"

"I think he feels they overstimulate you. I'm afraid that if you
told him how generous you were to me, it might give him another
reason to stop their coming."

She twisted her hand to grip my fingers. "Well then, we mustn't
tell him."

I hesitated. "Are you certain?"

"Good Lord, yes! I don't want anything to come between
me and my boys. You come to me when I call, child. You leave
Michel to me. I haven't signed those adoption papers yet, and he
knows it."

I smiled. "It will be our secret."

I FELT NICELY smug when I left Dorothy's room, and the brooch was a reassuring weight in my pocket. But my smugness lasted only a moment, because as I stepped into the hallway, I saw that Michel's bedroom door was open, and I heard him talking to one of the menservants. My body responded to his voice with a quick anticipation, a pull that was nearly irresistible. I could hardly be smug when he had this power over me.

The things I'd discussed with Dorothy were dangerous; I'd been plotting against him, and I knew that if he discovered it, he would try to stop me. The question was how. I retreated quickly to my room, but once I was there, I felt strange, light-headed and dizzy. I grabbed onto something—a chair—to steady myself as I felt the press from the other side; the bright light of day dimmed before my eyes. I heard her voice: *Listen to me. I've come to save you,* and I felt her flooding into me, taking over my thoughts and my pulse.

I was back in that boardinghouse room, and she was watching Michel from where she lay on the bed, and he on the end of it, writing feverishly with the nub of a pencil on the back of a broadside page, his sharply planed face too thin, taut with concentration, his hair falling forward to hide his eyes.

"Her family's wealthy," he was saying. "One of the oldest in New York City. Knickerbockers. And she married a Brahman." He made a sound, an amused snort. "A royal marriage of sorts."

Adele yawned. "What's a Knickerbocker?"

"Her sister lost two sons."

"Her sister? Does she live in Boston too?"

"She lost them to cholera and scarlet fever. Or diphtheria. *Mon dieu,* which is it?"

"Does it matter? She'll be amazed that you knew them to be dead at all."

He lifted his head to glare at her. "Do you say these things to annoy me, *chère,* or because you're truly stupid?"

She plunged out of bed, throwing herself at him so the paper crumpled and the pencil fell to the floor, and he had to catch her or be borne to the floor himself. "Why are you so mean to me? I hate it here, you know I do! Every day I expect to hear him knock on the door. I thought I saw him in the market—"

"It could've been anyone."

"He looked so angry! I can't go back to him. I won't! He hates me."

"I thought you said he loved you."

"He loves me, he hates me—oh, it's miserable! He's not a man. He's not like you. . . . Can't we just go now? You promised me France!"

"France takes money," he said coldly.

"He'll take me away. Doesn't that frighten you?"

He seemed to soften at her words. *"Oui."*

"Then let's go. We can find rich grieving women somewhere else."

"Where else, *chère?* To leave, we need money, eh? Or a patron. We've neither. This is our best chance."

"I don't need all this." She grabbed the paper from between them and crumpled it into a ball, which she pitched across the room. "The spirits come to me. You said so yourself. I hear their voices—"

"Oui."

"I heard Milo Grau's wife. And the Hawking child."

"After I told you about them," he pointed out. "Would you have heard them if I didn't tell you what to listen for?"

"You told me nothing about Ian."

"Your own son," he said patiently. "Who knew him better than you?"

She went very still upon his lap. "I could hear their voices without all your notes. They come to me."

"Would you care to try it, *chère?* In the middle of a circle, when they're all waiting to hear rapping from a loved one's spirit? Would you choose to leave it to chance?"

She pushed away from him, landing on the floor as gracefully as a cat. She paced to where she'd thrown the crumpled broadside and picked it up from the floor. "You doubt me?"

"It doesn't matter whether or not I do. You won't throw away the paper."

She marched to the chamber pot and lifted the lid. She threw the paper into it with a smile of satisfaction. "Really?"

Michel only smiled. "It's already in your head, *chère,* eh? Everything I told you."

"What if I forget it?"

"Then you'll fail. But if you fail, there'll be no money, and we'll stay here longer." He looked at the door. "Did I hear a knock?"

She froze, crossing her arms over her chemise-covered breasts. I felt her fear and saw how wild she looked with it until she realized he was laughing.

"How mean you are! I wonder sometimes if you hate me too."

His laughter died abruptly. "*Non.* Forgive me."

"What would you do if he came? Would you give me back to him?" She came to the bed. When he said nothing, she grabbed his shoulders, pressing her nails into his skin. "Would you?"

He wrapped his arms around her, pulling her onto the bed on top of him, but she held herself away. I felt her looking for truth as she stared into those elusive blue eyes. "Would you give me back to him?" she demanded.

"I would kill him," he said, and there was a matter-of-fact viciousness in his voice that thrilled her. "Would that make you happy, *chère?*"

THE VISION CLEARED, the shadows parted like mist in the sunlight, and I found myself bent over the chair, breathing hard and deeply nauseated from her possession. I barely made it to the chamber pot before I vomited. Afterward, I knelt there, pressing my hand to the tight band of my corset, gasping. The words

Michel had spoken in the vision stayed with me. *"I would kill him."* How easily he'd said them, as if murder was no more difficult than choosing the fabric for a frock coat.

The vision's heaviness was impossible; I could barely breathe. I wondered why she'd shown it to me, and when it had been. A year ago? Two? Or only months ago—even weeks? Who had they been talking about? What man had Michel been so ready to kill? An impossible thought came to me, but I could not dismiss it. I wondered if Robert Callahan had been right all those days ago, when he'd asked me if Peter had a mistress. Could that be the connection I'd sensed between Adele and my husband? Could she have been the reason Peter was killed?

I forced myself up. I went to the washbasin and splashed water into it and bathed my face, sprinkled tooth powder on my finger and rubbed it over my teeth, rinsed my mouth. I felt better then, but still I didn't know what it was Adele wanted from me, or what she meant to show me—except that Michel would kill to protect himself, that he had killed, and those things I knew already.

I needed desperately for someone to help me make sense of things. But Benjamin thought it was all an illusion bred of strain, and Michel . . . Michel was the guide I needed, but he was the one guide I could not use.

No, I must figure this out on my own. Adele was the key; I felt it now more than ever. I remembered what Michel had said, about her leaving some of her things, about how he'd kept them for the police that never came. I thought of the notebooks in his drawer—was she in those? Had he researched her as well as he'd researched me before he seduced her, before he made her his partner, before he sent her away? I felt the cool steadiness of deliberation come over me. *"You can do whatever you please,* chère. *Don't you know it yet?"* Yes, I did know it. I had managed Dorothy well enough, hadn't I? I opened my bedroom door and stood there for a moment, looking down the hallway. Dorothy's door was closed. The library was open. As was Michel's door. Which meant he must still be there.

I took a deep breath, and then I crossed the hall. If I must discover his plans for the day, the easiest thing to do would be to ask him.

He was inside. He was dressed but for his necktie, which he was twining about his neck, a great swath of a silver blue silk that matched the stripes in his vest. He glanced up when I appeared in his doorway, and then gestured impatiently for me to come in.

I stepped inside.

"Close the door," he said.

"I'd rather not. There's help everywhere."

He shrugged. "Then come closer. I don't wish to yell."

Obediently, I did as he asked, but I stayed near the desk as he watched himself in the bureau mirror.

"I heard Dorothy called for you," he said. "How was she?"

"Your dosage was perfect this morning. She seemed quite well."

He gave me a sideways glance as he looped his tie. "Charley said she sent him to the schoolroom to find the scarf. It's quite a breakthrough, *chère*. Congratulations. That room's been locked nearly twenty years."

"Yes. She was very happy."

"What did she say?"

"She said thank you."

"Ah." He finished the knot and turned to his bedside table, opening the drawer to search for a handkerchief. "She didn't offer you a gift?"

"She did. I refused it."

He looked at me in surprise. "Did you?"

"Yes, I've no need of such things." I glanced down at the inlay on the desk, tracing it with my finger.

"I'd say you had more need than most."

"I believe, after the trial, I'll have what I deserve."

"No doubt," he said quietly. Then, "Would you hand me that pin there? The sapphire."

I twisted around. The cloisonné box was open, his jewels spilled out as if he'd been going through them. The sapphire pin was there, tangled with rings and the watch chain—Peter's watch chain. My throat tightened when I saw it, and I could not help myself; I pulled it loose so the little fish dangled and sparkled, and the tears came suddenly to my eyes. I blinked them away and let the chain fall again from my fingers, and that was when I saw it:

A single gold cuff link with an opal.

The cuff links Ben had bought Peter. I hadn't remembered seeing them on Peter's wrist, but now I realized I *had* seen one before. I'd seen it here, on Michel's desk, in the cloisonné box, where it had no mate.

"Once we find that cuff link, or the gun, we'll know the truth of Peter's murder."

I felt queasy as I picked it up.

"Didn't you find it? It's right there." Michel was suddenly beside me. He reached past me for the sapphire pin. "These are the kinds of gifts Dorothy favors, eh? And she doesn't take no for an answer."

The opal sparkled against my palm. I couldn't take my eyes from it. "Not that you would ever say no."

"Non." I felt him pause. He plucked the jewel from my hand. "Where did that come from?"

I forced myself to say, "How would I know? It's yours."

"I must've picked it up somewhere. I don't remember it." He dropped it onto the desk. How nonchalant he was, what a consummate liar. Had I not known the truth, I would have believed him.

"It's quite beautiful."

"You're partial to opals?" He put one hand on my waist, drawing me close while the other swept my skirt, pressing. Against my lips, he whispered, "They aren't to my taste, but if you like, I'll wear them for you."

I tried to smile. "You've only one. I wonder where the mate is?"

"Perhaps you can persuade Dorothy to buy me its match," he

said. Then he stepped back—barely a step, and twisted his palm so that I saw what rested within it. The emerald brooch that had been in my pocket. "If she'll give you this, she'll give you whatever you ask."

I struggled for composure. "She didn't give me that. I brought it with me."

"You weren't allowed. You were to take nothing."

"No one knew I took it. It was my mother's."

His gaze swept my face; I forced myself not to look away. I saw the anger in his expression, and I knew it was because of the cuff link. I'd found it, and he knew I realized what it meant.

"Your mother? How did she afford such a piece?"

"I don't know. I was surprised myself."

Amazingly, I saw the anger pass from his eyes. "What a good liar you've turned out to be, *chère,*" he said with what sounded like genuine pride. The turnaround surprised me so much that I didn't move as he reached for me again. "Let me save us both from your guilty conscience, Evie. You earned it, and you deserve it. I would've told her to gift you had she not thought of it herself." He found again the slit of the pocket in my skirt and dropped the jewel back inside. Then he cupped my chin in his palm. His fingers pressed hard into my skin. "You've no need to lie to me, *chère*. I'm on your side—don't you know it yet?"

25

I'VE COME TO SAVE YOU

I returned hastily to my room. The proof I'd found that Michel was a murderer, incontrovertible at last, shook me in a way I could not explain. I'd known it already, hadn't I? Why then should this disturb me so?

My room felt too small to contain the mix of my anxiety and fear. There was a heaviness behind my eyes, the press of tears, which I kept back through sheer will. Finally I went downstairs and grabbed my cloak, resolving to go out into the garden, even as chilly as it was. I wanted clean air, something bracing to clear my head.

The day smelled of mud. The budless, bare tree branches bounced in a light breeze that was still sharp enough to cut through the heaviness of my cloak.

I glanced over my shoulder to the windows that winked unseeingly back at me—impossible to see through the glare of the world that they reflected. I could not tell if someone watched me from those windows, and the thought made me shudder and pull my hood closer about my face. I went to sit on one of the stone benches that dotted the yard, beneath the outstretched arm of Apollo, which was blackened and mottled with mildew and dirt.

The freezing cold of the stone seeped through my cloak and my skirts and my petticoats. A rose planted in the flower bed trailed its thorny canes to snag on the soft kid of my glove, its few brown-yellow leaves and withered hips a poor decoration.

I closed my eyes and let the smells and the feel of the breeze and the cold lull me. But I felt *her* there too, just beyond the world, waiting for me. *No, not now,* I told her. *I don't want to know any more. Not today.* I pushed her aside and rose from the bench; I made a promenade about the yard.

And then, though it seemed much too soon, I saw someone— a man—come from the side of the house into the backyard. His coat flapped with the hurry of his stride. His top hat glimmered.

Benjamin.

I nearly ran across the muddied grass to meet him and threw myself into his arms. He grasped me as if he didn't quite know what to do, and then he held me close. I smelled tobacco in the fur of his collar. I hadn't known he smoked. How odd not to know it.

"Dear God, I'm glad you've come," I said.

After a moment, he held me away. "Evelyn? You look as if you've seen a ghost."

The inadvertent aptness of his statement made me flinch. I led him back to the bench, where we sat down, and I glanced involuntarily up at the library window. Did I imagine it, or was there a flash of light there, like the sun glancing off a jewel—perhaps a sapphire?

I turned quickly back to Benjamin. "I found the cuff link. It's in his room, as you said it would be."

His face broke into a smile. "Excellent! You see, my dear, I told you! Oh, this is very good news. Where is it now?"

I felt a stab of uncertainty. "Should I have taken it?"

"No. No. You must leave it there for the police. They'll need to find it. Why do you look that way?"

"I was just so surprised to see it. I wasn't even looking for it—"

He went very still. "I don't know if I take your meaning."

"Michel was there when I found it," I said. "He asked me to get him a pin, and it was just there. As if he never meant to hide it at all."

"Why were you in his room, Evie, when he was there as well?"

I looked at him quickly. "He asked me to come in. He wanted to speak with me a moment."

"You were alone with him?"

"The door was open. And Dorothy's an invalid, Benjamin. We're often alone."

"But not in his bedchamber, I'll warrant. Or are you?" His cheeks were flushed.

"No. No, of course not."

He made a sound of exasperation. "Has he tried to seduce you, Evelyn?"

"You yourself warned me he would do so. It's in his nature."

"And has he succeeded?"

I took a deep breath. *Bodies don't lie,* Michel had said, and now I used that to my advantage. I looked at Benjamin directly, though it took great effort not to glance away, not to hesitate. "No, Benjamin. He has not."

I knew a profound relief when he sighed, when he said, "Forgive me. He's succeeded so often. . . ."

I touched his arm to reassure. "I understand."

"I am embarrassed," he said with a shamefaced smile. "It's only that I care a great deal for you. Do you mind?"

"Not at all. In fact, I'm glad to hear you say it."

He looked down at his gloved hands, his fingers clenching and unclenching. "I could not bear it if he . . ." He shook his head, letting the words remain unspoken. Then, grimly, he said, "I must admit to some disappointment that Jourdain knows you found the cuff link. No doubt he'll move it now, and, of course, it puts you in greater danger. I managed to speak with Hall today, but as you can imagine, he's quite against your leaving here, even if we could find another patron. He's insistent upon the Tombs. But never fear. Once I speak to Denham—"

"Have you told them what we've found so far?"

"We don't have enough to convince them, I'm afraid. And surely not enough to dismiss your case. We've only Dorothy to testify to the adoption and the commitment, and she will hardly agree to incriminate Jourdain. You haven't found the gun. You're living in the house—they might believe you put the cuff link there yourself. Unfortunately, there's no sign of the commitment papers at the office. Peter's assistant doesn't remember them at all. Peter must have done them alone and kept them secret."

I nodded, and then I summoned my courage. "There's one other thing, Benjamin. I think . . . I think Michel may have killed someone else. Someone besides Peter."

He looked surprised. "Who?"

"The spirit that came to me the other night. Adele."

Ben went very still. "Adele?"

"He said he'd known her. That they were together for a while, but then he sent her away. He said she was killed."

"Evie." Benjamin's voice was dangerously soft. "Don't tell me you're putting credence into a 'spirit visitation.' Not after our talk last night?"

"I know you think it's an illusion, Benjamin. But I know things I couldn't know—"

"Are you certain you haven't overheard these things somehow? The mind plays tricks all the time. Until I can talk to Denham, I've no choice but to leave you here. I'd be less concerned about it if you would do what I ask now and leave this all alone."

Doggedly, I persisted. "It doesn't feel like a hallucination."

"Are you still having nightmares? Are you sleeping?"

I looked away.

"You see, all this is easy to explain. You're not getting enough rest; you must deal with pretense every moment of the day. You must get some sleep or you truly will go mad."

"Sometimes I feel as if I already am."

"This is how such things work," he said gently. "One delusion grows upon another. Think of your father: would he be so quick to accept this? Or would he investigate until he found the reasons?"

His words lent me courage. "He would find the reasons."

"And that is what you must do as well. You're in a household that believes in spirit guidance. Jourdain is doing everything he can to convince Dorothy and the others of its truth. You're working tirelessly to save yourself. Doesn't it occur to you that these things may be feeding the hallucinations? That these visions have no outward cause, but are simply your own imagination? Don't you think Jourdain is doing what he can to cause them as well?"

"How would he do so?"

"Your lessons, for one thing. He's part mesmerist, Evie. Have you any doubt of his ability to use others? Look at the slave he's made of Dorothy." He sighed. "I'll get you out of this house as soon as I can, but in the meantime, stay away from him. These visions of yours will disappear when the strain does, I promise it."

I nodded obediently at his words, but I was troubled.

Ben smiled; it was thin. "Promise me you'll stay away from him."

"But Dorothy expects—"

"Promise me." Ben's eyes were bright with an intensity that made me uncomfortable.

"Very well," I said.

He let out a breath. "Excellent. Now I fear I must go. Shall I walk you inside?"

"Thank you, no. I think I'll stay in the garden a while longer."

He did something surprising then. He took me in his arms, pulling me into the cold wool of his coat, the broad expanse of his chest. My face was buried in the fur collar, and he held me so tightly I couldn't move to breathe. I felt his kiss upon my hair. It was an uncharacteristic display of affection, and one I had wished for. But when he released me, I was oddly relieved.

With a smile and a good-bye, he was gone.

I had not truly expected him to believe my suspicions about

Adele, but it disturbed me that he dismissed them so readily, the way a man might do when confronted with a slightly unbalanced woman. I felt foolish for confiding in him. And what he'd said about my overhearing conversations unknowingly bothered me too.

Was Benjamin right? Had Michel perhaps said Adele's name to me one day? Had I heard him call it? Was it all just a dream wrought of my imagination? Bits and pieces of things I'd heard or seen?

I looked up, past Apollo's grayed marble arm to the winter clouds sweeping over a watery blue sky. Every color seemed thin, like a watercolor wash over charcoal, as if I were watching it through a veil.

I heard her whisper in my ear.

I've come to save you.

I felt her nudge, the press against my skin. Everything before my eyes fell away. I saw only the haze, the distance that seemed to pull me with it as it receded, and then it changed like smoke shifting with the direction of the wind, and I was once again in the dream of her life, helpless to look away, because it filled my head, it was my memory now

She was in a room strange to me, but not to her. She knew it well. It wasn't the boardinghouse room, but a parlor, lavishly appointed, cluttered with bric-a-brac and gilded mirrors, paintings along every square inch of wall above the wainscoting, a huge Chinese vase with peacock feathers in the corner.

The heavy rust-colored drapes were drawn, and the room was dim, the gaslight off, the only light coming from the candles standing in the middle of a large round table. They flickered in the collective breaths of those gathered around it, jerking madly when someone—Michel—coughed, the light falling across their faces in an exchange of yellow and shadow, making them all look weird and fantastical. There was Michel, and Adele next to him, and then, alternating, three other men, three matronly women.

"Oh, spirits, please send one of you to guide us. Speak with us, spirit. Hear our call." It was Adele who spoke. I felt her confidence, her sheer exaltation at her power. Her voice rose until it seemed to fill the room. "Spirits, has one of you come to talk with us?"

There was a rap. I felt her thrill at it.

"Are you there, spirit?"

RAP RAP RAP.

"Who has come to speak with us tonight?"

RAP RAP RAP RAP RAP.

"It wants the alphabet." One of the women, resplendent in frills and heavy gold chains that rose and fell upon her ample bosom with every breath, spoke in a rush.

Someone else—a man—called out, "*A, B, C, D—*"

RAP.

"*D!*"

"*A—*"

RAP.

"*A, B, C, D . . .*" It went on, spelling out slowly and inexorably.

"Daniel," said the woman in the gold chains. "Dear Lord. Is this Daniel come to speak with us?"

Adele was confused. *Daniel? Who was Daniel?* She closed her eyes, trying to hear his voice, to see him as she'd seen others before. *Daniel?* She had not been expecting that name, but another. Hadn't Michel told her the name was Richard? Yes, Richard. A beloved uncle who'd died of consumption. Who was Daniel? Why had Michel rapped to that name?

RAP RAP RAP.

"Yes." The gold-chained woman's voice was breathless. "Oh, it is Daniel!"

"Ask him what happened," urged one of the men. "Everyone's wondered. Where was he?"

Nervously, Adele squeezed Michel's hand. "Can you tell us what happened to you, spirit?" she asked, and then she tried to listen for the voice. It didn't come. How could that be? Her mind was empty. She felt cold sweat in her armpits, trickling between her breasts.

"Where were you, my love?" whispered the gold-chained woman. "Please tell us what happened. I have wondered so."

Nothing.

"What's he saying?" another of the men asked. "Is he answering? Adele, what's he say? Did he die as they told us he did?"

Her mouth was dry. She licked her lips. "Yes. He says he died—"

"On the ship or in the raft after?"

"Ssshhh," one of the men hushed. "Remember, we're supposed to test the spirit first."

Adele swallowed. "On the ship," she said, taking a chance, hoping it was true, because no voice came to her, nothing. She didn't even know who this Daniel was. She slitted her eyes open, looking sideways at Michel, who said nothing, did nothing. She squeezed his hand again, asking for his help.

"On the ship?" the gold-chained woman asked, clearly incredulous. "But that's not what they told us!"

"Perhaps it's not really Daniel, Sally. We're to test the spirit first. Ask it something else."

The woman called Sally nodded. "Did you feel pain, my love?"

"We've no way of knowing that for certain," another woman said. "Sally, we need a test. Here, I'll do it. What was your job on earth, spirit?"

I felt Adele's panic. Her fingers dug into Michel's hand.

"What was your job, Daniel?"

Nothing. How could there be nothing? Where was the spirit? Why couldn't she hear him?

"Why isn't he answering?" One of the men turned to Michel. "What's wrong with her?"

They were waiting; she felt them all waiting. Why didn't Michel say something? Why didn't he help her?

"Is the spirit still here? Daniel, are you still here?" Sally asked plaintively.

She was failing. Failing, just as he'd said she would—

"I'm here." It was Michel's voice, but deeper, not completely his own. Adele's relief was so dizzying she barely heard it. The others at the table turned to him with alacrity.

"Daniel?"

"I was a sailor," Michel said. His eyes were closed, his breathing deep and even. "The ship broke apart. There was screaming, Mother—it was terrible. But I made it to the raft. I thought I would be saved. But no one came. Not for days and days."

Sally's voice caught on a sob.

Michel said, "I'm at peace now, Mother, and you should be too. The end was kind, and I was glad for it. And now I live in such love."

Adele stared at him. She had forgotten how good he was. In these last months, he had been only a man, her lover. He had been too busy training her, because he'd said people trusted a woman more than they did a man, and this aspect of him had disappeared.

"Oh, my dear love," Sally said. "To think of you suffering—"

"The suffering was nothing. The peace and love I feel now, that is what you should know, Mother. When your time comes to join me, you will understand."

Sally dissolved into quiet sobs. There was silence but for the sound. Then Adele felt Michel stir beside her. He opened his eyes, blinking, and then he said, in his own voice, "The spirit is gone."

The circle broke apart. The lights were turned up. They began to mill about, each of them buoyed by an eerie excitement, an energy born of contact with the spirits. Adele rose, anxious for their accolades, but no one turned to her. Instead, they flocked to Michel.

"How talented you are, my boy! Why did we never see it before now?"

"You spoke in his voice. My dear son's voice!" Sally clung to his arm, burying her face in his shoulder, and he wrapped his free arm about her and held her close, comforting her with a quiet smile.

"*Madame,* it wasn't me. The spirits find affinity where they will."

"Yes, it makes sense that he would find his way to you. You're so like him, really, Mr. Jourdain. So much like him."

I stood in the background, watching through Adele's eyes. I felt her growing envy, along with her anger. Michel glanced at her over the crowd surrounding him, and suddenly she knew: he had done this on purpose. He had told her about Richard, but not about Daniel. He had meant for her to fail.

"Could we speak with him again?" Sally asked, her eyes bright with tears and a fierce longing. "Can you call him for me?"

Michel said, "It would be difficult tonight." He began to cough. That horrible, consumptive cough he'd perfected, and Sally clung to his arm, watching him in dismay. When he reached for his handkerchief, saying, "Pardon, *Madame,*" she cried, "How ill you are!"

"It's nothing," he said into the handkerchief. "A hazard of boardinghouses, I'm afraid."

"Of course. I didn't think. How draining it must be for one of your constitution." She turned to the maid, who was bringing tea. "Bridget, prepare a room for Mr. Jourdain. The red one."

"*Madame—*"

"You must stay with me," she said. "I insist. You'll be my guest. Please, Mr. Jourdain, nothing would give me more pleasure."

Adele stepped forward. "If you please, Mrs. Bayley, we've our own rooms—"

Michel's glare cut her off. "But we'd be pleased to accept your offer, *Madame*. You're most kind."

"You must call me Sally," the woman said. "And you must stay as long as you like."

Then, it was later, and Adele lay in a bed canopied with red velvet and golden fringe, watching Michel as he stood at the window.

"You didn't tell me about Daniel," she accused.

"Of course I did. You weren't listening, *chère*."

"You meant to do this. You meant to make me look like a fool."

"You don't need my help for that."

She was enraged. She clutched the bedcovers to control her temper. "I don't want to stay here. I want to go home."

"Home? Where is that? You mean your little cottage?" His voice was mocking, needling. Adele's anger fled in cold fear.

"I meant the boardinghouse. *Our* rooms—"

"I'm not going back there," he said.

"You can't mean for us to stay here."

"*Non.* Not *us.*"

"What do you mean?"

"I mean I'm sending you back, *chère*. It was entertaining for a while, eh? But now I think your husband's been without you long enough. No doubt he misses your tempers and your silliness."

"You can't mean this, Michel." She pushed back the covers, running to him, clinging to him. He didn't even turn. He was hard as stone. "Please, dear heart, you can't. You need me!"

"Not anymore," he said, and his voice was soft and deadly.

THE SCENE SWEPT away like clouds before a wind, and once again Adele was in the dark alleys of the riverside. Once again she was running, and I felt her fear, her gasp of breath as if it were mine. And then he was there, grabbing her arm, pulling her back, and her cry was cut off so abruptly it was as if it had never been.

The vision dissolved, and I was pulled into myself again. I woke drained and nearly numb with cold. My legs were clumsy as I rose; I could no longer feel my fingers. I had no idea how long I'd been out here. The remnants of Adele still hovered about me, shadows I tried to fight through as I made my way into the house. It was time to discover what Adele meant for me to find.

26

WHAT SHE LEFT BEHIND

I took off my cloak and gloves and went upstairs. The door to Michel's bedroom was closed; as I passed, I stopped, trying the handle as quietly as I could. It was locked. Of course, it would be now that he knew what I'd found.

I heard a sound from the library, a movement. I went down the hall, stepping between the open double doors and into the green-and-gold-papered library, with its walls of polished maple shelves and leather-bound books and huge window that over-looked the backyard.

He was before the window, staring outside. The light haloed his hair and limned him. He could almost have been an angel standing there, except that I knew he was not.

I'd thought he hadn't heard me, but he turned. He was angry. "How's Dorothy?" I asked him.

"Sleeping the sleep of the blessed." His voice was sharp. "And your assignation with Rampling?"

Uncomfortably, I remembered the flash of light I'd seen through the window. "It went well enough. He came to discuss my case."

"Did he? Most clients don't go running into their lawyer's arms. But perhaps I'm wrong. I've so little experience with it, you see."

"Benjamin and I are good friends. You know that."

"*Oui.* The inevitable husband." He turned again to the window. His mood was strange. Not just angry, I realized, but something else. I took a risk and feigned ignorance. "Are you angry with me?"

He laughed—it was short and bitter. Then he made a sound of frustration, bringing his hands together, as if he were strangling an invisible neck. "*Jésus,* what you've done to me . . ."

I took an involuntary step back. "I've done nothing. You've brought it all on yourself."

He snorted. "D'you love him?"

"You're jealous!"

"I find I've a possessive soul after all." His smile was wry. "What am I to think? You lie to me. You leave my bed to run into his arms."

I had not expected this, but I knew well enough to take advantage of it.

"Suppose you tell me why you would lie to me about the jewel Dorothy gave you. Or what it was that brought Rampling today running to you like a slave?"

I touched his arm, and when he stiffened, I stroked up his sleeve to his shoulder. I felt his tension radiate into my fingertips. "I didn't tell you about the jewel because I was afraid you'd be angry. It's worth a great deal, Dorothy said, and I felt guilty. After all, if the adoption goes through, it would've been yours. And I need it so very much."

"Very pretty, *chère.* And Rampling?"

"After the circle last night, Benjamin and I argued. I wanted to reassure him."

"About what?"

"That we were still friends." I eased my fingers between the buttons on his vest. "And yes, that I still regard him as possibly more than that."

"Do you really think he'll marry you? Even if you aren't found guilty, you'll be an accused murderess. Do you think your upper ten'll forget it? Do you think he'll sacrifice everything he's gained to keep you?"

My fingers stilled on the buttons. "He's already taken on the upper ten for me. He's taken on the Athertons."

"That isn't the same as marrying you." He made a sound of disbelief. "Why don't you see that you don't need him? You could make them all dance to your tune, if you wanted. Look at how well you managed Dorothy! The game belongs to you, Evie. Why the hell do you want Rampling? He doesn't understand you."

I struggled to steady my breath, to remember my task. "You're at Dorothy's beck and call. Not only must I share you with her, but your former lover keeps her constant presence in my head. Do you think I've no cause to be jealous myself?"

"Dorothy's a task, you know that. And as for Adele, there's no reason for jealousy."

"She says differently."

"We parted badly. She would lie to you."

"You claim to understand people so well." I slipped one button of his vest loose, and then another. "But how well can you understand a woman, truly? You said it yourself. We've sensitive nerves; we feel things men don't." The buttons were all undone. I pressed my hand against his shirt, and then I trailed down to his trousers. "I think she meant something to you. After all, you kept the things she left behind."

"For the police." He sounded strangled.

"Ah, but how can I believe that, knowing you as I do? You were working on Dorothy Bennett even then, weren't you? How could you want the police anywhere around? I think you kept those things because you cared for her—"

He caught my wrist, stilling it. "How little you know of it, *chère*." He jerked me against him, kissing me with such violence that his teeth ground against mine, and when I tried to pull away, he wouldn't let me. When I managed to say, "The door—" he glanced up, and then without a word he grabbed my arm, pausing only a moment to be sure the hall was clear before he propelled me from the library and down the hallway toward his bedroom. Once we were there, he fished in his pocket for the key and then he hauled me inside impatiently.

He didn't loose his hold on my arm as he relocked the door, but I felt the way the simple turn of the key restored him. When he turned back to me, it was with a slow thoughtfulness, but I knew how hard had been his struggle to curb his violence and his temper. He was breathing as heavily as I was.

THE BRONZE CLOCK on the mantel of the fireplace read midnight. We had gone without supper, and he'd left me long enough to retrieve some bread and cheese from the kitchen, which we'd eaten by the low-wicked light of the oil lamp on the bedside table. My legs were tangled with his beneath the sheets, my body pressed into the lean hardness of his side. He was playing with my hair where it spread across his chest, spinning strands of it around his finger and then letting it fall loose only to spin it again; the gentle, rhythmic tugging lulled me into a half sleep.

Then he said, "What does she say to you?"

The question roused me. I heard his uncertainty, and I turned my head into his chest, smiling against his skin. I knew who he meant; I didn't bother to pretend otherwise.

"It's not what she says, it's what she shows me. How cruel you were."

"I was never cruel to her"—a pause—"or perhaps I was. We weren't a good match."

"So when you could no longer use her, you sent her away?"

"*Oui.*" His finger spun my hair. I felt the little sting at my scalp as he pulled too tight. "I don't doubt she hates me. Or that she wants vengeance. You mustn't trust her, *chère*. She'd lie to hurt me."

"Why?"

He was silent.

"Let me see what she left behind," I whispered.

He made a sound of frustration and pulled away, dislodging me as he climbed from the bed and went naked to the armoire in the corner. His movements were tight and angry as he opened the door, as he rummaged through it. Then, finally, he turned, holding a small carpetbag—the same one she'd been carrying in my vision?

"Here," he said, throwing it so it landed with a soft thump on the bed. "Do what you want with it. Burn it if you like."

I grabbed it and pulled it close. When I touched it, I smelled her perfume. Citrusy, woodsy. "What's inside?"

He shrugged. "Some clothes. A brush."

I sat up, pulling the sheet up to cover my breasts, and took the bag into my lap. Michel came and sat on the edge of the bed, rubbing his face in his hands, his back to me.

I felt the tension of his waiting, and my own curiosity, my certainty that Adele held the answers to my questions, made me undo the clasp; it clicked softly, and then I pulled it open.

Her scent wafted so powerfully I found myself lurching back, as if her spirit came with it. Then I reached inside. My fingers encountered softness—fabric, fine and thin—and I drew it out. A dressing gown, decorated with ribbons and lace, of a lawn so sheer it would be almost indecent to wear it. I ran it through my fingers, searching it for some clue, though I hardly knew what I was looking for. Bloodstains, perhaps? A rip in the fabric to show how she'd died? But then I remembered the vision, and I knew she'd been wearing a dress when she died. Not this. I would have recognized this.

"A pretty thing," I said softly.

He looked over his shoulder. "A gift I bought her. She wore it at the circles."

"This? But it's indecent."

"You've so much to learn. She wore a chemise under it. It was for the men, eh? When they wanted to contact a spirit. It made them more willing to believe."

"I imagine," I said dryly.

"For the women, it was different. She pretended to be my wife."

"Yes. She would need to be respectable for them."

"I may make a charlatan of you yet."

I pushed the dressing gown aside and reached in again, bringing out a silver-backed hand mirror, a brush that still held strands of her brown hair. It was a beautiful set, and old. I held the mirror in my hand, fingering the tooled silver. "She meant to come back. No woman leaves something like this."

He said nothing. The next thing I drew out was a scarf—a beautiful paisley in greens and blues. I set it aside.

There was nothing more. In disappointment, I shoved the bag away. But then I heard something slide within it, and with a frown, I drew it back again and felt all over the bottom, into the pocket that lined the inside. And there in the corner, I felt it. A fine chain gathered in a little pile. I pulled it out.

It was a silver chain, very lovely and delicate, and swinging from it was a locket, a silver oval, delicate as well. I placed it in my palm, letting the chain fall between my fingers.

"A locket." Carefully, I pried it open. Inside was a lock of hair, very like the lock of Peter's hair I kept in mine, but this was dark, and it was a little curl, tied with a tiny cream-colored ribbon. On the other side, there was an engraving. I leaned close to read it. *To my Addy—* It was hard to see. I tilted the locket closer to the lamplight, and when I did, the curl of hair fell out, revealing more writing beneath, the continuation of the sentiment. *Your husband, Ben.*

I glanced up at Michel, who was watching me closely. "What was her surname?"

"LaFleur, when I met her. After a while, she used mine."

"Was that her married name?"

"I never asked her. I assumed so."

I shoved the curl of hair back inside and closed the locket. "Did you meet her husband?"

"*Non*. I try to avoid duels if I can, *chère*."

I looked back down at the necklace.

Benjamin was a common enough name. No doubt there were hundreds of men named Benjamin with dark hair. And LaFleur was . . . what kind of name was that? It didn't seem common at all, but neither did it seem quite real. Michel had said she was a medium when he'd met her. Many mediums took assumed names. Perhaps even Michel's was one. And I knew from my visions that this medium was hiding from her husband. Suddenly my thought that she might have been Peter's mistress seemed wrong. But Peter had never said anything to me about Benjamin having had a wife. Benjamin himself had never alluded to it. It could not be the same Ben. Of course it was not.

"What is it, Evie?" Michel asked.

I glanced up at him. His face was gaunt in the shadows cast by the lamp.

"Nothing," I said, curling my hand around the locket. "The necklace is from her husband, that's all. Odd that she would keep it after she'd run away from him."

"Women do many odd things," he said. He motioned to Adele's things, spread as they were on the bed. "Did you learn what you expected?"

"She didn't want to leave you. She loved you."

His expression was veiled. "I'm irresistible, eh? But you knew that already."

"Yes. I knew that."

He swept aside the dressing gown, the scarf, the brush set, and crawled across the bed toward me. "So she meant to return and didn't. Perhaps she changed her mind."

"Or she couldn't. You said she was killed."

"Months after."

"Was it so long?"

"It was a long time ago. She doesn't matter to me. She never did." He kissed my shoulder. "Enough questions. Don't be jealous, *chère*. She isn't here. Don't let her come between us. Please, Evie. Control her."

His whisper was lulling, but I knew he had other reasons for wanting me to keep her out. I knew he was afraid. I felt it in the way he clutched me, as if his sheer possession was enough to command me, and I let him believe it. And as my body leaped to his touch, as I twisted beneath him, I felt her just beyond my consciousness, watching. She waited patiently, and she pushed inside. When I reached my release, she took it all, she filled my head, and I knew—though Michel did not—that it was not me with whom he'd just made love, but Adele.

I WOKE JUST before dawn. Michel was asleep beside me, and carefully I lifted his arm from where it curled about my body and moved from beneath it. He made a sound of protest, but he didn't wake. The carpetbag, Adele's things, had fallen to the floor, and I left them there—except for the locket, which I saw glimmering in the faint blue light in a wrinkle of the bedspread. I picked it up and climbed carefully from the bed, slipping into my chemise, which was piled upon the floor, and bundling my other clothes in my arms.

I heard no noise yet, and I crept down the hallway and into my bedroom. My clothes I hung carefully, but I kept the necklace tight in my hand as I went into my own bed. I lay there against the pillows, letting the chain swing from my fingers, watching the back and forth pendulum of the locket. I needed to know more about her, and I could not trust Michel for the answers.

I must have stared at that necklace for hours. Finally, I rose and went to the armoire. I had already tucked away the brooch Dorothy had given me in the pocket of one of my gowns, and now I did the same thing with the locket, and hung two other gowns over it. Michel had proved how easy it was for him to come into my room, locked or not; I did not think he would take the time to search through all my clothes, and any other hiding place was too obvious.

When Kitty came, I bade her dress me quickly and call me a carriage. I did not tell anyone I was going, and no one was around to question me as I left. As I boarded the carriage, I saw the police watchman start to attention. The morning was cold, the sky overcast with clouds that signaled icy rain. Though I'd seen the new shoots of daffodils and snowdrops in the yard, spring still felt very far away.

"Pearl Street. Atherton and Rampling," I told the driver, and we were speedily off.

It was nearing eleven as I climbed the steps to Peter's office, and the halls were swarming with businessmen. The handsome clerk at the desk looked up owlishly from behind his glasses as I opened the office door and stepped inside.

"Mrs. Atherton," he said, rising so quickly he knocked a pen off the desk. "How can I help you this morning?"

"I'm here to see Mr. Rampling," I told him.

At that moment, one of the doors beyond opened, and Benjamin came striding out as if I'd beckoned him. His hair was smooth and shining, his beard neatly trimmed, his frock coat brushed. He was the perfect example of a prosperous lawyer. He was conservative and well bred, and it was surprising that such a man had not taken a wife. Why had I not thought that before now?

Foolish, I told myself. There were a hundred Benjamins. What made me think he had anything to do with Adele? Why could I not dismiss the thought?

He frowned when he saw me. "Evie?"

I stepped past the young man. "Have you a moment?"

"I was on my way to the prosecutor's office, but I suppose he can wait." He turned to the clerk. "Wood, will you send a man over there to say I'll be late?"

"Absolutely, sir. I'll go myself."

Benjamin waited until the young man had disappeared through the door, and then he gestured for me to follow him into his office. When I was inside, he closed the door behind me.

"Did he move the cuff link?"

I had forgotten all about it. "I'm afraid I haven't had the chance to look again. He's been about, you see—" I took on the mien of distress, and though I felt guilty for the lie, my need to reassure myself about Benjamin was greater. "I've been . . . well, I know you told me Adele was an illusion. And I think I must believe you. But even knowing that, I still see her. Michel is quite insistent that she's real—"

"He obviously sees some purpose in it. I've told you that."

"I know. But he swears he's never said her name. He says she meant nothing to him, so why would he speak of her?"

"I hardly know."

"She was married, did I tell you that?"

He looked surprised. "No. Evelyn, is there a reason you've come to discuss this illusion with me? The prosecutor waits—"

"She was married, but her husband didn't come after her. Doesn't that strike you as odd?"

"Wives take lovers and run off frequently. You must have known that from your father's work. No doubt he was asked to investigate such things."

"Yes, but if you had a wife, and she ran off, wouldn't you try to find her?"

"Such a hypothetical is impossible for me to answer."

"You've never been married, have you, Benjamin?"

"No," he said shortly. "Which is why I have no idea of such things. When one makes suppositions based on fiction, one is bound to blunder."

"You're right, of course. I feel foolish. I'm not even certain why I came down here. Just to hear your voice, I suppose."

"Having heard it, are you reassured?"

"Yes. Yes, I am. Thank you. I'm so sorry to put you off your schedule. I know the prosecutor awaits. . . ."

"He does, but you are my first concern."

I smiled. "I feel much better now. Please, you should go. Don't worry about me."

"Then if you'll excuse me." He reached for the black case on his desk, and then he paused. "You'll tell me when you've located the cuff link again, or found the gun?"

"The moment I do."

Then, with an apology for not showing me to the door, he was gone.

I had told Benjamin that I had what I came for, and I did, but it was not what I'd wanted. It was not what I'd hoped for. *"Bodies don't lie."* Neither had his. I'd seen it clearly, the way he avoided my glance when I'd asked if he'd ever been married, the involuntary twitch of his jaw. He was not telling me the truth.

I left his office as quickly as I could, not wanting to be there a moment longer than I must. Dorothy's carriage was waiting in the street, as was the mounted police watchman, at a careful distance behind.

"Home, ma'am?" the driver asked as he took my arm to put me into the carriage.

"No," I said firmly. "I want to go to the *New York Times*. And quickly."

27

LIARS WILL LEAD YOU ASTRAY

THURSDAY, FEBRUARY 26, 1857

Research was the key; if nothing else, Michel and my father had taught me that. Benjamin had said it as well: *"One can find anything,"* he'd told me, and now I meant to see if the archives of the *New York Times* building on Printing House Square held the information I needed.

Steam rose like fog from the grates on the sidewalks above the pressroom of the *Times*; one could feel the thump of the great presses reverberating in the flagstones beneath one's feet. When Dorothy's driver let me off, I hurried into the offices, which bustled with people. I asked the man at the front desk for the archives, and he sent an assistant to take me there—a small room downstairs that was covered with shelves from floor to ceiling, and so full of the musty, dusty scent of old paper that I had to suppress a sneeze. He led me to one of the three tables in the room—there were other people there as well, all turning pages of yellowed newsprint, eyes searching the columns for information, and I thought how easy this was, how any clever person might find whatever they wanted about anyone. What privacy we had existed only in our own thoughts.

I hoped to find what I was seeking in a single news item: the account of a murder. I knew vaguely the time frame in which it had occurred. I knew also that it had happened either in Charlestown or Boston—and so whether it would even be in the *Times* depended greatly on its notoriety. I had no other choice; I was bound to this city by law and circumstance, and it was impossible for me to make a trip to Boston.

When the man asked me what months and years I wanted, I thought of my visions. Michel had been coughing, the women were clothed heavily, Adele had been cold, the streets icy. The winter months then, perhaps moving into spring. Michel had been researching Dorothy then, and he had known her for eight months. So I asked for the papers from the winter of a year ago. The pile, when he brought it, looked enormous. I thought it must take me days to go through it.

I began to scan the papers, one after another—the headlines first, and then, past the city news to the news of the country, and then the little notices from other towns. MURDER IN PORTSMOUTH, MURDER IN SALEM, . . . IN CONNECTICUT, . . . IN BOSTON, . . . IN BOSTON, . . . IN BOSTON. . . . There must have been twenty of them. All wrong. Not what I was looking for at all. After two hours of this, I grew tired, and the words began to swim before my eyes; the wavering gaslight and its heavy smell in the unventilated room began to make me feel slightly ill.

I took a deep breath and wished for some water, and then I picked up the next paper—dated January 14, 1856. The headlines seemed to gather together; I turned the first page, and then the next one, and then I saw it, part of a column of news from other cities: BODY FOUND IN CHARLES RIVER.

The back of my neck tingled. I blinked to clear my vision and pulled the newsprint closer.

BODY FOUND IN CHARLES RIVER

BOSTON—Local fishermen were thrown into great consternation Sunday morning by the horrible discovery of the body of a young woman caught in their nets. She has been identified as Adele Rampling, the wife of Charlestown attorney Benjamin Rampling. Mr. Rampling said she had run off some months previous with a Boston spiritualist, and that she had been performing as a spirit rapper herself under the name Madame LaFleur, but that he had recently recovered her.

Mrs. Rampling had disappeared Wednesday night after an argument, and her husband believed she had returned to Boston. This was confirmed by witnesses.

Mrs. Rampling was found mortally stabbed. Police believe that she is the victim of a robbery, as several items she had taken with her—including a silver locket—were missing. There are no suspects at this time.

I had to read the article again. And then the proof of Benjamin's lie—of the enormousness of it—was stunning. He *had* been married. To Adele. Whose death was so like Peter's it was remarkable— certainly the same person could have committed both murders. Any lawyer could have seen that, and yet Benjamin had never said a word—not of her, not of the similarity of the circumstances of Peter's death, nothing. That he had known of Adele's involvement with Michel was clear as well.

Benjamin had lied to me.

Why? Was it because he wanted vengeance against Michel more than justice? Because my fate had mattered to him only insofar as it allowed me to be used?

No wonder he'd been so angry when Adele's spirit had appeared at the circle. I remembered his words: *"Did he tell you those things? Did he put you up to it?"*

He'd been angry because he'd thought Michel had told me about her. He'd been angry because he believed I'd taken Michel's side, that he had lost my allegiance, that I was no longer his tool.

Dear God, what a fool I'd been.

But none of it made sense. Why not simply tell me the truth

about Michel and Adele? Certainly that story alone, and the similarity of her death to Peter's, was reason enough to suspect Michel. I would have understood.

And then I had another thought. Could Benjamin have been the one who killed his wife and Peter? It seemed impossible, and yet, he had a motive to kill Adele, and he'd lied to me. . . . I heard a shuffle behind me. There was a light touch on my shoulder that made me jump.

"Pardon me, ma'am, but are you well? Is there something I can do?" Behind me was the assistant who had brought me down here, looking very concerned.

"I'm fine, thank you," I told him, smiling so falsely it hurt. "Truly, I am."

He frowned, but he nodded and moved away, and I turned back to the newspaper. I read the words again, as if they might have changed in the interim to become something less noxious, more bearable, but of course they had not. Benjamin had lied to me, and I couldn't trust him, and the days were moving inexorably toward my trial. I smoothed the pages, folding the paper carefully, setting it back onto the pile with the others, as if it had not irrevocably changed everything I knew.

Then I gathered my bag and rose. The assistant waited at the door. "I'm finished, thank you," I said.

"Did you find what you wanted then, ma'am?" he asked politely.

"I found what I needed," I said.

IN THE WARM safety of Dorothy's carriage I tried restlessly to sort the mysteries surrounding Peter's death into some kind of order. Benjamin had been married to a woman who had run off with Michel, a woman who had died in the same grisly way as had Peter. I knew from the visions that Adele had not wanted to return to her husband. Was it because he was dangerous? She'd said he hated her. Hated and loved, I remembered. He'd wanted her back, and she didn't want to go. Why? Was it simply that she couldn't bear the idea of being removed from Michel?

I didn't know. Nor did I know whether Benjamin's determination to bring Michel to justice for Peter's murder had more to do with vengeance than with truth.

The only thing I did know was that the deaths of my husband and Adele were similar enough that it seemed unlikely to be mere coincidence, and I knew of only two people who had a connection to them both: Benjamin and Michel.

Benjamin had lied to me, and he was manipulating me. I had given him the chance today to tell me he'd had a wife, and he had not. The newspaper article said the police suspected a robbery. Yet I knew the location of Adele's missing locket. Was it in Michel's armoire because of the reason he'd stated? Or had he taken it from her to make her murder look like a robbery—the same way he'd taken the cuff link from Peter, a cuff link he claimed to have never seen?

The carriage slowed to a stop. When I looked out the window I saw that we were before the Bennett house. The gray of the rain seemed to soften its edges; the windows were lambent and welcoming, and I thought how that house was like everything else in my life, how nothing about it was as it seemed. I waited for the driver to open the door; when he helped me out, I realized the rain had grown heavier. The black feather on my hat drooped to brush my cheek. I stood there on the walk, staring up at the house, at the window I knew belonged to Dorothy's bedroom.

"Ma'am?" the driver asked.

I smiled brightly and gave him my hand.

The house was quiet when I entered, though the lights were blazing, the heat rising from the vents along the floor. When I gave my cloak and hat and gloves to Lambert, I asked, "How is Mrs. Bennett today?"

"Quite well, ma'am. Mr. Jourdain is with her now."

There it was, that little flicker of jealousy. I refused to feel it. I was relieved he was with her; it meant I would not encounter him on my way to my bedroom. Still, I lingered on the stairs. I did not want to see him, not at all; yet I was disappointed when I reached the safety of my bedroom without meeting him.

He could have killed them both. He had the motive for each of the murders: for Adele, because she had become difficult, and Peter, because he was in the way of the adoption, because he had drawn up commitment papers for Dorothy—

I paced fretfully to the fireplace. There was always a fire lit, whether I was in the room or not. I supposed because the central heating was not strong enough to reach well to the third floor; the heat was like the flutter of a fan, the air warm when you were close to the vents, insubstantial when one stepped a few feet away—

The truth is not always what you want to believe.

The thought winged through my mind, as if someone had sent it there. I looked to the desk, where the notebooks containing the spirit writing were on top, neatly laid out by Kitty. It had been some time since I'd looked at them. I went over and picked them up and took them to the chair by the fire, and then I opened them, poring over the words.

Liars will lead you astray. Do not be tempted.

Tempted by who? Who was the liar? How could I tell?

Trust those sent to guide you.

But if someone had been sent to help me, who was it? Who did the spirits mean? Adele? Michel? Benjamin? Dorothy?

Go farther than you will and be satisfied.

I slammed the books shut and shoved them onto the floor. They were as much a mystery as ever. I closed my eyes and tried to calm myself, to clear my mind.

"Peter had not seemed himself these last months."

The words came to me like a scent memory—the sudden whiff of a long-ago perfume caught in a breeze, an entire childhood told by the musky sweet tang of fallen apples in the sun. There, not there, a memory left dangling.

"I lost my love for him in that moment. I thought we were confidants."

I realized that I had forgotten one thing in my quest to solve Peter's death: his life. I had been—as Michel had so mockingly told me—willingly blind. I had not wanted to face the looming failure of my marriage, and so I ignored anything that might show the cracks. Peter's disappearances. His distraction. The truth was as I told Ben: I had not known my husband as well as I'd told myself I had.

But someone else did.

28

ASKING THE RIGHT QUESTIONS

I did not want to wait to speak to Dorothy. Lambert had said Michel was with her, and that meant he'd given her the cordial—soon, she would fall asleep, if she hadn't already, and my questions would have to burn within me 'til morning.

I went directly to her room, knocking softly upon the door.

Charley opened it. "Why, there you are, Mrs. Atherton! Mrs. Bennett's been asking for you all day."

I heard a muttered imprecation, and then Michel stepped past the screens. He wore no frock coat, and his vest and shirt were open—he'd obviously been tending to Dorothy. The worry in his face was replaced quickly by relief when he saw me. He started toward me, as if he meant to take me into his arms. Then he checked himself. "*Madame,* we were worried. You left no word."

"I had an urgent errand," I said.

"So urgent you couldn't tell Lambert?"

"I'm sorry if I distressed Dorothy. Or you. But I assure you it was necessary."

"Had Rampling something to do with it?"

I said, "Might I speak with Dorothy?"

He stepped back, but not enough to let me pass easily, and I knew it was deliberate and he was angry. I had to compress my skirts to get by him, and even then, he was so close my hand brushed his trousered thigh. I did not look at him as I went into the bedroom.

Dorothy's eyes were closed, and she looked very peaceful. I went to the chair and sat down, which put me even with her face. Gently, I touched her hand, which peeked from the bedcovers. "Dorothy," I whispered.

"Oh, I can hear you well enough, child. I'm not asleep." Her eyes opened. "Where've you been? I wanted to talk to Johnny this afternoon."

"You must forgive me. I had an—"

"Urgent errand. Yes, I heard."

"I didn't mean to neglect you. But I'd be happy to tell you of it"—I threw a glance at Michel—"in confidence."

He hesitated, but he inclined his head and put his hand on Dorothy's shoulder. "*Madame* wishes me to leave, *ma chère*. I'll return when you've finished your *tête-à-tête,* eh?"

She snaked a naked arm out to reach for his hand, clasping his fingers and bringing them to her lips. "Don't go far, dear boy," she said, releasing him.

I couldn't read his expression. Still, his displeasure was obvious as he left.

I waited until I heard the closing of the bedroom door, and then I said, "I've a question to ask you, Dorothy. It might be quite important."

She frowned at me, and then she closed her eyes. "You discovered something today?"

"Yes."

Dorothy sighed. "About Michel?"

"I don't know. Perhaps. There's something I must know about Peter. I've been thinking about the commitment papers. It's puzzled me from the start, why Peter would do such a thing."

"He wanted to protect me."

"By ruining you? It doesn't seem like him. It seems frankly cruel. I thought the two of you were friends. You said yourself that you were confidants."

"Yes, child, we were." Dorothy's voice was very soft.

"Then if he truly believed Michel to be a mountebank, why not punish him? It seems he was willing to sacrifice you, to leave Michel untouched, which makes no sense at all—"

"Oh, I understood it, my dear. I understood it."

"Then perhaps you could explain it to me."

"Oh, my dear child." Dorothy gave me a strangely sympathetic look. "You're so bright that sometimes I must remind myself how young you are. Where did he find you? In your father's office? Did you ever wonder why he married you, Evelyn?"

"He told me he was tired of the girls in society. He said I made him laugh."

"Good reasons. But do you really think they were good enough that he should take on his family and the upper ten for them? Ah, I suppose you were like any girl in love. Thinking of your fairy tale. Never asking the right questions."

"What questions would those be?" My voice was barely there.

"He never courted anyone but you. When he was a boy, he used to run with these other young bucks, the way boys do, but Peter never outgrew it. Always had these young men about him. And then he met Michel, and . . . Oh, my dear boy does cause his share of trouble, doesn't he? Such a pretty face. Such a voice. And there was that Tommy Miller too. That's who you should talk to, child."

"I don't understand. Who's Tommy Miller?"

Dorothy closed her eyes.

A little desperately, I said, "Did Peter return here that night after the circle? Did he see Michel?"

She shook her head. "He didn't come here."

"Perhaps he did, and you didn't realize—"

"Michel never left this room, child. Not that night. I'm not wrong about that." Her eyes opened wearily. "Peter went to the waterfront. You go see Tommy Miller. He'll tell you Peter knew the risks he was taking, going down there, but he didn't care."

"Why was he down by the river that night?"

"I suppose it's no wonder, given how often he went down there."

"Talk to those men who were Peter's friends, Evelyn. That's all I'll say. Now, will you call Michel? I ache so."

She clearly knew more than she was telling, but it was obvious she intended to reveal nothing else tonight. I rose. "Of course."

"I'd ask you to bring me my boys, but I'm so tired. But Evelyn—tomorrow? Tomorrow, you'll call them for me, won't you?"

I looked back at her, lying so feeble and small on the bed, waiting as she did for my lover, begging for my favor, and I hardly knew how to feel. Whether I should feel anger for what she was keeping from me, or jealousy over what I must share with her, or gratitude for the protection she'd offered, or even satisfaction at her dependence upon me. They were all there, jockeying for place.

"Tomorrow," I told her. Then I went to find Michel.

WHILE KITTY UNDRESSED me, I thought of my husband. I remembered how Michel had taunted me with the fact that Peter must have known what would happen to me when he left me his family's home, his mother's things. Though I felt certain he would not have expected I would be accused of his murder, that too felt like a final reproof, a censure from the grave—as if he couldn't forgive me for trying to love him, for trying to be the wife I thought he wanted.

But that was a lie too. I had married Peter because I wanted more from my life. The truth was that I had hidden in the role of the devoted, blind wife, the grieving widow, because it was easier to pretend than to admit that I had made a wrong choice, that I was unhappy.

We had both been miserable. No wonder his spirit had never returned to console me, or to guide me—

Except that he had.

I frowned in the mirror as Kitty unfastened the crinoline. I realized suddenly that Peter had not visited me for some time. Not since Michel and I had become lovers. Not since that first night. *"Don't trust him,"* he had said. Over and over again. But then, when I found myself in the arms of the man he had begged me not to trust, Peter's spirit had suddenly vanished.

Why?

Dorothy had told me to look for answers in the men Peter had befriended, in the places he'd frequented. Places near the river. Peter had not gone back to Dorothy's house that night, though if it was Michel he'd meant to question, as Ben had supposed, why not return here? Why make the trek to the waterfront? And how would I find this Tommy Miller to ask?

"Kitty," I asked quietly. "Do you know what happened to Cullen after the Athertons released him?"

She clucked as she stripped off my chemise and pulled my nightgown over my head. "A pity, what they did to him, ma'am. After him being Mr. Atherton's driver for twenty years."

"Where did he go?"

"He was lucky enough to find another situation, ma'am, though he's working for a tradesman—not quite the gentleman Cullen's used to, but he says he's happy enough."

"If I gave you a note to give to him, do you think you could find him?"

"Oh yes, ma'am. I know right where he is."

As she took down my hair and brushed it, I penned the note. When she left, it was with the missive tucked securely in her pocket.

"Take it first thing in the morning," I told her. "And please, tell him how anxious I am to see him."

Then I waited. But it was a restless hour. I knew he delayed to punish me, but I also knew he would come, and finally, he did.

The knock was perfunctory. He came inside nearly the same moment, closing the door again behind him. I turned from where I stood at the fireplace, pulling my dressing gown more closely about me, feeling suddenly too vulnerable, too uncertain, watching him turn down the gaslight so it began to flicker, almost low enough to snuff out.

He stepped over to where I stood. Then he took off his vest, which was still undone, and his shirt, and laid them neatly over the back of the chair.

"I hardly know whether to strangle you or make love to you," he said, taking the few steps to me. He lifted a curl of my hair from my shoulder, rubbing it between his fingers. "I find it a familiar feeling of late."

"I wonder that I should be the source of such confusion. Perhaps it's your own ambivalence that creates such a paradox."

"No doubt." His smile was small. "Where were you today?"

"I told you. I had an errand."

"Ah, *oui*. An urgent one. Occasioning not even a word to Lambert. Or to me."

"I would explain if I could."

"You don't trust me."

I pulled away. The strand of hair slipped from between his fingers. I looked into the fire. "I can't think why you should be surprised."

"I thought we understood each other."

"I don't know that I will ever understand you."

"Why do you torture yourself this way, *chère*?" His voice lowered. He touched my shoulder. "Come to bed with me."

"How good you are," I said, trying to make my words as cold as I felt his manipulation to be. "What am I to do now? Tell me so I know your intention—is this when I run mindlessly into your arms? When I stop asking questions? Is that how it's always worked before?"

I felt his sudden stillness, and I caught my breath at the danger. I wanted reassurance; I wanted him to tell me something I could believe. But I expected to feel the strength of his fingers about my throat. How had Peter died? And Adele? Had they gasped for a last breath? Or had the first thing they'd felt been the hot slice of a knife in the soft flesh beneath their ribs?

My vision wavered, soft and blurry now with tears. And then I felt his hands at my hips, pulling me back against him. He wrapped his arms around me, burying his face in the hollow of my shoulder. His hair tangled with mine.

"I'm falling in love with you, Evie," he murmured against my skin.

I couldn't tell—was it true, was it not; in that moment, the two things seemed the same. I began to cry in earnest; I was pliable as a babe as he turned me to face him, as he kissed me—my cheeks first, and then the trail of my tears, and then my lips, and I stumbled against him so that he bore all my weight and it seemed no trial for him at all.

The next thing I knew, we were on my bed, and he was undressing me slowly, lingering over my skin as if he meant to impress every inch upon his fingertips, and I let myself go mindless and cared nothing for whether or not it was his intention. I ignored what I believed he was and what I thought he had done, as I allowed myself—for one small moment, and perhaps only this once—to love him.

29

WHO WOULD BELIEVE ME?

FRIDAY, FEBRUARY 27, 1857
THREE WEEKS AND THREE DAYS BEFORE
EVELYN ATHERTON'S TRIAL

We didn't speak of it in the morning. Before dawn, he woke, and I roused sleepily as he kissed my shoulder before he got out of bed. I watched him pull on his trousers and gather his clothes, and at the door he turned to look at me. I knew he saw I was awake, but he said nothing, and when he was gone I fell back into a sleep so full of dreams and images that it was scarcely sleep at all.

But the dreams were my own. Adele did not visit me again. Nor did Peter. It seemed the spirits had left me to discover the rest on my own.

Which was exactly what I meant to do. The answers that would save me were there, just beyond my reach. Today, I meant to find them.

When I was fully awake and dressed—by the upstairs maid, Molly, because Kitty had gone on her errand to find Cullen—I went to the library to wait. Michel was with Dorothy, I knew, and I could not stay in my room, where memories of last night intruded. I went to the large window overlooking the backyard and tried to put such things aside. I could not think of them now; perhaps I would never think of them again.

It was nearing noon when Kitty returned, breathless and red cheeked, to find me.

"He says he's off at six, ma'am. He'll come to you then."

Six o'clock. Dear God, it seemed an eternity. A hundred things might happen between now and then. How was I to spend the hours?

Dorothy sent for me soon after. I walked into her room to find Michel still there, seated in the chair on the other side of the bed. He rose politely when I entered, but his expression was carefully blank; he might not have been the same man who had confessed his love for me last night.

"I want to talk to my sons," Dorothy told me as I sat. "I've kept Michel here to help."

"I'd hate to keep him from his other tasks. I think I hardly need him."

Dorothy said, "Well, we'll find out. Child, close the curtains."

I rose to do her bidding. At the same time, Michel turned down the gaslight and lit a candle on the bedside table.

"Shall we hold hands?" I asked.

To my surprise, Michel shook his head. "Let's try it without, eh?"

I nodded and closed my eyes. Dorothy began to sing a hymn, and Michel joined along, and I tried to let myself drown in the words, in the melody. But my mind kept spinning to the things I knew, the puzzles that twisted and turned. I thought of Cullen, and my planned visit with him tonight, and what more I might discover. I was growing close, I knew. Very close. All I must do was put the pieces in order—

"Is there a spirit come to talk with us?" Michel asked softly.

I was not in a mesmeric trance. I tried to make my mind blank, but the door of my thoughts blocked the way. I remembered Dorothy's disappointment at supper, my own plans for my future. I opened my eyes. "Could we try again, please?"

"Another hymn?" Dorothy asked.

"If you would. And perhaps the prayer."

But even then, my mind would not obey my will.

"Perhaps I could call them," Michel suggested.

"They'll come to me, I know it. If I could just clear my mind—"

"Of course." He rose in a fluid motion and came around the bed toward me. I frowned as he stepped behind me. "Allow me—" He placed his fingers on my temples, stroking back into my hair, and then down, tracing the bones of my face, reminding me forcibly of last night. "Close your eyes," he whispered, and I found myself doing so. I found myself falling into his rhythm. I heard Dorothy begin a hymn very quietly, a lone voice in the room, and I was slipping into a dream created by his soothing touch; the door was opening; I was wafting through it.

Here I am.

She was waiting for me, and she was angry. *You don't know him as I do. He's using you. He knows just what to do to keep you.*

"Is there a spirit here?" Michel asked.

I heard her voice pushing through my throat. "Yes, dear heart, I am here."

"We wish to speak to Johnny or Everett Bennett. Can you find their spirits for us? May we speak to them?"

"No. I don't wish to bring them. It's my turn to speak."

Dorothy cried out in dismay.

"Then speak, spirit," Michel's voice was preternaturally calm. "Tell us why you've come."

I felt her struggling to feel his touch through my body. I felt her greediness, her failing. "I am Adele."

"What do you want with us?" Dorothy asked. "Why can't you bring my boys?"

"I won't leave you again, dear heart." Adele's voice—my voice— was low and vicious. "Now that I'm here, I'm staying. You can't send me away this time. Not ever."

I watched from a distance. I felt my own dismay like a foreign sensation. I began to cross the divide. She held me at bay, her fury impossible to penetrate. *No. He belongs to me. You cannot come back. I won't let you in.*

"Evelyn." Michel's voice, soft and powerful. "Control her."

I could not find the door. I could not push inside.

"She cannot get back," Adele said. "I'm more powerful than she is."

"Evelyn, force your will," Michel said.

His voice was like a beacon. I followed it. I found the door.

"She must bend to you. She must be your servant," he said.

No. Adele fought me. *I will not go.*

"You're stronger than she is."

I pressed through. She filled my head; she would not give way, but my body belonged to me, and in the end I knew it better. *"Control her,"* he had said, and I did. I forced her back. I pushed her out. Her fury was her weakness, and I used it to command her. *Bring me the boys and go,* I told her, and though she fought me, though she hated me, she did as I beckoned. I felt her fade; I felt the benignness of a young man's spirit pressing close, begging entry, asking permission. I let him inside, but I didn't surrender myself; I kept vigil.

When I woke, it was to find Michel's hands still on me, and Dorothy beaming. I was sweating and exhausted, and when he withdrew his hands, I heard myself make an involuntary sound of protest. I felt immediately vulnerable, as if he were withdrawing his protection, and that was so contrary to what I knew of him that I was confused.

"I've something to give you, child," Dorothy said, and she held out her hand. Michel stepped around me. He reached into his coat pocket and drew out a box, which he put into her hands to give to me. From Tiffany, I noticed as I took it and opened it. Within lay a necklace so beautiful that I gasped. It was emeralds and diamonds, strung together in an elaborate web of gold. It was valuable, and ostentatious, and so completely to my taste that I could only look at her in surprise.

"I asked Michel to pick it for you," she said. "Look how it matches your eyes. Another little reward, eh? For bringing the boys."

I looked at him, startled and overwhelmed.

"It seems you need me after all, *Madame,*" he said, and there was no mockery in his tone, but only a matter-of-fact truth.

I let the necklace fall back into the box, and I replaced the lid and rose, clutching it in my hand. "I'm overwhelmed at your generosity. Truly. I hardly know what to say."

Dorothy said, "The two of you have given my days peace at last. The best thing I ever did, child, was to bring you here to help my boy. Now you must let him help you become what you're meant to be."

He had cemented his place even further and used me to do it. Willingly or no, I was bound to him, and the necklace in my hand was meant to be the manifestation of that bond—I knew that. I knew what he wanted from me: a partnership, both of the mind and the body. *"You and me, we're alike, chère,"* he had said, and perhaps it was true.

Perhaps he *was* the spiritual affinity I was meant to find.

But I could go no further with this. I could not commit myself. Not to Dorothy, not to him, not to the game we played together. Not until I knew the truth.

WHEN CULLEN CAME, I was waiting on the front stoop, shivering. I did not mean for anyone to hear our conversation, nor did I want anyone to stop me. As he came up the walk, I stepped onto the stair before him.

He started, stopping short. "Ma'am?"

"Thank you for coming," I said. "It was very kind of you, given the circumstances."

"I never blamed you for it, ma'am," he said. "And I found a good situation. Not the same as working for Mr. Atherton, but good enough."

I saw a dark movement across the street, the police watchman. "I'm in trouble, Cullen. You know they're accusing me of murdering my husband."

"None of us believe it, ma'am."

"That means a great deal to me."

"Whatever I can do to help you, Mrs. Atherton, I will."

"There is something," I said, lowering my voice, not knowing how well it might carry on the chill air. "I've recently come into some information about Mr. Atherton, and I wanted to ask you a question."

"Yes, ma'am?"

"That night, the night he died, Peter didn't return here, did he?"

"No, ma'am."

"He went to the waterfront, didn't he?"

Cullen hesitated. "Well, ma'am—"

"The truth, please, Cullen. If you want to save me from the gallows, you'll tell me the truth now."

"Mrs. Atherton, I don't think you want to know this."

"Oh, but you're wrong. I need to know it. In fact I think it's the key to what happened to him that night. I need you to take me there."

He looked alarmed. "It ain't no place for a lady."

"I must go there. There's a man I need to talk to. Tommy Miller. Do you know of him?"

His shock was almost humorous.

"You do know of him. Please, Cullen, you must take me there. If you care anything about what happens to me, you must."

I felt guilty trading upon his loyalty, but my guilt quickly faded at his slow acquiescence. He said, "Should I call us a carriage, ma'am?"

It took little time to hire a cab, and soon we were seated within it, leaving the Bennett house behind. The police watchman followed at a discreet distance, and for once I was happy for it. I had no real idea where we were going, or how dangerous it might be.

Twilight sheathed the streets in gray. As we went, the lamp-lighters made their rounds, their shadowed figures bearing flames on long poles. One by one, the gaslights flared to life, and the streets and nooks beyond their halos grew darker and harder to penetrate. I felt a tug of nervousness and pulled aside the leather curtain of the carriage to look out as we made our way into lower Manhattan. The thaw had left the streets more impenetrable than ever. Now, instead of hard ruts and ice, there was mud, and mud of the most viscous, sticky kind. The big square Belgian paving stones settled within it, and there were potholes everywhere.

The buildings began to change from the partitioned mansions and boardinghouses of the financial district to narrow-fronted stores with their filthy, sagging awnings and sidewalks littered with garbage from the barrels and boxes that had cluttered them during the day. Pushcarts and wagons began to appear on the corners, where peddlers sold the last of the oranges and lemons hanging in bags, straggling bunches of vegetables and onions, bruised apples—all at bargain prices. The upturned faces of the tired and haggard women gathering round them looked ghostly and disembodied, lit as they were by the small oil lamps hung at the corners of the carts. Match girls and hot corn girls, newsboys and men hawking tobacco called out their wares, and street Arabs lurked in the corners, waiting for an opportunity to steal an apple or pick a pocket.

When the storefronts gave way to beer cellars and small cafés and theaters and music halls, Cullen had the driver stop. His usually bland face was wrinkled in concern. "Are you sure you want to do this, Mrs. Atherton?"

I nodded grimly, stepping out into the filthy street. "Is it far?"

"The next block."

The flagstones of the sidewalks were crooked and cracked in this part of town, the piles of sewage and garbage tottering over the curb, great mounds of horse manure steaming in the street. Spittoons had been emptied onto the walk so that strangely sweet-smelling, sticky brown streams wound their way into still puddles that one had to be careful to step over. The acrid urine and blood smell of the tanneries and slaughterhouses was deadened some by the winter air, but still the tangy stink bit my nostrils, fighting with the stench of fried fish and beer. Cullen said nothing as he took me down the block, and though it was early yet, the walks were beginning to fill with dandified Bowery B'hoys and their girls, men looking for whores or entertainment. I heard music coming from the buildings we passed.

Then we turned onto another street, and I realized that the whores skulking in the shadows were no longer women, but men—tall, pretty youths and young boys. There were no longer any Bowery G'hals, but only men—men in rough clothes and working men with their eyes lowered and dandies in their tight trousers and brightly shined boots and colorful vests. Some even wore paint. I was as out of place as a cardinal among crows.

But now things began to fall into place. My memories unspooled: Peter's friendships with men, which seemed deep and constant and yet changed with regularity; the string of friends paraded through our home—Duncan Granger, whom I'd never seen again, despite their fast friendship, others like him; the intimate suppers where I had never wondered why these men never had wives, or why, after Peter's mother died, I was always the lone woman at the table; or how, in three years of marriage, I could count on my fingers the number of times my husband had come to my bed. I remembered how indifferent had been his lovemaking—I'd never questioned it; how could I, when I'd never had any to compare it to before now, before Michel? Peter had gone about it as if it were distasteful, a chore to be dispensed with quickly—

Cullen stopped. We were before a building with windows that were boarded and covered with the flyers and banners that decorated every other surface in New York City, notices fluttering and curling in the chill air advertising bathhouses and theaters and something called the Persian Poetry Club. The door was painted green, and peeling. There was no sign indicating what it was.

But then, two men walking arm in arm pushed past me and went through the door, and I heard laughter above the music eking from inside. I caught a flicker of light, a crowd, the smell of smoke and liquor.

I looked over my shoulder at Cullen. "Is this it?"

He nodded. Uncomfortably, he said, "The Neapolitan Club. Mr. Atherton liked to come here."

"And this is where he came that night?"

"Yes, ma'am."

Now I understood completely. "Very well." I made to go inside.

Cullen stepped forward. "Not alone."

I laughed bitterly. "Cullen, I imagine I'm safer here than nearly anywhere else in town."

"But they won't help you, ma'am. They recognize me from Mr. Atherton."

It made sense, and I let him escort me into the Neapolitan Club.

After the darkness of the streets, the room was bright, nearly dizzy with gaslight and clouds of tobacco smoke and music from a piano near the back of the room. It was notable both for the absence of spittoons and the fact that the couples on the dance floor consisted of men. Young men and boys with rouged cheeks and clothes too tight for modesty served drinks and whispered into their customers' ears. There were partitions along the sides of the room, all curtained, and I did not stop to think of what must go on there, of what Peter—

"Madame," said a voice near me. "I'm quite certain you've come to the wrong place."

I turned. A woman was leaning against the wall beside me. She wore a cheap blue satin gown with a low bodice. The lace trim was ragged and filthy. I thought at first she was a whore. Then, I realized she was not a woman at all.

He reached out, letting his hand fall against my breast, and when I jerked in surprise, he drawled, "Why, you're quite real. The sapphists are down the street."

Cullen stepped forward threateningly.

The man glanced up. "I know you, don't I?"

I said, "I'm looking for Tommy Miller. Is he here?"

The man shrugged. The gown he wore slipped from an angular shoulder. Then his eyes narrowed. "You his sister? You look just like him."

"Yes," I said. "I mean, no, I'm not his sister. But he's the one I'm looking for."

"He ain't here. He's next door. Could be with a customer. You might have to wait."

I was relieved when we were outside again.

"You might want to let me ask the questions, ma'am," Cullen said as we went next door. It was a café, and like the Neapolitan Club, it had boarded windows that looked dark and abandoned. But Cullen opened the door, and we were immediately assailed with the heavy, greasy aroma of fried fish, the sour hop of lager. The place was full; I saw a few curious glances, but most of these men were embroiled in their conversations and their food, and those glances slid away again.

Cullen made his way to the bar at the back, and I followed him. The bartender there wore the tightest trousers I'd ever seen. He glanced up as Cullen approached; I saw his gaze move over the driver assessingly, and then his brow rose as he saw me coming behind.

"What can I do for you?" he asked.

Cullen leaned on the bar. "We're looking for Tommy Miller. They sent us here from next door."

"Oh yeah? Who's looking for him?"

I stepped forward. "His sister. Do you know where we can find him?"

"I got a good idea. Only my guess is you don't want to find him just now."

"I need to find him. It's important."

He hesitated. He must have seen the desperation in my face, because finally, he jerked his head toward the narrow stairs behind the bar. "He's up there. But he's with someone."

"I just need to talk to him for a moment," I told him.

"You in trouble, sister?"

"Nothing Tommy can't solve," I said.

He said, "Go on up. Second door on the left."

I didn't wait for him to change his mind. I started over to the alcove behind the bar. Cullen put his hand on my arm, slowing me, and when I turned to look at him, he said, "You'd best let me go first, ma'am," and pushed past me to lead the way up the narrow, badly painted stairs.

They opened onto a hall not much wider than they were. It was dingy, and the plaster was peeling, and there was no light but that from a flickering gaslight at the far end, its globe so thick with soot that it seemed the flame was gasping for breath. The floor was warping, the hallway lined with doors that were all sagging, all seemingly squeezed into their swollen frames.

"Second on the left," I said, following Cullen to the door. He rapped sharply.

Silence. Then scurrying. Then, "Who is it?"

I opened my mouth to speak, but before I could, Cullen said, "Looking for Tommy Miller."

"Who wants him?"

"A friend. They sent me up from downstairs."

There was a curse, and then I heard the sound of staggering footsteps. The door was pulled open, and we were staring into the bland, downy bearded face of a young man wearing only a ragged dressing gown. His eyes were bleary and reddened. He frowned when he saw Cullen, and then more so when he saw me.

"Who're you?"

"Are you Tommy?" I asked.

He turned to look over his shoulder. "You expectin' someone, Tom?" and I pushed my way past him. The room was tiny and dim, lit only by a small oil lamp. The single window had been covered by a threadbare blanket. There was a mattress on the floor—other than that, there was no other furniture in the room. Sitting on the mattress, shirtless, with his trousers undone, was a young man, and I stopped, struck by how much he looked like me. He was small for a man, and slight. His hair was dark and long, and his skin was smooth as a woman's, his mouth wide and mobile. And as I drew closer, I saw his eyes, like mine, were a mottled green that no doubt changed color depending on what he wore. He was lolling against the wall, and he held a bottle in his hand, and he peered at me as if I were an apparition he couldn't quite make out. The sweetly spicy, medicinal scent of laudanum was unmistakable.

The man at the door giggled and nearly fell as Cullen came into the room behind me. "Oh, me, they've sent you a girl, Tommy. How long's it been since you tried that?"

"I ain't never tried it," Tommy said. He squinted at me again and tried to rise, gave up, fell back again to the wall. "Do I know you?"

"No," I said. I ignored the other fellow and glanced over my shoulder at Cullen, who closed the door. Then I stepped up to the mattress. "But you knew my husband. Peter Atherton."

The bottle fell from his hands. I saw something come into his eyes—fear, knowledge, *something*—and he struggled to sit upright. His voice became sullen. "Peter? I ain't seen 'im. Not for weeks. What d'you want to talk to me about 'im for?"

I knelt on the mattress. The movement sent the smell of musty, mildewed straw and sweat and musk into my nostrils. "Because he saw you the night he died," I said softly. Tommy's eyes widened; I had his attention. "And I think you know something of what happened to him."

Tommy swallowed. "Look, lady, I don't know why you come

'ere, but I got nothin' to say." He reached blindly for the laudanum. "I didn't see 'im."

"I think you did."

Tommy looked frightened.

I heard the other boy. "Hey. Hey! What're you—"

Cullen caught his arm, holding him in place. "Quiet, boy."

Tommy looked at Cullen and his friend and seemed to blanch.
Then he looked back at me. "Listen, I didn't . . . I didn't kill Peter.
I swear I didn't! It was the other one. The one 'e came for—"

"What other one?" I asked.

"You think 'e even looked at me twice once 'e 'ad 'im? We got
into a fight, 'ey—but it weren't nothin'! I swear I didn't kill 'im!"

I leaned closer. The smell of laudanum that came from his
breath was almost dizzying. "Think, Tommy. Tell me what happened. What night was it?"

He grappled for the bottle. I grabbed it first and held it away.
"Tell me. What night?"

"Right before the storm. It was cold. I remember that."

"You were at the club?"

"Yeah. I mean, no. Peter was supposed to meet me there, but 'e
never showed up, so I came over 'ere to get somethin' to eat and a
drop." He pushed his hand through his greasy hair. "I was gettin'
mad, you know? 'E was supposed to be there."

"What happened?"

"After a bit, 'e showed up. But 'e didn't want me. 'E was
lookin' for his new love."

"He wasn't that new," said the other boy.

"'E was goin' to leave 'im too."

"Not to come back to you, though."

I glanced over my shoulder at Cullen, who gripped the boy's
arm tighter and said, "Quiet, you."

I looked back at Tommy. "Who was Peter going to leave?"

"Benny. They was arguin' about some new fella. Petey was in
love." Tommy snorted. "Left me for Benny, so I knew 'e'd leave

'im too when 'e found somethin' new. Told Ben that too, but 'e didn't want to 'ear it, you know?"

Benny. The same name Willie Chesney, his *assistant,* had used for him.

"Benny," I said hoarsely. "Benjamin Rampling?"

"Was that 'is name?"

"Dark hair? Bearded?"

"Yeah. 'E was Petey's law partner. So 'e said. I never believed 'im none."

A wave of nausea swept me. "Who were they arguing over?"

"Don't know. Never saw 'im. Someone Petey was seein' at one of 'is fancy 'ouses. 'E was moony for 'im. Some spirit rapper." Tommy laughed drunkenly. "'E believed that shit, you know?"

"What happened?"

"Ben was downstairs, whinin' about another fight they 'ad about that rapper. I was 'appy they was fightin'—I thought maybe when Pete came down I'd get lucky. But 'e was madder 'an 'ell when 'e found Ben, and 'e didn't want me at all. I could just fuck myself and get lost."

"He was a bastard, Tommy," said the other boy.

Tommy looked at him as if he'd forgotten he was there. Then his green eyes filled with tears, which he dashed away angrily with the back of his hand. "Give me that bottle, will ya?"

I held it away. "What happened, Tommy?"

He seemed to melt against the wall. His eyes closed and his shoulders sagged; he fell to one arm. "The fight got rough. Matt told 'em to leave. 'E don't allow that shit. But then they was out in the street fightin', and I followed 'em. I thought maybe Benny'd go off pissed and I'd be there, you know. But Benny was mad as I've ever seen 'im. 'E kept sayin': 'You was supposed to 'elp me ruin 'im, not fall in love with 'im!' and grabbin' Pete's arm, and Petey kept jerkin' away and sayin' at least he never tried to kill nobody, an' 'e was goin' to the coppers."

I was gripping the laudanum bottle so tightly that my knuckles were white. "Then what?"

"Petey went runnin' off. Ben chased 'im. Looked to get nasty, and I'd lost my taste for it. I never liked Benny much. 'Ad a temper, that one, and I didn't want to get in the middle of it. I figured if Petey wanted me, 'e knew where I was. But 'e didn't come back." Tommy's voice went soft and plaintive. "I loved 'im, you know? I would've taken 'im back." His voice broke. "I would've."

I sat back on my heels. "Did you tell the police any of this?"

He shook his head. "Nah. Who would believe me? 'E was an Atherton, for Christ's sake. But if I 'ad to guess, it was Benny who did 'im. I'd lay money on it. 'E was jealous as I'd ever seen 'im. You want to find the one who killed Peter, lady, you find 'im."

30

THROUGH FRESH EYES

I understood now what Dorothy had known about Peter's life, the secret he had kept from me, from all of society. I understood why she had not dared to voice it, even to me. Such things were not talked about. They were barely acknowledged to be true. Peter's life had been a counterfeit, and I was part of it—I was the illusion.

It made me sad to think he had not trusted me with his secret, that he had allowed me to believe I was the one at fault in our marriage, but that sadness was overshadowed by the truth of his death, by the impossible news that Benjamin Rampling had been my husband's lover. And I knew now that Benjamin had killed both Peter and Adele, and that I had played into his hands. I felt sick at the extent of his betrayal, at how naive I'd been to trust him so completely. I had thought he'd made such a valiant sacrifice in choosing to defend me against the murder charge, and now I wondered: what had he meant to accomplish? Had he meant only to keep the investigation from turning to him? Had he meant truly to save me? Or was it all a lie—were all his machinations intended only to serve his vengeance against Michel? I could not believe he would have let me hang, but what had he said to me once? That I trusted too easily. I thought he'd been referring to Irene Cushing then, but now I realized he could have been talking about himself. Nothing had been as I'd thought it was.

Now it all came down to the fact that I must somehow find a way to use this information to save myself, and I knew I couldn't simply go to the police. It would have been one thing if Peter had talked to them, as Tommy claimed he'd intended to do. They would have listened to him. But they would not believe me, and even if they did, they would never proceed with such scandalous information—not when it involved such a prestigious Knicker-bocker. I would be ignored and scorned. I was a nobody. I was on my own once again.

"I'm falling in love with you, Evie."

Or perhaps I was not on my own anymore.

When Cullen dropped me at the Bennett door, I told him, "Thank you. I may need you again, you know, to talk to the police on my behalf."

"I know, ma'am," he said. "Kitty knows how to find me."

He waited there on the walk to see me inside safely. When I reached the front door, it opened before I touched the handle. Lambert stepped back to let me come inside.

"We've been looking for you, ma'am," he said.

Standing behind him in the hallway was Michel.

I had never seen him look so angry. As Lambert closed the door behind me, Michel said tightly, "Might I see you in the par-lor, *Madame?*"

Lambert took my cloak and my hat. Slowly, I pulled off my gloves and handed them to him. I felt the rise of Michel's temper as I tarried, but he kept it in check, waiting stiffly as I preceded him into the parlor. Once we were inside, he closed the door.

He waited barely a moment before he exploded, "Where the hell have you been? I've been looking for you for hours."

The evening caught up with me at last. I sank onto the settee. "I was out."

"Another errand? Who was that man in the yard?"

"It was Cullen."

"Cullen?"

"Peter's driver."

The confusion on his face was comical. "Peter's driver? You're sneaking out to meet a driver?"

"You mustn't be so jealous if we're to work together. I dislike men with tempers."

"Then perhaps you shouldn't provoke them," he said, and then he froze as he comprehended my words. "What's going on, Evie?"

I hesitated. I had no idea where to begin. Finally I just plunged in. "Were you my husband's lover?"

"What?" He stared at me in shock, and then he laughed. When I didn't laugh with him, he said, "*Non*—Evie, how can you even think it?"

"Did you know he was . . . that he liked . . ."

I felt him measuring his words. "I didn't know for sure. I suspected."

"I think he was in love with you."

"Ah." He looked wary. "Perhaps. I preferred to think of it as gratitude."

"Do you remember that cuff link in your room? The opal you said you didn't recognize?"

"What of it?"

"It was Peter's."

"Peter's?"

"And I imagine somewhere in your room we'll find his gun as well."

"*Mon dieu,* how many times must I say it before you believe me? I didn't kill your wretched husband—"

"I know."

He looked stunned. "You know?" Then, "Where did you go tonight?"

"To a little café on Chatham Street, where I met a charming boy by the name of Tommy Miller."

Michel went to the decanters on the sideboard and splashed a large amount of brandy into a glass. It was a measure of his discomposure that he offered nothing to me but only took a great gulp before he said, "Perhaps you should explain."

So I did. I told him of my visit to the newspaper office, and my discovery that Benjamin had been Adele's husband, and that she'd been found murdered in the same way Peter had been. I told him of finding Cullen and of my conversation with Tommy, and when I was finished, Michel sat next to me, leaning his head against the hard carved edge of the back, gimbeling his drink in his hand.

"I never knew," he said. "Her name was Rampling?"

"I'm disappointed at the spottiness of your research."

"I didn't research her. There was nothing I wanted from her but—" He broke off with a quick glance to me.

"Was it worth it, then?" I asked. "Knowing what you did to Benjamin? How much he hates you?"

"He doesn't hate me for her. It's Peter he hates me for."

"How it must have rankled him. Losing his wife to you, and then Peter too."

"And now you," Michel said quietly. When I looked at him, he was staring down into his glass. "Does he know, *chère?*"

I shivered. "I don't think so."

"Because once he finds out, you're in danger."

"He used me," I said bitterly. "All this time, I thought we were friends—more than that. I thought he was trying to help me. I thought he even—" The words were a lump in my throat; I could not say them.

"Perhaps he did you a favor, eh?" Michel took another sip; his gaze met mine over the edge of his glass. "You don't belong in that life, *chère*. You know it. Rampling only provided the way to see it."

"He must have put the cuff link in your room himself. During one of the circles, I suppose. It would have been easy enough to slip away. He's been asking me to look for Peter's gun."

"Then suppose we find it." Michel rose. He put his glass on a nearby table and offered his hand to help me to my feet, and together we went to his room.

Once we were there, he lit the gas and turned to survey the room critically. "He wouldn't have had much time to hide it. And he would've been sure to put it where he thought you'd find it."

I tried to look at the room through fresh eyes. The cuff link had been in the box on the desk, and I had searched the rest of the desk well for the key to the drawers.

"He was always saying how clever you were," I remembered. "He would have hidden it where I wouldn't have questioned that."

"Somewhere clever. Somewhere quick. Somewhere you would find it. Not much to consider, eh?"

"Where would you have hidden a gun?" I asked him.

"That doesn't signify. I wasn't meant to find it, *chère*—you were. The question is: where would you look?"

"In the armoire," I suggested. "Perhaps in a boot."

"That I might wear?" He lifted a brow. *"Non."*

"Then in the drawer beneath."

"Among my inexpressibles—*oui,* that is exactly where Rampling wants you, isn't it?"

"I've been through the desk already. It isn't there."

"Or in the bed stand drawer," he said dryly.

I glanced about the room. The mirror, the shaving strop, the basin. There was a side table upon which was a pile of books. No place there to hide a gun. On the back of the door hung Michel's dressing gown and nothing else. The fireplace mantel was empty but for more books and a china urn. I went to it and picked it up, turning it over. Nothing but dust and a spider fell out.

"Ah, you insult me, *chère,*" Michel said, his voice deep with amusement. "How clever is that?"

The chairs before the fireplace were richly upholstered, but the cushions were not deep enough to slip a gun between. The drapes were opened and closed every day—a gun would have been quickly discovered. There was no place else. No place except the bed.

It was fashioned of richly carved rosewood, with decorative panels set into the headboard, inlaid with ivory to match the desk. I flushed at the sudden memory that came to me, of pressing my hands against them as Michel—

I shook the thought away and sat down upon the bed, running my fingers over the headboard. The inlaid pieces were firmly set, not drawers as I'd thought they might be, but as I sat, the mattress eased away from the headboard, leaving a space between them.

I hesitated. The space between was just big enough, wasn't it? I reached into it, feeling along the planks of the bed stand beneath, along the edge of the mattress and just under the headboard, feeling for something that didn't belong there.

He must have just let it fall. There'd been no attempt to shove it beneath the mattress, to conceal it well. Had I not known, I would have thought Michel ingenious for choosing such a hiding spot—no one would have found this gun without having been in the bed—

And there the slyness of what Benjamin had done struck me.

I pulled the gun loose. Peter's gun, certainly. I had seen it enough to know. A small, short nose. A burled handle with his initials in gold. *PMA*. Peter Martin Atherton. I dropped it onto the coverlet, where it shone in the gaslight.

"Did you say he knew nothing about us?" Michel asked.

I looked up at him. "He must have suspected."

"And when you found the gun, he would've known for certain."

"He warned that you would seduce me."

"What did you tell him?"

"I told him you'd tried. It seemed best not to lie. It wasn't in your nature not to."

His smile was wry. "I don't seduce everyone, you know."

"It was what he told me. I believed him. I believed everything he said about you. It never occurred to me to think differently. And you must admit you did nothing to convince me otherwise."

He sat beside me and brushed a loose hair from my face. "I was overcome. And bedeviled. From the first moment."

I glanced at the gun. "What should we do with it?"

"Contact the police," he said. "Your watchman's outside. I can call him—"

I grabbed his arm to keep him from rising. "No. What would we tell him? That we found Peter's gun in your room? That we have the cuff link that was on him when he died? Who will they believe? You and me? Or Ben, when he says he knows nothing about it?"

He was quiet for a moment. Then thoughtfully, he said, "*Oui*—of course. There's a better way. Don't you know it?"

And suddenly, I did. "The circle."

Michel smiled. "The circle."

THAT NIGHT, I lay in his arms while we went over our plans.

"You can imagine her life," he told me, stroking my arm as he talked. "It was very like yours. It's why her spirit has an affinity for you. Her husband was distant; she was unhappy. She put her energies into her child, and when the boy died, she had nothing. She took to berating Rampling—she had a vicious tongue, that one, eh? He didn't satisfy her, and she let him know it. *Mon dieu,* how she must've tormented him before she left."

"So she ran off and fell into spiritualism—or mediumship, anyway. And then she met you."

"She was dead from that moment."

"Don't joke. It was true."

"I'm not joking," he said softly.

"She left her things because she was certain you would call her back."

"She returned to Rampling."

"Where else was she to go? She had nothing. I think . . ." I hesitated, sorting it in my mind for a moment before I went on. "I think she thought to make you jealous by returning to her husband. But she was in love with you, and she felt nothing but contempt for him, and she couldn't pretend otherwise."

"She was never good at pretending."

"And then he killed her. It's such a sad story. If she tormented him so, why couldn't he just let her go?"

His fingers drew lazy circles over my skin. "Ah, who knows? Perhaps it hurt his pride to lose her to another man."

"He knew you," I said, remembering how adamant Ben had been that Michel was a charlatan. "He'd told me you'd been run out of New Orleans. That you seduced a maid into pretending to be a spirit."

"Not run out. Though it seemed best to leave."

"And the maid?"

"One does what one must, eh? She was satisfied well enough."

"Is there anyone who hasn't found you irresistible?"

"Ah, *chère,* don't let it trouble you," he whispered against my ear. "It only matters to me that you do. One can't always regret the past, eh? It's a waste of time. Best to move forward."

"Ben said to me once that he regretted a great many things," I said, and my chest felt heavy—both sad and angry—at the memory. "He said he regretted that he waited so long to find his heart's desire. I thought he'd meant me. But he meant Peter. How desperate he must have felt when he thought he was losing him. And to you, of all people, the same man who stole his wife!"

Michel kissed my shoulder. "He should've asked me. I would've told him there was nothing to fear."

"That night, at the circle, the shooting—Peter was right—he was right to be afraid for you. He knew Ben had fired the shot, that it was meant for you."

Michel sighed. "I suspected then it had something to do with Peter. I told the police myself when I spoke to them."

"Did you? They said nothing of that to me." My eyes grew

blurry; I turned my face so he wouldn't see. "Dear God, what a fool I've been. I never suspected any of this. Not any of it. They hid it so well."

"They had to live in the world, just as you once told me you did."

"What about you?" I asked. "What secrets are you keeping from me? Is there nothing else for me to know? Are you hiding something?"

He gathered me into his arms and teased, "*Non*. How could I? It'd be like hiding from my own soul, eh?"

I laughed through my tears. "You are such a liar."

He sobered quickly. His arms tightened around me, and his eyes glittered. "I'm not lying about this, Evie. Not about this. We must do this perfectly on Tuesday night. No mistakes. I won't be without you. You know this?"

"Yes," I whispered against his lips. "I know it."

He pulled me close, and I felt her there, Adele, wanting him still, waiting for me to surrender, to let her in. *No,* I told her, and I felt her fury as I controlled her, as I kept her out, as I loved him. *He belongs to me now.*

WE PLANNED IT until I felt it had happened already. I knew every moment as it must unfold. I was amazed at the things he understood, the tricks he used, and once they were in my head I was astounded that anyone in the circle believed him, even for a moment. The ways were so transparent, so easy. I suppose what made them work so well was his confidence that they would.

31

THE CIRCLE

H e watched carefully as I prepared, as I undressed to my chemise and pulled on Adele's filmy dressing gown, tying the peach-colored ribbons over my breasts.

"There won't be a man there tonight who won't want you," he said approvingly as he took down my dark hair and spread it about my shoulders. "*Mon dieu,* Evie, look at you—when this is over you must never wear black again."

"I'm nervous," I said.

"Don't worry. You must believe it will work, *chère*. If you believe, they will."

"I don't know if I can face him."

"He wants to destroy me. He cares nothing if he destroys you too."

"I know. But to pretend I still trust him—"

"If you love me, you'll pretend." He turned me to face the mirror. "Look. See what I see."

I was startled at the sight of myself. The woman who stared back at me from the mirror was not the woman I'd been—the woman who haunted the candlelit mirrors at Rose Reid's ball, pale faced and desperate to belong; the woman who had allowed her husband to ignore her; the woman who believed she'd been lacking in her marriage. In her place was someone dangerous. Someone provocative. Without the armor of corset and crinolines, my body was revealed, my curves my own, not forced into a shape by boning. Whatever the game might be, the woman in the mirror was ready to play it, and to use whatever she must to win. Here, wearing another woman's gown, I was more myself than I had ever been.

"Do you doubt you can do this?" Michel whispered.

"No," I said. "I don't doubt it."

I suppose, in the end, that was the only thing I needed to remember.

I stayed in my room while the others arrived. That was part of it, he explained, because things would be different tonight, and everyone must be off their guard. The easiest way to do that was to provide the unexpected. He went down to greet them, and to help Dorothy to the second-floor parlor, and I paced my room, trying to relax. So much was at stake. If this did not work—

But it must work. I went to the window, pulling aside the drapes just enough to see out to the Avenue. There he was, the police watchman, in his usual place.

The clock struck eight. It was time.

I dropped the drape back into place and glanced once more at the mirror, feeling once again for the reassuring heaviness in my pocket—my own insurance, though I hoped I would have no need of it. I was calm as I left my room and went down the stairs. I heard them in the parlor, talking among themselves, chattering away, as if this was any other circle, and I felt a little stab of anticipation as I hesitated outside the door.

Then I stepped inside.

Michel glanced up. He was speaking with Jacob Colville and Dudley, and when he saw me his eyes lit with admiration, his lips curved in subtle encouragement.

The two other men turned to follow his glance, and I saw

their palpable surprise, and then the warm touch of their appreciation. Michel said something to them in a low voice, and Dudley stepped forward, crossing the room to take my hands.

"How lovely you look this evening, Evie!"

"A more comfortable dress to find the spirits with," Michel explained to them.

"Most assuredly," Jacob said fervently. "I wonder that we'd never thought of it before."

I heard the swish of skirts behind me, and I turned to see Sarah with Wilson Maull. Wilson seemed struck speechless, but Sarah was beaming. "How beautiful you are, Evie. Nearly like a spirit yourself."

"Perhaps you'd care to greet Rampling," Michel said to me, and I followed his glance across the room, to where Benjamin stood with Dorothy and Grace Dudley. They had all stopped talking to stare at me—Benjamin, in fact, looked stunned.

I had been prepared to see him, of course, but I had not been prepared for the anger I felt at the sight of him. How ordinary he looked, self-possessed and confident in his frock coat and his staid vest, his beard closely groomed, his thick hair gleaming. Not at all like a murderer—or a man who so easily betrayed those who loved him.

Michel said, "Bring them over. It's nearly time to begin."

His words were a quiet reminder. I smiled at the others and then went quickly, marveling at how much easier it was to move without crinolines or corset. I could breathe—which was helpful, as I was tense enough at the thought of what we must accomplish tonight.

"My dear child," Dorothy said as I approached. "What *are* you wearing?"

"It's exhausting to bring the spirits. I thought if I were comfortable, I might control them better."

Grace said, "I've often wondered about that. How hard it is to breathe deep!"

"Michel wishes us to start, now that everyone's here," I said. "Shall we go to the table?"

Dorothy's cadre of nurses gathered to help her, and Grace went ahead. But as I started, Benjamin caught my elbow, holding me back. "What's this about, Evie? A dressing gown? Why it's indecent. Who suggested this to you? Jourdain?"

"I've already explained. He thought I would do better if I were comfortable—"

"You didn't even bother to do up your hair!"

"I'm only attempting to perfect the illusion," I said.

He glanced about, as if afraid someone might overhear. "I hardly expected you to take it to heart this way. You must remember, Evie, who you are, what your hopes are for the future. This won't do at all."

"Benjamin," I said, turning to lay my hand upon his arm. I curled my fingers lingeringly, and I met his gaze with a limpid one of my own. I saw the moment he was reassured, though I saw too his discomfort. He did not understand this, and it unnerved him, and that was good; it was what I wanted. "I'm doing what I must. Please trust me."

"I do trust you, Evelyn. It's *him* I don't trust. Have you found the gun?"

"I haven't had the chance to look. Dorothy's been asking me nearly every day to bring her sons, and it requires a great deal of my time."

"Her sons?"

"And there are other spirits that come as well," I said. "I've tried to do as you say and ignore her, but Adele's been very determined."

Was it my imagination, or did his breathing quicken? "Adele?"

Michel called, "Rampling, you're delaying things. You can speak to *Madame* Atherton about her case after the circle."

I took my hand from Benjamin's arm and smiled. "We'll speak later." Then I moved away from him, the fine lawn of Adele's dressing gown twisting about my chemise-covered legs as I went to the table.

Michel held out the chair for me. As I sat, he leaned close, whispering, "Bravo, *chère*."

The others took their seats, and when Dudley settled himself beside me, he gave me an almost intimate smile. When he took my hand, his own was moist, as it had never been before. I was aware of how my attire had changed the feeling in the room. There was a different tension this evening, one colored with desire and, perhaps, guilt over feeling such. *"It'll make them all feel exposed,"* Michel had promised me. *"And exposed people are susceptible ones,* chère. *Never forget it."*

"Whose spirit shall we call tonight?" Grace asked.

"I think we'll see who comes," Michel said. "Will someone dim the lights?"

Sarah did the honors tonight. The candles burned in the middle of the table, their flames twisting this way and that with the currents of our breathing, then wisping into smoke as Jacob blew them out, and we were cast in shadows. Michel's thigh pressed mine—clad as I was only in my chemise and Adele's dressing gown, I felt the heat of him, an intimacy that was strangely exciting as we sat among the others. He squeezed my hand, and as the hymn began, he whispered to me, "Remember. Control them." His thumb began its caress, the touch that took me into trance. This time, I was to go only so far, no farther. This time, I must keep my own spirit present, as he'd taught me.

I felt myself fade; I felt the slow descent into slumbering wakefulness. The door was opening, wavering like heat vapors between this world and the spheres. I felt the seductive pull, and I resisted it; I did not let it take me out. But I pushed aside, I made room. And then, at last, I felt her there.

Leave them to me, she said.

And I said, *Join me.*

She was surprised and agitated; it was not what she wanted.

She pushed at me, and I held my ground. I told her, *Tonight, you shall have your say.*

I felt her satisfaction.

Then I heard Michel's voice. "Has a spirit come to speak with us tonight?"

She began to speak. I held her back. *Wait.*

There was silence. Then I felt the muscles flex in Michel's thigh as he tapped the lever.

RAP RAP RAP.

"One has come," Sarah said—always so excited, as if she expected each time that no spirit might visit, and was surprised anew when one did.

"Who has come to us tonight?"

"Is it one of my boys?" Dorothy asked.

Let me speak, Adele begged me.

I made her wait again.

"Spirit, who has come?"

Now, I told her.

She pushed anxiously against my throat. I felt my mouth open, as if in a dream. I heard her voice. "I am here."

"Who are you, spirit? Can you tell us your name?"

"Adele."

I heard one of the women gasp. I found myself searching for Benjamin, but he was hard to see in the dimness, and my eyes were not fully my own.

"Who have you come to see?"

"I come for you, of course," Adele said. "I always come for you."

Michel's voice was smooth and even, unperturbed. "What message have you for me?"

This was not what she'd expected. She wanted him afraid. She wanted him repentant. "Don't you know?"

"I'm afraid I don't."

"Don't you regret what you did to me?"

The others were avid.

Michel said, "*Non*. But you must know that. We were never meant to be."

She flailed within me. She tried to push me out. I felt Michel's hand strong on my own. *You'll bend to me now,* I told her.

She fought me. I felt her jealousy and her anger.

She said, "All those times you touched me, you kissed me. The boardinghouse room. None of that meant anything to you?"

"This isn't our business," Dorothy said tersely. "Watch yourself, spirit. You're among others."

She cared nothing for Dorothy's admonition. She was hungry for Michel. She said, "Did it mean nothing to you?"

"We passed the time together for a while," he told her.

"You didn't love me?"

"Such feelings keep you from passing into the next sphere. Put this behind you, spirit. Move on. Release me."

"Tell me you were jealous—even a little—when I went back to him."

"Move on, Adele," Michel said softly.

I felt her confusion and her hurt. I said to her, *There is something you must do for me. If I let you touch him, will you do it?*

She struggled to say no. But I felt how badly she wanted him. How she still hungered so for him.

Her voice said, "I would like to touch you."

"As you wish," he said.

His hand released mine. I felt his stealthy movements in the dimness, though I knew he looked in the opposite direction to distract the others, focusing on a distant spot, as if waiting for her to appear there. I felt him slip the fine chain of the locket over my head. I felt the oval dangle between my breasts. I kept my eyes closed. With my own free hand, I pulled the scarf from beneath the cushion of my chair.

She began to speak. I silenced her.

Michel stretched out his hand, and I slid my own from Dudley's, as if I were restless and must reposition it, always keeping contact, until Michel's fingers took the place of mine, and I was freed, and Dudley still thought I was there. I slipped from my shoes, leaving the one still touching Dudley's foot. Then, barefoot, I rose slowly, as if I were emerging from a bath, trusting that in the dim light I could hardly be seen, that what was seen was a filmy dressing gown that moved as if of its own accord, hoping that Michel had distracted them with his own feigned astonishment.

I took the scarf and put it over my head to hide my face. Then I moved behind Michel, and I wrapped my arms around his shoulders and pressed myself against him, and then I bade her say what she would, and she did not surprise me; she spoke through my voice.

"I loved you. Why did you let me go? Why did you send me back to let him kill me?"

"Who killed you, *chère?*"

"My husband."

"I knew of no husband, spirit."

"Oh, how you lie. What sweet lies you always told."

"Who was your husband, spirit?"

Tell him, I commanded her, and I felt her surprise at my insistence.

You know who he is.

I know, but you must tell him, I said to her. *Tell him now.*

"I have his necklace about my throat," she said. "Look—the locket he gave me. Can you not read it?"

"It's too dark for reading, spirit."

"His name is Benjamin. I think you must know him now."

The others in the circle moved restlessly.

She began to speak again. Again, I made her wait.

RAP.

"Another spirit?" Dudley asked. "Who can this one be?"

RAP RAP RAP RAP RAP.

"A weaker spirit," Dorothy said hoarsely. "It wants the alphabet."

"*A, B, C, D . . .*

"*M, N, O, P—*"

RAP.

"I see who comes now," Michel said.

"*A, B, C, D, E—*"

RAP.

"Is this the spirit of Peter Atherton?" Michel asked.

RAP RAP RAP.

The excitement in the room grew. I felt Adele waiting in my head, trying to see through my eyes, which were hazy and blurred. She had not the power to direct them well.

Michel spoke. "Yes. I am here."

It was uncanny. He sounded so much like Peter that even I nearly believed it.

Dudley said, "Atherton! We've been waiting for you for some time."

"I was lost. I came only in dreams."

I know this spirit, Adele said in my head. *I have seen him.*

I let her speak. "I know him."

"You know him, Adele?" Jacob Colville now. "Are you together in the spheres?"

"He has already passed into the next. But we were murdered by the same man."

"The same man?" Jacob's voice was a squeak. "Who murdered you, spirit? Who murdered Peter Atherton?"

"This is ridiculous!" Benjamin burst out. He leaped to his feet, wrenching loose from the circle, and the disruption was like thunder breaking. "No one should believe this claptrap. How can you believe it?"

I felt Adele's fear. The intensity of it surprised me, and I was caught up in it. I felt when I lost control of her, when her fear possessed me—I let go of Michel; I backed away in the darkness.

"Don't let him come near me!" Adele cried.

Jacob Colville rose. "What's going on here?"

"He's the one," Adele said, pointing at Benjamin through the darkness. "He was my husband in your world—"

"This is a lie! I won't listen to this!" Benjamin shouted. "I had no wife—she was a whore!"

"Rampling, calm down—"

I tried to gain control of the spirit in my head, but she was too afraid. She screamed, "Keep him away from me!"

I felt his rage through the darkness, and it was like the vision all over again. Her fear and panic, running through the darkness, though there was only carpet beneath her feet now. She had me running toward the door, but the ice and mud that had slowed him before was gone; he was on me in a moment, and at his touch, my waking trance was broken. Adele disappeared, swept away, and I was myself again, blinking and weakened. He jerked the scarf from my head, and then he grabbed for the locket, snapping its chain. His hands were around my throat, squeezing, and as I grabbed at them and tried to pry them loose, he slammed me against the wall so hard my head bounced against it. I saw stars in the darkness. I heard shouting, but it sounded far away, like spirits through the mist. What I heard was Benjamin's voice, low and steady with vicious rage.

"Shut up, you lying bitch! Dear God, you'll torment me no longer! I'll see you truly dead this time!"

I knew he didn't see me; he saw only Adele. His eyes shone in the darkness. His teeth were very white. His thumbs pressed hard into my throat, choking me. I couldn't breathe. I grabbed at his fingers with one hand; with the other I tried to reach the pocket of my dressing gown. But the world spun and tilted, the shadows grew dimmer.

I heard a crash. A white light flashed through the darkness.

Benjamin fell away. I could no longer feel his fingers. I gasped for breath. I thought, *This is it, then. I must be dead.*

Then, almost in the same moment, I realized that I was still in the parlor, that there was shouting, that Michel was beside me.

His hand was on my arm, holding me steady as my legs went weak. And then I realized that Benjamin was collapsed on the floor, and there was a pool of something dark spreading from beneath his head. Lying beside him was Peter's gun.

The others were rushing over. There was shouting, chaos. Someone turned up the lights. It was too sudden, too bright. I collapsed into Michel's arms, turning my head into his chest.

"Someone must call the police," Jacob said.

"There's a watchman outside. I saw him when we came up."

"Go call him." I felt the rumble of Michel's voice against my cheek.

Someone went running. I looked down to see Wilson Maull kneeling beside Ben. He looked up with an expression of disgusted dismay. "He's quite dead."

Grace sobbed and flung herself at her husband.

"Is Evelyn all right? She wasn't hurt? Evelyn, are you all right?" Sarah's face was pale with concern.

I nodded. "I think I'm . . . fine."

"Dear Lord, did you see the way he went after you? I thought certain he'd killed you."

"It was the spirit he was after. His wife's spirit."

I heard the sound of running on the stairs. One of Dorothy's nurses came racing into the room, the watchman close on his heels.

"There's been a terrible accident," Michel said quietly as the policeman came inside, and the others backed away to give him access to Benjamin's body.

The watchman recoiled. "Jesus Christ. What the hell happened here?"

"He shot himself," Michel said. I looked at him in surprise, and his arm tightened about me in warning. "Didn't he, *Madame*?"

I said, "Yes. It was quite horrible."

"I hardly saw it myself, I was too concerned with *Madame* Atherton."

"He tried to kill her," Sarah said. "He tried to strangle her!"

"Here now—" the policeman said. "He shot himself, you say?"

"Yes, I saw it. I thought he meant to shoot Evelyn, but instead he turned the gun on himself," said Wilson Maull.

"Why would he do that?"

"I suppose he couldn't live with himself after what he'd done," Michel said calmly. "Killing two people that way—we all heard him confess, didn't we?"

"I heard it," Robert Dudley said.

"Me too," said his wife.

"He said he killed Peter Atherton," Dorothy said. She was leaning heavily on Charley's arm, and she was pale as death. "He admitted to it."

"And his own wife, a year ago," Michel said.

I listened to him in awe. He made them all believe it. Every word. I said, "How terribly guilty he must have felt all this time."

"Not guilty enough to take the blame, though," Dorothy said sharply. "He left that for you, didn't he?"

Sarah nodded. "We saw it all. We heard him say it."

The police watchman knelt at Benjamin's side. "Nearly blew 'is 'ead off."

Grace made a sound of horror.

"If you don't mind, sir," Dudley said.

"Oh, o' course. Pardon me," said the policeman. He sighed and got to his feet. "Is there someone we can send for my captain?"

"Lambert will go." Dorothy nodded to the nurse who'd brought the police officer and who now stood by the door. "Go send him to the station, Matthew, will you?"

The nurse left quickly. The police officer reached into his pocket and took out his notebook. "You say he's the one killed Peter Atherton?"

"Whose wife stands just there—accused herself," Jacob said in indignation. "Who has borne all manner of insults these past weeks while the real killer posed as her lawyer!"

"This is Benjamin Rampling?" the policeman asked. He looked at me.

I nodded. "My husband's partner."

"He admitted he killed your husband?"

"Yes."

"Did he happen to say why?"

"I don't know. It was all so sudden, but there was something about a falling-out—"

"They'd argued wretchedly," Sarah said.

"I believe Atherton tried to end the partnership," Dudley offered.

"No doubt an accident," Michel said. "He had quite a temper. He admitted to killing his wife in a rage."

"He was still furious with her," Grace said. "We could all see it."

I glanced down at Benjamin, at the blood soaking into Dorothy's velvet tapestry carpet, turning the pale cabbage roses red, and I said weakly, "Could someone cover him, please?"

"*Madame* should sit down," Michel said. "Might I take her to the settee?"

"Of course." The officer waved us away. Wilson Maull took a knitted throw from a nearby chair and spread it over Benjamin's body, tucking it in, as if he meant to prepare him for a good night's sleep instead of one for eternity.

He paused. "What's this?" He reached for something—the necklace where it had fallen to the floor, just next to Ben's hand. "The spirit's locket," Wilson said almost reverently as he picked it up. Without a word, Michel took it from him and gave it to me. Then he led me to the settee, away from the others. I heard them arguing among themselves, providing the policeman with details, tripping over one another to embellish further what was nothing more than the delusion Michel had hand-fed them. They had seen nothing. It was too dark. Only I had seen it. Only I had seen Michel rush to my defense. Only I had seen him pull Peter's gun from his frock coat pocket—the gun I had not known he carried—and set it against Benjamin's temple. He had not hesitated; he had made no warning, he had never given Benjamin the chance to release me.

He had simply pulled the trigger.

32

To Live Within the World

It was nearly three in the morning before the police finished their questioning and the coroner had come to take the body away.

"Looks cut-and-dried enough," he said as he'd stared down at the body. "They all saw him do it, eh?"

Dorothy had collapsed at two o'clock, and Michel had gone with her nurses to take her to bed, and to give her the cordial that calmed her nerves and helped her sleep. But she had not gone without patting my hand and saying, "You're free now, Evelyn, child. They'll drop the charges against you." Then her face had crumpled, and she'd gripped my fingers hard. "You won't leave me, will you, my dear? You'll stay?"

"I've no plans to go anywhere," I told her.

"You're like a daughter to me," she said.

Michel had taken her away then, and I leaned back upon the settee, exhausted, watching as the policemen did their work, and the circle disbanded one by one as each was questioned and released. Lambert had called the maids and the driver and the gardener into service, and they moved the furniture and labored to roll the ruined carpet and take it away, but there was still a stain upon the wood beneath. When I finally rose to go to my own room, Bella was working upon it, scrubbing with tired resignation—though the household was so disconcerted by Benjamin's "suicide" that I doubted anyone would sleep tonight.

Including myself. Wearily, I went upstairs, grateful that I was dressed so simply that all I must do was fall into my bed. But I was afraid of sleep. I didn't know who might visit me in my dreams—Peter again? Or Adele? Or worse yet, Benjamin? There was some justice, I supposed, in them all being together, if in fact they were. They had tortured one another well enough in the material world; now that they had returned to one another, I hoped they might find peace. Certainly I deserved it, if they did not.

It wasn't until I reached my bedroom and took off Adele's dressing gown that I realized the fine lawn was spattered with Benjamin's blood. I let it fall to the floor—tomorrow I would burn it—and then I stumbled wearily into my bed. The locket was still in my hand; I lifted it, letting it dangle for a moment to glimmer dimly in the subdued light of the streetlamps eking around the edges of the curtains. Benjamin had loved her once, I supposed, though no doubt that love was like Peter's had been for me—an attempt to live within the world, a necessary evil, given that he was forbidden from revealing the truth of his heart. To love so secretly, and then to lose Peter to a man who would not love him back, to have no recourse. How Benjamin must have hated Michel.

I closed my eyes for a moment. I thought of how Ben and I had walked together. Now I realized it was not shyness that had been in his eyes when he said, "I regret it took me so long to find my heart's desire," but sorrow. Perhaps we were all the same when it came to that. Perhaps there were those who never found it.

I put the locket on the bedside table, letting the chain fall in a steady stream from my hand to pool around it, and then I lay there in the darkness, staring up at a ceiling I could not see—it could almost have been the way to heaven, so far it seemed above my head—and waited.

It was nearly dawn before he stepped inside the door.

He moved quietly, as if he thought I slept and didn't want to wake me, and I didn't disabuse him; I liked to watch him move within the shadows. That grace, that silky confidence, as if he never considered that I might refuse him. He undressed, laying his clothes upon the chair, and then moved to the side of the bed and pulled aside the covers carefully, crawling between them. I sighed, and moved into his arms, and he held me close, stroking my hair.

"I'll keep the nightmares away, *chère*," he said.

It was only then that I slept.

33

How Lovely It Is When Families Get Along

Thursday, March 5, 1857

New York Times

ATHERTON MURDER SOLVED!

Murder Most Foul Ends in CONFESSION! Wife's Lawyer the Killer

MANHATTAN—New York City was stunned this morning to discover that the murderer of prominent Knickerbocker attorney Peter Atherton confessed to the grisly crime Tuesday night.

Benjamin Rampling, who had been Mr. Atherton's partner in the recently formed law firm of Atherton and Rampling, confessed at Dorothy Bennett's home, in front of several witnesses, that he had killed Mr. Atherton during an argument in which Mr. Atherton suggested their law partnership be dissolved.

The murder took place on the night of January 15th, as Mr. Atherton and Mr. Rampling returned from a social engagement. They argued, and Mr. Rampling became enraged and stabbed Mr. Atherton viciously in the gut, after which he removed from him any valuables and threw him into the East River, hoping those who found the body would take it for a robbery.

Witnesses to the confession, including Mr. and Mrs. Robert Dudley, Mrs. Dorothy Bennett, and Mr. Jacob Colville, say they begged Mr. Rampling to consider handing himself over to police custody, to no avail. Before the horrified witnesses, Mr. Rampling shot himself in the head with the gun he had taken from Mr. Atherton's pocket the night of the murder.

Also present was Mrs. Peter Atherton, who had been charged with her husband's murder in February, and who was awaiting trial. She declared herself shocked and sickened by the spectacle. "I know now Mr. Rampling offered to defend me only because of the guilt he felt," she said. "That he was willing to let me go to trial for the crime he committed is beyond comprehension. I am only sorry he waited so long before confessing his guilt."

Mr. Rampling also admitted to killing his wife, Adele Rampling, who died in a similar unsolved murder in January of last year.

Charges have been dropped against Mrs. Atherton, and police say they consider the matter closed.

Y ou're a free woman," Michel said as I put the newspaper aside. He sat across the table from me, eating heartily of a late breakfast I had no appetite for. "A relief, I imagine, eh?"

"I don't quite know yet," I told him.

"Time enough to come to terms with it," Dorothy said. I had been surprised that she made her way downstairs this morning, but she seemed anxious to take breakfast with us, though she only picked at her food and barely drank her tea. "It'll be months before you live down the notoriety. Until then, no one but those in the faster circles will have anything to do with you."

Michel glanced up at me. "Give them time. The rest'll come looking for you before long. Once they hear of your talent, they'll want to see it for themselves."

I met his gaze. "Well then, I shall give them a show worth waiting for."

He smiled.

Dorothy said, "Mark my words, the two of you will have them all convinced by year's end."

Lambert came to the door. "Pardon me, Mrs. Atherton, but there's a Mrs. Burden here to see you."

I looked up in surprise. "Mrs. Burden? Pamela?"

"How quickly they descend," Michel said wryly. "Even earlier than you predicted."

I rose, setting aside the damask napkin. To Lambert, I said, "I'll see her."

"She's waiting in the parlor, ma'am."

Michel said, "Remember what's owed you, *Madame*. We aren't done yet."

I met his gaze. "Oh, I know."

"Don't give in to them, Evelyn," Dorothy called after me as I went to the door. "They're vultures, the lot of them."

I could not help but smile at the image as I went into the parlor, especially when I saw Pamela standing by the window, dressed in mourning, her hat so bedecked with black feathers that she looked very like some strange kind of bird.

"Hello, Pamela," I said. "How odd to see you. I cannot think what you must have come for. Except perhaps to apologize."

She lifted her chin. "Can we not be civil to each other, Evelyn?"

"Why, I don't know. Can we?"

"The family's sent me to try to make amends. We were wrong about your role in Peter's murder."

"How kind of you to realize it. Especially now that you've ruined me."

Her full lips thinned to near invisibility. "Must you make this difficult?"

"I'm only returning the favor."

"Evelyn, please. We're quite sorry for what we put you through. Though it seems to me you've done well enough since." She gestured to the parlor. "From what I understand, Dorothy Bennett has treated you like a daughter."

"She was kind enough to help me when I needed it."

"I've heard many reports of your new talents. We all have. You seem to have recovered quite well on your own."

"Oh, yes," I said sarcastically. "As you can see, all of society is clamoring at my door to apologize for its appalling behavior."

She had the grace to flush. "We—the family, that is—wish to extend our hands to you again, Evelyn. We had hoped we might be able to reach some kind of accommodation."

"Oh? What accommodation is that?"

"In regards to Peter's will. Given everything you've been through, we thought—well, John and Paul thought—you must be anxious to put all this behind you. To start life over, as it were."

"I see. You intend to let the will stand?"

She glanced up again, her eyes flashing angrily before she recomposed herself. "Goodness, Evelyn, even you can't believe we would so willingly hand over Mama's house and everything else to you. Peter's allowance is nearly seventy thousand a year."

"Then I've no idea what accommodation you can mean."

"All this . . . attention . . . you've endured must be wearing. I can't think that you'd want to continue it. You'll get no support among the upper ten if you decide to fight. What can you hope to gain but a disgraceful reputation? It's time for healing, Evelyn. We're willing to"—she took a deep breath, as if the word was difficult for her to say—"sanction your return to society—after a proper period of mourning, of course—if you will sign a paper relinquishing your claim. It will save us all a great deal of time and trouble."

"I see. I'll be the repentant Atherton returned to the fold?"

"Your life will be as before," she said. "With Dorothy Bennett's support, and ours, you can move freely in society again. It's a generous offer, Evelyn. You must know it."

"More than generous. I hardly expected it."

Pamela looked surprised. "Then you'll consider it?"

How easy it was to maneuver her, after all. Just as Michel had said it would be. I smiled at her. "Do you think you could bring the family here? As you must realize, it's difficult for me to leave the house just now. And I'd like Dorothy to be present. She's been so kind to me, after all, but she's very ill, and I don't like to trouble her more than I must."

"Of course," Pamela said with alacrity. "I'm certain they'd be anxious to do whatever makes you comfortable."

"Perhaps this afternoon?"

"I'll send a driver round to the others. Would six be acceptable?"

"Perfectly," I said.

"Then I'll take my leave." She went to the door and paused there, turning back to me. "I'm relieved you're being so gracious about this, Evelyn. I confess I didn't expect it."

"One doesn't experience life without learning valuable lessons, Pamela. I expect you'll find I've changed a great deal."

"I'm gratified to know it," she said.

"Yes," I told her. "So am I."

I HEARD THEM arrive that afternoon, though I did not greet them. I wore black bombazine and jet beads around my neck and in my ears, as befitted a proper widow, though I wished nothing more than to be done with mourning. I waited in the upstairs parlor, running my finger along the polished surface of the great round table that had made my future. I let them gather and talk among themselves. I imagined I could feel the shiver of their expectation as they anticipated my surrender.

Then Michel appeared in the doorway. He was dressed exquisitely, as always, in dark blue that accented the paleness of his eyes. "Dorothy's downstairs with them. Are you ready?"

"I've never been more so."

He held out his arm to me. When I took it, he kissed me lightly upon my forehead. "I'm there with you, *chère*."

"I know it," I said.

Together, we went downstairs, to the parlor, where Bella was just exiting after having brought the tea. I heard John's voice. "Well, it's about time. A merry chase, wasn't it, but—"

He stopped as we entered. They were all there, Dorothy on the chaise and all of Peter's family: Pamela, her china-doll eyes filled with self-satisfaction; her husband, John, composed as always; Paul, as quiet and watchful as ever; and Penny, humorless and severe.

"Evelyn," John said, rising, along with Paul.

"This is Michel Jourdain," I said. "I expect you all know of him by now."

"I thought this was to be a family discussion," John said.

"But Michel is my family," I said. "And Dorothy too, as my old family abandoned me. I'm very loyal, you know, unless I'm given cause not to be."

Pamela said, "For goodness sakes, Evelyn, we've discussed this."

I looked at the teapot steaming on the table, the unused cups beside it, the plate of untouched cakes. "Would anyone like tea?"

Michel smiled and withdrew to the corner near the French doors, where he leaned almost indolently against the wall. Paul's gaze followed him before he turned back to me. I saw the speculation in those eyes that reminded me so much of Peter's, the quick flash of envy.

Dorothy said, "None of them want refreshment, child."

"I've brought the papers," John said, reaching for his briefcase. "They're quite simple to understand. All they require is your signature—"

"I won't be signing anything," I said.

John glanced at Pamela. "But Pam said—"

I went to the settee and sat, arranging my skirts carefully. Paul and John took their seats again, but warily now.

"We didn't come here for games, Evelyn," Paul said.

"Well of course you did," I said. "You came here to win one. But I'm afraid I've some conditions for my surrender."

"You're in no position to make conditions," John said.

"You think not?" I smiled. "Perhaps you'll change your mind when I tell you I've no interest in the house. You can keep it. Dorothy's offered me a place here with her, and I've accepted. I will take the things that are rightfully mine, of course. The gifts Peter gave me, the jewelry, some of the furniture—I'll have an inventory done and let you know what I intend to bring with me. And oh—I'll have Peter's allowance as well. What was it? Seventy thousand a year, I believe? In perpetuity."

Their expressions were dumbfounded, various degrees of Atherton dropped mouths, opened eyes—strange variations on a theme. Even John looked like an Atherton in that moment—as if he had gradually taken on their characteristics simply by virtue of living among them. In the corner, Michel smiled.

"You must be mad," Paul sputtered finally. "You truly must be mad. Why should we do such a thing?"

"If you won't do it because your brother would have wanted it, then I have no choice but to force you to his will."

"And how, exactly, do you intend to do that?" Pamela asked acidly. "Our offer was quite fair, though it would have cost us considerably to save you from the attention you've received lately. This spirit calling, Evelyn, your association with this"—she motioned to Michel—"this charlatan. It's all the talk. People believe you must be insane yourself. You've no allies to speak of."

Penny said snidely, "What will you do? Call Peter's spirit down among us?"

"Oh, I don't think I need go that far," I said. I glanced at Michel, who looked as if he might burst out laughing at any moment, and then at Dorothy, who seemed uncomfortable but determined. "I think the mortal world will serve just as well, if not better."

John sighed. "Enough of this, Evelyn. I think we've given you quite long enough. If you don't mean to sign these papers, we are truly wasting our time. We'll see you in court." He rose.

"Sit down, John," I said, and this time I let all my contempt for him ring in my voice.

He frowned at me in surprise.

I said, "Did none of you suppose there might have been a reason why Peter married me? I mean, after years of being presented with the best pedigrees in New York City, why would he choose an investigator's daughter?"

"You bewitched him," Paul said.

John sank back down onto his chair.

I smiled. "Have you any idea what goes on in those little cabarets on Chatham Street?"

Penny frowned, but I saw Paul's sudden attention where he sat beside her.

"Or the bathhouses?" I went on. "There's a place called the Persian Poetry Club. Very Turkish in its style, I heard. For those with a Greek temperament. They make a point of studying the more obscure Byronic texts, I'm told. The ones celebrating romantic love. In all its forms. I believe Peter even hired some of the club's members as legal assistants. Not clever boys, but very pretty. Your brother liked them pretty."

Slowly, slowly, I saw my words' effect. I saw Penny and Pamela reach a dawning understanding. For Paul and John, it did not take so very long. Perhaps they'd wondered before now. They were men of the city, after all.

"You know, just the other day I was talking to a boy—a friend of Peter's—and he said the most interesting thing. He asked me who would believe him if he told the truth about Peter's preferences? And I thought: why, everyone would."

"How dare you!" Pamela said. Her color rose. She looked as if she were swelling. "How dare you say those things about my brother!"

"Your brother was a sodomite," I said sharply. "It was why he married me. It was why Benjamin Rampling killed him. Not over the law practice, but because they were lovers, and they were fighting over another man. I've kept it out of the papers, but all it would take is a word. Can you imagine what the *Herald* would do with such a story?"

"You're lying." This from Penny. She had gone so pale that she looked like a corpse. "I, for one, won't stand for it!"

But John's face was chiseled stone. "Quiet, Penny," he said in a strangled voice. He looked at me. "I don't imagine you've any proof of this?"

"It's all true, John," Dorothy said with a sigh. "I've known it for years. I've quieted the talk whenever there was any. But I won't see you cheat Evelyn. It's distasteful to mention such things, but I'm too old to be fastidious. I'll do what I must to protect her."

I added, "I know where to find his lovers. I'm certain they can produce evidence enough, if you truly require it."

John said, "I want a list of all these people."

"Oh, I don't think so. How else am I to keep you from cheating me?"

"You have my word."

"It's not enough. The Atherton name means nothing to me now that Peter's gone. Don't think I would hesitate to besmirch it."

Pamela seemed to explode. "You are a . . . a—"

"An Atherton?" I smiled sweetly. "Unfortunately, that's true. I like to think I've taken on the very best traits of your family. I expect it will take me far."

John said, "If we do this, you can rely on us for nothing else."

"You're not setting the conditions. Do what I want or I'll tell the truth about Peter. It's quite simple, John. Even your scheming brain ought to grasp it."

Penny put her face in her hands. Pamela looked ashen.

Paul stood angrily. "I'd like to talk to you a moment, Evelyn. Alone." He reached for my arm.

Michel roused from his place against the wall. "Sit down," he said, and though his voice was pleasant enough, the danger in it was unmistakable.

Paul looked startled, but he withdrew and sat again.

With a smile, I said, "As you can see, I've all the allies I need."

John spoke through clenched teeth. "Tell me again what you require."

"Seventy thousand a year, and the things from the house I desire. You can keep the rest. Quite a fair bargain, I think."

John nodded so stiffly I thought his neck would snap. "Very well. You have your conditions."

"Wonderful," I said. I smiled and picked up the teapot to pour. "I must say—how lovely it is when families get along."

34

AFFINITY

MAY 1857

"My dear Evelyn, how quickly even my most expansive hopes have been surpassed. Such talent as yours should be shouted from the rooftops!"

I smiled as Henry Reid bowed over my hand. The parlor was empty now but for the two of us. The night's circle had disbanded; the only spirits remaining were those lingering in the smell of the liqueur on his breath. I pressed my fingers warmly into his palm. "You're far too generous. I'm merely a telegraph. Your cousin's spirit was so anxious to speak to you that I believe she would have found some other means to do so, in time."

"It's you who're too generous. After the way we treated you after dear Peter's death—I'm grateful beyond measure that you should see fit to welcome us again so readily."

"The spirits teach us to live in everlasting love with one another. I merely follow their dictates."

His eyes were hazel beneath his heavy gray brows, and just now they were filled with the most tender reverence. "I feel I must do something to thank you for what you've done."

I fingered the sapphires—his earlier gift to me—that lay warm and heavy against my bare collarbone. I had worn deep blue satin to match them, and I knew—because I'd seen Henry Reid's stunned expression when he'd first stepped into the parlor that night—that the effect was remarkable. I dropped my eyes demurely. "The spirits know you for an unselfish man already."

He made a sound deep in his throat. When he spoke, his voice was thick. "My dear, do you remember what my cousin said through you?"

"Oh, hardly. It's like a dream. Some parts come back to me. Others . . ."

"She asked that I try to spread the word of this miracle, and I believe I've thought of a way."

"Have you?"

"Jourdain was kind enough to suggest some things. I had thought—what do you say to the idea of starting a spiritualist retreat at Saratoga? Everyone who's anyone will be there this summer—most have left the city already. We've stayed so long for you, but why not continue the circles there? It would take some funds, of course, but I daresay I could manage it. And I've other friends as well I think I could convince. I would, of course, be most honored if you and Jourdain would help me. Why, to have you preside over the circle there, at least for a time! Oh, I know you've your commitments here, especially with the Spiritualist Convention, but New York in the summer is unbearable, and what with the legislature taking over the police and the new liquor laws and Mayor Wood's posturing, well, the city's unstable enough now. It may well prove a powder keg these next months."

"I'm honored that you would consider me. But I hardly think—"

"I'm in a position to pay you quite well for your involvement," he said quietly. "And Jourdain too, of course."

"I don't know that we could leave Dorothy."

"Saratoga'd be just the thing for her. She's delighted in it in the past. It's time she got out of this house, don't you agree?

She seems so much better now. I could procure her a private rail car."

I smiled. "I think Dorothy could afford her own car."

He flushed. "I only meant . . . I know she's adopted Jourdain and provided for you quite handsomely, and that you must feel an obligation to her, but she cannot mean to keep you just for herself, Evelyn. The world awaits your gift. Having given it to us, she would be selfish to withdraw it."

"I owe her a great deal. And she depends upon Michel."

He reached for my hand again. His palms were moist; he squeezed my fingers hard. "We all owe her, my dear. She helped to discover you. But did you never mean to move on? To share your gift with everyone? To teach us all the wonder of the Summerland?"

"The spirits bid me do as they will," I said. "But they do tend to look favorably upon generosity"—I touched the sapphires again—"in all its forms."

"Then I will do all in my power to influence them," he said.

I drew my hand from his, and nodded to where Rose stood in the doorway. "I believe your wife's waiting for you."

Reid bowed once more. "Until the next time, then."

I followed him to the doorway and watched as he took Rose's arm and led her from the parlor and down the stairs. I heard the others at the door as they said their good-byes, their exhilarated laughter, their assurances of return, and I felt a heady satisfaction that only grew when their voices disappeared into the night, and the door was closed behind them, and I heard the footsteps I waited for come back up the stairs.

He was nearly to the landing when I said, "I understand the spirits mentioned Saratoga tonight."

He took the last steps easily. "*Oui*. They did."

"Reid said he would get a private rail car for Dorothy."

He laughed. "I'm sure she'd appreciate it."

"And he'd pay quite well for our 'involvement.'"

He came up to me, slipping his arms around me, and I leaned into him. "Ah, I intend so, *chère*. Next time, suggest that a suite would be just the thing—it must be large enough for a circle, eh?"

"Why, that's up to the spirits. I'm only the conduit."

"*Oui,* of course. But make him suffer a little first, eh? Tell him we'll hold no circle next week. What should we say—ah, tell him that with the police so distracted, the streets are too dangerous."

"He'll be impatient."

He lifted the heavy strand of gems around my neck and let them fall again, a gentle thud against my skin. "Impatient men are generous ones. Or haven't you learned that by now?"

"Should I make you wait, then? Now that you're a rich Bennett?"

"Rich as Croesus," he agreed. He kissed the hollow of my throat, brushing his lips against the gold links of my necklace. "And thanks to you, *ma coeur,* about to be richer."

I took his head in my hands. My fingers tangled in the silkiness of his hair. I kept his mouth close against me. "And then? After that—what will we do then?"

"Whatever we wish. I told you once we could have the world. We're just beginning to own it. Would you stop now?"

"No," I said. "No."

I felt him smile against my skin. "I thought not. You're a wolf like me after all, Evie. Will you finally admit it?"

I closed my eyes. I remembered the look that had been on his face as he'd pulled the trigger that night, and I knew what he'd done for me. It was what I would have done for him, given the chance, had I been able to reach the gold-chased penknife I'd hidden in the pocket of the dressing gown, had I a single moment longer. I wondered: had the spirits known that when they sent Michel to me? Had they known this guide of theirs would fit me so well? Had they seen the affinity between us?

It hardly mattered, I supposed. The spirits were as capricious and selfish in their world as they had been in ours. Their purposes were their own. The only truth was whatever you could make someone believe.

"Come to bed," I said to him, and then I took his hand and led him there.

Tomorrow was soon enough to own the world.

How we would make it dance.

ABOUT THE AUTHOR

MEGAN CHANCE is a former television news photographer. She lives in the Pacific Northwest with her husband and two daughters. She is also the author of *An Inconvenient Wife* and *Susannah Morrow*.